HETAERA:
Daughter of the Gods

J. A. COFFEY

Cover image: "The Favourite Poet, 1888" Sir Lawrence Alma-Tadema
Text copyright © 2013 Julie A. Coffey

All Rights Reserved

ISBN-13 978-1482785395
ISBN-10 1482785390

DEDICATIONS

As is the way of writers, we recognize that we stand on the shoulders of others to achieve our dreams. This book would not have been possible without the following people:

To my mother, a stalwart champion of all my endeavors. You are the model for following my dreams.

To my sister, she of the red-gold hair, whom I always admired and aspired to be. You are a Thracian in my heart.

To the many authors and editors who encouraged me to persevere in an industry which often doesn't support budding authors--the incomparable Jody Wallace (sorry it took me so long to get it right!) and my critique partners of RWA; editor Mary Theresa Hussey, for comparing me to one of my giants and thereby giving me hope; editor Anna Genoese (for calling me out and making me want to be better); to authors Mary Renault and Jacqueline Carey-women who showed me it was possible to write the book of my heart; to Sarah for an eagle's eye and a red pen (and whose work I hope to one day read--you have been called!); and to Hope for friendship and support.

To STM for the mistakes and pain—both given and received.

But mostly to my husband, Robert, for unfailing love and with whom the yoke of a marriage bed is a most joyous and lighthearted place. I love you, I love you. I couldn't do it without you.

CONTENTS

CHAPTER 1

What soul can say for certain where her trail will end, or upon which paths the sands of her life will blow? My life was one of humble beginnings and yet I find myself at the point of scribing my name with gods and murderers in the tombs of kings.

I have been given many titles in my life - daughter, slave, and lover. Never have I held a child of my own in my arms. How strange to think, then, she who has never borne life shall mother an entire nation.

How I came to Egypt is not a mystery, in itself. I was born in a coastal village in Thrace, near the shoreline fortress of Perperek. We were often subject to slave raids from the neighboring Greeks and Macedonians, the Spartans to the west, and the Persians across the cold salt waters of the Sea of Marmara. All of them hungered for the strength of our backs and the fire in our Thracian blood.

But, though we labored on the rocky slopes of the Rhodopes Mountains, we loved as fiercely as we fought in homage to our honored Dionysus, god of death, rebirth and of passion--my downfall.

Life in Perperek's shadow was not easy. There were those in our village who gained sustenance from the providence of the *ktístai*, sacred priests in the temple. Fashioners of precious metals. And holy ones, priestesses like my mother, a Bacchae, who crept the treacherous mountain paths to worship the gods with wild beauty and song. Someday, I hoped I would be like her. I dreamed of a time when I could live in leisure, with enough food to fill my belly and, perhaps, lovely adornments for my body. Thracians have a love of beauty, and I was no exception.

The village was filled with simple folk. We tended, planted and gathered. But of all who toiled within the village, our warriors were most revered. Warriors like my father. With pride I remember him, foremost of those who fought for Perperek. His powerful arms. The precise color of his red-gold hair, my legacy, shorn from his head in the warrior topknot. His laughter. How much I loved him. But in my twelfth year, I set my feet upon a course that would forever change us.

"What harm can there be in one last trip to the temple before the storms come, Delus?" my mother asked. "There is talk in the village of her." She jerked her chin at me. "And of us." She continued pulling provisions from our dry storage for the evening meal.

"Sita, please. There is always the chatter of crows in Perperek." Milk of the gods, red and thick as blood, clotted my father's close-cropped beard. He motioned for her to refill the wineskin. "Let the women talk. The Bacchae can wait. Perhaps in another year, we can spare her."

"The devotees of Dionysus will _not_ wait. It is time I took Doricha with me to the temple. She is nigh a woman and must earn her place, as I once did. She is of an age that she can be taught the temple diktat."

My father smiled at me, his agate blue eyes sparkling like sunlight on the waves of the sea. One large hand pawed the air as he motioned for me to come forth. He seemed uncomfortable without the shaft of his _sarisa_, his long spear.

"Have you memorized your mother's teachings, Dori?"

I nodded and ran to him. Twining my fingers into the long tresses of his topknot, I marveled in the rich, warm protection of his broad shoulders. His arms encircled me like bronze bands. The scent of roasting goat wafted from the spit where my mother buried onions and garlic in the tender meat, and I felt safe and as peaceful as I can remember being in my life.

"You are a treasure, Doricha," my father said. I loved him for it. "I cannot let you go to the temples yet. Do you hate me for denying you your birthright?"

"No, Papita." And I didn't.

His teeth flashed white against his ruddy skin as I snuggled like a wolf kit into his lap. Though we were a spear's point away to starving as any in the village, my father saw a king's ransom when he looked at me.

I knew what starving was. Starving was thin, patched wool cloth, and no meat. Starving meant freezing to death on the mountainside at night, for lack of shelter and fire. True, we did not share the luxuries of those who lived within the shoreline fortress of Perperek--but we were not starving. Not quite yet. Once I was temple trained, my future would be determined by my efforts to pay homage to the gods with my grace and beauty—or the strength of my husband's spear.

Still, I could not deny the warmth of my father's smile as he winked at me behind my mother's back.

"The girl must take her place in the temple, as others before her have done." My mother wiped the fat grease from her hands with a sharp, brittle movement. "Please, Delus. You must see the reason in this. We can ill afford to anger them a second time." She put away the scraps from preparing our meal.

"I care not whom I anger. I am still your husband. Or have you forgotten?" My father shook his head again and took another long pull at the wineskin.

I burrowed further under the space beneath his chin, tucking the skirt of my chiton around my knees. My mother's lips tightened and I confess I feared to see it, for it meant she was resolved to have her way.

Do not mistake my heart in this. I loved my mother as well as any daughter can, but in her eyes, I was first and foremost a servant to Dionysus. It was heresy for me to refuse the path to temple service when it was offered, when so many others had already been pressed into the fold. Especially the daughter of a Bacchae. Yet to my mother, it seemed, I was dissimilar to a king's ransom as could be. I crouched there, safe and content in my father's arms, and glared at my mother's back as she smoothed her hands on her skirts, and turned to the chest containing her things.

"I have not forgotten, Delus," she murmured. Her movements were fluid and beautiful, as were those of all the Bacchae.

My father's eyes were on her as she bustled around our small hut. She knew it well, too. Maintaining her slight distance, she uncoiled her bound hair until it fell in a shimmering crimson curtain in front of her face, and picked up a carved wooden comb. Her limbs unfurled with canny grace, mesmerizing to my eyes and to my father's. With long strokes she brushed her hair until it crackled with life, and the blue tattooed patterns on her hands undulated in the firelight.

"Temple training has served us well, my love." She stared at him as her hands stroked up and down her exquisite silken locks. Her voice was breathy and low. "And you are my husband. Still, we have a duty to our people, Delus. We should not invite trouble where trouble does not dwell."

I shifted in my father's lap, uncertain of what was to come next. His eyes never left my mother, but he took another long pull at the wineskin. Some of the liquid dribbled out the side of his mouth and he flicked a red-stained tongue to catch it. I was uneasy then, and acutely aware of the smoking cook fire, my father's unwashed but not unpleasant scent, and the odor of soured grapes.

The firewood snapped, and I flinched. Father laughed and embraced me even tighter. He crushed me against his barrel chest in a bear-like embrace, while his rough whiskers tickled my cheek. "Very well, Sita. You may take Doricha, but not until tomorrow. Tonight," he smiled wide, "we celebrate our victory over the Greeks!"

Mother's cheeks were flushed. "Whist, Delus, for shame! The battle has not yet begun, and will not until the moon shines bright in the sky and the blood of Dionysus flows in your veins."

My father's laughter rattled the walls. "Think you, they can best a Thracian? Come to me, Sita, that I may impress you with the strength of my spear."

My mother ran to him, her lovely face alight with inner fire. She giggled like a young girl, sweeping herbs from the table onto the floor in her haste. Father nudged me out of his lap to make room for her. I huddled on the floor by their feet, forgotten, and busied myself with separating the plants, until their soft laughter ceased. They rose and drew the goatskin curtain back from the sleeping quarters. Father grabbed the wine.

"Doricha, go and fetch some water from the well. And stay clear of the trees. There are Greeks about." Father's voice thickened with so much wine in him. A glance revealed naught of my mother save her long, slender limbs disappearing under the animal hides in the sleeping alcove.

I sighed, and grabbed the heavy wooden bucket from its customary place, feeling surly from his oft repeated warning not to venture into the unknown cypress groves at night. I'd never penetrated the thick trees that hid us from the west, but kept always to the low bracken on the forest's edge as I made my way to the well.

Life in our village was ever solitary and unchanging. In my few years of life, I'd busied myself with toiling at gathering herbs or tending the small animals, as the villagers eschewed playing with the daughter of a Bacchae. Now, here I was poised on the precipice of womanhood. The pale moon hung just above the forest line, as I slipped from our hut with a strange tight knot forming in the pit of my stomach, feeling both loved and unwanted at the same time. In the twelve winters I lived in Perperek's shadow, I had yet to disobey my father, but tonight, with the soft mewlings of my mother erupting from our tiny hut, I felt a burning in my middle I could not explain.

With tears pricking my eyes, I entered the bower of midnight cypress just beyond our village. I wandered through the silent trees and scuffed up the dried fallen leaves that filled the air with a musty scent of decay.

An image of my father's face flashed before my eyes and I hurled the bucket into the trees. I tromped further into the grove, taking no pains to be quiet. So, there were Greeks about? Well, they never came so close to our village and our men would raise the alarm if they did. Besides, my father was so enthralled with my mother's company, he would not even notice if I was taken. Such were my thoughts and I am heartily sorry for them now.

Many times I have wished to recapture that moment when first I chose to leave the safety of the path, but I was a child then and had not a woman's experience to make me wary.

I walked on in a night-blind stupor, until the crack of a twig pierced my solitude. With a start, I realized I was much further into the forest than I'd thought. Perhaps, too far. Where were my bucket and the path that would lead me home?

I wandered for what seemed hours, thinking one way, and then the next was the path I sought. Scuttling blindly through the underbrush, rising panic beat a steady tattoo in my chest. Surely my father would search for me? His concern over my tardiness would steal him from my mother's embrace, I thought. He loved me. He would come.

I waited, but he did not appear.

Unable to find my way home, I climbed the bough of the nearest tree and sought refuge from the cold night and the prowling beasts that preyed on human flesh. Perhaps in the morning light I would recognize the way back to the village. Insects and other creatures of the forest clicked and chirruped. Long moments passed, how many I cannot say, whilst I shivered and sniffled into my damp woolen chiton, cursing the passion between the two people I loved most in this world.

At once, I heard a strange noise, like a scuffle in the underbrush, and held my breath. Who was about? Could it be my father? Then another thudding hiss.

At the soft jangle of unsheathed metal, I thought with a child's hope it might be my father come to claim me. Slipping from my perch, I crept toward the footsteps and whispers that emanated from the forest grove.

"*Papita*?" I called softly.

Closer I moved toward the sounds and closer still, until at last, I came upon a sight that burnt itself behind my eyes forever. It was not one man, but many gathered in the woods that night.

The Greeks had come.

A group of twenty men from the village, men I had known most of my life, burst from the trees. Their faces were painted with mud and gore. They erupted in a wild frenzy, and howled like wild beasts as they fought a horde of armored Grecian invaders. The odor of blood and filth infiltrated the night air.

I froze.

Blood poured like red wine from split skin and bones. Someone bellowed behind me and I scrambled behind the nearest tree trunk and covered my mouth with my hands to stifle a scream as the sounds of battle grew nearer. I did not want to look, but somewhere my father might be fighting nearby. Keeping my back safely against the cypress trunk, I peered through the dark at the carnage.

Some men carried swords, others their long spears, but nowhere did I see my own father's sarisa. All sounds froze in my ears, and feeling fled from my limbs. I heard only my own ragged breathing as I watched men screaming, hacking and dying.

Please, I begged the unhearing gods, as if my entreaty could move their immortal hearts. *Let him be home enjoying the embrace of my mother's body. Spare him.*

But Bendis, Huntress of the Earth, and Dionysus turned their cruel faces away from me.

My father entered the starlit clearing. He towered over the Greek invaders. The gore of battle covered his ruddy skin. With a wild cry, he thrust his *sarisa* into the neck of the nearest Greek. A spout of night-black crimson spattered his face and tunic, transforming him to a living specter of Death.

He bared his teeth and growled a challenge. Two Greeks attacked, swinging their swords and hacking at him. Father dispatched them at once, his movements strong and sure. Another Greek, and yet another succumbed to the tip of his spear. He was a fearsome sight. The men from our village cheered as the grove began to clear of invaders. Bracing his stained leather boots against the helm of a fallen raider, Father jerked his *sarisa* free and leapt out of the reach of the next invader. He veered into the worst of the battle and spun. There, he jabbed with the tip of his long spear, to worry the men who followed him. I'd never been so afraid, nor so proud. My father, Delus, the pride of Perperek.

Father slipped once, twice in the muck on the forest floor, reeling a little out of control, as the blood of Dionysus sang in his veins. I wanted to call to him, but no sound came from my useless mouth. Instead, I shivered and hid my face in the shadows and underbrush, clutching the rough trunk of the nearest tree until my palms were red and marked with blood. A clang of metal and one of the Perperek soldiers fell heavily at my feet. I thought his name was Borlok. His eyes wide and unblinking.

I think I screamed.

I must have, for my father turned suddenly and fixed his gaze on me. He mouthed my name, *Doricha*, though I could not hear it over the din of the battle, the clang of metal weapons on metal armor, the squish of blades striking flesh, and the hoarse screams of those that fought and those that fell. He never saw the swords float out of the inky night and flash behind his back, brandished by unseen hands.

Stark terror drove a blade into my heart and I stood and pointed to the area just beyond his familiar broad shoulders. My father's brows drew together for the briefest of seconds before he turned. His topknot swung like a stinging whip, dark with sweat and blood. He brought up his spear and deflected the first blow. His muscles bunched underneath his taut skin. Like a fierce bull, he planted both of his bare hands on the haft of his *sarisa* and forced the Greeks back.

A flash of silver danced at my father's side, and a bloody black line appeared on the grime of his pale tunic. He staggered, clutching his abdomen. He leapt out of reach and spared another tortured glance in my direction.

Then the Greeks spotted me.

My father beat the haft of his _sarisa_ against his armor, trying to draw their attention, but to no avail. Moonlight streamed through the trees and gleamed off the surface of the raiders' polished bronze helmets. One lifted an arm and pointed in my direction. He shouted an unintelligible word. Time seemed to stop.

Blood pounded in my ears. I felt as if my hands were cupped around my eyes; I could see neither left nor right, only ahead, where my father struggled to reach me before the Grecian soldiers.

"Dori!" My father roared. "No!" His leather sandals churned up the stinking, blood-damp forest floor. He slashed wildly at the soldier in front of him. The Greek crumpled to the ground. Father vaulted the fallen soldier and jabbed at the unprotected hip of the next.

"_Papita_," I whispered.

Tears stung the back of my eyes and spilled onto my cheeks. My feet were rooted to the soil. I was so afraid. I could not make them move. My hand made a small gesture unbidden, reaching out to him as if he could indeed make it to me in time to save us both. For a moment, I thought he would.

More invaders fell, Grecian pigs slaughtered by my father's fearsome rage. And then, the Greeks reached my hiding place. The world rushed back to me with such force that I was knocked to my knees. Time resumed its deadly march.

I peered up from my crouched position to see a pair of cold, dark eyes boring into my skull. The five invaders shouldered each other, jockeying for position before my father plowed into them from the side, like a storm from the sea. One sidestepped the blow—the same who had spotted me. He said something to me that I could not understand, grabbed my bare arm and began to drag me from the clearing.

"Doricha," my father called after me as they drew him further away. His voice was tinged with a helpless timbre. "Doricha, fight! Don't let them take you!"

I tried to twist my arm free and run. My captor stopped and slapped me, open handed across my left cheek. He laughed as my father continued to fight the remaining pack, desperate to retrieve me. The blood from my father's side soaked his tunic, but he called curses to them in challenge. The Greek was diverted.

He halted at what he judged a safe distance, removed his helmet, and tucked it under the arm that bound me to him. With a nasty grin at me, he wiped his pale face on the back of his hand and turned back to watch my father's torment. Moonlight gleamed off the dark oiled hair curled against his white forehead.

I had to find a way to free myself. I resolved to fight him, though I'd little chance against an armed Grecian soldier. At full age, we Thracians are half again a Greek's height and breadth but as scarce more than a child, I was no match for him. Or so he thought.

Suddenly, I spied the bucket I took to gather water, lying unnoticed in the bracken. By stretching out my toes, I was able to hook the long handle around my ankle. I bobbled, unbalanced on one foot, and looped the rough wooden handle into my sweating hand.

My captor took no notice, transfixed by his companions' efforts to subdue my father. I glanced at Father once more, as the night's glow surrounded his sweat drenched skin. His face, crowned by the glorious, shining topknot of red-gold, his broad lips curled in a grimace, and the flash of his _sarisa_. At that moment he seemed more splendid than even Dionysus himself. I prayed to be as brave and strong as he.

Wielding the bucket like Boreas, the harbinger of storms, I jerked my wrist free, and screamed my father's war chant.

"Live free!" I aimed for the back of the Greek's head.

He turned in surprise. I swallowed hard, closed my eyes, and swung the heavy wooden bucket with all my strength.

As fortune would have it, my captor leaned over to recapture my wrist just as the wide wooden brim of the bucket clouted him on the side of the temple. The heavy wooden edge boomed like thunder against his skull. His ivory skin split beneath the force, and his dark eyes grew vague. He staggered and blood dripped from the wound to taint his cheeks. Then it seemed the left side of his body ceased to function, for his hand went as nerveless as a palsied elder.

Again, I hefted the bucket and prepared to strike, but there was no need. On the second step, my captor fell to the ground with a most puzzled expression and ceased to move again. I think I shall never forget his death stare.

I was free! And yet my joy was short-lived.

The two remaining Grecian soldiers, unaware of their companion's plight, had gained the upper hand. I turned, just in time to see them plunge both their blades deep into my father's abdomen.

Father's agate eyes locked on mine, strange and terrible, and he gripped a sword pommel and tried to pull it from his body. His lips quivered as his hands scrabbled at the blade thrust through his organs.

"Run," he said in the tongue of my forefathers. "Run, Dori! Don't look back." He coughed and bloody spittle ran from the side of his lips, so much like the crimson wine before. Though I was more than twenty paces away, I could hear his voice as clearly as if we were still snuggled together on the hearth.

The Grecian soldiers taunted him. "The Thracian dog begs for mercy."

They laughed at his pain, and yanked their blades free. My father sank to his knees in the red-running earth. The coppery scent of his life's blood clogged my nostrils. The sea wind moaned like a wounded animal, and rage such as I'd never known scorched the sorrow in my heart.

I would kill them, too. The cleansing flame spread through my arms and legs and filled me with vengeance. I picked up the sword of my dead captor and took one bold step forward out of the shadows.

My father's head shook, the feeble motion begging me without words to stop. Gasping for breath, he clutched his hands over the gaping wounds, trying to hold his flesh together long enough to save me still.

"Run." His chest heaved like a small bird I'd captured once in my palms. "Live free."

He might have said more, but coughing overtook him. Horror struck me. My father lay dying in a pool of his own blood. I'd killed a man. No one would protect me from the cruel whims of the gods. No one, except myself. *Run*, he'd said. With that thought entrenched in my mind, I dropped the cursed Greek sword and fled the clearing, as silent as a wraith, though my throat ached to wail my sorrow to the skies.

Run.

I stumbled and plunged through the black forest.

I could scarce see two steps in front of me. Surrounded by the drowning sounds of battle, my arms flailed. I heard Grecian soldiers in the whispers of every blowing branch and leaf. I feared for my mother and our peaceful village. Was I running to another Grecian trap? And, oh, my father was dead!

Live.

I don't know which direction I fled. Somewhere in the darkness, a wolf howled. I clenched my jaw to keep from joining in. Silence descended, heavy and strange to my ears after the screams of the dying. Great gasping sobs racked my chest, and my legs burned from the steep pitch of the land, but I did not stop. I could not. My father, oh, my beloved father!

Panic and desperation beat at me with icy claws, until I heard a familiar sound to the south. Sounds of the tide. The fortress was near the shoreline, and our village lay directly between the forest and Perperek. I covered my mouth with my hands and focused on the call of rousing sea birds to guide me home.

And all the while, my father's war chant became my mantra.

Live free.

Live free.

It was his dying wish for me. And so, I vowed, I would.

CHAPTER 2

After the initial fear of capture subsided, I followed the tide until at last, I stumbled across the worn earthen path that led to home. The sun was just beginning to break. Pale, silver fingers of light infiltrated the familiar terrain. I shivered and my knees turned to water.

What would I say to my mother? What _could_ I say? My mind turned again and again to the night's devastation.

I had been foolish and it had led my father to his death. Oh, if only I had heeded his warning! Though my eyes were open, I saw only my father sinking to his knees, the hilt of a Grecian blade that protruded from his gut and spilled his steaming blood and innards to the earth.

A tight knot hardened in the pit of my stomach and then uncoiled with such fury I dropped to the earth myself and vomited. Icy, shivering sweat bloomed on my body. My hands and hair were rusted from old blood, whether mine or that of the man I had killed, I do not know. I rolled to the side and curled my knees to my chest, praying I would die before my mother should discover the awful truth.

Some many moments later, I realized Bendis, Mother Huntress, would not take me to her bosom. I reasoned my actions had made me unclean in the eyes of the gods, and so I rose, stiff and aching, to continue.

Where else could I go?

At the top of the next rise, our home materialized out of the low-lying mist. I pictured my mother, still drowsing in the aftermath of spent passion. Or perhaps worse, she could be setting the fire, awaiting me and preparing for my father's victorious return. If not for me, he would return to us. I was sure of it. I bit down hard on a dingy knuckle and stifled the cry that again threatened to erupt from my raw, aching throat.

My father was by all accounts the most accomplished warrior in Perperek. Though we were poor, his exploits had afforded him the luxury of a beautiful Bacchae as a wife instead of one of the sturdy village women who populated this territory. Without him, I did not know how we would survive. That is, if the Greeks did not infiltrate our village and enslave our people. For if my father, the mightiest of men, had fallen so had the others. I'd escaped, but perhaps only to be recaptured as a slave.

Live free, my father had commanded with his last breath.

Could I? Our hut was deathly silent as I approached and no cook fire burned. I trembled, fearing the worst.

"Doricha!" My mother, who never moved without unconscious grace, rushed out of our hut. Her face was ashen. "Gods be praised, you've escaped! You must hurry."

I wanted to speak. My throat closed, and I felt tears prick my swollen eyes.

"Doricha." She enveloped me in a fragrant embrace of herbs and sorrow. "Something has gone amiss. None of the men returned last night and the Greeks could be upon us at any minute. Come now, quickly." Her light eyes darted about the hillside, as she shooed me towards our hut.

I froze in my tracks just outside the threshold, the door my father would never again walk through, because of my willful disobedience.

"Whist, Dori, did you not hear me?" My mother gripped me, quick and brutal and shook me hard enough to set my teeth to clattering.

"*Mamita*..."

My voice was a pitiful sob, even to my own ears. But what right did I have for mercy? My mother turned me around then, and her eyes loomed large and terrible in her divine face. She knelt before me.

"Hear me, Doricha. None of the men returned. *None*. Do you understand?"

I nodded and tears streamed down my cheeks.

"Then you know what that means for us. The fortress has fallen. The others have already fled into the mountains. I waited for you. Hurry now. I've already gathered our belongings."

I was grateful then, so very grateful that she was efficient in her fear. The Greeks would be upon us at any moment. She had always been first and foremost a Bacchae, but the morning's bloody sun revealed my mother's true feelings to me. As I bent to gather my meager pack from the hearth, a darker blot crossed my mind. She didn't know I was the cause of her sorrow. I vowed then never to tell her.

We padded stealthily into the unknown hills to the southwest, beyond the familiar rises of fields where I'd gathered herbs and played solitary games.

My mother was so afraid of capture that she never sought to question my haggard and filthy appearance. I hadn't even had time to wash the evidence of my betrayal from my palms. I rubbed the dried blood from my skin as if I could erase the memories along with my guilt.

Storm season was upon us. I sought to lose myself in the raging wind as we made our escape into the hills. My mother's frigid hand tugged incessantly at mine throughout the day, and she urged me in whispers to hurry. Her concern began to mock me. What would she do if she knew the awful truth? The mountain air scarred my cheeks with taloned claws that could not reach the desperate secret buried in my stomach. It gnawed at me with every step, every murmur of my mother's voice.

When we reached the broken, jagged cliffs of the Rhodopes, I pulled away from her steadying hand and stood at the edge of the rocky mountain path. My beloved homeland stretched green and gold far into the distance. I wavered there. It would be easy to slip off here, into oblivion.

"Doricha?" My mother beckoned to me with her eyes wide and full of fear. "Come away, Daughter."

I did not want to go to her. I wanted to be away from all of this--away from the dying screams of men and crimson fog clouding my vision. But I had not the courage to hurl myself over the welcoming heights of the cliffs. Hot bubbling acids ate at my stomach. I could taste them in the back of my throat as I rejected salvation and returned to the path of my mother's footfalls.

A day and night, a night and day, we walked on in silence with only the birds to note our progress. When she offered me a slice of bread and goat cheese, I refused. A crease formed between her delicate arching brows, but she said nothing and let me walk on in hunger and guilty silence.

The hills were treacherous and I stumbled and slipped on the scree, until my mother bade me clutch onto her skirts as we climbed. Sharp rocks pierced the soles of my sandals and the wind tore my stained woolen chiton to ragged shreds and still we journeyed towards the setting sun. I took no food, only a little watered wine, until my mother's concern over me outgrew her sorrow at losing her heart mate.

She knelt before me in the dust and pressed her face against my chest.

"Please, Doricha. You must eat. For my sake, if not your own." Her light eyes were awash with tears. "I cannot lose you, too."

I could not stand to see her humbled. I choked down the hard stale bread and smelly cheese to ease her mind, though it stuck in my throat. We headed onward, I knew, to the one place that might offer us some protection-- the temple of the Bacchae.

As we labored on beneath the third slowly dying sun, I followed my mother without question. At some point, we must have passed out of immediate danger, because the set of her shoulders relaxed. Perhaps the proximity of the temple reassured her. I was too sick and exhausted to care. We continued, it seemed, for eternity though in truth the night's horror had yet to fade in my mind.

When at last I thought I could go no further and it seemed I would march into the gates of Hades for my sins, we reached the torch-lit sanctuary. It was dusk, a time when the veils between worlds are drawn back and fearful things tread upon mortal soil. The cliffs, once solid and eternal rock, grew filmy before my weary eyes, and I fancied the air grew thin and sharp, as if in anticipation as we drew near.

The Temple to Dionysus was hidden deep within a natural cavern of the Rhodopes Mountains. The entrance was a gaping black hole that seemed to swallow every trace of daylight in its inky maw. Torches lit the narrow path of crushed stone. Thracian artists had enhanced the rugged beauty of the entrance with enormous carvings of the gods in various stages of repose or pursuit. Beyond the columned entry, Dionysus lay on a verdant hillside attended by the blue-inked Bacchae. Feeling unclean, I took no comfort from the depictions.

I stared at the exquisite illustration and then at my mother. She noted my gaze and patted my shoulder.

"It's what you were born for, Dori. To live in grace and beauty as a Bacchae."

I turned again to the carved friezes adorning the chamber entrance. Here, a Bacchae fed grapes to a satyr. There, Dionysus danced, ringed by five women, whilst others played musical instruments. Each was a vision of beauty, grace and gaiety. I swallowed hard. Each bore a pattern of cobalt across the backs of their hands. After the grisly images in the night forest, I felt as if I'd entered the blessed afterworld.

These women were the epitome of perfection. Oh, how I longed to be one of them! With every fiber in my being I wished to find myself worthy. But I was all elbows and knees and stringy hair. My limbs were too long, my nose too snub, and my teeth too large. I did not know how to play music or dance. And worse, I was unclean--both outside and in, for I had led my father to his doom.

I closed my eyes, shutting out the beautiful images. In my mind's eye, I saw them turning away from me, shielding their pure faces from the stain of my presence.

"I will never be one of them," I muttered.

"Whist, daughter. You mustn't say such things."

A glimmer of hope pierced the haze of despair in my heart. If I were a Bacchae, I could beg my lord Dionysus to watch over my father's shade. I could earn back my honor.

I let myself be consoled by my mother, who shooed away my failings with a pale, slim hand. Deafening booms resounded off the craggy cliffs, like peals of thunder, too evenly spaced. My body shuddered with each beat. I imagined them as the voice-blood of the Bacchae, mocking me for my impurity.

"Come," my mother said and led me to the gods' door.

It is a strange thing what guilt, youth, and starvation can do to one's perception of truth. Smothering darkness enveloped my mother and me. As the heat of the day passed from our bodies, we entered the temple. The path sloped downward, deep into the mountain. Chill bumps grew along my bared arms and legs. The crunch of our sandaled feet on the stone path mingled with the whoosh and sizzle of unseen torches in the earth-scented air ahead of us.

"This is the Throat of Orpheus," my mother whispered as dim torchlight penetrated the darkness. "It is a sacred place, one of the last places he walked, before the Maenads slaughtered him. Dionysus, our lord, accepted the death of Orpheus as a sacrifice for his people. Pass these walls and pray for joy to return again to your heart."

"Will no one come to greet us?" I asked.

"Whist, Dori. You heard them sound the gongs, did you not?" But her nostrils were white and pinched.

So, not thunder, as I had thought before, but the hammerings of mortal men upon a polished disc of bronze. I wondered what portent the alarm held for us, but feared to ask. We traversed the long hall in silence, my mother praying and myself, eyes downcast, feigning penitence for I was certain the priests would know of my unworthiness. I scurried beside her and shrank from the serpentine shadows that seemed to follow my every movement.

The sudden appearance of a robed figure in the tunnel startled me. A priest materialized out of the shadows like a wraith, tall and sinuous. I skidded to a stop to avoid colliding with his pale robed legs. His eyes were deeply set and obscured by the shadow of his brows, but they flickered once like burning pitch over me before settling on my mother.

"Greetings, Sita," he said after an uncomfortable length of time.

"May the gods find favor on you," replied my mother. She bowed her head.

"You've brought the girl for induction." It was not a question.

"Please, we...I must speak with the Branch Order. Will you take us?"

He considered her for a moment longer before answering. "As you wish."

My mother exhaled audibly, and her icy fingers gripped my hand as we stepped from Orpheus' Throat into the temple's embrace.

My first impression was that I had shrunk in stature. The temple had an enormous central hall painstakingly carved out of the natural cavern. Pale granite columns supported the entire cavern, jutting like wolf's teeth from the polished stone floor. The air felt moist and cool upon my skin, as if I walked inside a tomb. Our footsteps echoed as we crossed the stone floor, and I could hear the far off whistle of an *avlos* being played. The priest shortened his stride, to accommodate my pace. It made me only a little less afraid.

The ceiling lay hidden in the black beyond the torchlight, so high I could not see it no matter how I strained my weary eyes. The sharp acrid stench of burning pitch stung my nostrils. Hundreds of torches shed their smoky illumination on the adorned stone walls. Painted grapevines blossomed in earthy red, ochre, and black, resplendent in their full harvest beauty. Stag and hare cavorted on mountain hillsides beyond. I followed their painted forms to aerial depictions of birds soaring toward the sea. They reminded me of my seaside village, now gone, so I turned away.

Attendants, all with the close-cropped, curling locks of the *ktístai*, swept the floors with rush bundled brooms. Their pallid robes flowed with the same unconscious grace that marked my mother and the priest we followed. The *ktístai* took pride in their work, completing each task with meticulous care. So will mortal man ever toil to make life upon the earth worthy of the gods' notice.

A large altar, complete with a sensuous carved effigy of Dionysus, stood near the rear of the colonnade. Several young maidens strung a garland of pale blooming flowers over the deity's crown and shoulders. Others swayed as they cleared away the wilted blossoms from the previous day. I would discover later this was a special task reserved for the most promising of inductees. For now, it was enough to mark that each of these girls was a study in classical perfection. Their skin was the faultless rose-pink of our race, and though their hair ranged from spun gold to crimson, each was ode to the gods in her own right.

I stumbled, feeling weary in my grimy chiton, but I wore my guilt and filth like a mantle to shield my pride. The immaculate priest raised a brow in my direction and continued.

We came to an inner chamber, not far off the immense temple. The priest told me to wait in the hall, and I sank gratefully onto the cold stone floor. Then the priest and my mother disappeared behind a wooden door. A gap the span of my palm existed between the door and the stone tiles, so, in my cross-legged position, I could hear much of what went on inside.

"Welcome, Sita. At last you have brought your daughter for training?" asked a woman's voice from the other side of the door. Perhaps it was the chill interior of the cavern, but the welcome spoken in words did not ring in her voice.

"If it pleases our lord, we have both journeyed to enter in his service," my mother responded.

"*Both*?"

"Yes." Her voice caught a little, much like the weight in my heart. "The Greeks raided our village. Delus is gone. I beg entry from the Bacchae for

19

my daughter and myself."

There was a long pause.

Would they give us sanctuary? If they refused us, I could not think of where we would go. If the temple turned us away, we were surely lost.

The voice spoke again.

"We cannot. Your daughter may stay as is her due, but you are unwelcome here."

I heard my mother sob and bit my lip hard. I would not stay without her.

"Please," she said. "I wish to rededicate myself to the gods' service. I will do whatever tasks you set, so long as my daughter and I may take refuge in the temple. I…I will teach or-"

"We have no need of your teachings here," interrupted the woman.

Another long pause, followed by murmurs of many voices. I could not make them out, muffled as they were through the thick wooden door.

"Please," my mother said in a voice I'd never heard her use. "I will do anything."

The babble began anew. One man's voice seemed to carry over the others. I rubbed my hands on the undersides of my chilled legs and fought the urge to peek into the gap. What would become of my poor mother if the Bacchae turned her away?

"You were favored once by the gods, Sita," said the woman. "More than most can claim to be. Now you are spoilt by your time amongst the villagers. Your hands are chapped and your body made slack for all your youthful appearance."

How those words must have stung my mother's heart, for the villagers had hated her so for her beauty. Now she was deemed unfit for the Bacchae, the glory for which she was trained.

The voice continued. "Still, for the sake of the girl, you may stay and take such tasks as will make you useful to the temple. Perhaps your daughter will achieve the greater glory you forsook to breed a soldier's get."

I wondered at the venom in that voice. I'd always assumed my father had the temple blessing to take my mother to wife.

My mother murmured her thanks, and the door flew open. The priest who'd led us through the temple peered down at me, still crouched in the corridor. His eyes flickered once to the door and the corners of his mouth deepened.

"You," he said. "Follow me." He started off down the passage without explanation.

"My…my mother?" I stood and brushed the dust off my knees. I was determined not to stay without her. The priest stopped. Though his manner was abrupt, his eyes were not unkind when he turned to look at me.

"She will be given a place. Your place is with the other supplicants. Over there." He pointed to one of the halls where I had heard music earlier. He waited until I shuffled forward before continuing. "You've come at a fortunate time," he said, as we once again crossed the great center hall. "There's to be a festival in honor of the last harvest. This winter we should press twice the number of grapes than the previous year."

This was fortunate news indeed, as there is nothing quite so fine as good Thracian wine. Indeed, it is our lord Dionysus' blood that runs in our veins and causes such jealousy in the hearts of other men. And after our life in the village, I could not believe that I would be given such fine clothes and good food. My exhaustion waned in anticipation of seeing my first Bacchanal. I was certain it would live in my memory forever, and so it has, but not for the reason I thought it would.

After being seen to my quarters, which were little more than a small alcove in a room of five other inductees, I was given a clean chiton and sent to bathe. A meager repast of bread, lamb, and cheese was brought to curb my hunger.

I'd just brushed the crumbs from my lips when weariness descended upon me, but I could not stop worrying for my poor mother. I begged news from one of the women setting out figs and thyme for the meal and was informed that she was settled into her own quarters. I should rest, as my inspection and training would begin on the morrow. I yawned so hard, I thought my jaw would crack from my skull. One of the temple priestesses saw and sent me to my pallet until the feast.

I set my guilt aside and slept like the dead until the moon sailed high in a curtain of the night sky. At least I thought it must be evening. Who could tell? It was odd residing underneath the mountains, like a serpent hiding under a rock. When my mother appeared to lead me to the Bacchanal, all my misgivings vanished. Lines of grief still etched her features, but her eyes were rested and alert. She seemed resigned and composed among the frenetic excitement of the feast.

"You must be silent, unless spoken to, Dori," she admonished.

"What part will I take in the Bacchanal?" I asked.

Mother compressed her lips. "I do not know, but for certain you should be as unobtrusive as you can."

"Is it not safe, here?" I wondered.

"It is not safe anywhere, Dori." Her voice quavered with sorrow. "But here, you may find a place, if only you will devote yourself."

"*We*," I corrected her. "We may find a place here, together."

My mother nodded and put a slim arm around my shoulders, but she did not smile.

We entered the vast cavern of the central chamber, which sparkled from the glow of torchlight reflected on the polished stone floors. Hundreds of bodies sashayed to the tables piled high with Thracian delicacies. There were hanks of roast lamb stuffed with raisins, garlic and figs, smoked pork, and wild green salats with olive oil and tangy vinegar. Crimson wine poured freely into hammered bronze and carved wooden goblets. Each hand had only to stretch forth and the blood of the gods flowed comfortably into reach. The sound of laughter drowned out the cries of the dying soldiers still ringing in my ears, and I reached often to refill my cup.

For hours, the temple folk feasted and laughed, while musicians played and the Bacchae danced. I ate, but no amount of mirth could tease a smile to my face. The other neophytes were rapt with attention, and I remembered my mother's grace. It was a tribute to the gods, the skill with which Bacchae played, and sang, and danced. Oh, the dancing! As graceful as birds on the wing over the vast seas.

I did so want her to be proud of me.

Late into the night, the air grew thick from the many torches, the scent of spiced foods and the press of bodies. I watched a temple priest sprinkling powder on the flames. A heavy perfumed smoke permeated the chamber. Soon, my vision wavered and my ears rang with the noise of the revelry. My head began to ache. Several participants had wandered off in twos and threes, no doubt to clear their senses, and so as the drums began to pound in time to my heartbeat, I moved to the nearest hall to do the same.

Away from the miasma of smoke and dazzling beauty of the feast, the pain of my father's death sliced my heart. I didn't belong here, in this sacred and beautiful place. I don't know why I thought of him, then. Perhaps the sight of my mother, whose feet should have been dancing. She'd sat alone on her stool and watched the men and women with a wistful expression, as the music rattled the base of the mountain. Then she'd risen and disappeared down one of the far halls. I'd felt too full of guilt to follow her. So I dwelled on death, alone in the corridor of black granite. I flung myself prostrate on the rough stone of the hallway and prayed for Dionysus to take pity on me.

Dionysus, who governs our passions, both rage and pleasure, chaos and love, if you accept me into your beloved arms, I promise never to turn away from my faith. Watch over my father.

The smoke in the hallway made my chest began to burn. I fancied I could hear the heart of Dionysus beating in my ears. The world spun, and the very stones seemed to vibrate and come to life. I laid my aching head on the cold stone. It felt so nice and cool beneath my cheek. My hands stretched backwards, palms up and the blood rushed in my veins in time to the quickening crescendo of drum beats emanating from the central hall. My pulse beat. The wild pounding inside the temple swallowed me whole.

Then, without warning, the drums stopped.

I rose, dizzy, with my ears still ringing and scuttled to the temple chamber. The air in the feast hall seemed charged with frightening energy. I remember the scent, still, to this day. Heavy and pervasive, sweet like the delicate hillside blossoms and thick with cloying human musk. A fug of stinking herbed smoke permeated the room, hanging over our heads like a pseudo-sky. Musicians sounded their flutes and harps. Chaotic harmonies swelled and receded like the waves of the sea. And then I heard the cries.

It seemed I'd entered a battlefield, though I saw no weapons. My heart thundered in my chest. Half-clothed bodies lay in a tangled mound on the cold stone floor, their wine goblets still clutched in their fists. I could not discern male from female at first. They were all connected by limbs and hips.

I was dizzy, so very dizzy. In my herb-muddled thoughts, some great tragedy had befallen us. The floor tilted under my feet and I stumbled. I blinked once, trying to clear my bleary vision and the smoky room became the nightmare forest battlefield I'd escaped in Perperek. The jutting columns became black limbs of the misty cypress grove. Crimson blood covered everyone and ran down the stone floors to puddle at my feet. Surely, I heard the mournful cries of the dying. My ears felt stuffed with wool.

I shook my head and the bloody scene vanished.

In its place was a scene I have difficulty describing, even now.

I crept behind a large urn to search for my mother, fearing most to see her amongst the tangled bodies. Fate was with me and she was not to be found amongst them. I watched in fascinated horror as the mass of temple denizens heaved and bucked. Many voices called out as if in torturous pain. This was so very unlike my memories of the Greek invasion, yet in my mind it seemed one and the same.

My vision wavered, and I clutched the columns for support.

The room spun. I felt ill.

All around me, time seemed to slow.

The mound of exposed flesh and limbs writhed. They seemed to grapple with one another, vying for some higher unattainable ground. Appendages flexed and extended with agonizing slowness. My stomach clenched. Swirling fumes coiled around each naked body, like demons. Men and women, women and women, and yes, even men together sweated and slithered in a great pooling of grunts and thrusts and sighs. The hairs on my neck prickled and I sensed that I was both welcome and not.

The floor pitched beneath my feet. I toppled sideways, and rolled before crawling on my hands and knees to escape. One of the Bacchae nearest me reached out her hand towards me. Her beautiful eyes were glazed in what I thought was the throes of death. How could I refuse?

I crept near to her and she grasped my hand. Her pink tongue slipped between her lips to moisten them and she kept her eyes focused on mine. I heard a grunt and my eyes traveled the length of her exposed breasts to her trim abdomen. I glanced at the priest sweating between her legs, at her robes hiked up to expose her womanhood.

"Stop," I whispered. The floor bucked beneath me and I swayed on my knees.

The priest's eyes bored into me like a *sarisa*. He groaned and his head lolled on his neck as he bucked against the Bacchae. I panted with him, as pressure aching to be released simmered in my midsection. His buttocks flexed and his hands held her legs wide like a butterfly's wings. They flapped as he continued his onslaught. She moaned low in her throat and squeezed my hand harder.

"You're killing her," I whispered. My voice refused to work properly.

I tried to let go of her hand, to beat at him with my fists, but her grip was too strong for me to break. She pinioned me with the huge ebony pupils of her gray eyes. Tears of frustration stung my eyes and poured down my cheeks as she arched her back against the cold stone floor and tried to buck him off. Her hips rose and pumped. Then she gave a small cry that sent liquid heat rushing between my legs.

Her body strained and then fell limp. Her eyes unfocused and then closed. I thought the Bacchae dead with the sheen of sweat still dewy on her lips and breasts. The man gave a hoarse bark and then slid away from her. I saw the spurting tip of his erect phallus as he spilled his glistening, pearly seed onto the ground. His eyes rolled back into his head and he crumpled to the tiles.

My hands shook as I pried at the Bacchae's fingers. I lifted my gaze, only to meet my mother's across the room. She smiled at me, a terrible pride shining in her gaze. It was then the haze of perfumed smoke lifted, and I realized what I had witnessed. My blood ran colder than a sea storm.

Not a battlefield at all, but a levy to the wild rites of Dionysus. I had heard of men who spilt themselves on the earth, as a recompense for Orpheus who was murdered and brought back to us as a god. For just as the seed of man brings life, so it does rebirth. It was one of the most sacred of rituals. One where Dionysus himself moved in our veins.

I knew these truths from the lessons of my mother. And now I'd seen how it was done.

I felt shaky and sickened as I wrenched my hand free of the Bacchae's grasp and stumbled from the hall. Was this was what my mother had meant for me, even before our village was taken? Before necessity forced us to take refuge in the temple. My intended destiny was to sweat and seethe beneath a temple priest, no better than a receptacle for lust?

With my heart lodged in my throat, I went to find her and demand the truth. I made it two steps before the world dimmed and I slid to the floor.

CHAPTER 3

"It was the wine." My mother set aside her mending.

Her chamber was not as small as my own but still not as large as some I had seen. She had a straw pallet, as did we all, but also a low wooden stool and a candle.

"The wine?" I was puzzled. "Was it poisoned like the smoke?"

My mother's lips twisted in a wry smile.

"You have so much to learn." She shook her head. "Not poisoned. Mixed with special herbs to give it the power of Dionysus' blood during the Bacchanal. It helps us to commune with our lord. I felt so close to him...closer than I have in years." Tears glittered in her eyes. "I am proud you were chosen to join in. It is a great boon!"

"A boon! I thought he was killing her! I was frightened!" I plucked at a loose thread in my chiton.

I knew what the rutting of animals was, having tended more than my share in our village. And I knew of the passion between men and women, being a child of two lovers. But the herbs in the wine and smoke had twisted it all in my mind. I was conflicted--sickened, and yet strangely thrilled by what I witnessed at the Bacchanal.

"Mamita, must I lay with any _ktístai_ who desires me?" I asked, worriedly. "How could you wish such a thing for me? I'm still a child." I was afraid of what I must do in the temple to earn our keep. Was this the life of a Bacchae?

"You are old enough to be wed." My mother shook her head and clucked like an offended thrush. "Have you remembered nothing of my lessons? Whist, Dori, these teachings are far beneath your years. We give honor to the gods through our grace and beauty. It is good we have come."

I could not believe my ears.

Had she forgotten the very reason for our flight to the temple? Had she forgotten my father's heart so soon? I wanted to find love in a marriage bed, the same passion that bound my father to my mother. I was afraid of what my part in the temple rites might be, but much more terrifying was the heat running through my veins. I'd never thought to see such lust, nor did I think to take part in it. Such things were the tales of women.

"Good? Good that my father should have died at the hands of the Greeks?" My voice was shrill and hot tears welled up to blur my vision. "You think it a fine thing that I should offer up my body to the service of the gods? If my father were alive he would never have allowed you to sell me to the temple priests for your own survival."

I do not know where the words came from, perhaps the black stain on my guilty soul. My mother rounded on me, and slapped me hard across the cheek.

Thracian children are not beaten, as are the Spartans and Greeks. Her loss of control was a marked sign of the pain my words caused her. But the anguish of my father's death was too new, too raw for me to care about her pain.

"Never speak such words to me again." She pointed a long tapered finger at me and her eyes flashed. "It is a blessing the temple accepted us. For you to witness the most holy of rites. To be respected and beloved by the gods. Think you, on where we would be now, if not for here? Brutalized by some Grecian dog? Fodder for the worms?" She turned away from me, and I heard her stifle a sob. "Not a sun will set that I will not ache for my husband's arms to comfort me. I will *never* feel them again. But you hold hope in your future, should you have the courage to grasp it. You know the entrance to the temple, Doricha. There are no gates to hinder you should you choose to go."

What can I say, but that I was a child then, and I fled from her anger and her pain. I padded through the hallways, confused and alone. I had not meant to argue with her, and yet I could not stop myself from hasty words to test the bond between us.

I staggered against the walls, unseen by any. My head pounded from both her blow and the thoughts turning round in my brain. I'd wanted to wound her. I wanted to scream at her, *why did you not keep him home with you that night?*

And what's worse, I found my anger had tainted even my father's memory. The temple was my duty, my birth right as the daughter of a Bacchae. Dionysus was our lord and master, so handsome and so virile. Who was my father to keep me from such a god's embrace? I felt angry, ignorant and ill-used. And then, a moment later, came the shame.

"Forgive me," I whispered into the darkness. I don't know which of them I meant.

I covered my face with my hands and wept for my dead father, my poor, beautiful mother, and myself, still lost between the both of them.

A priestess found me there, with my face buried against the stone wall. She mistook my tears and led me back to my quarters. I laid myself out on my pallet, wretched and expecting the gods to curse me for my blasphemous thoughts.

I must have dozed, because I awoke to the sounds of someone entering my chamber. Soft hesitant footfalls padded across the silent expanse of my small room. I bolted upright and peered into the darkness.

"Who's there?" I whispered. The familiar scent of sorrow enfolded me.

"Shh, Daughter." My mother's words floated out of the darkness like welcome birdsong. Her voice was hoarse; I could tell she had been weeping. "I should not have exposed you to our sacred rites without preparing you first. It was a mistake. Allow me to stay with you this last time. Tomorrow your training will begin."

She slipped onto the straw pallet, and I felt the soft warmth of her body mold against my back and legs. Tears pricked my eyes anew. We lay side by side for long moments, while she stroked my hair. She let it run through her fingers like water, and the movement soothed my troubled heart.

"I am sorry," I said.

She sighed and rested her arm over my waist. "So am I, Doricha. So am I."

"I _do_ want to make you proud to call me 'Daughter'." And I did, deep in my heart. I fancied I could hear her smiling in the darkness.

"And so you shall. You are special, Doricha. One day, all the world will know your name," she promised.

We fell asleep smiling at our own absurdity.

In the wee morning hours, I arose to an empty bed. My mother entered the room with a neophyte's robes. She held them out for me to try.

I slipped into the fresh robes and allowed her to brush my hair out. She left it long and shining. If her eyes were a touch wistful at the sight of my red-gold tresses, I pretended not to notice. There had been enough harsh words between us regarding my father, and I would offer up no more to wound her with.

"Aidne will see you first. She will determine your strengths and skills, if she establishes you have any." Mother placed her hand under my chin and tipped my head back. "You have very fine eyes, I think, and your skin is fair. Well," she said with a sigh. "We shall see."

I was too nervous to eat much the first meal, but with crease worrying my mother's forehead, I managed to gulp down some wine and a bit of coarse bread. Then, a pretty blushing girl with a devotee's robes came to lead me away.

"My name is Mara," said the girl. She took my hand and smiled. I could not help but smile back at her dimpled cheeks. She did not appear the least bit nervous to see this Aidne, and it eased my trepidation.

"I am Doricha, but my mother calls me Dori."

"Then so shall I call you, if you'll have it. I can tell we shall be near-sisters in no time." Mara tucked my hand in the crook of her elbow and whispered, "Don't be nervous."

"Why? Is not Aidne very stern?"

"Oh no! She is _very_ stern. And she is likely to be rough with you as well, considering…but nervousness will not please her."

"Considering what?" I asked, beginning to feel faint in my sandals.

"Your mother," she replied.

I had not time to ask her more, for we arrived at Aidne's chamber. Mara knocked on the wood, and waited until she was bid entry. She closed the door soundly in my face, and alas, there was no hand-sized crevice through which to listen. I stood in the hall and shifted in my sandals unsure if I should knock on the door myself. And all the while, a sinking fear I might disgrace my mother churned my stomach.

At last the door was opened, but not by Mara. It was another devotee, a girl of no more than sixteen winters, with dull red hair and a surly frown. She gestured for me to enter.

"Come close where I can see you." I turned my head and found a woman of advanced age. Her pale hair had faded to grey near her temples, but her face bore the beauty of our race like a shield to battle. Faint lines etched the skin around her mouth and eyes. Those eyes were sharp and not kind when she turned to me.

"Step quick, girl! The gods wait for no one, least of all you." I recognized that voice as the faceless woman who had almost denied us entrance to the temple.

Oh, how I fought the urge to scurry to her side, like a kit cleaves to its mother when nipped. Instead, I forced myself to walk at a sedate pace and tried my best to emulate my mother's graceful sway. In the corner of the room, Mara shifted her weight to the balls of her feet as if she could force me to hurry.

"Same eyes," grunted the old woman. "More green than grey. Pah!" She made a shooing motion with her hand. "That's his hair, too, I'll wager." She scrutinized every inch of my face. I felt my flesh crawl under the touch of her gaze and I resisted the urge to scratch my nose.

Aidne circled me, slowly like a serpent. "Well, strip off your robes."

I must have displayed my shock, because as I felt my brows draw up, hers narrowed until I could see the glimmer of her black pupils. _She hates me_, I thought. My arms felt wooden as I moved to unpin my woven pleats and my cheeks burned fiercer than the hottest flame.

"Here, I will help her," Mara volunteered. She scooted to my side and I felt better to have her step between Aidne and me, as if she could shield me from the old woman's displeasure. Aidne moved away from us to scold the red-haired girl.

"She despises me," I hissed. My eyes darted beyond Mara's pale pink shoulder to where Aidne muttered.

"Perhaps," whispered Mara, unclasping my robes. "She was devastated when your mother left the temple, or so they say."

"She knew my mother?" I risked another furtive glance. Aidne frowned at me and strode over to the pair of us. The sullen red-haired girl glared at us. Mara bit her lip and glided back to the wall like a shadow.

"Drop your hands," Aidne commanded. I realized I was clutching my robes over my body. Well, if she was determined to hate me, I would not give her the satisfaction of seeing me cringe.

I lowered my hands, and my robes followed. The soft woven material puddled at my feet. The room was cold, but I would not show her my discomfort. Chill bumps grew on my legs. I thrust out my budding breasts and lifted my chin, feeling my nipples pucker. My vision, I affixed to a far off spot on the chamber wall, as my audacity did not extend to meeting her eyes.

"Your limbs are long and spindly. You will be tall, I think." She sniffed. "That is something, at least. Your buttocks are round and high. Good. You will be especially suited to dance, if you have any grace about you at all. Time will tell, girl, what blood runs through those veins of yours. Now, open your mouth."

I blushed with pride at her assessment.

Aidne counted my teeth and peered down my throat. She pinched the flesh of my arms and legs. Oh, would this inspection never cease? I felt like a brood nanny goat. When she was satisfied, at least as much as she could be, she instructed me to sing.

My heart sank, for song is not one of my finest gifts. My legs quivered and my throat closed with nervousness, but I sang. I sang loudly, though perhaps not well. When I finished, Aidne folded her arms across her chest.

"Well, you will never be exceptional, but you will not be the lowliest among us, unless you are idle," she said. Her eyes flitted to the red-haired girl. I caught Mara stifling a smile.

"You may report to Lukra for dance this morning. After the midday meal, I wish you to study our sacred histories with Merikos, the priest who met you at the tunnels."

Merikos. The priest with the kind eyes. I repeated his name until I was certain not to forget.

"In the days that follow, you will be assigned a different tutor for song, or harp and flute, for tumbling and _gymnastikas_. If you show promise, you will be set new tasks and find a position in the temple. But if you are idle, you will be sent to the kitchens and serve the priests with menial chores for the rest of your days. What do they call you, girl?"

"Doricha."

Aidne grunted. "Very well, Doricha. You may go."

I'd never minded the sound of my own name, until I heard it spoken from her lips. Mara moved to escort me out.

"Stay, Mara. Let Suvra take her. I have need of you elsewhere."

My heart plummeted again.

Suvra the Surly, as I came to call her in my own mind, shuffled forward with no pretense at grace and led me from the chamber. I had one last glance at a meek-eyed Mara before the door was closed.

"I saw you smile." Suvra lifted her squared chin several notches. "You think I am the lowliest of the devotees? Humph! I serve my grandmother well enough."

Disbelief hit me like a thunderclap. "Aidne is your...?"

"My grandmother." She sneered. "You're lucky she asked to see you. They would not have let you or your mother stay if my grandmother had declined to see you. Think on that, little devotee." Suvra smiled, a sight which, I'm sorry to say, did not improve her looks.

"Why would she do such a thing?" I mused aloud.

"Why would she not!" Suvra cried indignantly. "Your mother was her sister's child, and most beloved when she forsook our ways to lay with a mere village warrior. She, who was trained to service gods and kings!"

A pair of priests entered the cold, damp hall and stared at us. They veered away, frowning.

"My mother," I murmured. "I must speak with her...."

"In there." Suvra grabbed my shoulder. She pointed to a chamber where I could hear the steady staccato of wood striking stone. "Or will you shame both our names by refusing your first instruction?"

My mind was as scattered as the leaves of a cypress before winter's frozen mantle lays all aside. I was to report to Lukra for dance. I wanted to speak with my mother, but even more desperate was the desire to do well, to be worthy. To become a woman of honor, a beloved Bacchae. If Aidne saw merit in me, I would not fail her or my mother.

Dionysus, if it be your will let me bring glory to your service. And so I prayed and stepped over the threshold.

CHAPTER 4

"Stand up straight!" Lukra clapped her hands in a steady rhythm. "Make your spine a _sarisa_, to battle against age and ugliness. Your limbs should float like foam on the waves. No, no. Not that like. Like this." She jabbed between my shoulder blades. "Now, again."

Sweat trickled down my back and soaked into my robes as I performed the agonizingly slow steps. Next to me, Mara's face shone with perspiration and her customary merry expression. I had been at the temple for ninety days, with little time to rest or see my mother. I learned quickly and, indeed, Aidne had spoken true. I did have some gift for dance.

Mara had become my near-sister, indeed. We took most our meals together and could oft be found whispering in the halls, when we were not training or serving. She was my first true friend, as the village children were somewhat fearful of my mother's training. Mara, like me, was finding joy in newly gained secrets taught to the temple devotees.

In addition to being required to serve in the temple professions, the Bacchae taught us the rudiments of the five arts of love making: the movements and positions, with special emphasis on the _kelēs_--the female superior "race horse" position. Mara and I had giggled through them at first, but upon recalling the Bacchanal, I quickly sobered. I was becoming a woman now.

Second, we were instructed in the arts of song and dance, though Sophriae despaired of my learning to sing well. Then, instruction in cosmetics and hygiene, the art of persuasive speech, poetry, and recitation, and how to use empathy, sensitivity and all the ruses and charms of amorous relations. Now that I was perceived a woman, I could not wait to employ my new found knowledge.

I devoted myself to learning my letters and learned to write my own name. I even helped Aidne to sort herbs, fragrant artemesia, fennel for protection, golden flowered rue for healing, and pennyroyal used in Bacchanal initiation and to prevent babes. One of them made my nose tickle and drip until Aidne cursed and sent me away. Weeks passed as I exhausted my body and mind, too filled with temple training to mourn my lost father and the freedom of my youth.

Every afternoon, I slipped away from the mid-day meal to arrive early for my lessons with Merikos. He began with the history every Thracian child is taught, how roving tribes of men settled in this most sacred place and paid tribute to Dionysus. Satisfied I had memorized those simple tales, he ventured into the lesser-known aspects of our religion; those studied only by the holy temple devotees who must spread the word of the gods to those less fortunate. He had changed since our acceptance into the temple, or perhaps it was only my knowing him better that made it so. I was reminded of the lithe form of Dionysus, older than me in years but still youthful with his handsome form and unlined skin.

That was Merikos.

And even more secret, he spoke of Orpheus, son of the muse Kalliope and Oiagros, a river god. Orpheus, who charmed the wild animals, beguiled the trees and flowers with his lyre, and drew followers with the beauty of his song. Orpheus, who sailed with the Grecian Argonauts to search for the Golden Fleece and protected them from the Sirens with his magic song. When he descended into Hades to rescue his beloved Eurydice, Dionysus was angered. Our lord turned his face from his favored son of Thrace, and the Maenads murdered Orpheus. Some priests still paid homage to Orpheus in secret and I guessed Merikos was one of them.

For if it is not here, where our dense forests, fertile valleys and gentle shores ring the power of the gods, then where? If not in our towering mountains with their wide green gorges and slopes tilting under the weight of poplars, willows, and humble shrubs that perfume the breeze, then it is not anywhere on this earth. Such were the teachings of Merikos and my ears never tired of hearing them, or my lips of repeating them to Mara.

"I do not believe a man could hold sway over the gods merely with his voice." Mara fluffed her hair with her hands.

It was very late. We had lingered over the evening meal until none were left, save the old crone who cleared away the platters. She gave us a dark look and we jumped to our feet and moved towards the devotees' hall.

"Why not?" I asked.

"I just don't. Besides, it is Dionysus who rules our heart and bodies, not a mere mortal with a lyre." She sighed. "When do you suppose they will hold another Bacchanal?"

I shook my head. "What do I care? We will not be asked to participate."

"I shall," Mara said with confidence. We passed out of the hall and into the alcove that housed her pallet.

"You won't!" I was horrified by the thought of my beloved friend sweating beneath a temple priest. I wrinkled my nose.

"I will," she said again. She dropped to her pallet and patted the area beside her. I flopped down next to her, glad to be off my feet. "See how my breasts have grown this year? Phrygia says I shall be a full woman, soon."

She took my hand and cupped it to her breast. I could feel her heart beating beneath the layer of rough wool. The heat of her surprised me. I put my other hand to my own breast. I could not tell if they were of a size. They felt the same to me, but I'd never considered myself womanly. Not yet. No, no...mine must be smaller.

"I do not think I have grown," I said miserably. Mara would be a woman without me.

She placed her palm over my hand, still cupping my breast.

"You have." She nodded sagely and gave me a gentle squeeze. "I'll bet even Merikos has noticed."

"He hasn't!"

"Hm." Mara made a noncommittal noise and lay back on the pallet. I followed her and we stared for some time at the darkened ceiling of rock above us. In truth, I stared at nothing, just enjoyed the company of her soft breath next to me.

"Did you know I have grown woman's hair," Mara said. "Down there."

"Have you?" I could not believe it. Surely she did not have that yet? "I never noticed."

"Well, you wouldn't," Mara said. "See?" She hiked her chiton over her hips and took my hand in hers. Our intertwined fingers slid slowly over her smooth skin, over the soft arc of her belly to the mound of her sex.

My fingers halted in the crisp thatch covering her nether lips. She was soft, so soft down there, hidden by the rough burr of hair. I felt a warmth blossom below my stomach. It spread like too much wine in my veins, and made me feel weak and languorous. I did not move my hand. Mara did not ask me to.

"You are a woman, now." I agreed. My throat felt tight.

We sat there for some many long moments, and I let the heat of her infuse me.

"Do you ever think of lying with a man?" Mara asked.

I swallowed hard. I hadn't. Not really. Not unless you counted the time I'd gazed at Merikos and wondered at what was hidden beneath his robes-- if he was as perfect as the effigy of Dionysus.

"Yes," I lied.

"Me too," Mara said. I was glad then, that I'd lied.

She pressed my fingertips more firmly, as if she were smoothing her chiton over her pubic mound. But there was no chiton between our fingers. There was only the crinkly hair and soft, slick nub she rubbed against my fingers. I heard her breathing quicken. My knees turned to water, and saliva flooded my mouth. I swallowed and had the sudden urge to kiss her. I wanted to kiss her, my near-sister.

Mara's other hand stole between my own legs now, and I was surprised to find it as moist as the feeling of liquid heat that threaded them. I feared I'd wet myself and was about to protest when Mara rolled on top of me. Her lips touched mine, and I forgot everything I was to say to her.

I'd never been kissed before. Mara kissed my neck and ground her hips against me. My buttocks rose off the floor to meet her and we undulated, our bodies slicked with the essence of our sex. My hands rose up to grasp her hips and urge her to the spot where I felt the world come undone each time she moved or moaned. She was round and hard with muscles from dancing. The scent of her skin, so familiar to me, was now laced with sweat and desire.

Faster and faster, our hips bucked until stars exploded behind my eyes. I stopped, my body rigid with release, but Mara continued for a few more thrusts until she gave a weak cry and rolled off me, still breathing as though she'd run to Sparta and back.

"I've never done that." She laughed and wiped sweat from her brow. "It was like riding the great horses of Athenos!" She clasped my sweating hand.

I laughed weakly and squeezed her hand. "I wonder how it will be with a man."

"Who knows?" Mara giggled. "But let us swear, whichever of us is the first to lay with a man will tell the other how it is."

"And if it is not as nice as this?" I unlaced my hand from hers and climbed to my feet, feeling a little wobbly and as weak as a newborn kitten.

Mara stood and embraced me. "We shall always be near-sisters," was her only reply.

I thought often about that night. Later when I was alone in my room, I would place my hands between my thighs and try to achieve the same liquid heat. Without Mara, the flame would not spread. Would this be the glory between a woman and a man, or a special bond between near-sisters?

I dared not ask my mother.

Indeed, I saw her scarce enough to ask, though of late she could sometimes be found in Merikos' chamber, where she stole away precious moments from her labor to sit cross-legged on the floor and escape with me through the magic of his words. If the priest minded her presence, he covered it well, though his words faltered a little when her eyes were upon him.

So another week passed. After my body had expended the last of its energy in dance, I promised to meet Mara for the meal and quit Lukra's chamber. I bathed quickly and ate with such surprising speed that Mara raised a brow at my haste. For despite my body's weariness, I was alive with the desire to crouch at Merikos' knee and escape to the past, when gods walked upon the earth like mortal men. Mara gave me a curious glance as I left the dining hall.

My mother's voice emanated from Merikos' chambers, as I drew nearer. My heart was glad for she had not attended for many days. I burst into the chamber.

My mother's hands were laced with his and her eyes shone with an emotion I could not define. He dropped her hands at my approach and scooted the stool for me to sit.

"If you please, Doricha, we will delay our teachings for a little. Your mother must speak to you." He bowed and departed the room, leaving me more than a little confused.

"Dori, I've just come from the temple healer…." My mother began.

"Are you ill?" I cried and jumped up to embrace her.

"Whist, Dori! Will you think the worst when I have such news to tell?" She smiled and patted my cheeks with her soft hands. "Do you remember when I despaired of ever feeling your father's embrace again?"

I nodded. "I do, but what has this to do with the healer?"

"I will tell you, if you will hold your tongue. I may not have your father, but fate has brought him to us, just the same. I am with child, Dori. His child and the healers prophesy it shall be a boy." Her face was alight with life and beauty. "What do you think?"

What did I think?

A boy! My brother, with the strength of my father and my mother's heart. I thought of the great love Orpheus held for Eurydice and how my father had planted his seed within my mother's womb that final day, to remind her of his love for us.

"We are blessed by the gods!" I threw myself into her embrace. She laughed, then. I knelt, pressed my face to her center, and whispered to the babe growing there. And that is how Merikos found us, when he returned, with my mother laughing and crying at the same time and me trying to speak to her soul.

My brother, her soul. As her body swelled, so did our anticipation for him. Merikos spoke to the *ktístai*, and offered to sponsor the boy until he was old enough to follow the path of the sacred priests. It was good he did, for later events would prove that had Merikos not charmed them with the music of his words, they would have banished us all from the gods' door long before my mother's time came.

I spent the rest of the year in a sort of ecstatic oblivion, content with my lot in life, and weak with anticipation for my brother's birth. Not even Suvra the Surly, who made a point to single out my faults whenever we met, could dampen my spirits. Only once, when Aidne herself visited my mother, did my joy wane.

Seven months had flown by in a haze of anticipation. Mother and I were seated in her chambers. It was very late in the day, the time when most had long since retired, but I gave up those minutes of slumber for the chance to watch my brother form himself under the sheath of her soft pink skin.

Aidne appeared at the doorway like a wraith. She did not enter, but stood under the lintel, her eyes glittering in the shadows.

"So. It is true, what they say," Aidne remarked. My mother squared her shoulders, as I had seen my father do, so many times before battle. "Breeding a soldier's get into the temple. And with Merikos to speak for you, so that none think to say 'nay' to the travesty."

"As you can see." Mother's hand strayed over her belly, as if to protect the child in her womb. "Delus' son."

"How _proud_ you must be." Aidne spoke the words with venom.

I wanted to shrink from her, but I forced myself to be still.

Aidne's eyes glittered. "I must say I wonder…are you certain it is Delus' child you carry in your womb? We have heard of your visits to Merikos. How he spoke before the Branch Order to sway them to your side. He ran to meet you at the gates when you were seen on the mountain pass before the temple. Picked up his robes and ran like a girl." Her eyes flickered to me, and I wondered what had been between the two of them, that she should hate my mother so.

"It _is_ Delus' child," my mother repeated and her chin lifted another notch.

Aidne continued as if she had not heard.

"Did you part your legs for Merikos, little niece? Did you sell your god-given talents once again, trading a soldier's coarseness for a long-limbed _ktístaí_? Did you wheedle your way back into Merikos' heart just as before?"

I recoiled as if I had been struck. My mother's cheeks blazed and she voiced her denial, but still I wondered. Merikos had loved my mother? Surely not. There was nothing between the two of them that I, myself, had not witnessed. They were pleasant and respectful to one another, nothing more. Or was there? I remembered the way his voice faltered when she looked at him and the time Merikos held my mother's hands. Just before she'd told me about the babe.

"How dare you spread such lies?" My mother stood and clenched her fist. "Step further into this chamber and I shall strike you a blow that will silence your treacherous tongue forever."

"You threaten _me_? We shall see, Sita, whom the gods choose to favor. And we shall see whom the child favors as well." With that, Aidne stepped from our chamber and disappeared into the tunnel.

My mother's fists trembled as she paced the floor. I was unsure of what to do. As much as I admired Merikos, the thought of my mother betraying my father made me ill.

"Will she *never* forgive me?" my mother muttered to herself.

"Forgive what, Mamita?" My heart began a slow descent into my stomach.

My mother waved away my concerns. "It is nothing," she lied.

Forcing a smile, she splayed her hands over the slight mound rounding her womb. "I'm tired, Dori, and you must be spry tomorrow for your instruction. Merikos tells me they plan to start your *gymnastikas* training. You're doing well, to begin another tutor so soon." She sighed.

My face must have fallen at the way she brushed my questions aside, for she tilted her head and gazed at me. She was not sleeping well; her skin was paler than usual. Weariness stained the skin around her eyes.

I placed my hands atop hers and swallowed my misgivings. I would not harm her, or the life she carried, with my childish questions. I trotted back to my chamber with anxiety trailing in my wake like an unseen standard.

I went to visit Merikos early the following morning. I could not help the dark thoughts turning round and round in my mind. In my mind's eye, I saw my mother and Merikos clasping hands, and pondered their shy smiles. It made my insides ache. I needed to hear Merikos speak, to let his voice soothe my turmoil with gentle words that brought me peace. So I surprised him in his chamber when he had just finished his morning prayers.

"Dori," he smiled at me, disguising his shock. "It's nice to see you. Are you enjoying the *gymn-?*"

"Do you love my mother?" I interrupted.

Fear is a pithy weapon. The words blurted out before I could stop them. I had not thought to question him. I simply wanted to see him again, to hear his magical voice reassure me that all was well.

"Dori, please. Come in and sit. Let us speak as friends. It does no good to have you, or your words, lingering in the hall."

I followed the music of his voice, though I struggled against it.

He scooted the stool nearer to the hearth and my legs gave out beneath me. The comfort of his familiar actions soothed me. Nevertheless, it was not kindness or patience or scholarly zeal playing beneath the calm exterior of Merikos' face.

It was guilt.

Merikos poured himself a goblet of wine, but I had not an adult's patience or restraint. His expression made me wildly fearful of what he might say to me. I had to know. I *had* to.

"Tell me, Merikos. You cannot put me aside. Are you the father of my unborn brother?"

Merikos turned. His hands shook and he opened his mouth to speak.

"Dori," he said. His eyes were solemn.

I felt my legs grow weak as water. My knees relaxed and I slipped from the stool.

Merikos rushed to aid me.

"Don't touch me," I protested, too angry to accept even his hand.

He drew it back with a sharp, graceless motion. His entire body went rigid and stiff, as if he had been carrying a burden for some time and had only now sought release enough to straighten.

"Doricha, try to understand. All of this had little or nothing to do with you."

"Nothing to do with me?" I cried. "How could you say such a thing? It has _everything_ to do with me!"

"You were not yet conceived, Dori. I loved your mother years ago, when she and I were still devotees of the temple. I'm sorry if my words cause you pain, but I cannot change the man I was. Not even for the sake of your tender feelings or your mother's indifference."

"She was not so indifferent as to lie with you!" I was on fire with the anguish of my mother's betrayal, and with his.

"Lie with me? We have never! I meant only that I loved your mother. I did not assent to enjoying her body or her womb!" He rounded on me and became as menacing and dark a figure as I had once thought him, long ago in the Throat of Orpheus. "That is Aidne's poison you spew forth. Has she turned your heart as well, then?"

My face must have shown the fear I felt, because Merikos composed his features into their customary placid expression.

"I have never touched your mother, save in friendship. She would not have it so, and I love her too much to force my attentions on her. I did not, though I am a sacred priest and could do as I wished with no one to say nay."

Warm relief flooded through my veins like blood.

"Then my brother _is_ my father's son," I whispered.

"For all that I might have wished otherwise." Merikos' lips twisted into a wry smile. "Come, Dori. Do you dislike me so much?"

How could he think such thoughts? Then, I remembered the hateful words I'd spoken. Indeed, how could he not? I loved Merikos a little, I think. As a wanderer, who has lost her bright guiding star and finds comfort in the dim warmth of firelight. Merikos would not replace my father or my gods, but my loss was lessened by his presence. Shame burned at my cheeks and scorched the ashes of my rage away.

"No, Merikos," I said and embraced him. "It is because I love you too well."

He stiffened as my arms circled him. "And you are dear to me, as well." Merikos patted my shoulder awkwardly and motioned to the stool. "Now sit and we will continue some lessons. It is still early. You will not be missed at the morning meal. I have some bread and broth here, if you care to eat."

I sat again and sipped at the cooled broth while he spun his magic voice into the air. He spoke at length. It was a story of no importance to me, for I had more pressing questions circling my brain. Now that my anger had cooled, I yearned to know what only Merikos could tell me. Merikos or my mother, though I dared not to ask her.

"Why does Aidne loathe my mother so?" I interrupted. I fixed my eyes on him, keen for any betraying emotion that might flit across his features.

Merikos stopped in mid-gesture and folded his arms slowly to his body, like a bird going to nest. He paused and I wondered if he was going to answer me.

"That is for your mother to answer, Doricha," he stammered.

Merikos, who never spoke without magic!

"Oh, please," I begged. Years of living torn between my parents had taught me how to best serve my own purposes. "I would not disturb her or my unborn brother with these ill thoughts."

Merikos considered me for another long moment, and I tried not to squirm under his gaze. Then he spoke, low and resigned, though his voice was taut with unspoken emotion.

"When your mother first came to the temple, the daughter of one of the finest spearmen in the Thracian army, she was immediately singled out as the prize of our devotees. Such grace she had and also such wondrous beauty, like a blossom yet unplucked."

His eyes grew vague, as if he could indeed see back those many years to the day my mother had entered the temple service.

"And did you love her then?" I asked.

"Many loved her then, but I was not to follow until later. It was your mother's heart that lured me to her, not her beauty." He sighed. "Sita was like a rare jewel. She shone like the sun. But more than that, she was curious about everything. She sopped up her tutelage like wine from the gods. Her mind was honed to meld with kings, and even the gods themselves, should Dionysus choose to grace us with his presence. Only the best of tutors would do. And one of those fine tutors was Aidne."

Ah! I thought. *Now we come to the thorn in the story.*

"Did Aidne hate her because she was lovely and clever?" I asked. Merikos gave a short laugh.

"Nay, young Doricha. She loved her for it." His voice trailed away, and I had to strain to hear it. "More than any of us realized."

Aidne *loved* my mother? It seemed nigh impossible!

"Tell me more," I said. "How did Aidne come to hate my mother?"

"Aidne's heart was blackened when your mother left the temple to marry your father."

"But *why*?" I persisted.

"Think, Doricha. Delus was a common soldier, although a very good one. He came to the temple to offer a sacrifice before the last war with the Spartans." Merikos flushed, and I recognized the stain of jealousy in his face. How he must have cursed the day my father came to the mountain temple. "When his eyes fell upon your young mother, nothing would do but that he would have her. So your father prayed, deep within the heart of the temple, to give him victory over the Spartans, that he might claim Sita as his bride."

"And the _ktístai_ allowed this?" I asked.

"It is not for us to dictate the prayers of a man's heart. Your father was truly blessed by the gods. He must have been, to prevail against the Spartan forces when no other army could. And blessed twice over, to win the heart of your mother."

You allowed this, you, who loved her? I thought. He must not have been near the powerful priest he was now, to have let her go so easily.

"He came late one evening to claim Sita. They fled away into the night, and she went willingly, for as he loved her, Sita's heart held no other but him. They escaped, leaving Aidne to discover only your mother's empty chamber in the chill morning's light."

I could tell Merikos was speaking with godly magic in his voice. He trained the story to make music to my ears. And I, knowing full well that deep within the mountain temple there _was_ no morning light save from the ever burning torches, immersed myself in it nonetheless.

How clearly I could picture my proud father with the hand of my mother safely ensconced in his grasp. He'd guarded her with the same fiery jealousy from the men of Perperek. But that still did not explain the rage in Aidne's eyes, or the poison in her tongue.

"And Aidne was enraged by the loss of her best pupil?" I asked.

"Her best pupil, beloved of the gods and more…yes, that is when Aidne's heart turned to stone."

"The Bacchae come and go as they please. Why should my mother be any different to Aidne, even if she was a blood relation?"

"That is for your mother to say," Merikos replied. His eyes were hooded.

"You know the answer." I pouted, twisting my face in an ugly grimace of frustration. After all the music of his tale, to be denied the final crumb of knowledge!

"I have my suspicions only. It is for your mother to give you truth. But be warned, for it may not be the truth you would wish to hear from a mother's lips. Now, go." He patted me on the shoulder. "For it will soon be time for your lessons. Do not give Suvra chance to scold you. Oh, yes," he said at my surprised expression, "We are a tight fit, all of us, under the mountain embrace. There is naught that goes unnoticed. Remember that, in the days to come."

And I did remember those words, but much later, and not in time to save any of us.

CHAPTER 5

Many days and nights passed. At last the blot on my soul seemed to recede. I revolved in a blissful cycle of absorbing lessons and watching my mother grow round with the weight of my unborn brother. Each day I looked forward to the challenges of my tutors, and each night I sank happily into sleep, with the memory of my hands cradling her burgeoning womb.

I was doing so well at the temple. Many times, Amphis or Phryne complimented me, saying I was as lovely as my mother had once been. I was aglow with happiness. I'd failed my father, but I would not fail my brother. I was oblivious to all else but the approaching birth with which I sought to redeem myself. So I grew strong and limber under the tutelage of the Bacchae, and my mother's weary eyes began to shine more in my presence. I sensed her approval and reveled in it, so sparingly had it been handed to me before our flight to the temple.

Merikos, too, marked the change in my demeanor.

"You are growing more beautiful each day, Doricha. Just as your mother was. Though perhaps without her innocence about you."

His words startled me. I had not told anyone of my guilt or the part I had played in my father's demise. Not even Mara, my closest friend.

"I cannot think what you mean, Merikos." I fought the shame that flooded me. Why should he question my innocence? Fear pricked at the guilt I'd buried deep within my own mind.

"Your father's death. It has touched you here." Merikos touched a gentle finger to the soft skin of my cheek. "And here." He laid a warm palm to my chest.

I flinched and he removed it at once.

"Of course my father's death marked me. Did you think I would be unmoved?" I asked.

"I meant no offense, Dori. Do not let my words cause you pain." A frown creased his forehead. "It was only a difference in your resemblance to Sita I meant to remark upon."

"Why should you compare me to her at all?" I was still angry with him. The room seemed unaccountably small and I turned away from my stool at the fire.

Merikos shook his head. "You are more like her than you might imagine. But, come and sit. Let us not quarrel. I have more to teach you." The corners of his mouth deepened.

"Will you tell me why Aidne loved my mother?"

I knew that would provoke him. Merikos was ever patient and kind with all the devotees, but Aidne was a sore place to him, like a splinter lodged deep under the skin.

"That again? Ah!" Merikos threw up his hands. "I have told you. It is not my place to say."

"You don't *want* me to know!" I challenged.

"Enough! Either sit or leave. I will not be lectured by a child!"

"A child? I am woman enough to feel your hand upon my breast."

Merikos looked stunned.

I don't know why I said it. Perhaps I did feel in some way he was using me as a substitute for the affection he could not show my mother. Or perhaps it was that angry black blot bubbling up from my soul to taint everything that I loved and turn it to dust.

I spun on my heels and ran from him, wishing I could slam one of those heavy wooden doors between us. But alas, there were no doors to personal chambers. We trusted in the gods to protect us. Devotees had few personal belongings that were not conscribed into the temple wealth. What need had we for privacy and doors?

So I ran blindly, not caring that Suvra stood just beyond in the shadows, with a faint ugly smile on her lips.

I spent the morning crying. No one scolded me on my missed lessons. If I threw myself wholeheartedly into my dancing lesson, no one commented on it either, but Mara.

"Are you angry with me?" Mara asked. I stared at her.

"At you? No. Why do you ask?" I covered her hand with mine, so she might see I meant my words.

"You've been absent at meals. And just now, in dance, your face flushed. I thought you were going to hurl me across the room when we spun about!"

"I'm sorry. I...I argued with Merikos. I did not mean to take it out on you."

"Oh, Dori." Mara looked troubled. "You mustn't! Merikos is powerful.

43

You'd not do well to anger him."

Mustn't, mustn't. I was forever being told what I could not do. But still, Merikos was powerful, and more importantly, kind when it came to me. I needed to apologize, but I could not face him just yet.

"I know you are right," I said. "I will visit him tomorrow."

Mara was silent for a moment. Then her eyes twinkled merrily. "Ordis looked at me today," she whispered.

"What of it? He looks at you every morning." My head was full of my own woe, I did not want to gossip with Mara.

"No," she giggled and covered my hand with hers. "He *looked* at me. In that way. I think he wishes to lie with me."

"Oh," I said, feeling odd. "Will the priests sanction your union?" Had Merikos ever looked at my mother in that way? I tried to picture it, but the thought made my chest ache.

"I don't know," Mara admitted. And she went back to her alcove, while I dithered, deep in thought.

I'd wronged Merikos, wounded him with my words. I could not stand this ugly thing between us. I just wanted everything to go back as it was before I knew of temple lies and secrets. Back to the days when Merikos filled my head with dreams.

But the next day, I did not see Merikos before the morning meal. I set out as usual, hoping to catch him before his morning prayers. Suvra caught me before I left the devotees hall.

"Aidne bids you to come to her chambers. *Now.*" She wore a smirk. I clenched my hand to keep from slapping it off her face.

"Why does Aidne wish to see me?" I asked.

"You'll see," Suvra responded. Her eyes glinted in the darkness.

I knew personal chambers had no wooden doors, and so I peeped at the one before me now and wondered at the marked difference in Aidne's status. Why did she merit such privacy and why had I never noticed before now? My nose tickled, and I resisted the urge to scratch it, whilst Suvra went inside to announce me. Then the narrow wooden door opened a crack.

"Enter, Doricha."

I was startled by the pleasant timbre of Aidne's customary gruff voice. I swayed as gracefully as I could into the chamber, conscious of my gait under her scrutiny. Whatever I had done to merit her unwelcome attention, I would not provoke her further if I could help it.

"Are you unhappy here at the temple, Doricha?" Aidne asked after a moment. Her breath was very warm on the back of my neck. She was very close indeed, and the hairs of my arms stood on end.

"Unhappy? No! I am content here." I tried to sound like a proper devotee.

"Even with the loss of your beloved father? What a strange girl you must be." Aidne's voice was mild, but as treacherous as a hidden snake. I would have to take care that she did not twist my words.

"To lose a parent to death or slavery is a risk all Thracian children must face at one time or another." I raised my eyes then and did nothing to mask the pride in my gaze. "I have learned to be content."

"*Content?*" Aidne's voice hardened.

"Yes."

I focused my eyes on the twin lines running down her cheeks and watched as they deepened. She pursed her lips a little, giving me a glimpse of what Suvra's face would be in the years to come. Then Aidne spoke again.

"And how fare your lessons with the priest Merikos?"

"I am pleased to learn of our sacred myths, Aidne."

"Pleased? *Pleased!* I think that a very odd choice for you, girl."

I couldn't think of why she should say such a thing to me. "Odd? Not at all! I am happy to learn the mysteries of the temple with Merikos."

"Are you, indeed?" Her eyes slid like oil to where Suvra stood. "Then you are very like your mother. She too visited Merikos' chambers, both as a girl and now." She paused.

I tried to follow her line of reason, but it was beyond me. "I...I am flattered by your compliment."

"Pah, you are more stupid then I imagined." Aidne put her hands on her hips and glared at me.

I tried not to shift my weight from hip to hip, nor fidget beneath her reptilian gaze. And all the while, my mind raced over the portent of her words.

"Go," she said brusquely. Her lips turned sour in an expression I guessed to be disappointment. "I have finished with you, for now."

I confess that I ran back to my chambers, as fast as the crowded passageways would allow, and not at all with the decorum of a temple devotee.

That night I visited my mother's chambers, as was my customary habit. She looked pale and more weary than usual. I should have guessed something was amiss.

"You work too much," I grumbled and pressed my cheek to her soul.

My mother made a noncommittal sound. She lay on her side on the stiff straw pallet. I buried my face into the folds of her skirt, inhaling the soft scent of her skin. My nose tickled, and I wiped it with the back of my hand as my mother reached for a goblet of herbed wine.

"What is that?" I asked, sniffing it. The scent made my nose itch again, so I handed it back before I dropped it. The odor reminded me of the musty scent of herbs in Aidne's chamber.

"For my back. It eases away the pains from the babe." She put her hand over her swollen middle.

"Does he disturb you often?" I stroked her hair away from her cheek

"A little," she admitted. Her eyes brightened. "It will not be long now."

"How soon?" I said.

"We have a few weeks left before my waters spill. Time enough for you to begin your patterns."

Oh, how my joy overflowed!

Each Bacchae bore a tattooed pattern across the back of their hands. My hands would be inked in cobalt, not intricate yet, but a symbol of my devotion to the temple. And best of all, my brother would soon arrive. I was so caught up in anticipation that I put the encounter with Aidne completely out of my mind.

The following week, the priests announced that Mara, I, and several others would receive our first marks. It was a time of celebration. The older girls gossiped amongst themselves, speculating on whose would be the most intricate, whose would boast the finest shade of blue-black. As for me, I delighted in the fact my brother would soon be born.

At last the day came for my marking ceremony. Even so, my mother was not allowed to set aside her chores to see me to the temple artisan. I was led outside the mountain's protection to a small hut near the entrance to the temple. The frigid wind shocked the air from my lungs, and I staggered against the priest who led me away. It felt strange to breathe in air that did not reek of earth or humanity, to see the cold brittle sunlight of winter and hear the plaintive cries of birds above me. My senses reeled from the headiness of it all and from the excitement of being marked as the temple's own.

The hut was very small and leaned against the rocky mountainside, as a child will cleave to its mother. A very old man, an aged priest most likely, beckoned us out of the wind and frost. The temple guard sent me inside and announced he would return forthwith.

"Come in, come in. Let me see." The old man peered at me with eyes that seemed much too rheumy to be of use. He bade me sit in a high backed wooden chair.

When I obeyed, he motioned for me to place my palms on the rough wooden table.

"Fine, fine…." He studied the skin on the backs of my hands. "Well then, shall we begin? Don't look so frightened, girl! It only stings a little."

I armed my nerves with his words and thought to make my mother proud. I was well on my way to becoming a Bacchae, to fulfilling my destiny…I would return, serene and triumphant and display my marks with pride. The priest lowered his instruments to my flesh. She would see I was worthy, that I was…I was…in pain!

The priest had _lied_!

My hands were on fire. And as soon as he'd pierced the back of one so often that I felt on the brink of fainting, he grabbed the other and began the same. The scratch of his needles seemed to dig clear to the bones of my hands. And oh, the blood that ran free beneath his fingers! He wiped it often to see the lines etched beneath the bloody skin.

Scratch, scratch. Wipe, wipe. The cloth abraded my swollen flesh. And then, far worse, his fingers rubbed, smearing the blue-black powder into my veins, only to repeat again, a fraction to the side of the previous sore spot.

Scratch, scratch. Wipe.

"Steady, child," the priest muttered, intent on his designs.

Oh, the long, drawn out pain of it!

I fancied that I could see monsters howling and the very pits of the Underworld opening up to expose my flesh-stripped fingers. Tears pricked at my eyes like the needles in my flesh. My eyes rolled back in my head, and I wanted to wipe my sweating upper lip on the folds of my robe. My jaw ached from biting back screams of agony. And just when I felt darkness crowding at the edges of my vision, the priest spoke again.

"You are finished. Such a difficult pattern I have not attempted for many years, but your skin was so pink and fine, I thought…Gods, are you ill? No? Well, there's a good girl. Off with you."

He patted my hands with a wet cloth, revealing a lovely web of cobalt on my reddened swollen flesh. When I winced, he clucked his tongue. He wrapped my hands gingerly in linens and told me to give them time to heal.

"They'll give you herbs to take with your evening wine. Be careful you don't overdo them, or you won't wake for a week's time, if you wake at all."

I stifled a sob and allowed him to lead me to the door. If I'd thought the frigid winter air uncomfortable before, it was now doubly so with sweat soaking my chiton. The chill was unbearable but the cold made my hands ache less.

I went to my chamber and drank the herbed wine that was laid out for me. Then I lied down upon my pallet and waited for sleep to overcome my agony. The world went dim and my chamber seemed to spin behind my closed eyes. My stomach roiled and I thought I might be sick. And then I dreamt.

I cannot remember now, how the dream started, save that I ran towards my father and someone held me back. I thought it might have been my mother, but when I turned to face her, there was no one there, only a flash of light. I heard a child's laughter echoing through the mist, and then my own beloved father's voice calling to me. The thunderous sound of the sea filled my ears, and then it became the sounds of a battle ringing through the tree branches. Father's voice rang in my herb-clouded brain.

"Dori," he said. "My treasure!"

I could not see him. I could not see _anything_. I was lost in a haze of mist.

"Papita?" I could not find him.

"Doricha," he called. And someone shook my shoulder hard.

I whirled and saw Aidne standing beside me.

"Doricha!" She reached for me with clawed fingers. Her mouth curled into a triumphant smile. I struggled to free myself. Her hands gripped my shoulders like iron.

"Dori!" Aidne screamed my name again.

I shuddered.

"Dori…." she called. "Dori!"

I jolted awake, my lungs heaving for breath.

The voice was both a woman's and real.

CHAPTER 6

Not a woman, but Mara, her forehead creased in worry.

"Are you awake?" she asked.

"Yes," I answered. My tongue felt thick. I reached for wine to ease my raw throat. My nose was stuffy and my head ached abominably. "What is it? Have I missed the meal?"

Mara helped me to stand. "You must come at once! It's your mother. Her pains began early this morning, but she did not want to ruin your ceremony." She glanced meaningfully at my bandaged hands.

"Is everything all right? Is my brother born?" How could I have missed his birth?

Concern gave my feet wings and erased the last traces of my night visions. I cupped my bandaged hands around the goblet and tried not to slosh the wine over the edge of my cup.

"Her labor is coming too early--her birth canal has not yet softened. She's holding up well, though. The healers say it will be some time before the babe arrives. I thought you'd like to be there."

"I can't thank you enough," I said.

Mara eyed my bandaged palms. "Does it hurt much?"

I took a sip of wine and winced. My nose began to tingle.

"What? Oh, no. Not much." I swiped my fingertips under my nose and tried to sound brave. No use frightening Mara before her own patterns were inked. A dubious look crossed her sweet face, but she nodded and fell silent as we approached my mother's chamber.

"Mamita!" I flew to across the room to her, heedless of the wine dripping on to the stone floor like fragrant drops of blood. I scarcely noticed the two women crouched on the far side of the room, or the girl by the fire.

My mother lay on her side on the straw pallet. Her lovely hair was plastered to her head with perspiration, and her face seemed very pale and drawn. But she smiled at the sound of my voice and turned her enormous eyes on me. I set my goblet of wine to the side and knelt beside her.

"Doricha." She reached out a hand to me. "I knew you would come. How…" she paused and blew her breath out in one forceful huff. "How went your assignment with the artisan?"

It was a point in itself, the attention she lavished on me despite my brother's impending birth and her own pain. I held out my bandaged hands for her to unwrap.

"Oh," she breathed. "They will be lovely, when you heal. They remind me a little of my own." I glanced at the patterns crusted with my dried blood and shook my head. They were not nearly as fine as hers.

"I shall believe it when the swelling is gone." I smiled to reassure her. "How is my brother?"

"He is…." Another gasp of pain escaped her lips. "He is well, I think. They say his head has not turned to the proper placement for birth. I will not lie to you, Doricha. It will not be an easy time. You must be brave for me." Her words sliced my heart. I hated that she was in such pain.

"Humph!" said one of the women, wiping my mother's brow. "Her pains come too close. It will not be long."

"The girl should go. There will be much blood here," remarked the other with a frown.

"No!" My mother and I voiced the same objection. "Please, let her stay. She is a strong daughter. She will not faint or turn away at the sight of blood. Will you, Doricha?"

I thought of the crimson rivers I had seen on the night my father was killed. I pictured the cooling life's blood seeping from the man I struck down and shivered.

"No." I shook my head. "I will not turn away."

"She will be a hindrance! What can she do with her hands bandaged thus?" asked the first. "Send her away, Sita, until the child is born."

"I will not." My mother grimaced again.

"Be reasonable! There is little enough room here." They continued to argue until the girl turned from the fire that glinted along the dull lengths of her red hair.

"Let her stay. She may aid me." It was Suvra!

A look passed between the two women. It was a glance I have often thought back on, and wondered at its portent. But such mysteries are hidden from me now, just as they were then. I was too shocked by Suvra's interference and too full of the birth of my brother that I did not think to question their swift acquiescence.

"Very well, heat some water, girl, if you can manage. The other one must leave." The woman shooed Mara out of the room.

"She will manage." Suvra grabbed at the vessel. I followed her to the fire. Her oily gaze settled on my bandaged hands. "How do you fare?" she whispered.

"They only sting a little, now. The wine helped." I glanced at my mother being helped to a squatting position. One of the women held a cup to my mother's lips. How close was the birth?

"The herbs. Aidne sent them to ease your pain."

"Oh," I mumbled, my eyes on my mother as she grunted her way through another birth pain. "I didn't know she cared so much for my comfort."

"Oh, yes. She insisted I have the wine prepared for your return. She mixed the batch herself." Suvra's face flushed. "After all, you *are* kin."

My mother gave a sharp cry. She clutched her middle and the women hovered around her like insects.

"Bring the water," one of them snapped.

I rushed to her, afraid to do anything, afraid to do nothing.

"Ohhhh," my mother panted and clutched her abdomen. "The pain!"

The room was unbearably hot and thick with the stench of womanhood and sweat. My nose and cheeks tingled as if swollen, and tears threatened to spill from my eyes.

The two women hovered, one at each elbow balancing my mother in a crouch between them. My mother's legs buckled and all three of them nigh collapsed.

"Steady, Sita! You cannot rest just yet."

My mother moaned and panted like a wild animal. Her lank hair hung over her eyes. Another cry erupted from her throat and suddenly there was a wet, smacking sound. I stared at the chiton rucked up between her legs and saw it was stained and dripping. Fluid puddled on the stone floor beneath her.

"There now, your waters have burst. The babe will move down out of your womb."

"Something…wrong. I can…*ugh*!…feel it." My mother slurred her words and continued to clutch her stomach.

"Give her more wine!" I cried.

"We have no more to give her, girl. I doubt it would do much good anyway. She won't keep it down." One of the women wiped the sweat from my mother's brow.

My mother wailed again.

"Use mine," I said and thrust my goblet in their hands.

Another look passed between the midwives before they reacted.

"As you say, girl." They poured it down her throat, and I encouraged them, thinking it would ease her pain, as it had mine.

"Look!" one of the women cried. She pointed to the mess on the floor.

There, in the life giving waters of my mother's womb was the unmistakable tinge of red.

My mother screamed again, and trembled between the unforgiving women. A gush of bright blood flooded the skirt of her chiton and ran down her legs. She cried aloud.

"Mother!" I moved to her side. Her fists flailed out and caught me full on the left cheekbone. I think she struck me out of agony, but the women misunderstood.

"Get back, you foolish girl!" one chided. "She doesn't want you. Here, Sita. Bend your knees and try to relax your womb."

"Gods," my mother shrieked. "Help me!"

I covered my face with my hands as the panic in her voice set chill bumps along my arm. Agony and fear drowned the murmurs of the two women and everywhere was blood, blood....

"Get Aidne," one of the women barked at Suvra.

"But...she said...." Suvra's voice trailed away and she eyed the overturned wine goblet on the floor.

"It is not right! This is too much. Now go, and the gods claim us all if you are too late!"

Suvra glanced once at me and then hiked up her skirts and ran from the room.

My mother grunted and strained, her body working to free her unborn child from the confines of her unyielding womb. Her face turned red from the strain. As she pushed, I prayed.

Dionysus, hear my plea. Help us. Bendis, Earth Mother, watch over us.

It seemed like several lifetimes before Aidne arrived carrying a goatskin pouch. Hours of watching helplessly as my mother strained and raved like a wild woman. It takes only moments to get from one section of the hall, from another. Aidne did not appear to have hurried.

"So," Aidne said, after my mother finished bearing down. "It comes to this."

My poor mother was exhausted. I did not think she could possibly face Aidne's hatred and so I moved between them.

"Please," I begged. "Do something. If you know what is to be done, do it!"

Aidne considered me for a moment and then moved to where my mother dangled between the two women. She brushed the hair from my mother's face and gazed at her unfocused eyes. Her hand lingered on my mother's cheek.

"Ah, Sita...how you must wish Delus had never come between us," she crooned. "To see you brought so low by his seed...."

I do not know if my mother was coherent; she was too far gone with pain and the wine. I think perhaps she was, for she drew her bobbing head back as far as she could and spat in Aidne's direction. It spattered across Aidne's face and neck like a bitter storm. And then, my mother laughed.

"You were never so close to my heart as you might...*ugnh*...have wished, Aidne. You taught me the skills of a Bacchae, nothing more." And she laughed again and cried at the same time.

I froze.

Aidne's face turned to creamy stone. "You were the most beloved of devotees! You were meant to serve the gods, not some mere mortal!" Her eyes bored into my mother with such force that I was sure it would kill.

"And what of you, Aidne? Were you not a mere mortal?" my mother asked weakly. The women on either side turned their faces to the walls, as Aidne's gaze raked across them, over Suvra crouched by the door, and finally rested on me.

Fear lanced my heart. She took a menacing step towards me, and the toe of her sandal caught the overturned wine cup on the floor. Aidne glanced once at it, and a crease appeared between her brows. Her eyes flickered towards me. Then, like a serpent uncoiling, she smiled. Sadness touched her eyes, but she smiled.

Aidne whirled to face her two assistants. "You two. Take the babe."

"*What*?" I cried. She would not dare!

"You should not do this, Aidne. It is not for you to say." One of the women glowered at her. "Get the *ktístai*. Bring Merikos."

"*No*! Leave Merikos out of this. He has done nothing to merit your wrath, Aidne." My mother lunged at her, but the women held her and another pain forced her to her knees.

"Has he not? "Aidne seemed unconvinced. "We shall see." Aidne jerked her chin towards the door. Suvra blinked once and rushed from the room. "Now, lay Sita back on the pallet."

"No," I said. "Wait." I struggled to make sense of what was happening, but my head felt stuffed with wool.

Aidne turned her dark eyes on me. "You stay silent or it will be the worst for you."

Mother was too exhausted to fight them. My mind rambled from shock of the situation and herbed wine. I put a hand on my cheeks, where my face ached both from the strike of her fist and from the constant tickle in my nose.

Aidne drew forth a small parcel of goatskin. She laid it on the stool and knelt beside the thrashing body of my mother. With steady hands, Aidne unfolded the many flaps of the parcel to reveal its contents.

It was a set of sharpened stone blades.

"No." My mother moaned. "Aidne, please, no! You cannot do this!" Her hands fisted in the manacles of the other women's grasp.

Aidne was unmoved.

"He's just a child. A babe. The gods will never condone your actions. Please," my mother babbled. "Please, Aidne. For my sake."

Aidne's hands paused.

"You are nothing to me, Sita. No more than a cow giving birth. You brought this upon yourself when you turned your back on the Bacchae to lie with that unsanctified wretch."

My mother sobbed and sank back on the pallet. "Take me, if you need your revenge, then."

Aidne spat in the dust and drew the stained chiton up and over the mound of my mother's abdomen. She removed a small animal bladder from her pack. When she had loosened the leather thong, she dipped a long finger into the bladder and drew forth a nasty black powder.

"How much did she drink?" Aidne asked, dodging my mother's feeble kicks. She drew a greasy, dark line down my mother's heaving abdomen. The older women looked frightened. I forced myself to inch closer.

"How much?" Aidne demanded again. "How much before it spilled?"

"Almost the cup."

"And before? Did she take wine before then?"

The women glanced at each other before answering. "She's been taking doses for weeks. Two full goblets since this morning, and then the girl brought more."

Aidne's eyes slid towards me.

"Yes...I saw." The way she drew out her words sounded even more serpentine than usual. "Listen well! Sita's had too much pennyroyal. She will most likely die, though I meant only for her to suffer the loss of Delus' seed. The girl's wine was laced with it for her initiation. If Sita drank it...we must take the child now."

"What?" I cried. "No!"

My mother began a keening high pitched wail that rattled the walls of the chamber. I covered my ears with my hands and sobbed beside her, determined not to let this terrible thing happen. Aidne lied, she had always lied. She meant to murder my mother, and I vowed to do whatever I must to stop her.

The stone knife glinted in the firelight, sharp and polished fine. Aidne wet both sides of it with her tongue, drawing her own blood. It stained her teeth.

Where to strike first, to save my mother and my unborn brother? The back of her head? Would she drop the knife, then?

A commotion at the entrance halted Aidne's hands as surely as my fist would have.

"What goes here?" Merikos' voice rang with disbelief.

Behind him, Suvra and several white robed *ktístai* hovered in the hall. Merikos' eyes were filled with rage at the sight of us. My mother, wailing and bloody, sitting upright on the pallet, Aidne with the knife poised in her hand, and myself hovering behind her with my fists clenched and raised.

"Why have we been summoned?" he demanded. My heart lifted at the tone of his magical voice. He would protect us; he could aid my mother!

"It is Sita." Aidne said. She lifted her chin and stared defiantly at Merikos. "The child has not turned and Sita's waters have burst. We must take the child, and now, or they will both surely die."

She did not mention her poisoned wine. Merikos' face turned ashen. Behind him the sacred priests began whispering.

Merikos knelt beside my mother, murmuring in his gentle way, and soon my mother stopped her wild cries and fell silent. Her body still racked from the labors of birthing, she let him stroke the hair from her face. "Gentle, now," he said. "Gentle."

"Leave me, Merikos. She has us all," my mother slurred. Her head drooped to her chest and she struggled to raise it again.

"Wh-what's wrong with her?" Merikos' voice cracked.

"She has been drugged!" I exclaimed, finally finding my lost courage. "I heard them talking. Aidne put herbs in her wine and it's killing her." I pointed a finger at the woman still poised with a knife suspended over my precious brother.

"How _dare_ you spread such lies, girl!" Aidne barked. "It was your own hand that poisoned your mother. Not mine!" Everyone stared at me.

"I did not," I said. "How could I?"

"There. In your own cup. You forced these women to pour wine from your cup into your mother. A full cup, they said. Do you deny it?"

My legs started to tremble. I could not deny it. "I…I did not…I thought only to ease her pain."

"Everyone knows the perils of ingesting too much pennyroyal," Aidne spat.

Merikos looked horrified, full of disbelief. "You cannot expect us to believe the girl poisoned her own mother. What reason would she have for such a god-cursed act?" His voice was strained.

And Aidne smiled, a slow, mocking twist carving the flesh of her cheeks into a feral curve.

"What reason, _indeed_, Merikos? Can you think of none?"

Merikos was silent. He frowned at Aidne and then glanced between her and me. It was as if the entire balance of the world rested on that one moment.

Aidne stood and placed the knife on the stool. "This girl has entered into an unsanctioned alliance with the priest Merikos. I have heard it from one who heard it from the girl's own lips."

"That is a lie!" Merikos thundered.

"I do not lie," Suvra called. She pushed her way into the already crowded room. "I heard Doricha tell him she loved him, and later, he put his hands on her. Here." She fondled her breast.

"The girl as much as admitted to me that Merikos has been her lover." Aidne lied. "He could not have the one, so he took the other." Merikos squinted at me and shook his head.

"You," he whispered. His face was white as death. "You said this about me?"

"No!" I said. "I would never!" My heart raged. *I did not do this thing.*

"There are other witnesses if you wish to call them before you, if my words are not enough. But the mother and child will both die before all is made plain." Aidne rocked back on her heels, confident in the power of her voice, of her commanding presence over us all in that tiny, blood dark room. Merikos' eyes darted back and forth between the priests and Aidne and I saw his fists clench.

But I could not refute the twisted words Aidne spewed like venom into an already gaping wound. She was a powerful priestess. I was only an inductee and I had no proof. For once, I was innocent, and yet I could do nothing. Of all the betrayals I've experienced in my life, I think this one to be the most painful.

"Sita," he began. He stopped and eyed the faces in the chamber, and those of the priests in the hallway. Then, shamefaced and red, Merikos rose and stepped to the tunnel. His eyes were no longer kind, but hard and angry, solidified by the thought I had ruined him.

"I'm sorry, Sita," he said. He spared one last glance for my mother who shook her head at him and turned her face to the wall. "Do as you must. I am finished here."

And he fled.

Just as before, he let someone take my mother from him. He was nothing more than a coward. The world spun. I would like to say I fainted, and I did not witness the murder of my family, but I cannot. They held me fast between them. The sacred priests speared me with black glances, while Aidne laid the blade to my mother's womb.

"The gods take you, Sita. Stop fighting me and let me ease your pain." Aidne said.

My mother gagged and one of the women held a basin for her to vomit into. Several of the priests edged closer to the hall.

My mother's arms and legs began to shake uncontrollably and she shook her head. "I will never stop fighting, Aidne."

"Then let me save your son, if I can."

I do not know what I wanted, only that I prayed for my mother to live, as my father did not. I wanted her to smile at me and whisper of my future as a Bacchae whilst we dandled my brother on her knees. I wanted so much to live in happiness without the stain of my guilt touching every secret desire of my soul.

"You wished him to die," my mother whispered. Aidne said nothing, but her eyes glittered. "But you will save him now, for me?"

Aidne considered for a moment. "There need be only one sacrifice," she said.

My mother nodded and closed her eyes.

"No!" I cried and struggled to go to her. They let me drop down beside the pallet. "Do not let them!"

My mother's eyes opened and she gazed at me. There was a terrible blue tinge around her lips, and her sour breath was labored and weak.

"Whist, Dori. I must do this thing. I am already lost." Her breath was labored. "You must be strong. For him and for me. Let me live on in his eyes. Be strong." And then she closed her eyes again and nodded at Aidne.

"Stay," I begged her. It no longer mattered that my brother should be born alive. She could bear other sons, even Merikos', I thought graciously. I would allow anything if only she should live.

"My daughter." She opened her eyes and reached up to finger a tendril of my hair. "So much like the two hearts that bore you. Remind him of me." Her hand dropped to the pallet.

"No, Mamita," I sobbed. "No."

"Do it, now, Aidne." My mother squeezed her eyes shut.

I gripped her hand while Aidne cut her apart, slicing her terrible blade along the painted line. I stayed, though my mother screamed and lashed between the grip of the two women. Aidne enjoyed it, I think, though at one point I saw a single tear slide down her cheek. Perhaps it was only perspiration.

When she had gutted my mother with the precision of a sailor, she drew forth my brother from the ruptured womb. For the child was, indeed a son as prophesied. My mother raised her head in the final moments to peer over the bleeding mound of her split stomach. She saw the cord, purple and slippery with blood, wrapped tight around his neck. He was not breathing. He never did.

"Ahhh…no." My mother cried. "Delus. Forgive me." She turned to look at Aidne, who stared at her with something akin to pity and triumph.

Mother fell back against the pallet and closed her eyes, her lovely face turned towards me. The moment I had looked forward to with anticipation and excitement was cut short in one fell swoop by the hand of a jealous priestess. My mother bled to death. She joined my brother and my father in the Underworld, and I was left to carry on here without them.

I could do nothing but tremble and weep.

At some point Aidne shook herself visibly and rose to wash and leave. "Toss that abomination on the hillsides for the wolves." She jerked her chin at my brother's tiny body.

"What shall we do with the girl?" someone asked.

I was amazed that anyone remembered me. Everyone I'd ever loved was dead and Merikos had abandoned me to Aidne's revenge.

"She is unclean to us. Unfit for the gods. Take her to the slave pits," Aidne said. "Let her spend her days serving a lesser master and keep her unworthiness far from our sacred grounds."

And so, they did.

CHAPTER 7

I didn't think they would do it.

I spent the night racked with sobs so fierce that my throat was raw and my eyes were swollen shut by the time they came to fetch me. Aidne had dosed my mother with pennyroyal to make her lose the baby, and my own initiation cup--which I'd thought to ease my mother's pain--had killed her. If only I had been clever enough to spot the truths behind the temple's lies. I tore out hanks of hair and wished the pain could dull the agony of my soul. My actions left me with only a sore, matted scalp and a speared heart.

After the morning broth, which I refused, a pair of temple guards positioned my right hand over my left and bound them with backs together, so my wrists were tethered and my healing tattoos did not show.

My mind was numb with grief and fear. My entire family was horribly, wrongfully murdered. I feared to face the grim light of morning outside the temple mountain, as a slave and alone.

I saw Mara. Her face blanched as white as the marble effigy of Dionysus when they led me out of the Throat of Orpheus. Her hand twitched as if to take mine when I passed, but a stern whisper from one of the Bacchae stopped her.

I willed her to remember me kindly despite what the others might say. I knew my name would be blackened from the temple.

Terrible thoughts dogged my heavy footsteps on the path to slavery. I was sold to a dark haired trader named Cyrus, garnered outside the temple. We traveled south along with three other slaves--an elderly Samothraki and two young males, scarcely out of boyhood, who never spoke. They stank of fear and resignation.

Cyrus was a harsh and unforgiving man. Grecian blood tainted his features and stained his skin a sallow shade of amber. He never asked what crimes I'd committed to be ousted from the temple, nor did he see to my basic needs.

We stopped so infrequently throughout the next three days that I was forced to wet myself. Urine burned my legs and soaked the bottom of my chiton. Cyrus puffed his lips in annoyance. Shame burned my cheeks. I wanted to curl up into a ball and die. The acrid stench burned my nose and sunlight seared my eyes. It was no more than I deserved.

Cyrus' damnable rope dragged me ever onward. We journeyed over rocky paths that bruised my heels. I trudged under a blinding hot sun until my shoulders turned to red fire and blistered in fierce, white pustules.

I was a stupid girl. If I had been more cautious, more vigilant, I would have seen the signs that pointed to this end. Aidne's words, the odd scent lingering around her like a mantle of cloth. Herbs that made my nose tingle and my eyes burn--herbs that when ingested by some could be as poisonous as a serpent's kiss.

"Eat." Cyrus tossed me an overripe onion and a strip of dried meat. "We reach Abdera soon." I made no move to catch them with my bound hands, but his aim was good. I let them fall from my fingers into the dirt.

Cyrus took one menacing step towards me.

"Here, I will help." The old Samothraki slave gathered them both and poked the dried meat at my chapped lips. Cyrus' eyes narrowed but he moved away.

"I don't want it." I brushed the meat away. My shoulders ached from the tether rope and I stank from urine, sweat and my mother's birthing blood.

"The trader gains _nothing_ if you perish on the road to Abdera," the old Samothraki whispered. His eyes darted back to Cyrus. "He will feed you and shelter you only until you are sold. You must eat if you wish to escape your bonds."

I surprised him with a bitter laugh. "I do not wish to escape, old man. I wish to die."

His eyes widened. "There are quicker ways to die than starvation. Cyrus will not exercise that force, for all that you might wish him to, girl. You are no use to him dead. Eat now. You'll find death soon enough."

But I vowed I would not eat. Not then, and not the rest of our journey out of the mountains. I prayed daily for death until at last I gave up voicing my pleas to the gods. When Cyrus held me down and forced water between my cracked and bleeding lips, I gave up the gods altogether. The days were a blur of piercing azure skies and rocky terrain. They passed in a haze of despair and desperation that never gave me respite from my guilty conscience.

I was utterly alone.

Once Cyrus came to me at night and laid on top of me, stinking of sour wine and murmuring filth and curses into my ears. I fought at him with my bound hands. He pinched my nipple so hard I thought it would burst. I remembered how Mara and I had giggled about taking a lover. So, this was to be my first.

Tears leaked from my eyes into my hair and my cracked, bleeding lips moved in a soundless wail. When the old Samothraki remarked into the evening air that I would fetch a better price with my maidenhood intact, Cyrus rose from my motionless, stiff body and dealt the old man a blow that should have killed him. The trader let me be afterwards.

For the old Samothraki's sake, I managed to swallow a bit of dried meat with water that morning.

We marched for almost a week. Seven hundred _stades_ of blistering trek over snow-covered mountain passes and ragged countryside until at last, bleeding and emaciated, we arrived in the port city of Abdera.

After months of frigid earthy air in the temple depths, the lure of the sea breeze in Abdera was a welcome change from the desperate cold of my despair. Abdera, the city founded by Herakles after his companion, Abderus, was slain by Diomedes' mare. It was larger than any city I had seen. Not even Perperek compared to its size and bustle. Our pace quickened as we wound our way down the mountains to the city.

We passed the main gates with little trouble. The cacophony was deafening. Abdera was arranged in a maze of paved streets and stone walls, much like the fortress of Perperek, and segregated patches of land into property. The main roads and alleyways led down towards the large open air marketplace, the _agora_.

Birds screeched and wheeled over the mobs clogging the roadway. Scents of humanity, exotic spices and perfumes, and filth of beasts assaulted my nose. My empty stomach churned, but I could not stop gaping. That is, until Cyrus laughed unkindly at my open mouth and tugged harder on the ropes binding my wrists together.

Then I remembered the purpose in my journey and I closed my mouth with a snap.

"The slave market will be nearer the water," said the old Samothraki. "On the far side of the _agora_."

I shrugged. What did I care on which side of the marketplace it was? My family was dead. I wanted to join them.

I'd violated my father's dying wish and I'd lost my family and my heart forever.

We trudged through the side streets, dodging other beasts and travelers. Around the _agora_ on all sides stood several temples, military headquarters, the city records office and a prison—like the fortress of Perperek but on a much grander scale. The inner walls were decorated with murals depicting the city's history. As we passed the law courts, I heard the crowds shouting at the unpopular speakers at the morning's assembly.

Market stalls constructed of timber, rope, and cloth or straw canopies afforded some shade from the oppressive heat. Slaves carried baskets of strange fish, eels, and mussels through the crowds. They stacked jugs of wine, olive oil, and vinegar for sale and hung twisted ropes of onions and garlic from wooden pegs. Slave boys darted through the crowded market place, avoiding the curses and cuffs of citizens and house slaves alike.

One winding, lopsided avenue held the stalls of the *metoikoi*, the tradesmen. The poor also labored in workshops beside the *metoikoi*, crafting leather sandals, dyeing cloth and other tasks, in hopes of learning a trade or gaining enough coin to feed their families. The two worked in such harmony that it was difficult to tell the difference between *metoikoi* and those too destitute to claim citizenship.

I was so preoccupied with the stalls that Cyrus jerked my lead hard and I fell to my knees into a puddle by the tanner. A wealthy woman squawked angrily at me, her brass and copper adornments jangling, and sidestepped to avoid my splash. Cyrus slapped at my ears. I scrambled to my feet to avoid another blow. My scraped knees began to flush and burn from the lye in the scummy puddle.

"*Move*." Cyrus muttered. "This way."

Slaves are common in Thrace and Greece. Even some of the families in my village had housed slaves, though I'd scarce took notice of them. And now I would be sold to some family, to cook food, mend clothing, and tend their children. My life would no longer be my own. Oh, how my father would be crushed!

When we reached the slave pits, the sheer numbers of people for sale shocked me. Most slaves were barbarians captured by pirates or soldiers. Others were the children of slaves or had been abandoned and rescued by slavers like Cyrus, who roamed the rugged hillsides looking for souls to ply his trade. I had no idea there would be so many of us.

Live free, my father wished for me with his last breath. And I'd failed him, as I'd failed my mother and unborn brother.

Hot tears blinded me as Cyrus maneuvered us towards the pits. I bowed my head, thinking to hide my face behind the curtain of my filthy hair.

"Sssst, girl," the old Samothraki hissed. "Cease your tears else it will go worse for you. Wipe your face. Pray for a kind master."

"Pray? To whom?" I moaned. What god would save me from the Hell I had created in my naivety?

My ears still rang from Cyrus' blow. My reddened knees felt as if a hundred stinging insects crawled on my flesh. I stank. I hurt. I could not face this humiliation, not without someone to guide my steps. What I wouldn't do for my near-sister to comfort me, now. But Mara was far away, hidden in a nest of traitorous vipers.

Cyrus pulled me to a long table, where they wrote my name and a price on potshard. The shard had a hole through it and a leather lace to suspend it from my neck.

Thracian girl, I read. *One hundred drachmas*.

One hundred drachmas? So much? Cyrus was a madman. The scribe raised his brows at Cyrus' price, but wrote it just the same. I felt his dark eyes on me when he finished and handed the shard to Cyrus.

Cyrus gathered up the shard for the old Samothraki and set a price on the two boys, to be sold as a pair. Even together, their price was not half of my own.

"This way," Cyrus ordered. He tugged my lead toward the rocky stretch of beach beyond the slave stockyard. The old Samothraki shrugged his shoulders at me. Apparently this was not typical.

"Where are you taking me?" I dared to ask.

Cyrus gave me a dark look and wrinkled his nose. Then we took a short detour and went around the backsides of what appeared to be private homes. The walls were low and coated in white plaster that reflected the sun's rays. They were crumbling in a few areas from neglect, or the sea salt in the air, I guessed, and some of the small gardens were overgrown. Still a few had courtyards that seemed tidy enough.

When he found the gate he was looking for, Cyrus whistled sharp and high. The shrill sound nearly split my ears. A woman poked her head out the rear door of the dwelling.

She frowned. "What do you want?"

"She needs a bath and a fresh chiton," said Cyrus. "Nothing fine. How much?"

The woman's eyes shifted toward me. She shrugged in indifference and named a price that made Cyrus tighten his hands on my lead. As they haggled back and forth, the old Samothraki edged closer to me.

"You will fetch a higher price when your beauty no longer hides behind your filth. Be thankful you have such a clever trader to bargain on your behalf."

Oh, yes. Cyrus was clever.

"He has only spared me the worst of his attentions," I whispered back. "It will not save me from being sold against my will."

The Samothraki tightened his lips at my words, but his irritation did not make them any less true. Coin was coin for a slave trader.

A tub of unheated water was brought. I was given a cake of soap and made to strip in the rear yard, with Cyrus leering at me all the while. My skin grew pink both from shame and the frigid water. By the time I'd finished bathing, there was no part of me that Cyrus, or anyone else who happened by, did not see. I dressed quickly in a simple coarse chiton that was too large for me by a hand span. The draped neckline was so loose; it persisted in slipping off one or the other of my shoulders. I cringed when Cyrus' eyes took on a very keen shine.

The woman came out and helped me rinse and dress my hair. Her eyes flickered at my tattooed hands and she darted a glance at Cyrus. When she picked up an oil ewer, he nodded and she rubbed olive oil through my hair. Then she jerked my gleaming tresses into a sloppy braid. My scalp stung from her ungentle ministrations, but at least I was clean.

Cyrus tossed a coin to the woman who caught it with a quick hand. She harrumphed her way back into the dwelling and I was led once more towards the slave stocks, with the Samothraki and the two silent boys creeping along behind us.

My first impression of the slave stocks was riotous noise. The clamor of the morning crowds was deafening, even more overwhelming than the stench of humanity pressed together in a sweating, perfumed throng.

Cyrus slipped the shards over our necks and led us to a large wooden platform. Slaves of every race imaginable were led in a single file line across the platform. Buyers shouted, inspected, and threw down coins before the most desirable of candidates.

I thought I might vomit.

My knees shook like willow limbs as I was led to the foot of the stairs. I glanced down the line at the black Nubians, the almond-eyed Persians captured during their last unsuccessful campaign, and the more familiar Greeks, Spartans, and Moesians on display. Most were men, although there were a handful of tired women and even a few children.

The children made my heart even heavier.

A trader with a thick wooden staff sauntered behind his stock. He positioned their bodies for best display, even going so far as to prod between the shoulder blades of an aged, worn man so his shoulders might square and thus make him appear fit.

"He'll be sent to toil in the silver mines," whispered the old Samothraki.

"How do you know?" I asked, in spite of my fear.

"The mine owners buy those that no other master will keep. They work them to death in the tunnels." He whistled through the gap in bottom teeth.

I thought he might be afraid for his own fate, but didn't ask.

"You are a pretty thing," he said. "My daughter was pretty like you. She went to a good household. Do you know Greek law claims a slave can earn enough coin to buy back their freedom? But not in the mines." He gave me a meaningful look. "Never in the mines."

Coin was coin, for a slave trader. I could not help but think that if anyone knew of my crimes, I, too, might be sent to the mines. I hated the thought of working in the deep, silent tunnels under the mountains. Halls so much like the cursed temple that stole my mother and brother from me.

I could not die unloved and forgotten under the earth. I would not. Whatever it took, I swore, I would not.

Live free, my father had wished.

His words echoed in my head. I saw my mother's face and I swore I could smell the sweet scent of her skin. I don't know exactly how my thoughts turned from death to regaining my life. But with that thought planted firmly in my mind, I was led onto the platform.

As soon as my sandaled feet hit the rough timber planks, I thrust my shoulders back, as Lukra had taught me. I swayed across the wooden stage, tipped my chin and stared unabashedly at the crowd before me.

There were so many in the marketplace. Wealthy Greek men, with their curled hair. Some scarce out of boyhood with the smooth cheeks of babes and others with shaggy beards, well-oiled and perfumed. Even a few jeweled women, with house slaves and scribes in tow--widows to whom moral conventions did not restrict to their homes. I sighed inwardly. Perhaps a wealthy woman would have need for me. I knew enough to serve a lady's household.

I tried to catch their eyes, to show them that I knew enough of womanly things to be a good purchase.

"What are you doing? Lower your eyes!" whispered the old Samothraki.

I didn't. It seemed ever to be my nature to not do as I must.

Well, I would meet my fate with my head lifted. Interested citizens intent on purchase of a new slave gathered at the wooden platform, their heads on level with my knees. I forced myself to unclench my fingers from my chiton and stand still, and even felt a moment's thanks for Cyrus' self-serving gift of a bath and clean clothes.

The two silent boys were bought first, by a hardened man wearing official robes. Once their price was met, the buyer eyed me, leaning close to peer at the shard around my neck. He grimaced, and moved away shaking his head. Then, went the old Samothraki, to a woman, no less. His eyes flickered once in my direction as he stooped to pick up a heavy basket of the woman's belongings. Cyrus stood to my left, in a knot of other traders hawking their stock. His eyes narrowed and stroked his stubbled chin in a way that made my knees quake, until a voice drew my attention.

"See here, Iadmon. A trembling Thracian flower," hooted a man, standing near the stocks.

He was dressed richly, if not well. The dark shade of wool draped on his shoulders did nothing to complement him, for he was short and pale in every regard. He called to a white-haired man with elegantly pleated robes and an exceedingly ugly personal servant whose features I recognized as vaguely Thracian.

The elderly man glanced at me and looked away in disinterest.

"I have no need for such, at present, Tyrsius," he said. He turned his back and continued conversing with a horse trader. The ugly servant gazed at me with an unreadable expression.

"Hoo hoo, what a face!" Tyrsius, the man in front of me, called to no one in particular. "I think I shall buy her and give poor Lydia a respite."

He staggered over to the stairs and onto the platform, slopping wine over the edge of a bronze goblet at every step. Other patrons averted their eyes, clearly embarrassed by his public drunkenness. When he reached me, he squinted his eyes and peered at the shard on my chest.

"Great Zeus, what a price! Surely this can't be right." He stumbled and I shifted my position to prevent him from trodding on my foot.

Cyrus strutted onto the platform. "She is untouched, good citizen. Temple trained and, as you can see, a beauty."

The man looked at me again. "Untouched, you say? How can this be true? Is not a Thracian woman synonymous with 'slave'?"

I felt my cheeks flush.

It was true; many city-states raided our villages to steal away Thracian women, for the Greeks have ever nurtured a love for that which is lovely and elegant. They equated the number of Thracian 'flowers' adorning Grecian homes as a measure of status. And now, the moment was here. I was to be sold and to this pig of a man.

I couldn't bear it!

By now a crowd had gathered at my feet. Buyers haggling over sturdy men had stopped to eye the noisome man in front of me. Everywhere, my eyes searched for some good and proper woman to take me into her household. But, there were none.

"I assure you, she is pure," Cyrus insisted. I could tell the gathering throng had heightened his excitement. He fairly rubbed his hands together in expectation.

Even the elderly man, Iadmon, and his ugly Thracian servant concluded their business with the horse trader and drew nearer to the platform.

I stood there, and did my best not to fidget under the scrutiny of so many eyes. Slavery or death, I wondered. Those not fit for better service would be sent to die in the mines. Die alone and in the dark. Which would be worse, I wondered.

I was nervous and so very afraid. My mind flitted for something unconnected to me, something mundane on which to ponder, that I might calm my racing heart. I found I could not keep my eyes from the Thracian servant.

He had a misshapen face, like fresh clay left to sag. His head was set at an odd tilt, as if something within him was broken, once, but his eyes were keen and sharp as a blade. I forced myself again to unclench my fingers from the fabric of my chiton. His gaze flickered to my hands and his brows lifted well into the folds of his forehead. He stared at me for some long moments while the drunken man fumbled with his sack of coins and haggled with Cyrus.

"A Thracian flower, indeed," rumbled the Thracian. "What say you, Iadmon? Is she a fine piece to be sweated over by these foolish boys, like a pack of dogs over a bone?"

I had never heard such a voice before, nor ever since. Not even Merikos rivaled this man for depth and complexity of tone. He spoke softly, and yet it seemed his words carried over the noise and cacophony of the _agora_. Though he did not address his master with reverence, it seemed to matter little to Iadmon. I wondered what could be between a master and his personal servant that such liberties were taken in public.

Iadmon shrugged. "Another riddle, dear Aesop?"

Aesop smiled broadly, transforming his face into a modicum of attractiveness. "Merely a question to muse, this time. Does not your wife have need of some new domestic?"

The back of my neck prickled. He played with Iadmon, much the way Merikos and I had bantered words during my lessons. Could I gain the interest of this Iadmon as I had my former tutor? Surely this elderly gent's wife would not abuse me as the drunken fool before me intended.

"Leave off, Aesop," slurred Tyrsius, drawing out his purse from beneath his robes. "Give the girl over to her fate."

"Fate?" Aesop replied. "Ah, now there's a question to be pondered."

Iadmon crossed his arms before his chest as if enjoying what was to come.

"What is fate, after all? Are we not all, men and women, made from the same clay?" charmed Aesop. The crowd chuckled with laughter.

Tyrsius tried to interject, but Iadmon waved him away with a stylish hand.

"What noise is this, Aesop?" said Iadmon. "You propose that men of all nations should be treated with the same privileges as the citizens of our beloved Greece?"

Aesop inclined his head and the corners of his eyes crinkled into deeper ruts in the fleshy skin around his cheeks.

"A spotted cur is the same as a black, is it not? Do they not all snarl and snap in fear, or bark when threatened?" he responded. The crowd murmured, and a few nodded. "Can you best judge a dog by the color of its coat or by the nature of his behavior?"

Iadmon stroked his grizzled chin, clearly encouraging his attendant's rebuttal.

Cold clarity flooded over me. This was no game they played at. I did not know yet, what these two bantered, but I knew the rules. To answer each question, in turn with another rhetorical question. An answer that posed a response only through speculation, not absolutes. They spoke in riddles, but

I could glean somewhat of what was being said beneath the play of words. I had but one moment in which to make myself worthy of their attention, or relegate myself to the anonymity of a flower fit to be plucked.

I cleared my throat, swallowing the hard lump of anxiety lodged just below my chin. I must phrase my response carefully. Enough to gain interest, but not enough to humiliate either party, for what if Tyrsius should buy me after all? No man will tolerate a woman who will make him look a fool.

"And which will best determine the fate of that beast?" I ventured. "Nature? Or the care by which the animal is received?"

All three men, and a good portion of the crowd, gaped at my response, more so I think because a woman dared to speak than the cleverness of my phrase. Cyrus' cheeks mottled with an angry red stain. The drunken Tyrsius stared at me with a slackened jaw.

Save me, I thought. *I should never have spoken.*

They would neither of them have me, now. I knotted my icy fingers into my chiton. Better to be a plucked flower than to toil unto death in the mines. I shifted my feet and waited for the worst to come.

Then, inexplicably, Aesop laughed.

It was a loud, rich, booming laugh, one that startled the crowd with the breadth of it. Iadmon glanced at his servant and then he too began to snigger. Soon, it was a full blown chuckle and the whole crowd laughed until they cried, all save Tyrsius, who wheeled from person to person shouting.

"What? *What is it?*"

Aesop laughed even harder. Even I could not stop a smile from touching my lips. Iadmon roared and slapped his attendant on the back with glee. And Cyrus glared at me with such fury; I thought he would kill me on the spot. Indeed, he raised his hand to strike me a blow.

"Hold," gasped Iadmon. He wiped at the tears running from his twinkling eyes. "Do not strike her. She has done her sex much good this day. And Tyrsius is a fool who drinks too deeply from the wine cart seller's horn. Aesop, pay the man her fee and see that she is brought round to our home before any other 'dogs' gather."

Quick as a wink, Aesop sobered and tossed a bag of coins to Cyrus. I think he planned this from the start, to be so ready with purse in hand.

"Wait," Tyrsius protested feebly. "She was to be mine!"

But the deed was done.

"Come, girl." Aesop took my arm and led me to the tally master. "Sign your mark to the tablet to record your sale. Can you write?"

I nodded dumbly.

"Good," said Aesop. "Be quick about it before that buffoon says another word. Unless you were hoping to have Tyrsius' affections? To elevate yourself through his bedchamber?"

"No." I shook my head vehemently.

"Humph." Aesop stroked his beard. "Then you do have some wit about you. Let's go home. We shall see what a little care can do for you, as well."

CHAPTER 8

My new home, as it turned out, was a rented dwelling in the finest district of Abdera. Iadmon was a philosopher of sorts and quite wealthy. His wife ran his main household on the island of Samos, but for now, Iadmon traveled with Aesop in search of higher learning. His son, Young Iadmon, we rarely saw although I heard he visited on occasion.

Aesop introduced me to the other slaves and concubines, most of their names I promptly forgot. I hoped I wouldn't need to learn them. Now that I was safely away from the stock markets, I planned to run away within the week, perhaps back to Perperek. With the press of so many bodies in the city, I could be long gone before they even noticed I was missing.

The question at hand was where to run. I trusted no one and my family was dead. Still determined, I secreted flat bread and a few olives from our midday meals into the folds of my chiton while I plotted my escape. I'd need food to make the journey, and it would take time to find an unused waterskin. After the second day in Iadmon's household, Aesop asked me to accompany him to the _agora_. It was an unusual request.

When we turned the corner, I saw several large men beating a young slave boy in the streets. He wailed in pain. Again and again their fists struck, sending the boy to his knees. I couldn't bear it.

"What goes here?" I cried. "Aesop, make them stop."

But Aesop would not.

He watched, face impassive as granite, as a man clubbed the boy with a stout stick. When the slave boy's bloody, bruised face struck the stones at my feet, I squealed and turned my face to Aesop's broad shoulder, until at last, Aesop drew me away.

"What did he do?" I asked. My hands began to tremble.

"He ran, Doricha." Aesop looked at me for a very long time. "He ran."

I stopped sneaking bread during meals.

The rest of the week, Aesop taught me much about the life of a Greek slave. I must never use my given name in front of my master. Iadmon was to assign me one. Until then, the other slaves took to calling me "girl", except for Aesop, who enjoyed some special status among us.

There were twelve slaves in the house of Iadmon--seven women and five men, one of which was the cook. Two female concubines attended Iadmon's personal grooming. There were men for the yard, the animals, and to work the wine and olive presses, but such domestics were not for me.

I was assigned the lowliest of household tasks--cleaning the privies and chamber pots. The many pots must be collected from various parts of the house and taken outside. I tossed the contents onto the huge refuse pile near the back alley, usually spattering my chiton in the process, especially if the wind blew in from the sea. Then I had to rinse and dry the pots, and return them to their positions. After I began my chores, most of the others avoided me.

Huge, shit-sucking black flies swarmed my eyes and mouth as I drew nearer the refuse heap. How I loathe insects! I kept my lips pressed in a firm grimace and tried not to breathe until I could move a few steps away-- only to be forced to return several times throughout the day and night to repeat the process anew.

It was worse when it rained, which was often during the storm season. Then the refuse pile became an oozing puddle of foul rivulets and squirming, pale maggots. I bathed dutifully every morning and evening, but the scent of decay clung to my hair and my skin. I felt like death itself, both inside my heart and out. I reeked. The others kept their distance, which was no hardship for me. I could not trust anyone, anymore. What did I care if they wanted conversation?

After the shock of my second week of slavery passed, my stomach burned with Aidne's treachery and Merikos' betrayal. If they'd dared to journey to Abdera, I swear, I would have killed them upon sight. My right hand prickled and burned as my healing tattoos festered. I suspected it was from the filth they were submerged in daily.

I screamed when the healer lanced my red streaked, swollen blisters. I was on fire! He poured wine on the wounds and wrapped them in a poultice. It made little difference, the following day I was back at my chores, although I did them with my good hand as much as I could. I wrapped and rewrapped my sores with clean linens each night before I dropped into an exhausted, fitful sleep.

Finally my wounds healed. The old, achingly familiar blue patterns of Dionysus danced across the backs of my hands. If the other slaves knew what my marks meant, they never said. Such a pattern would be revered in Thrace, but these ignorant barbarians did not recognize the god's touch on my skin. I wanted to go home. I ached for my mother's smile and my father's embrace. I'd give my hair to see Mara again and feared the worst for her.

I begged the other slaves for news whenever they returned from the agora. "Were there any Thracian girls there? Did you see a girl, with hair of gold, at the slave market?"

"There are always girls like that," they scoffed and fanned their hands in front of their noses. Had Mara been sold after I left? I kept after the others, hungry for any tidbit of news. When one of the men grew frustrated with my pestering and shoved me so hard I fell to the ground, I stopped asking for news. I was a slave. What good would the knowledge do me anyway?

My life was an endless cycle of flinging excrement and gagging from the stench. Still, it was better than mining or working in the fields beside the men. Anything was better than that. As there was no lady of the house, Cook oversaw the division of chores--for everyone except Aesop, who reported only to Iadmon. Well, if Aesop could rise to such a state, so could I. I needed only to prove myself worthy.

What a futile wish!

"You have been lazing in the sun," Cook shouted, even though I'd emptied the last pots as fast as I could. "No meal for you tonight!"

My mouth dropped open in disbelief. I'd risen before sunrise to get an early start!

His hand shot out and he slapped me across both cheeks. "Close that insolent mouth. No food tomorrow, either."

The sting of his palm seared away my righteous anger. I glared at him, but didn't speak.

Iadmon, like few well-to-do masters, had ordered that we be given adequate meals instead of the leftover scraps. I suspected it was more out of his love for Aesop, than for decency sake. Some of the other slaves I'd met at the well were not half so fortunate. But what good are food and luck when you're starved into submission?

I went hungry often. The scent of stewed bull-fish and crabs filled me with anguish. I tried to be dutiful, honestly I did. But somehow there was always another pot of piss or vomit to be gathered from the nightly parties and gatherings. I swear Cook must have emptied his bladder more than the goats gave milk, for how else do you explain the filled vessel that I'd only just returned?

If I slept past the cock's crow, I was beaten with a willow sapling until crimson cuts ribboned my back and legs. Sometimes Cook beat me for no other reason than I was a Thracian woman and unprotected. My hands grew raw and chapped and my back constantly ached from either bending or an unwarranted switching. I saw Aesop's jaw clench when I winced during a simple offering ceremony--one of the few luxuries the household staff was allowed to attend. His eyes darted towards the cook, but he said nothing.

I learned to keep my mouth closed and my ears open. Better this, than to starve to death on a mountainside. My infrequent meals would sustain me better than exposure to men and wild beasts, and at least I had shelter from the elements.

My only blessing was that the others could not stand my stench, so I was given a very small alcove all to myself. My sleeping mat was a worn straw pallet, but it was all my own, free of snoring, gassy bodies. At night, I curled into a miserable ball and tried to picture my mother's face. I yearned to feel my father's warm embrace, but only the bite of the stone against my back comforted me. I drifted to sleep often too weary and hungry to even dream.

Live. Well, at least I could fulfill one of my father's wishes. I _would_ live. I had to survive, if I ever wished to regain my freedom.

In the next months, Cook's attentions grew worse. He caught me several times going about my business. At times, I swore he sought me out. I began to dread the sound of his footfalls. What purpose would he have to accost me when there was any number of much more pleasantly scented women about the house? But, there he was…with rough hands and mean eyes.

At the end of one year, I'd reached utter humiliation. My stained chiton started to pull across my breasts, a sure sign they were growing. My beatings lessened, but now the cook would pinch and grope me whenever I was nearby. I went to the other women to beg help, but as I turned the corner, I saw him grab the buttock of Lyphinna, one of Iadmon's concubines. She bobbled and almost dropped a tray of olive oil and combs, but righted herself in time. She said nothing and did not even look his way as she left the open air kitchen.

I caught up with her in the hall. "Cook cannot do that. He touches us whenever and however he pleases. We should tell the master."

"Hush, girl," Lyphinna grunted and cast a dark glance behind her. "We have no status here. Such is the man's right of dominance."

"It is not his right to fondle me," I claimed. "Even I know marriage is forbidden amongst slaves!"

She laughed. "Marriage? Ha, you are a stupid girl!"

"I am not stupid! I am temple trained for a god's pleasure not some filthy Greek!"

Lyphinna turned her eyes on me. I have seen such eyes many times, in the faces of those who have been slaves for most of their lives. They were without compassion, without hope--without any emotion at all. Her expression remained as blank as the stone walls surrounding us and just as hard.

"Pray to your gods, then. Go on, pray." She turned slowly and continued down the hall. "See if they answer you."

"I will," I said to her retreating figure. But I wondered if Dionysus would hear the prayers of an outcast.

The next week, Lyphinna returned late from the well. She set a large amphora of water on the floor as soon as she entered the house, instead of in its customary spot. The sight of her stopped me in my tracks.

Her face and neck were scored with red welts and one of her large brown eyes was almost swollen shut. Her chiton had been torn away from her upper body on the left side, and she held it over her breasts with a trembling hand. She had a bleeding gash in her shoulder joint, just above her breast. The wound looked suspiciously like teeth marks, set close and deep, though from what kind of animal, I could not say.

I set down my pots and ran to help her. Why did the others not move?

"Lyphinna?" I gasped. My hands froze in mid-reach. I was afraid to touch her. She was trembling all over and I thought for certain she would collapse.

Instead, she brushed my hands away and wiped the bloody spittle from her lips with the back of her quaking hand. Then she tottered down the hall, as if each step was trod upon broken shards of pottery.

"Lyphinna," I said again. I stared around the room, as one by one the others began to move. One of the men shook his head and picked up an amphora before going out to the stables.

"Go back to your chamber pots, girl. There is nothing you can do." I did not see who spoke. I did not have to.

In a daze of despair and regret, I picked up my chamber pot and went out the side yard towards the refuse pile. As I left the rear courtyard, I saw Cook come in, brushing dust from the front of his short chiton. He stopped and looked at me for a moment, like a wolf trying to determine if he should expend the effort to catch his prey. My eyes flew from him to the house and back. I began to shake. The contents of the pot sloshed over the edges and soaked the front of my chiton.

The cook curled his lip.

"No meal tonight," he grunted and went into the house.

When Aesop walked in the next morning and found me pinned against a column, and Cook with his hand on my breast, his bushy brows furrowed like dark clouds gathering before a storm. Aesop gave Cook a scolding about the rights of slave property and sent me to the women's quarters to darn and weave from now on. Thus my chamber pot duties ended, and all because Cook found my breasts worthy.

I was so grateful, I didn't care.

My fingers peeled and blistered from carding wool and twisting it to be spun, but the tasks were superior in comparison to emptying piss, so I did not complain. Weaving was not the greater glory of dance or song, true, but better this than to die alone and unloved in the streets of Abdera. It was a trade skill, and a useful one at that. Perhaps I could take in extra coins to buy my freedom.

I dreamed nightly of Mara, my father and, of course, my precious mother. How many of these low tasks did she perform at the temple, so that I might have been trained? I was selfish not to have seen her disgrace. Was this how she felt--forced to the lowest drudgery at the temple where once she'd been a prize? I had been blind in so many ways.

In the months that followed, I kept well out of Cook's way, or made certain Aesop was within hearing. It meant I had to sneak cheese and bread to my alcove at night, or go hungry, but that was a small price to pay to reduce Cook's attentions to me. It was not Cook's notice that I most secretly hoped to gain, for he was also a slave and therefore could be of no use to me.

After two months, I noticed a goodly amount of frothy spew in the chamber pots, most of them near the women's quarters. When I commented on Lyphinna's pale and sweating face, I was told to hush. Two weeks later the news was confirmed. Lyphinna was with child. Normally such would be cause for joy, but for a concubine or slave it is dreadful news. We are not only forbidden to marry, we are not allowed to nurture children. Lyphinna's babe would be sold or left out in the elements to die-- its fate for Iadmon, our master, to decide.

"How horrid the life of a slave is," I whispered to no one in particular. Lyphinna had just fled the morning meal after taking one look at the raw, salted onions and bread. The sounds of her retching rent the air. I never wanted children. First my mother's death and now this...I would go to my grave a virgin, like Bendis, or the Greek goddess Athena, who was herself a virgin warrior.

Aesop stared at me for a long time before he raised his cup to his lips. I shivered and wondered if he could read my thoughts.

The next morning, which marked the sixth season of my service to Iadmon, Aesop reviewed my progress and pronounced me fit to serve at banquets, which meant I was to enjoy a small salary. My heart trilled, for my weaving skills had never progressed beyond the rudiments of carding and spinning.

"A man wants to see a pretty face and figure as he enjoys his wine," was Aesop's rationale. Well, there would be any number of 'two-obol girls' willing to hitch up their skirts and serve the pleasures of a rich man's banquet. They could oft be called from the brothels and streets. Still, it had been so long since someone found me worthy, I could not help but smile.

So, for the next few months, I served at raucous banquets, informal celebrations and the receptions Iadmon held for Aesop, who dispersed his 'wisdoms' with an acerbic tongue. Ha! If only I should have been a man and free, I would have spoken just the same.

Many times, I was sent to fetch goods from the *agora*. I learned to haggle quite well. More often than not, I returned home with my supplies and a good deal of coin, some of which Iadmon let me keep. After the misery of my first year, I dreamed now of the day when I might buy back my freedom.

My wages, of course, were quite small. I comforted myself with the thought that at least Iadmon never visited my chambers at night. I'd heard the other women gossiping at the well where the entire city of Abdera drew its water. The tales they told made me cringe with disgust. As much as I wanted to feel the passion of Dionysus which I'd experienced with Mara, my curiosity did not extend to bearing babes who would never know me. I missed my near-sister, with her quick wit and comforting arms.

Lyphinna's babe came late one evening, on the night my life changed.

A wicked storm raged outside. Thunder rattled the ceiling beams and lightning bolts sizzled across the sky. Rain fell in a relentless deluge, forcing us to abandon the open air kitchen and eat meals from our preserves of dried fish along with uncooked fruits and vegetables. There was no meat and very little bread.

Lyphinna had been in labor all day. With the steady rain, we'd been trapped in the house as she screamed and moaned. Even Cook seemed anxious, although it was probably the weather and his ruined quail eggs.

We gathered in the weaving room until the birth was over. I fussed over a particularly stubborn clump in my wool, as I had never been particularly skilled with making thread.

"Fie," I grumbled at the tangled mess. One of the other women took it from me before I ruined it with my tugging.

Lyphinna's shrieks rose and ebbed in quick succession. Something was happening now! All went still for a moment. I waited, scarcely daring to draw breath. Had she died? Had they cut her as they had my mother? Then I heard it. The lusty wail of an infant. I glanced around the room, unable to keep the ghost of a smile from touching my lips. One of the women murmured something and kissed her knuckle. We waited some more. No one came.

I sighed, cross and weary of damp cold air and the noise coming from the next room. I needed to stretch my legs. Restless, I moved into the hallway to get my tattered *peplos*, my shawl, from my alcove. At least it would keep away some of the chill.

"I've never had a son," Cook's voice trailed down the hallway, despite the fact that he spoke softly. "If it were a girl, I'd say leave it for the wolves…but, Aesop, surely you can understand. Give me the boy. I'll send him to my sister and her husband to foster."

"Your son will be a slave, as you are." Aesop's voice was firm.

I crept a step closer.

"*Please*, Aesop," Cook wheedled.

Aesop sighed, after a long pause. "I will ask. But, it is for Iadmon to say." He did not sound pleased.

I leaned against the cold, stone wall and pressed my hand to my stomach. An image of Cook's calculating smirk flashed before my eyes, followed by Lyphinna's bruised face. Gods forgive me, but at that moment I was overwhelmed with guilty relief. He'd raped Lyphinna, but it could just as easily have been me.

The following morning I slept in by accident. I'd spent the night tossing and turning, so as dawn broke, I was still abed. My shoulders and neck were stiff from sleeping in the chilled, rain- damp air, and I rubbed my gritty eyes as I went to the kitchen for the morning meal. Hopefully, everyone else had as uneasy a night--I didn't want to face Cook alone, not after what I'd overheard last night.

Cook was gone. In his place was squat woman with graying hair and a lined face. She looked gruff, but nodded pleasantly as she handed me a hunk of fresh cheese-smeared bread and a pair of small, dried apple.

"Where's Cook?" I asked, nibbling at my breakfast.

"Gone." The woman grunted. "I'm here, now."

So, Aesop had finally seen to Cook. I smiled at her, not even caring where her predecessor was now. Hopefully rotting in some dank prison, the rutting pig. Wherever he resided now, it was no doubt too kind for him. Relief made me happier than I'd been in years.

"Good," I said and meant it.

CHAPTER 9

"Call me Kailoise," said the new cook.

Though her words were abrupt, I soon found out she had a kind heart and patient hand when it came to me, although she rarely spoke. Her affection towards me was shown in other ways, such as an extra portion of meat or fish, or a small sweet found waiting in my alcove.

My days as a slave became less of a nightmare. After Lyphinna was sold, it seemed my position was secure. I did not live free, but at least I no longer lived in terror. I now had Lyphinna's chores, to keep me occupied. I attended Iadmon's dress, pleating his robes with precision and trimming his white whiskered chin, in addition to serving at meals and symposiums. I took to it well enough, I daresay, even Aesop remarked on my new vigor. His praise gladdened my heart.

Aesop was not free, for all that he acted thus. Considered something of an oddity by the rest of the house staff, he was exceedingly clever and well spoken, traits that earned him the nickname of the 'Fabulist'. Learned men gathered each morning after the assembly, to spout questions at one another and try their best to thrill Aesop with their wit and humor. They rarely did so. Not even Young Iadmon who had recently returned from Syracuse to live in the house of his father.

Young Iadmon, the master's son, was a boy scarce older than myself. And while his features were youthful and fine, inside he seemed as dark as the storm shadows that blew in from the sea. We, all of us slaves, avoided him when we could, praising the gods that his father had assigned a male concubine to groom and dress him, for he was known to give an unprovoked beating.

Still, I glimpsed a life of wonder during those symposiums with Aesop. Any respectable woman in the household would have been sent from the chamber, but as a slave, my presence was tolerated. I poured watered wine into the communal friendship bowl, as I was told only a drunkard or a Thracian would dare to drink it pure, and watched the men furrow their brows as they puzzled over the meanings of Aesop's tales.

Soon, I found the Fabulist just as charming as his tales. I'd thought Aesop ugly and misshapen upon our first meeting. But as the seasons passed, I found myself drawn by his wit and charm. His countenance improved, or perhaps it was just my getting used to him that made him so. More months passed in a regular cycle of endless drudgery and toil, which was nothing like the greater glory for which I had been trained. My only respite, it seemed, was to exercise my mind.

Once, I almost dropped a platter of figs down the front of Citizen Aeschylus when I realized I had reasoned out the question before any of the others. I caught Young Iadmon, the master's son, staring at me, and I feared he'd discovered my secret. I vowed to keep my attention on my tasks, but the lure of Aesop's fables was too great to withstand.

I pondered over tales of oxen and ass, tortoise, hares, and yes, even dogs. It became almost a game with me, to see if my thoughts were of a turn, or better than, the wealthy patrons I served. I began to love calculation and philosophy, anything to keep me from musing on the loss of my family and Mara.

And then one evening, glorious beauty and the hope for my salvation came to visit.

A pair of women, languid, and resplendent in their perfumes and adornments, dined with Iadmon and his son. They were perfectly groomed, and dined with delicate precision, knowing precisely the fashionable crook of the correct finger with which to catch up a crab or fish or meat from the communal plates, and reclining gently on the left elbow, as I'd seen Iadmon himself do.

I'd scarcely seen my master's son since he'd caught me listening in to Aesop's wisdoms, for my tasks kept me much occupied in his father's quarters or in the marketplace. But tonight, I attended the lovely women during the feast. I felt their limpid eyes on me, and heard the intellect with which they jested and the music of their laughter. How long had it been since I'd laughed so freely myself? Surely not since my life in the village, before I knew of death and treachery.

"Who are they," I asked, as one of the women took up the lyre to play.

"They are _Hetaerae_," Kailoise whispered reverently, coming up behind me to take an emptied platter of stuffed sow's womb, a dish for which she was particularly noted, from my limp grasp.

"_Hetaerae?_" I asked.

"A special class of companions. They are more than common whores. They are courtesans educated in the arts of pleasure and womanly arts. This pair hails from Athens. The master has paid a pretty price for the both of them."

"They are lovely," I said.

"A *hetaera* likes old wine, but not old men." She quipped and I smothered a giggle. "Perhaps this will be well for our household." Kailoise speculated. "For your sake, I pray it might be."

I slipped away to follow her to the kitchen for a fresh dish of cakes and to beg more details.

Hetaerae, Kailoise reported, were renowned for their grace, beauty and talent, and, even more fascinating, their intelligence. Far removed from the common *pornai*, who roam the open streets or sex stalls and sell their bodies, *hetaerae* are revered. Grecian women have no place in society except to bear children and keep a household, but *hetaerae* were not only allowed to attend public events, they were honored at them. More than one *hetaera* was reputed to have political influence with high ranking politicians, as much as the Bacchae held sway over the spirits of the gods in Thrace.

I wondered if my temple training made me a worthy candidate in the eyes of the *hetaerae*, or if a Thracian woman could even dare to aspire to such greatness. Carefully, I watched each motion of their hands and toss of the head, vowing I would emulate them. I would much rather spend my time in pleasant company, pampered and appreciated, than closeted from all social contact. These women bantered with Iadmon and son, as well as any man in the symposiums. Perhaps I could get one of the women alone at the night's end and ask how it might be done.

I never got the chance.

At the evening's end, the pair of *hetaerae* disappeared with Young Iadmon, in a common practice of sexual tutelage for young men. Later, I found a knotted *peplos*, half-hidden under the courtyard bushes. It was so lovely and so very fine. Surely, they would miss it. I gathered the shawl in my hands and sat on a stool near the front gates, so that I might return it to its rightful owner.

But, I did not see the *hetaerae* leave in the morning, and indeed, they never returned to Iadmon's household again. That did not bode well for Young Iadmon's sexual prowess, but as he was reported to have a mean temper, I did not trouble myself over the loss. I concealed the finely woven shawl, still scented with sweet perfume, in my sleeping alcove. It reminded me of Mara, and made me feel a little less alone.

I thanked the gods Young Iadmon departed for Minos soon after that night. We did not see him off, but Kailoise reported on his comings and goings, which was oft a welcome warning. For now, it was enough that he was gone. Another span of weeks passed without change in the monotony of my chores and the familiar bustle of the city. Still, I at least I had more time to myself. With Young Iadmon away, our master entertained less frequently, so I was relegated to weaving once again, though it bored me to tears.

The other women worked in silence, so I began to make up my own tales, repeating them over and over as I thrust the shuttle from one end of the loom to the other. I wondered what Aesop would think of the fables I had spun. And I wondered too, about that day long ago in the stocks, when he intervened to save me from a drunken fool. Aesop was cordial to me, as much as he could be, given our situation. The other slaves gossiped about his status in the household, but I paid no mind to them. After all, he was the Fabulist. Still, I wondered why he had troubled himself to influence Iadmon's notice of me that day in the slave stocks.

Why should he risk himself, for me?

At last, I could bear it no longer. I've never been a patient creature. I felt I must speak out. So, the day came when I dared ask Aesop a question of my own. We slaves had just finished our morning meal in the dark hours before my true chores began.

"You are different these days, Doricha," he said, as we cleared our rough communal platter. "You dined most elegantly this morning."

"I have always been a quick study," I replied, wiping the crumbs from the table into my hand and tossing them into the fire. "And we Thracians have a love of that which is beautiful."

Aesop considered me for a moment. "That we do," he agreed.

"Aesop, why did you lead Iadmon to purchase me?" I asked when all the others had filed out to begin the day.

"I led him?" Aesop responded in his usual questioning fashion. He stroked his stubbled chin.

"Come now," I whispered and peered over my shoulder. "There is no one about. You and I both know how much Iadmon values your advice. It was your words that spared me from the mines, as much as his coin."

Aesop considered me for a moment. "You are Thracian," he replied and turned away, as if that was explanation enough.

I shook my head. "No. There were others there. Why me?"

Aesop smiled. "Let me tell you a tale."

I sighed. "As you wish."

"An Ant went to the bank of a river to quench its thirst, and being carried away by the rush of the stream, was on the point of drowning. A Dove sitting on a tree overhanging the water plucked a leaf and let it fall into the stream close to her. The Ant climbed onto it and floated in safety to the bank. Shortly afterwards, a bird catcher crept under the tree. He laid his lime-twigs for the Dove, which sat in the branches. The Ant perceived his design and stung him in the foot. In pain, the bird catcher threw down the twigs, and the noise made the Dove take wing."

I stared at him. _This_ was the reason for my life being spared the torments of the mines? What had an insect and a bird to do with me?

81

"I do not understand," I sulked. "You did not give a proper answer."

Aesop rose and cleared his empty bowl from the table. He handed it to me for washing. "Give it thought, if you have any. You will have your answer."

And that was the way of Aesop's tutoring. In the four years I spent in the house of Iadmon, I absorbed bits of information. I served the men watered wine, whilst they spoke of higher purposes and the fate of man. I learned to be casual in my observations, else I should be sent from the room. But Aesop knew I listened. Knew, and nurtured my hunger for his words until I begged him to teach me in earnest.

"Please, Aesop," I cajoled.

"Bah! I cannot teach a girl. You have even less sense about you than a woman."

"You don't believe that," I said, with a pert smile. "I am simply a dog of another coat."

Aesop laughed at my jest. My heart flooded with pride that I could do what so few men could--amuse the great Fabulist.

"And how will you pay?" he asked.

"Pay?" I echoed. I hadn't thought of payment.

"Yes, Doricha. How will you repay me for filling your mind with knowledge that befits a king?"

My heart sank. I had nothing of value to give save the few coins I'd saved from clever haggling. And those I hoarded to buy back my freedom.

"You teach the others, the men who visit Iadmon," I retorted. "They do not pay."

Aesop crossed his arms over his barrel chest. "My master bids me to teach them. Tell me, what do you offer, Little Flower?"

My thoughts centered on that word, 'flower'. Aesop did not use words lightly.

So, a Thracian flower to be plucked.

"I will wash and cook for you," I ventured, knowing it was useless. "And mend your garments."

Aesop reached out and touched a strand of my hair. "You will do that anyway. You are a slave and a woman."

An unpleasant feeling twisted my stomach. I thought of Merikos suddenly and the time he'd put his hand on my breast. My cheeks burned.

"I have never known a man," I whispered. Aesop did not respond. He stared at me with unreadable eyes. "But I...I know what it is, what you want."

"Do you?" Aesop asked. I jumped at the sound of his voice.

"Yes," I licked my lips nervously. I wasn't exactly sure how it was to be done, save for the animals in the courtyard rutting violently. An image of the Bacchanal flashed in my mind. A pair of pale slender legs flapping like butterfly wings.

Again, Aesop stared at me. Stared until I shifted in my spot.

At last, something unreadable flickered in his gaze. "Dance for me."

"Wha-at?" I asked.

"It has been many years since I've seen a Thracian woman dance. I would lay odds you are exceptionally fine at it." He eyed my hands. "Very fine indeed."

"I cannot dance," I protested. My heart was heavy with memories of the temple, of my happiness there so swiftly shattered. I had not practiced any of Lukra's lessons for nearly three years. I couldn't dance for him!

Aesop gathered my hands together and turned them palm down. The betraying blue tattoos danced along my nervous flesh.

"A man is not wise, who assumes his clothing will disguise his nature. This is doubly so for a woman. You cannot hide your training any more than you can disguise the natural grace of your figure."

His eyes traveled the length of me. He was a large man, great of mind, body, and spirit. I thought of the lithe, sensuous body of Dionysus. Aesop could not be further from that graceful, merciless god than an eel is to a goat.

"Dance?" I repeated. "That is all?"

Aesop smiled. "For now."

So, I danced.

After my wretched first years of slavery, I feared to be resold to some cruel master. Those who crossed the Fabulist found themselves on the slave platform before the cock crowed, a lesson learned by Cook. Aesop curried much favor with Iadmon, and he was kind to me. I wanted to please him, almost as much as I was afraid not to.

And perhaps part of me did wish to impress him with my skills.

So, I danced.

I wore the *hetaera's peplos* I'd secreted away and felt almost beautiful. Aesop watched me with his grey eyes glittering in the moonlight. We dared not play music, for it was late in the evening, the time when sleep came to most others. I crept to the courtyard, where the night breeze cooled my flesh and perfumed the air with the scents of basil, thyme, and mint.

Aesop hummed low in his throat. I danced to the rhythm in my mind, hesitant at first, until I could almost sense Lukra's sharp staccato on the packed earth floor of the courtyard. How easily it all came back to me, the lessons in my memory. I imagined the twang of the lyre strings and the whistle of the *avlos*, the pipes. I positioned my arms as if I still clasped the hands of my beloved Mara. I danced until my arms ached and my legs quavered. I danced until sweat soaked my chiton and Aesop's breathing was as labored as my own.

"Enough," he said and reached for his goblet of wine. "I will teach you, Doricha. The mere sight of you dancing is enough."

Some of the crimson liquid dribbled out the side of his lips. He wiped his beard with the back of his hand.

I had a sudden image of my smiling father doing the same. Oh, how I missed him! His loss came crashing down on me with the weight of a thousand stones.

"Doricha?" Aesop put down his goblet. "What is it?"

I could not answer. I ran from him with my hands covering my face. I fled blindly through the dark courtyard, not knowing or caring whence I went until my body encountered an unmovable force.

I ran headlong into Young Iadmon, my master's son. He had returned to plague us again!

"Hie there, Rufus," he said. 'Rufus' was an ugly reference to a red-haired Thracian. His hands manacled my bare upper arms. "Why are you up so late? Where have you been? Stealing from our larder?"

My breath caught. Aesop was nowhere to be seen. "I…I was dancing, Young Iadmon. In the moonlight."

His lips drew back in a leer and snorted, a habit that had earned him the moniker of "The Swine", amongst the slaves.

"Another of your heathen Thracian rites, no doubt. Very well then, Rufus. Dance for me." His hands slid down to my wrists and he dragged me into the center of the courtyard. I pulled away.

"No, please! I do not wish to dance now. Please let me return to my quarters. Please, Citizen." I hoped to remind him of his status, but Young Iadmon would not listen. His eyes fixed on my pilfered shawl, though I doubt he recognized it.

"You will call me master, Rufus," he said. "Shall I make it clear to you?"

"I am minded to tell you a fable, Young Iadmon." Aesop's thick voice suddenly floated out of the shadows by the wall. He stepped into the moonlight, his face as impassive as the rock wall behind him.

"Fable?" Young Iadmon's gaze darted from Aesop to me, and his eyes narrowed. "What is this?" he asked suspiciously.

"You see," said Aesop. "An Ass, having put on the Lion's skin, roamed about in the forest and amused himself by frightening all the foolish animals he met in his wanderings."

"Be still, old fool," Young Iadmon said and tugged on my wrists again. "My father is abed, and I have no wish to hear your lectures. Leave us."

Aesop continued as if nothing at all were amiss. "He came upon a Fox. The Ass tried to frighten him also, but the Fox no sooner heard the sound of his voice than he exclaimed, 'I might possibly have been frightened myself, if I had not heard your bray.'"

The Swine thought for a long moment while I writhed in his grip. Then his countenance turned dark in the moonlight. "You call me an ass, slave?" He sneered. "I am your master!"

"There is only one master here," Aesop remarked. "Shall we rouse him from his bed?"

Young Iadmon's cheeks paled. "She is our property."

Aesop's brows drew together like a thundercloud. "She is a slave, not some mere concubine without protection."

Young Iadmon's gaze darted from me to Aesop. I held my breath, afraid to rouse him further. "Back to your quarters," he ordered, at last. And he marched away with his narrow shoulders stiff with futile rage.

When he had departed, I turned to Aesop with breathless gratitude. "Thank you."

"Bah!" Aesop grumbled, throwing a dark glance at the direction Young Iadmon had fled. "He should know better than to attack his father's property without provocation. There are laws against this, as he well knows."

"But, how did you know?" I wondered.

"Know what, Little Flower?" Aesop rubbed a gentle hand over the marked flesh of my wrists. His touch both piqued and soothed me.

"How did you know he wouldn't wish to rouse his father?"

"Did you notice his tunic, Doricha?" Aesop asked. "It was torn and bloodied. The Swine is well known for his temper in these parts. And our master wearies himself with paying coin to cover for his son's escapades."

"I didn't notice," I mumbled, my embarrassment tempered slightly by the small joy of newly acquired knowledge.

"Well," Aesop patted me on the head. "Those lovely eyes of yours should be of more use to you than mere decoration. Do you not agree?"

Oh, how I did.

CHAPTER 10

Three has never been a good number for me, even to this day. I'd lost three members of my family. Three sorrow filled paths I've chosen to walk. And three times have I loved, but all for naught. So, naturally, there were three occasions The Swine sought me out in the house of Iadmon.

My heart still mourned for Mara and my lost family, but I was more resigned to my plight.

Months of Aesop's tutoring had given me much to divert my mind. Just this week, we'd discussed whether a man's nature could be altered by his surroundings or if simple creation determined a man's character. I was of the mind that gifts of the gods determined our character, but Aesop had raised his brow in such a maddening way that I questioned the very walls before me.

I still pondered that infuriating brow lift when Young Iadmon caught me changing the bed linens.

"Rufus," he said and startled me. I fumbled the packet of herbs I'd meant to sprinkle on the linens to keep away vermin.

The Swine crossed the room quickly. His lips compressed in a hard line. I glanced at the door, praying to find someone, anyone, passing in the hall beyond.

"I called you, girl. Answer me," he demanded.

I lowered my eyes, dutifully, though in truth I ached to find an escape. "What is it you require?" I gave the customary bow.

"What I require," said The Swine, reaching a hand towards the leather thong binding my hair, "is for you to serve me."

I swallowed hard and fought the urge to shy from his touch. His fingers probed the knot in the leather and freed my long hair with a single tug. My eyes stung. These past months with Aesop's protection, a man had never been so bold as to touch me without my permission.

"I do serve this household, citizen, for Iadmon is my master," I replied truthfully. I hoped my words would appease him.

A satisfied smirk appeared on The Swine's face.

"Yes," he said. "And as your master, I bid you please me." He tangled his fingers in my red-gold hair and drew me close to him.

"Please, I-I am expected in the servant's hall," I stammered. I escaped his grip and bent to retrieve my herb packet, but The Swine was not deterred. A wicked light gleamed in his eyes.

"I bid you serve me, Rufus. Stay there, on your knees. It suits me just as well." And he grabbed both the back of my head and his codpiece, just as his father entered the chamber.

"What goes here, my son?" Iadmon asked angrily, his hands clenched.

"I was just having a bit of sport." The Swine eyed me. His handsome features turned sullen, as a child sneaking a sweet.

"Unhand my slave." Iadmon's voice was as hard as his son's eyes. "Leave us, girl."

I rose and darted from the chamber as fast as my unsteady legs could carry me.

Aesop had once told me Greeks believed a slave should be treated firmly, even beaten if necessary to gain obedience. But no master dared to inflict a serious injustice upon his slaves, or else face the wrath of their gods upon final judgment.

Thanks to Iadmon's fear of the gods, I'd escaped his son's attentions a second time. My legs quaked as I rounded the hallway towards my alcove, trying to move as silently as I could.

The morning gathering had just ended. Aesop was bidding a hearty farewell to our master's guests when he caught sight of me passing the arcade. I must have looked distressed, for he placed a tender arm around my shoulders and led me to the kitchen. My heart ached for my mother's embrace and a woman's knowledge to help me understand.

But I had only Aesop.

I told him all that had happened and after he poured me a bracing cup of mellow aged wine, I felt stronger.

"Fortunate for you our master happened by," Aesop said, when I had finished my cup and my tale.

I nodded. "Still, I wonder. What did The Swine want?" The kitchen was small and comforting to me. There were no corners that held hidden dangers.

"What did he want?" Aesop echoed and frowned at me. "You cannot be that innocent."

My cheeks burned. I didn't want to appear stupid—not to Aesop. "I didn't understand. When he said being on my knees suited him just as well?"

"Oh, that. Well, I suppose he meant for you to take him in your mouth."

My curiosity was roused. "Take what in my mouth?"

"His manhood. What else, you silly girl?" Aesop stroked his beard.

I thought for a long moment. "Can it really be done?" I could not picture such a thing.

"Yes, it can be done. As easily a man's kiss, though perhaps with a bit more depth." He wiped a hand over his chin.

"I've never done it," I responded.

"No….no I should think not." Aesop grabbed up the cup, and poured himself a draught.

"I mean, I've never been kissed by a man." I scuffed at cobbled floor.

He corked the wine. "Haven't you?"

"No."

"Would you like to?" he asked.

"With you?" I asked. An image of Dionysus' lithe form flashed through my thoughts. Aesop was my teacher, my only friend. _Did I?_

Aesop looked around the empty kitchen. "There is no one else about unless you prefer to find The Swine. He would be more than willing to teach you whatever you wish to learn and perhaps a bit more. Come now, Doricha. Do you dislike me so?"

I caught my breath at those words. They were similar to those Merikos had spoken to me in the temple. Merikos, who'd loved my mother. My father and even Aidne, that treacherous serpent, had loved her. I knew betrayal, but what did I know of love, save for my adolescent passion with Mara?

I eyed Aesop, the man they called Fabulist. He was a massive man, olive complexioned--odd for a Thracian, and with a shock of unruly hair kinked like wiry strands of copper from his scalp. Though he walked like a lopsided mountain, he had a gregarious smile that infected me with his wry humor. And there was his mind and his voice…. He was not _so_ very ugly, I thought. Not handsome, but not _so_ ugly. Could he teach me the mysteries of the flesh?

I took a deep breath and closed my eyes.

"Very well. I am ready to be kissed," I announced.

Nothing happened. I cracked an eyelid.

"I think not, Little Flower." Aesop chuckled. "But you will be, soon. Keep your eyes closed if it suits you."

His face loomed closer and I dutifully kept my eyes shut tight.

I felt the raw scratch of his beard tickling my cheeks and inhaled the scent of sharp Grecian wine a moment before something soft and warm pressed on my lips. The pressure was not unpleasant, but certainly nothing like I'd imagined. It was nowhere near what I'd experienced with Mara, those years ago in the temple. I stiffened a little, at the memory, and the warm pressure disappeared.

"There now," Aesop announced proudly. "You have been kissed."

"That was all?" I cracked an eye open just in time to see Aesop's cheeks flush.

"For all that you stood there like an unforgiving stone. Yes, that was all." He sounded offended.

"Try again," I ordered and closed my eyes a second time.

This time as Aesop pressed his moist lips against mine, I tried my best to conjure up the image of my lithe Dionysus. Heat rushed through my body as Aesop's hands rubbed my breasts through my chiton. I reached my hands out to touch the perfect white flesh in my memory, but encountered a very hairy forearm instead.

"Oh." I drew back as disappointment flushed the image of my lord from my mind. "That _is_ all." I frowned at Aesop. "It hardly inspires my passion."

Aesop made a growling noise, deep in his throat.

"Shall we try again?" I was less than enthusiastic. "I do wish to be pleased."

Aesop's countenance darkened like Boreas' thunderclouds. "Be gone, girl!" He pushed me none-too-gently towards the doorway. "You come to me with tears staining your cheeks and tales of despair, and yet you expect to be wooed? Go away and return when you are ready for a proper instruction. Go!"

"But Aesop, I only wished to...."

"Go!" he rumbled again.

I fled back to my quarters, thinking something must be very wrong with me, if The Swine wished to abuse me and Aesop did not wish to please me with kisses.

A week passed, days and nights when I felt eyes on my back; whether they were Aesop's or those of my master's son I could not say. I had lost the favor of Aesop's protection. The other slaves began to whisper and avoid me, especially after The Swine made a show of pinching my bottom in the dining hall. He left a nasty bruise.

Aesop avoided me. If I entered the kitchens, he jerked to his feet and stomped out. If I was to serve at symposium, Aesop refused to even glance in my direction. I must be truly horrible, I thought. First Merikos and now Aesop, my only friend and teacher. Was it the nature of all men to leave behind those most in need of their care and protection? Well, if I was to be alone, then I would carry on.

I swore I didn't need Aesop's protection.

So I was, again, quite alone when The Swine found me next. I'd been sent to the _agora_ to buy fresh eel and fish for the day's meal. Aesop, Iadmon, and his son had gone to assembly and were not expected home until later.

The wind blew in from the ocean, and reminded me somewhat of Perperek. For a brief moment, I was a child again, wending the seaside village paths. I felt rather free as I traversed the winding streets down to the marketplace, twirling my fish basket before me. With a twinge of guilt, I remembered my first view of the large open area that housed the slave stocks. I wondered what had happened to the old Samothraki, and I prayed that he'd been spared from the mines.

Dionysus, if it be your will, send him some measure of your grace.

I'd begun to pray to the gods again, in these last few days, and so caught up with my belated pleas I was that I did not recognize the man lounging in the doorframe ahead of me until he grabbed my arm.

"Young Iadmon!" I drew away from him and my sandals skidded on the crushed limestone path. The basket dropped from my fingers and lay abandoned in the street as he dragged me away to a nearby alley.

His thick fingers bit into the soft flesh of my shoulder. When he pushed me back against the rough stone building I had the sense to open my mouth to scream. Most of the city peacekeepers are slaves. An unprovoked attack on a slave was forbidden!

The Swine covered my lower jaw with a bruising hand before I uttered a sound.

"I will have you, you red bitch. You will not twitch your skirts and offer yourself solely to that misshapen tale spinner."

I tried to deny him, but his fingers obscured my words into an unintelligible groan.

"Be silent!" he hissed. His eyes darted from side to side and the fingers of his spare hand ground further into my shoulder joints. I moaned at the flash of pain radiating down to my fingers.

The Swine wedged a knee between my legs, nudging the fabric of my chiton up to my thighs. He rested the length of one forearm against my throat.

"Make no sound, do you hear? Not one," he said.

His fingers peeled away from my aching jaw and I felt the sea breeze cool my hot, sweaty skin.

"You're so pink," he said, his gaze roaming my face. "So very soft and pink. I've longed to feel you yield beneath my touch."

"Please," I begged and tears stung my eyes. My voice was hoarse from the crushing pressure of his arm against my throat. "Please let me go. I will not tell, I swear it. Just let me go!"

His hand returned with a blinding slap and clamped over my lips.

"I said, 'be silent.' Now, I must find a way to keep you quiet."

His face was so close to me. Too close. I could smell the stink of Greek onions and olives on his breath and see the red rims of his eyes.

My fingers clawed at him. I had to get away, yet I could not strike him.

And then he kissed me, if one could call it a kiss.

His hand peeled away at the last instant before his mouth bruised my lips. I tasted salt and the copper tang of blood. He'd pressed so hard my teeth had punctured my bottom lip.

He savaged my lips. Saliva trailed from my nostrils to my chin. I wanted to retch. Then he thrust his tongue inside my mouth and I gagged. He drew back and boxed my ears. They popped and the world became muffled, as though stuffed with wool. I cried out at the stabbing pain and felt a wet stickiness in my left ear.

The Swine drew his hands back and scrabbled at the front of my clothing. I wept as he tore the top of my chiton away. His ragged nails scratched crimson lines into my flesh and my breasts puckered at the exposure to the cold air.

It hit me then. He was going to take me, here on the rocky hillside overlooking the path to the _agora_, like a common street whore, a _pornai_. I understood enough of what went on between men and women to understand this.

Dionysus, if it be your will, I began to pray. But I could not think the words to finish. The world began to tilt crazily as The Swine's fingers began to grope and squeeze. I scraped my back sliding down the rough stone wall. The ground rose up to meet me.

And all the while he cursed until my ringing ears were full up with the sound of them.

"I will have you. I will. I _will_.".A strange light glittered in his eyes.

The world grew dim.

His voice seemed very far away. Further off, I heard the braying of dogs and then, blissfully, I heard and saw no more.

"Bring some wine. She's coming round." A familiar warm voice filled my aching head and penetrated the fog in my ears.

"Aesop?" I tried to crack an eye open but a stab of pain made them water so fiercely, I kept them closed. "Aesop, where am I?"

"Shh, Doricha. You're safe. We've brought you home."

"What hap-?" My voice cracked.

If the Swine had succeeded I would know soon enough. I shifted and found I was sore at the juncture between my legs. I could not stop the tears that leaked out of my eyes and spilled onto my cheeks.

"Leave us," Aesop spoke to some unseen servant. He paused for a moment and I felt his cool, dry hand pass over my brow. I was sore there too, just above my left temple. I winced.

"You have a nasty bruise over your eye," Aesop said. "And your body is scratched and sore. But you are…intact for all purposes." He sighed. "Fortunate we were passing and heard your cries."

"We?"

"Iadmon, Aeschylus, and myself. Iadmon became worried when his son did not arrive at the assembly."

"Oh," I turned my face away in a direction I hoped was toward the wall. If Aeschylus knew, soon the entire city would know of my shame. "Where is The Swine now?" *Would he creep upon me in my very bed?*

"His father has sent him away to Phrygia."

Relief, followed swiftly by cold fear washed over my limbs. "Because of me?"

"Iadmon ordered his son to oversee a shipment of tablets. But, yes. Because of you." Aesop touched a cool rag to my eye.

I was glad I had not been raped. While we do not prize virginity as much as the Greeks, I did not wish to be taken unless I desired it. And I most definitely did not wish The Swine to take me. What little I'd experienced of his attentions had left me bruised and sickened.

"Will Iadmon send me away as well? I didn't do anything, Aesop. Please, you must tell him!"

"You are to stay here, for now. And that is all I can say, Doricha."

It would have to do. I sighed heavily and tried to rest. As long as The Swine was away, I would not be touched. My body ached but I leaned over and pulled the *hetaera's peplos* from under my cot. I buried my nose in it to comfort myself with the faint scent and stroked the soft material until I fell asleep.

The following morning, Iadmon himself came to visit me. My master had called a healer from the temples of Abdera to serve me, a mere slave. Iadmon was a good man, a kind man. I tried to remember that in later months. Kailoise sent me seed cakes for my breakfast, and glared at any man within ten paces of me, so Iadmon nodded briskly at the physician's report and left.

In the months that followed, the household treated me with kindness. Aesop and I never spoke again of that morning when he'd kissed me, or of The Swine's attack, but the rest of the slaves regarded me with a grudging tolerance they had never shown before.

My body healed, even my ear, which the healer proclaimed burst. After a week's time, they poured sweet olive oil in my ear cavity, and when the golden liquid drained there was no blood and no pain.

Though my bruises faded, my memories did not. I shied away from dark corners. My body grew thin with anxiety The Swine would complete his father's bidding and return to us in Abdera.

Aesop tried to turn my thoughts away from my fears with increasingly difficult puzzles and indeed my mind grew sharp as my body waned. I learned much under his tutelage. On more than one occasion, Aesop's bushy brow raised and he would laugh like thunder booming down from the mount in reaction to my words. Things resumed their normal pace.

After a time, I stopped watching the shadows.

But the fear never left me, and I think Aesop knew it. If he felt sorrow over the cause of it, he never said, but I never went anywhere without him or one of the other slaves to accompany me. At least not in those months.

Then my first woman's blood began.

I woke after a feverish night where I'd dreamt Dionysus had stepped off his stone platform in the temple and caught me by the wrists. He bade me dance for him, and I did gladly, until my legs ached and my throat was dry and parched. My body was hot, much too hot, and I quivered under the touch of my lord. The heat ignited my innards like flame, consuming my strength with it as it burned.

When I begged my lord for rest, he turned his face to me, and his face was that of The Swine. The lithe, marble hands of Dionysus became bird's claws that raked my flesh to crimson ribbons.

"Dance for me, Rufus," he ordered and pulled me stumbling along, until I collapsed on the floor in a shivering heap.

I awoke in a puddle of sweat and sodden, blood-rich bed linens. My chiton was half-dried to my legs and the air was thick with the meaty odor of spoiled flesh.

My first woman's blood.

By moonlight, I climbed out of my cot, washed myself off as best I could, and changed into a fresh chiton. I tore linen into strips and tied them around my waist to secure them under my crotch like an infant's swaddling. Then I carried my linens out to the rear courtyard to wash.

My body felt wobbly and out of joint and my stomach churned and ached from my nightmare and the pains cramping my womb. My mother had spoken of a woman's courses before we fled to the temple, so I knew well what the blood signified. I could bear children. I was not afraid, but still I wept as I scrubbed the stains out of my old clothing and my bed linens. If only my beautiful mother were here to guide me.

At last, I was a woman.

Some weeks later, after a long day spent shuttling between the agora and the weaving room, Kailoise sent me to the courtyard gardens to collect herbs for a Lydian meat stew. The dusk air was heavy with humidity and the clean scent of parsley. I was tired after a long day, and did not attend to my surroundings. So it was that I bundled up the plants and stuffed them into my basket, with little note what lie just beyond the shadow of the pillars.

"Night becomes you, Rufus." It was the voice of my dream.

My blood ran cold and my teeth chattered in terror. He should not be here. We'd had no warning! He _could_ not be....I felt a hysterical scream bubbling up my throat as Young Iadmon stepped from behind a shadowed portico.

"You...here?" I croaked. I held my herb basket before me like a shield.

"And where else should I be, but in the house of my father?" He reached out to finger a lock of my hair and I flinched from his touch.

The Swine's brows drew together and he slapped the basket away. It hit the stones with a muffled thunk. My throat closed in fear and I swallowed hard.

"Ah, little Rufus. There is only one place I desire to be tonight. Between those lovely pink thighs of yours. Or have you had your fill of the Fabulist? Perhaps even my honorable father, as well. They both seem to champion you to extraordinary lengths." He turned and spat. "They sent me away to Phrygia on a god-forsaken mission for some crumbling tablets of stone, when I had a much more a precious treasure waiting for me here."

I stumbled backwards to a column and gripped it to steady myself.

Think. This is simply another puzzle.

He delighted in torturing me with unwelcome attention. What would he do if I were to turn the tables? What if I feigned interest in his attentions? He was scarce a man and interested only in that he should not take. Well, I was his for the taking in any case; what did it matter if I failed? Perhaps, with this ruse, I could buy some time until someone discovered I was missing.

"I have been awaiting your return." I leaned back against the column in what I hoped was an alluring manner, but in truth the stone lent strength to my quaking knees.

The Swine were wary and more than a little puzzled. His eyes darted back and forth across the courtyard and he wet his lips with his tongue before speaking, as if his mouth had suddenly gone dry.

"You are thinner than I recall. Are you not so much a woman, then?"

"I have begun my courses." I tossed my hair. "I am fertile now and ready to bear you many sons." I wanted to retch at the thought, but I forced a smile to my lips.

He curled his lip and wrinkled his nose. I felt a flash of hope.

"I wish no sons from you, Rufus. Zeus knows they would all be born into slavery and marked by your accursed red hair." He gave my long locks a sharp tug. I winced.

I have never been gifted in theatrical arts. When he pushed me further against the column, I forgot all my plans to distract him and screamed.

"Don't touch me!" I shrieked and flailed with all my meager strength against his smooth muscular arms. My ploy to deter him had failed, but I would not go silently. He would beat me no matter what I did. So I screamed, as if the hound of Hades, Cerberus, was nipping at my throat.

I screamed high and loud, and prayed that someone would come.

His hand bound my wrists. Birds twittered in alarm and took flight, roused from their nested slumber. The Swine sought to quiet me. He clamped his hand over my mouth. I shook my head and bit at him like a rabid dog.

Oh yes, I thought. *I may be a dog of another coat, but this bitch will not go down without a fight.* I growled in fury, and prepared to strike, as I had that Greek long ago in the midnight forest. I shouted like Boreas, God of Thunder, and….

Then, Young Iadmon drew his fist back and struck me, as if I were a man.

The blow stunned me and I fell to the limestone pavers, like my basket a few moments before, with the same muffled thud.

I tasted blood and spat. Moonlight gleamed on a bit of pearl in the bloody spew.

My tooth.

My head and jaw raged in pain. I reeled from the blow, dizzy and unable to gain my feet, and without even the sense to crawl away. I cried out as my tongue probed the tender spot on the side of my mouth, where a tooth used to be. Young Iadmon struck me again. I rolled and used the nearby column to drag myself to my feet.

The Swine pounced on me. I toppled over backwards. My elbows hit the stones. I tried to knee him, but he twisted away and struck me again. My head rebounded off the pavers and the night went completely black, save for the lights whirling behind my eyes. I felt his hands tugging at my chiton, rucking it up above my hips. Then my legs were pried apart.

"I will have you," he claimed.

"No-o," I slurred. I could not open my left eye. My ears felt thick and stuffed with wool.

He crushed me with his weight. I felt a piercing pain between my legs. I could not breathe, I could not scream. The whole of his body invaded me in a way I never thought to be broached. Again and again, he thrust inside me. Each motion struck lightning pain through my legs and back.

I sobbed. I cursed. I cried words that even I did not understand. I beat at him with my fists until he wrapped his hands around my throat and began to squeeze, gently at first, but more and more until I thought I would die. I prayed for it.

Dionysus, I pleaded. *If it be your will. Let this end. Let me come home.*

I saw the face of my mother and father in the darkness fogging my vision.

"Mother," I whispered and reached to her.

A thousand needles pricked my flesh. My parents smiled at me. I ceased to feel the raw thrusting pressure between my legs. I smiled back to them. My father stretched out his strong hands to me. I ceased to feel anything at all.

"Doricha," he whispered. But my mother shook her head.

"No, Doricha." She shook her head sorrowfully. "No."

Tears leaked from my eyes and the world rushed back to me with the mighty roar of a familiar voice.

"Doricha! _No!_"

I turned my head and saw a pair of sandaled feet running towards me on the pavers. The Swine still hovered over me, his eyes shining like pools of ebon blood in the moonlight. He groaned and convulsed between my legs, oblivious to all. His fingers dug into my shoulders.

"Doricha!" It was Aesop.

He hefted a limestone paver. Our eyes locked, his expression dark and terrible.

Then, he brought the stone down on top of Young Iadmon's head.

The Swine groaned and slumped to the side, withdrawing himself from my body as he went. I winced as his member trailed warm fluids across my thigh.

Aesop stared down at me. His face was crumpled. I had never seen such fear, such grief, etched in the fine lines surrounding his eyes. His hands twitched as if he wished to pick me up off the cold, pitted courtyard. A sudden breeze blew the scent of parsley and blood to my nostrils.

"It is over," I said. My voice sounded strange and far away.

Aesop looked at the unmoving body of young Iadmon and back at me. "Not yet, Little Flower." He turned and shouted over his shoulder for help. There was a sound of sandals slapping on the cobbles.

And overhead, somewhere unseen, a bird cried three times and flew away into the night.

CHAPTER 11

I was tended by the same healer who'd come before.

The old man clucked his tongue at me, but said nothing. When he finished, I saw Aesop pay him far more than his time was worth, no doubt to keep his mouth sealed.

My bruises faded after a few weeks. I was sore and felt chilled for days. Kailoise gave me a union of herbs, oil, and wine to leech the ill humors from my body, but it did me little good. My breasts were so sore and tender, I wondered if The Swine had bitten them. Even the soft wool of my chiton was nigh unbearable.

The Swine lived. They told me how the slaves carted his unconscious body to the temple hospital, the *asklepeia*, named for Asclepius, their god of healing. Iadmon's face had turned as grey as Aesop's eyes when they reported the night's disturbance. He did not seem surprised, though. And this time, he did not visit me.

After the fifth week, I found myself dizzy and off balance, while going about my duties. I thought perhaps the rape had addled my brain. But, on the third morning of vomiting my morning broth, Aesop told me the news.

I was with child.

The punishment of the gods could be no worse!

How well I remembered my joy at my brother's impending birth, and the pain and death of my mother. Despair and fear gripped me tighter than The Swine's claws had held me against my will to bear his seed.

I avoided the courtyard. I could not stand to see the spot where I'd been taken. The very sight of the colonnade made me sick, though it could have been the accursed child within me. The household tolerated my restless, sleepless nights of wandering and my days of frantic activity. I could not bear to be alone, yet I could not stand the company of anyone, save Aesop.

He, alone, attended to my wretchedness.

I prayed for death in the days and nights that followed. A servant was sent to watch over me during the night hours when I was wont to wander off into the shadows. Even Aesop could not comfort me.

He did his best. He spoke of duty and accepting one's fate in life. He spoke of far off lands and even posed riddles which I never bothered to answer. I could not fathom my own lot in life, what did I care about another man's fate?

In three month's time, my belly began to round ever so slightly despite my inability to keep anything down. The chills in my body continued to plague me. My cheeks and forehead flamed. Smudges lined my eyes and made me look a harpy. When I went to gather the water, I tossed the bucket in at my reflection. The other slaves began to whisper and draw symbols in the air when I passed. How much I hated them for their hostility and their fear. How much I understood it.

I hated myself.

"You should pray to Hera, mother of the gods, to give you a fine son," one of the women advised me, after the umpteenth time of sicking up my meal. *A fine son?* This cursed creature would be the epitome of his father. What would any goddess find blessed about it?

My own lovely red-gold hair grew listless and fell out in hanks when they bathed me. I had no desire to bathe myself. I had no desire to do anything other than weep and vomit, or so it seemed.

I paced the halls in a filthy chiton with the *hetaera's peplos* wrapped around me. It was the only thing that brought me any measure of comfort. I lost myself in dreams of the past where my mother stroked my hair and told me that one day the world would know my name.

At times, I swore she spoke to me.

Another month passed and I grew weaker. The babe seemed to feed off my infirmity and drew strength from every tear I shed. Strange rapid flutters, like butterfly wings in my abdomen, kept me awake at night, and then ceased, which was worse still.

My body was not my own. I housed a child of hate and revulsion. I was convinced it would bear the same brutality as its father. What would he do to me when the child was born? I longed to be rid of it, to return to my former self. My only salvation was the knowledge that I would not need to raise the child, myself, for it would be sold or cast off as soon as it quit my womb.

Perhaps then, I thought, I could convince Iadmon to send me home. Surely there was someone back in Perperek who would take me in, wretched and cursed as I was.

One day, as I tended to Iadmon's grooming, I thought to ask him. Instead, he shared news that his son would recover, but had lost the use of his right arm. I thought of the blows that hand had struck against me and could not muster compassion for him. When my master saw my frigid demeanor, he sent me from the room, and so I could not beg my freedom, after all.

I went to my alcove, heedless of the work still to be done. After I allowed Kailoise to brush out my hair, I curled up in the peplos. Later, Aesop visited, and tried to comfort me with another story, but I closed my eyes and he went away. I offered a prayer to the gods that I might never wake.

Dionysus, hear my plea, I began. Then I realized with cold clarity, that my lord was not master here in Abdera. The Greeks had their own gods. Perhaps my assault was simply their will.

I dredged up memories of attending the family religious ceremonies and slave gossip, culling faceless names to my lips. Then, I slipped onto my knees on the cold floor, ignoring the bite of the stone into my knees and prayed.

Great Zeus, I began. For I would not pray to Hera, the mother goddess! *Hear me Poseidon or Aphrodite. Show mercy! Show mercy....*

I prayed until my head ached and my throat was dry. I prayed until my knees were stiff and my back cramped from touching my forehead to the stones. Then I crept back onto my cot, feeling somewhat better, and slept.

That night, I dreamed.

I stood on the rocky beach of a barren black sea. Three birds circled and veered before a setting sun turned their feathers to rose-gold--an owl, a sparrow, and a gull. They cried as the wind blew my red-gold hair into a tangled web. I did not recognize this place, but I felt certain if I turned away I would find the house of Iadmon behind me.

How I wished to be free. Free of my life in Abdera, and yes, free of the child in my womb.

"Whom will you choose?" cried the wind. *Choose.*

I shaded my eyes with my hand and stared up at the blazing sky. I don't know why the voice did not startle me.

"Choose," the wind commanded me.

Three birds etched in silhouette against the sky. Three, an ill-luck number. I fixed my eyes to one of them, the smallest, and pointed a finger at its rose-gold plumage. Perhaps the smallest of the three would take pity on me.

The other two cried once and veered away on the wind.

The smallest, the sparrow, swooped low over me.

"How will you pay, Little Flower?" This time a woman's voice echoed over the crash and thunder of the churning waves. Foam danced on the tide and beckoned me deeper into the cold, dark sea.

I stretched my hands out over the agate waters. A shining pearl glimmered in my palm.

The sparrow called once overhead.

Then, it was not a pearl, but my lost tooth knocked free during the attack. I let it slip from my hand into the agate waters and tasted salt on my lips.

"It is done," said the voice. I thought I saw a woman striding across the sea. Her lips were curved in a sly smile. She wore a girdle of bright gold that matched her hair and carried a small bronze mirror. Her eyes were as blue as the sea and she wore a pearl circlet over her unbound hair. A sparrow perched upon her finger.

"You chose well, Beauty. Only _I_ would show compassion."

Her words rang in my ears like a hundred brass bells, yet her lips did not move.

She pointed her mirror at me. I felt my insides twist as if I needed desperately to void my bowels. I shifted, and crouched on the rocky beach, pulling the _peplos_ tighter around my shoulders. The pain in my gut grew. I rocked back and forth on my heels.

The woman knelt gracefully on the waves and the sparrow lifted from her finger, and flew away. She cupped a hand to the water below her.

Taking the salt water into her mouth, she stood and spat it at me. The water trickled over my face and body like warm rain. Droplets dribbled between my eyes and down my neck. I bowed my head and let the water drip off my nose and chin.

"It is done," the woman repeated.

And the sea she spat became a flood that washed me away from Abdera.

When I woke with a start, it was not yet morning.

My stomach still churned and twisted. When I stood on trembling legs, the pain was worse. My skin felt prickly and I burned and froze by turns. Something was not right.

I stumbled into the hall, and tripped over the slave sent to watch me for the evening. He blinked sleepily and rubbed his foot before standing.

"Where is Aesop?" I asked. Another pain. I grimaced and pressed my hand to my stomach. To my great relief my monitor hurried down the hall, his chiton flapping behind him.

In minutes, Aesop arrived. I was shaking and I felt something wet and warm trickling down the inside of my thigh. It reminded me of the rain from my dream. Aesop frowned at me and ordered the slave to get the Kailoise and the healer. Then he gripped my arm and led me back into my chamber.

"What have you done, Doricha?" he said. "What have you done?" His face was ashen.

"I did nothing. It was a dream," I cried. "Only a dream."

Aesop shook his head and helped me back onto my cot. "This is not a dream."

He stayed with me. That is something I shall never forget, whatever else happened later. Aesop stayed.

He bathed my forehead, held my hand when the pain became unbearable, and suffered my tears. But he turned his head when the female slaves came and sopped the blood from between my legs.

In time, the healer arrived with a pair of women. They peeped under the thin linen sheet and shook their heads. The pair whispered something to the healer, who left the room. When he had gone, they glared at Aesop. I suppose they blamed him for my condition.

"I will fetch her some wine," Aesop mumbled. He left then in haste.

The women carried a brass chamber pot to my bedside. They bade me rise, telling me to squat as if I needed to void my bowels. The cramps were so bad, I thought I would vomit, but I didn't. I hiked up my stained chiton. My head swam. I forced my shaking legs to support me and squatted over the pot.

As soon as I was in place, I felt a warm rush of clotted blood exit my body. Blood splashed up over the sides of the pot and onto my calves.

"What is happening to me?" I moaned as another swell of pain overtook me.

"Hush, girl." They forced me into a deeper crouch. "It's only the babe you lose."

I'd never been so grateful to be ill.

When I finished releasing the spawn of hatred from my womb, they cleaned and changed me into fresh clothing. My cot was stripped while I sat idly on a stool, my hands folded over the subsiding cramps in my abdomen.

"It was a girl, most likely. The gods do not look favorably on a girl child. Rest now," ordered one of the women. "You should be well enough for mild tasks by the morrow." They helped me to lie back on the cot.

"And do not trouble yourself," said the other, covering me with a fresh linen. "You are young still and will bear many sons. Keep to yourself for a few weeks. You don't want to fill your womb until you've healed."

I covered my eyes with my arm, to shut out the sight of them. If they thought to bring me comfort with their words, they were mistaken. I was glad to be rid of it.

"Take away the pot away," I said. "I do not grieve. I never wish to bear a child."

The women were silent as they left my chamber. A sudden breeze sifted into my window, bringing the scent of salt water. I lifted my arm off my head and stared at the moon sinking in a cold, dark sky.

"It is done, Little Flower." I heard the golden woman's voice in my head. A sparrow trilled outside my window, unusual after dark. "But how you will pay."

I was assigned menial tasks, to prevent more bleeding. Even a slave may not stop laboring for her keep, not mater the cause. Kailoise more than made up for my lack of industry. She tended me as well as any mother, and scolded those she deemed unfit. By three week's time, a slave came to fetch me away from my simple chores. As he led me to the chamber, I heard Aesop's voice rebound off the stone walls.

"And what should I have done? Left her to be murdered by your son? Master, surely you know I struck him for his own good as much as for the well-being of your slave!"

"He was simply asserting his male dominance." It was Iadmon, my master. He sounded annoyed. I heard the clank of brass on crockery. "It happens often enough in every house and brothel in Greece."

"There are laws against such, as you well know." There was a pregnant pause. "You are still a visitor to these lands, master. I know not what the Abderans would do, if the truth was known about the _hetaerae_."

"Yes, yes. You have always been a faithful servant of my interests, Aesop.".Iadmon sighed. "But there has been much talk about you, of late. Talk of the strength of your words. Of the degree of freedoms I afford you. You face a greater danger than my son ever will. I do not know if I can protect you from them, if they come for you. You are a slave and forbidden to strike any man." Iadmon sounded weary and old. "If they know of him, they know of you and your actions, as well."

I glanced at the slave who accompanied me. He tipped his chin at me and left but I did not go into the chamber. Instead, I lingered in the corridor with my hand pressed against the cool stone wall for support.

"He would have killed the girl, had I not intervened! You know this!" Aesop's voice continued. "He...he is unwell, Iadmon. And he will not leave her be! Remember the amount of coin you had to pay restitution to appease the other women's families? Send the boy back to his mother on Samos."

"Aesop, you have been a faithful teacher and I know your words are true. But I will not confine my son to a bit of floating rock. He is my heir. My only son."

"Better that rock, than a prison. He will face ostracism, here. Especially after it becomes known he beat that courtesan to death."

The breath whooshed from my lungs. The lovely woman, whose shawl I'd coveted..._dead?_ She'd never returned. I'd thought her very wealthy, to have forgotten such a treasure. _Dead?_ Perspiration broke out under my arms.

"Why should they care so much about one _chamaitype_? There are hundreds of whores roaming the city." But Iadmon sounded afraid.

"She was not a simple whore and you know it. She was a _hetaera_. The Abderans regard them almost as highly as the Athenians do."

Iadmon sighed. "Then we shall leave Abdera. We can go to Thebes or Knossos. I hear they have a very fine assembly there. You can teach him to be a proper man, be his mentor."

"And then?" Aesop was angry now. "Will the assembly protect the women of Knossos from your son? Will they protect your slave, Doricha? Your property?" Aesop thundered. "Will both you and your son be denied the Elysian Fields because of injustices inflicted on your chattel?"

"Calm down, Aesop. We are upstanding citizens; we are good and pious people. We make many sacrifices. They would not dare!"

"Who knows what may be in the hearts of the gods?" Aesop resorted to his maddening defense of dispute by way of questioning. "Are they rulers of men, or by men do they rule? Think carefully. You may well risk your soul on the answer."

There was another long pause.

So, we were all to move away to another city, another terror-filled, rented house where The Swine would attack me as he pleased, simply because his father refused to send him away. I could not bear to live in this house, or to move to any other. Ah, such was the life of a slave, and how well I'd learnt it. What is a female slave compared to a son?

I'd had enough of skulking in hallways. Being privy to my master's thoughts did me little good for I could not speak for myself. I might as well find out what fate awaited me.

"You sent for me?" I entered and knelt before Iadmon, affixing my vision to the stone tiles at Iadmon's feet.

I remembered the anguish in my father's voice as he called for me to run, to live free. _He knew_, I thought. _He knew._

"Come in, girl." Iadmon spoke, breaking the awkward silence. "I have decided."

I bowed my head, no ready argument on my lips. His decision was fixed already. What could I say to sway him?

"A slave is not his own man." Iadmon continued. "He can make no choice on where to build his home, nor the path by which he will earn his food and keep. There is danger in the world, for a slave. I have decided, therefore, I will grant you your freedom."

I could not believe my ears!

My breath caught in my throat. My heart nearly burst from my chest. The gods shone on me this day, to grant me the freedom I so desperately desired. An overwhelming wave of relief flooded me. I would not have to stay in this household. I would not have to stay, at all!

Then, I lifted my gaze from the floor and saw my master's stare directed not at me, but at Aesop. My old mentor appeared almost as shocked as I.

Then, I saw red.

The color flushed and crawled its way up Aesop's neck to the skin under his beard and stained his cheeks. He opened his lips, closed them, and opened them again, but for once, he had nothing to say.

I fisted my hands at my sides. I burned and froze inside my soul. Aesop was my friend, my mentor! He was the only one who protected me. Without him I would be utterly alone.

"They cannot come for you if you are not here, Aesop. In this one thing, let me be your teacher. This solves everything. You are free, my friend. Wander far from Greece. Your knowledge is wasted on us all."

Aesop took one stumbling step forward. He almost tripped over me as I knelt before Iadmon. I think he'd quite forgotten me.

Aesop clasped Iadmon's hand and embraced him. They towered over me, like a rocking column of manhood. As a mere woman, I was still on my knees, alone, and cowering beneath them.

"Now, then. As to the other matter. Take this girl to Samos. Let her work in my wife's household." Iadmon released him.

Aesop frowned. "That is unwise. They are one and the same. Your son will follow her there."

"Why should he? He detests his mother's house. And there are plenty of women here or wherever we travel. She will be forgotten, if she has not already." Iadmon sipped from his cup.

Aesop eyed me. Perhaps he felt a flash of guilt.

"No, Iadmon. There are very few like this one. She will only grow more beautiful, and your son's vanity has been cheated. He will not let her be. You owe her this much for the wounds he has already inflicted."

Iadmon considered me. It was as if he'd never seen me before. I flinched at the depth with which his eyes touched me. "Take her to Samos," he ordered. He ran a shaking palm over his brows and turned away from us both.

Aesop made a noise to protest and Iadmon held up a hand.

"No, no…not to my wife. Bring her to Xanthes. He is a friend. Tell him to take Doricha away and sell her to someone who will care for her. Someone who can afford to protect her. A man without sons. Promise me, Aesop, as a last request from your master. For the sake of my soul and that of my son's, promise me, you will do this thing."

Aesop glanced at me. "As you wish."

We boarded a ship for the island of Samos a week later, when at last my bleeding had stopped. I had no fond farewells for any save for Kailoise. Her face flushed and she put a kitchen rag over her head and wept, as we hurried out of the gates. It seemed I should always be leaving someone I cared for behind. Aesop and I shouldered our meager things and walked the city streets to the docks. White seabirds cried and wheeled overhead, as if to mock me.

He was in a fine mood, whistling as we loaded provisions for the short trip onto a small vessel with a square white sail. He stopped when I glared at him.

"I have been a slave since I was born," he said as if by way of an apology.

"You were *never* a slave," I replied, allowing my anger to taint my words with bitterness. "You lived better than any slave, a friend and teacher to your wealthy master." I tossed a sack of onions into the hull. "What do you know of slavery?"

"And what do you know of my life? I was born into slavery, the son of the son of a slave!" Aesop tucked a crate of chickens into the boat cargo, a gift for Xanthes the Samian. "Do not think you know my heart so well!"

My innards ignited with righteous fire.

"It should have been *me*," I spat. "The Swine never harmed you. *My* life was risked--*my* body violated. It should have been me who was given freedom."

Aesop rounded on me. "You are a foolish girl. Do you think to be the only woman who has ever cried to the gods for mercy from the prick of an unwanted spear? The goddesses themselves were raped. Lido, Alcmene...Bah! Even my own mother. You are not so much a child as to misunderstand these things. You are simply a woman. And this world was not made for women."

"Woman or no, I was born free and sold against my will!" I retorted. "Which of us has the right to freedom? You, who have never known it, or one who had it snatched from her?"

It was true! What could a lifelong slave know of my suffering? Me, who once tread the hallowed paths of the gods, now forced to this low and base status. I should not be, I vowed. For the sake of my proud father and my beautiful mother, it should not.

Aesop was silent. He stared out across the docks into the sea for a long time.

"There are some who say to teach a woman is to give more poison to a serpent. Now I can see why," he said. "You shame me with your words, Doricha. Me. A *man*. May the gods have mercy on me for giving you the power to do so."

We loaded the rest of the vessel in silence and climbed aboard.

The oar master set upon his drum with a fury which matched my own. I wondered what he'd heard of our exchange, but his face remained as impassive. The wretched creatures, dock slaves, hunched in rows behind of long, wooden paddles, muscles bunching with strain as we sailed far from shore and everything I'd ever known.

I'd never sailed before.

My stomach lurched as we pushed off.

It is no small thing to leave the soil of one's birth behind. My tears were bitterer than any ocean spray. The gentle swell and splash of the water took the place of solid rock beneath my feet. I have heard sailors fear a woman on ship. If they gave me any dark looks, I did not notice, but stared out over the waters and offered my sorrow to the gods.

It wasn't fair, I thought.

I did not understand what I had done to be so cursed by the gods. Did I not honor them with my face and figure? Did I not attend the religious services in Iadmon's household dutifully, as I ought?

But after many hours measured by the oarsmen's drum, the angry fire in my breast burnt itself out.

I eyed Aesop, standing at the railing furthest from shore. The decision had rested entirely with Iadmon, I knew this. Aesop had done his best to spare me further pain. He was my protector. It was not his fault that men receive the blessings while women must bear the curses. I'd wronged him, and I do hate to be wrong.

So, I went to the prow of the vessel to make my peace with him.

"See there, Doricha? It is the walls of Troy we pass," he said. "Soon we will skirt the island of Lesbos. Have you traveled there?" His words were amiable, even if his eyes were a touch cautious.

I shook my head. I'd never been outside of my own village until my flight to the temple.

"No?" Aesop continued. "Well, the Greeks rested there after they defeated Troy. It's an important trade port. A city of politics, culture and finery. Why, Sappho herself hails from the island. You would do Sappho proud with your words, you know."

"Sappho?"

"A famed poetess and more. She carries power in the city of Mytilene-- no small feat for a woman, as you can well imagine."

"A _woman_?" Such a thing might be harder for a man to consider, than I. Still, I was surprised. "Is she _hetaerae_?" I asked.

"No, no. She hosts an _academia_ of sorts for young women of the upper echelons. Lovers, poets, musicians...they compose new marriage hymns and play music without peer, or so I'm told. Perhaps we should stop there for the midday meal. I would not be unwelcome in her home." He glanced at me out of the corner of his eye, as if to judge my reaction.

I could not stay angry at him.

"I am sorry if my words caused you pain, Aesop. You are not the one I blame." My apology curdled in my mouth.

How I loathed admitting fault! If only I could learn to curb my tongue, I should never have to apologize again.

"I know." He looked satisfied.

We circumnavigated the isle of Lesbos until we reached the docks of the white, shining city of Mytilene on the northeastern side of the island. The city itself gleamed on the side of the hilltop, like a maze of pearled steps leading upwards to the gods.

Aesop spoke true. Mytilene was very beautiful.

I was glad Aesop had suggested we stop. My stomach was not accustomed to sea travel. I came close to spewing my morning meal. I was already tired of the salt crusting my hair and my clothing. The sun's rays reflected off the waves, and I felt sweat, slick and dripping, beneath my armpits and the backs of my knees.

The rowers and captain elected to stay aboard. One of them made a reference to a newly born calf, and they snickered at us as we departed. Our unsteady legs amused them after the many hours spent at sea. Aesop led me through the busy streets to a public bathhouse where he spent some of the coin Iadmon had given him.

We began in the *laconicums*, the separate sweat baths for males and females, built in the form of a rotunda, with a roof that tapered off into a cone shape with a round opening at the top. A bronze lid operated by chains could seal the opening, controlling the temperature.

Aesop sent a slave to inquire at the home of Sappho and we cleansed ourselves while we waited for a response. I sighed, and allowed the knots in my shoulders to loosen in the warm, scented humidity. After a suitable sheen built on my skin, we moved to a tepid water bath, followed by a massage of scented oils. Flowers were strung through my hair, which curled prettily around my face. I felt almost myself.

Soon enough, the slave returned with an invitation inviting Aesop and I to call upon the Poetess of Mytilene.

A leisurely walk through the winding city streets took us to an uppermost hill overlooking the central city. I reveled in the feeling of the breeze on my clean, scented skin. For once, the salt-fish odor was not unwelcome in my nose. With Aesop safely at my side, I felt a moment's peace as the noise and bustle of the city fell away behind us. The feeling grew the higher we climbed up the path to the poetess' house.

"You are lovely, once again, Little Flower." Aesop nodded. "A fitting tribute to the Poetess Sappho and her household."

"How could a woman rise to such a high estate?" I asked, watching sparrows flit gaily from tree to tree. I burned with curiosity to see this great, this powerful woman who swayed men with the strength of her words.

"Ah, Sappho is the eldest in an aristocratic family. Her brother Charaxus trades in wine with the East and South. The youngest brother, Larichus, is a public cup-bearer."

"Oh," I said.

Aesop glanced at me out of the corner of his eye. "And her husband was a wealthy merchant who drank far too much wine and made himself a fool. She inherited much when he died." He winked.

I smothered a smile. That made more sense to me. I could not wait to meet her.

Sappho's abode was as lovely as one could imagine. White plastered walls housed a lush courtyard with cypress, blooming shrubs and olive trees. A fountain spouted clear burbling water mingled with the scent of the sea to perfume the air. The path leading to the gates was well tended, with pale golden stones that clinked as we walked. To one side, I could see a fine garden, with ropes of grapevines in bloom drooping over the outer wall. From somewhere within, the faint sounds of a lyre could be heard.

We announced ourselves, and waited. Finally, a slave ushered us in the domicile.

Well and why not? A decent Grecian woman would not show herself in public. Still, I was disappointed. I'd imagined from Aesop's brief tales that Sappho might be different. Surely, as a widow, she'd be afforded more freedom to greet her own requested guests.

We left the heat of the day behind, winding our way through shadowed halls to the center courtyard. Sunlight filtered through the open colonnade and lent the whole abode an otherworldly air. The scent of oleander and myrrh filtered though the portico.

Once inside, Sappho herself greeted us without benefit of her chaperone. This was unusual and I smiled to myself, certain my curiosity would be satisfied.

It was.

She was short and dark and lovely, even if her figure was a little softened with age. A thin band of polished gold held Sappho's hair so the curls framed her forehead in a becoming fashion. Brown eyes, deep and intelligent, appraised me openly, in a way that reminded me of Aidne. I shivered and rubbed my hands over my arms.

"Aesop." Sappho's voice was low and fluid as water. She clasped his hand in greeting. "It has been many months since I saw you last."

"You are as beautiful as I remember in my dreams." Aesop smiled.

I gaped at him. Was the fool actually flattering her? She was pretty, I supposed, in a bird-like way. She reminded me of a swallow. But *beautiful?* Obviously, the sea wind and the rowers' drums had addled his brains.

I straightened my shoulders and lifted my chin a notch. Sappho's dark eyes flickered over to me once more but she addressed only Aesop.

"Flatterer!"She sounded pleased. "And how fares Iadmon, your master?"

"He is my master no longer. I am free."

Sappho did not appear surprised. "I wondered when he would….never mind. So, you have come at once to attend me, then?" She smiled. "I am glad for it. Come, let us have some refreshment."

She led us, that is to say, she led Aesop to low cushioned bench. I simply trailed after them, feeling invisible.

"Is this your girl, Aesop?" Sappho asked at long last, when Aesop took his time to settle his bulk onto the chaise. She signaled for wine and fruit.

"No, she belongs to Iadmon. We're traveling to the stocks on Samos."

Sappho considered me for a long moment, where to my chagrin I found myself positioning my figure to its advantage. I don't know why I cared what she thought. Perhaps it was because she _had_ thought, unlike most Grecian women. Or perhaps it was because I could see Aesop gave credence to her opinion.

Either way, a little thrill ran down my spine when she drew near and touched my shoulder with her small, soft hand. Her perfume tickled my nostrils.

"She is…pretty," Sappho said.

"She is more than that, as well you know, Sappho." Aesop's eyes were affectionate.

"I suppose, if she did not have the look of half-starved dog about her. See how her clothing hangs. Is she ill?"

I'd not thought to prepare a new chiton after my old one had been let out to accommodate the babe in my womb. I'd not wanted to make myself appealing to anyone. Disgrace burned in my cheeks.

"She is well, Sappho. It is nothing a little rest will not cure." Aesop bit into a fig. So, he would not parade my shame in front of others. I blessed him silently.

"Hmm," she mused. A burst of giggles wafted from the hall.

Sappho clapped her hands and a pair of young women ran to her sides. They giggled again as she held out her hands to each and kissed them lightly on the mouth. A third ambled into the room with a lyre and a dreamy expression.

"They are lovely girls, all of them, Sappho," Aesop said. He sucked noisily on the fig.

"Erinna of Telos and Damophyla of Pamphylia. Of course, my own daughter, Kleis, you know." She indicated the girl with the lyre at the last. "But Anaktoria has left us, and I feel her absence keenly." Sappho's eyes grew moist.

"You feel all things keenly, poetess. Especially matters of love."

"And why should I not, when all that is noble in life is touched by the hand of the Cyprian?" Just like that, her tears evaporated, replaced by a beatific smile.

"So you still sing to your goddess Aphrodite, then?" Aesop asked. "Well, you are a good servant of that one's fickle attention." Aesop reclined further in his chaise, his chin resting on his left elbow.

"Bite your tongue, Fabulist, lest you bring shame to my household!" Sappho scolded, but her eyes twinkled. "I say it is what one loves, that does them credit in the eyes of the gods. Is it not so? Did not Helen leave behind her family, her fortune, even her own child for the sake of him she loved? Ah, one day I shall write of this and you will see I speak true."

I found myself infused with the excitement of this discourse, but Aesop waved away the servants who hovered over him with a measure of laconic skepticism.

"She did and found herself cursed for it," Aesop retorted. "You say love is mightier than the hand of man? This insipid love that poets and women croon and fawn over and call themselves wiser for the pain of it?" Aesop shook his head. "It is not so."

"Pah," Sappho shooed away his disbelief with a slim hand. "You are a man, yourself, so how can you judge? Tell me, on what do you waste your love? An army of black horsemen? A fleet of fine ships? A jug of wine?"

Oh, the sharp, silvered tongue of this poetess! Would that I was like her. I thought perhaps I was expected to stay silent, but as is ever my nature, I could not. I might look like a starved cur, but I could nip and bark as well as she.

"Neither, lady," I ventured. "It is knowledge, or the pursuit of it, that strikes fervor in his heart."

At this, both Aesop and Sappho paused.

Then Aesop threw his head back and howled with laughter. I saw Sappho eye me with renewed interest, and I confess I burned a little under her gaze.

"The girl speaks truly, Sappho." Aesop wiped at his eyes. "She knows me well."

"If what she speaks is so, then I shall pray one day you may experience the true gifts of Aphrodite." Sappho gave me a lingering, approving glance. "We've composed new *epithalamia* to be sung at the marriage of Tisias," she said, changing the subject. "Would you care to hear it?"

Aesop nodded his approval, and the girls sang as Kleis accompanied them on the lyre. I must say it was an astounding rendition, although I was but a slave and unused to hearing such niceties, save what bits I caught when Iadmon entertained. It reminded me a little of the *hetaerae*. I thought of that poor dead woman whose *peplos* I'd cherished and I shivered.

When the music ended, Sappho stood before me. I had to clench the muscles in my legs and back not to shiver again.

"You did not like the hymn?" she asked, with a pert frown.

I risked a glance at Aesop who seemed overly interested in spitting the seeds of his fig onto a silver platter.

"Who is to say I did not, great lady?" I replied and met her eyes. To my great surprise, her face lit up.

"So," said she. "A question for a question."

Her languid eyes flickered at Aesop and he preened for all the world like the prize cockerel we'd carted from Abdera. At that, Sappho laughed and clasped my hand between her soft, cool palms, and bade me sit by her feet.

I did not know if I liked her approval or not, but it made the next hours pass easier. The girls sang and played for us again. I watched Sappho as she bantered and jested with Aesop. Her eyes were on me often enough, especially when I was asked to dance for them, and I daresay I should have guessed what was to come, but I did not.

Sappho herself played the lyre, while I danced.

The music was low and melodic, much like the voice of the Poetess. She played well, and I did my best to honor it with my body. I think, perhaps, Lukra would've approved.

Afterwards, the girls, Erinna and Damophyla, grew bored with us and wandered away. I marveled at their freedom to do so. How long had it been since I had the freedom to wander where I wished? To come and go as I pleased without fear of retribution or displeasure?

Sappho showed them no displeasure but released their supple wrists and hands as they slid from her grasp and meandered away. Their intertwined limbs reminded me of my near sister, Mara, and my heart clenched. I wondered how she'd fared after I'd left the temple.

Aesop shielded his eyes with his palm and checked the sky. "The hour grows late, great Sappho. Moreover, you have graced us with your hospitality and your presence. We should go before the dinner hour." He stood and brushed the crumbs from his beard, motioning for me to prepare to depart.

Sappho rose gracefully from her chaise. "If you say, dear Aesop. But, I have no cause to retire just yet. I beg you to stay a moment."

Aesop's brows drew together. I could sense this was most unplanned.

"I find myself drawn to this girl," Sappho said, moving to stand by me. "She is young and clever. I have a need for such a girl at present. Will you sell her to me?"

I was dumbstruck. When sense returned to me, I turned to find Aesop considering Sappho with an expression not unlike my own. He shook his head.

"I cannot, fair poetess. She is bound for Xanthes the Samian, by order of Iadmon himself." He placed a hand in the small of my back and drew me nearer to the colonnade.

"To what end? One sale is as good as another. There is somewhat about her expression--there, you see it?--in the eyes. I could learn to love such a face, I think. You will not deny me." She smiled sweetly, very sweetly indeed.

Aesop furrowed his brow further. "I cannot, dear lady. I gave my word."

"Then, take the words back again. For me." This time Sappho's smile did not quite reach her eyes.

"No, Poetess, I cannot take back my promise." Aesop gave a slight bow. "Not even for you. My words are all of what I am."

Sappho reached over and fingered a lock of my hair. I did not dare to draw back from her touch. Her eyes roamed my face, as if to memorize it.

"And what say you? Will you be sent to warm some man's bed, to bear him sons while Aphrodite's songbird rejoices at the mere sight of you?" She sounded a touch scornful, and her brow arched like a sparrow's wing.

"You cannot ask me, for I am another man's property." The room grew unaccountably warm. I felt perspiration bead my upper lip as I followed Aesop to the gates.

"What can I say to persuade you both?" asked Sappho, following after us with her hands on her hips. "Come, Aesop, you are a man of some reputed intelligence. Give me this girl, for my heart's sake, if not your purse's. Let me spare her from the childbirth grave and I shall love her with all the music in my soul."

Though a life of beauty and comfort tantalized me, I found I did not trust this woman. I did not like the way she dismissed Aesop's excuses, as if they had no merit whatsoever. She meant to have her way with me, regardless of objections. How did that make her any different than The Swine, save that she had no phallus to spear me with? I suspected the weapon of her intellect would be sharp enough.

"I will bear no son of Greece, Lady." I could not halt the rush of words from my heedless tongue as we crossed the threshold out of her abode. I heard the crash of the ocean in my ears and the cry of sea birds overhead. It made me dizzy. "I have made my bargain with the gods. My womb shall close to all man's seed until Love should open it. Can your fine words do any less for my heart?"

Sappho blanched at my speech.

"You dare...?" she whispered as she trailed us to the entrance of her lair. "You dare to speak to me of love? I am beloved by the Cyprian! I speak with her voice, her soul, her very heart. You are naught but a mote of dust buffeted in Aphrodite's breath!"

A flock of sparrows set up such a firestorm of chirping that anything else that might have been said by the poetess died away. Aesop bowed and mumbled a hasty goodbye. He pushed me out of the gate before him. We were halfway down the lane when Sappho's words wafted to our ears on the perfumed breeze.

"She is marked, Aesop. I have heard it," she called loudly. "The gods of Greece declare doom for any man or woman who loves such a creature. Sell her to some unlucky wretch and be done with her."

I took three steps before I risked a glance at Aesop. He caught me looking.

"We set sail for Samos in the morning," was all he said.

CHAPTER 12

"You shouldn't have spoken to her like that." Aesop stared out over the water in a direction I can only presume was towards Samos.

"What can she do to us now? We've sailed from Lesbos." The waves lapped at the sides of our small ship. I glared at the water churned to froth by the oars.

I'd lost the only likely chance of gaining some measure of freedom back, and all because I feared a lyricist's touch. He was right, of course, but I was filled with dread as we sailed away towards a new slave stock. What did I care about Sappho when I would soon be sold, my life no longer my own? I shouldn't have refused her. Perhaps then I might be free to slip from her grasp as did those other girls.

"The Poetess holds much power in certain forums. It's said they've even built a shrine to her on Syracuse. Who can say how far her influence spreads? She could make trouble for you."

"She briefly desired me and I was rude. It will pass." I tossed a crust of hard bread at the birds circling overhead. "Besides, she thought no more of me than The Swine. Fie!"

"Sappho has ever possessed a flair for the dramatic," Aesop agreed. "Especially in regards to unrequited love."

"She knows nothing about love, Aesop. One cannot coerce such emotion. It must be freely given and I have no inclination to give my love to her. She would turn me out as soon as another nubile girl caught her eye." I tried to make myself believe it. Sunlight glittered off the waves, its beauty like a *sarisa's* tip in my eyes.

Aesop frowned. "You do not want this woman as your enemy. Why are you so reluctant to heed me?"

"This woman's trouble will be the least of my worries once the Samian sells me to a new master. Kind or not, he will still own me, body and soul.

What is a poetess' wrath compared to that?"

"She is not 'a' poetess, Doricha," he chided. "But 'the' Poetess."

"Do not banter words with me, Aesop. I have not the heart for it, just now."

And I didn't. I'd sold my chance at freedom for a sharp quip. Would I never learn to do as I must? I turned away and watched the coastline disappear into the distance.

"Ah, Doricha. Do not be so discouraged. You are young still and alive. That is saying much. You will forget the pain of the past."

A breeze arose and the sailors scrambled to unfurl the sails and take a few moments of respite from rowing. The flap of the sails reminded me of the sound of bird's wings.

"Let me tell you a tale," Aesop began.

"No more of your stories!" I tried to wave him away, but he silenced me and began again.

"A Crab, forsaking the seashore, chose a neighboring green meadow as its feeding ground. A Fox came across him and, being very hungry, gobbled him up. Just as he was on the point of being swallowed, the Crab said, 'I well deserve my fate, for what business had I on the land, when by my nature and habits I am only adapted for the sea?' Do you understand me, Doricha?"

"I suppose," I mumbled.

"I have been a slave my whole existence until now. Contentment with our lot in life is an element of happiness in itself. If you cannot change your station, you must try to find some measure of satisfaction, Doricha." He patted my hand awkwardly, but I pulled away.

"It is an easier thing to do when one is free, Aesop. I only hope I do not need to give my life to find it, as did your Crab."

He crossed his arms over his barrel chest. "Freedom does not always mean happiness. You would do well to remember that."

"It does to me," I whispered.

It had been over four years, now, since I'd been free and more since I'd been happy. I wiped the salt spray off my cheeks and turned my back on Aesop. What did he know?

I resumed my watch of the coastline until the sailors shouted that the island of Samos drew nigh.

Samos.

What can I say about it, but that I dreaded its rocky shoreline? Samos, home of the woman who birthed the Swine who took me against my will. Another island, yes, and on it was a trade port, another marketplace, and another slave trader who would mark my name and price on a shard of pottery.

Dark-skinned Xanthes the Samian was rough, as men who spend much time on the sea are wont to be. His robes were fine, if not elegantly pleated, but he needed to trim his grizzled beard. He appraised me with an eye of a horse trader.

Aesop ordered the vessel on its way after paying our fare, for he planned to journey east by caravan to Lydia and then perhaps Egypt. I'd never heard of such places, and could only dream of what his life would be like. I suppose after a lifetime of slavery he was due to wander the world a little, but I could not help feeling forlorn as Xanthes, after a quiet discussion with Aesop, went about setting a price that made even the seasoned slave traders protest.

"See here," they shouted. One shook his fist at the burly Samian. "You're ruining the market with her," he said.

But Xanthes fingered his stout club and paid them no heed.

I hunched my shoulders miserably as he slung the thong over my neck and settled it between my breasts, flinching when his hands lingered too long around my neck. Aesop was deserting me. I would be vulnerable again. Panic turned my innards to ice, despite the sultry heat of the afternoon.

"She is just a woman and a Thracian at that!" another said, eyeing me with distaste.

Why should he not? I wasn't his stock, and the price set upon me was exorbitant.

It was Aesop who answered. "If this is all you see, then you do not see her." The men eyed his burly physique, and ceased their grumbling.

So, I stood there all morning.

I watched while other men, women, and children became another man's property. I stood there and endured the black stares, curses, and perverse interest of those looking to buy. I do not know which was worse--the first time I'd been sold, or now. Then, I'd still had the innocence to hope for mercy. Now, I knew better. I knew my life would never be my own again. I was a plucked flower, there for any man's taking.

I slouched in my place and tried to take as little notice of my surroundings as possible. By plastering a vacant expression on my face, I hoped to seem a poor purchase. Perhaps the high price would work to my advantage and repel any patrons.

A desperate surge of hope flooded my heart as each would-be buyer passed me by. My plans were hastily laid. If Xanthes could not sell me, perhaps I could journey onward with Aesop. I had little hope he had enough coin to buy me, but surely Xanthes would be glad to be rid of me.

I spent the rest of the morning crossing my eyes whenever the traders weren't watching me. I wanted to clap my hands in relief, as midday passed and I was not yet sold. With relief, I was allowed to sit and take some bread and wine. A little luck, and Aesop could not desert me, not until I was resold.

But luck had deserted me. If not for the hot temper of a man and the birds pecking at crumbs nearby, I might have gone unnoticed and unbartered for that day.

It was early afternoon, the hour when most forsake their work to spend a few moments of rest away from the hot sun. Most shops in the _agora_ closed and would remain so until the early evening when the sea breeze cooled the city marketplace. At this hour, the market was a furnace of blazing sun reflected off the plaster buildings and gravel.

An odor of rot gut infused the air. I wrinkled my nose, still unused to the stench of fishy brine in my nostrils. How I longed for clean mountain air!

"Do you curl your lip at me, girl?" asked a testy patron of the slave pits. He had a surly expression and the fronts of his robes were spattered with food grease from some previous meal. I glanced around the _agora_. There was no one else about. Why should he not mistake my expression for one of displeasure towards him?

He strode nearer to my platform. "Great Zeus! What madmen ask so much coin for an insolent girl?" He glared at Xanthes. Aesop put down his cup of wine and hitched up the pleats of his robe.

"I have set the price. Pay it or be gone," said Xanthes.

"I have half a mind to pay it!" shouted the patron. "Do you not teach this girl better manners, I shall!"

Sea birds scattered at the force of his words. They took to the air, screeching and flapping. The flock roused the attention of some nearby sailors loading goods onto a large trireme on the docks.

My head began to ache from the heat.

"The sun has addled your brain," I said wearily, too overheated by the burning sun to hold my tongue. "I smelled a foul odor and that is all. It is a hot day. Perhaps you should rest."

My words brought a chuckle from the sailors. One suggested the patron soak his head in cask of wine to cool his temper.

The patron's cheeks mottled and he drew back his head and spat at me. It landed on my sandaled foot, the spittle soaking into the leather strap. Aesop strode over and I saw Xanthes loosen his club. This could mean trouble, both for me and the newly freed Aesop. Of a surety it would not bode well for poor Xanthes who was only following the directive of his friend. The sailors stopped their laughing chatter and drew nearer to the platform.

"Your slave has insulted me," the patron insisted. "I demand restitution. Give her to me."

"You see her price, citizen. Pay it or leave." Xanthes fingered his club.

"You owe me for her insult, trader. I will give you two hundred drachmas for her. That is still a hefty price."

Xanthes considered the man's words. I saw him glance at the nearest stall where several helmeted peacekeepers put down their wineskins.

"Aesop...?" Xanthes murmured.

"Have you sons, patron? This girl is bound for a family without heirs, by order of her master," Aesop replied. He did not look pleased.

The patron smiled. "I have none," he said. "As of yet."

"Aesop, be reasonable. There have been no others," Xanthes whispered. Aesop waved his hand in irritation. "It is a good offer."

The patron reached for his coin purse, which was drawn as tightly as his smile. One of the sailors hissed through his teeth.

"You men, why have you stopped loading these wine casks?" A voice from the docks startled me. "The Pharaoh's table awaits us. Get a move on now or...by the Cyprian's kiss, what goes here? <u>Aesop</u>? Is that you?"

We turned. A man strode off the gangplank towards my platform, his hand shading his eyes against the sun. I could not make out his features at first. When he drew near, I could see his skin was tanned and his eyes were dark. His features were sculpted in fine aristocratic fashion, not coarse as the other sailors. His curled hair gleamed in the sunlight.

Aesop glanced at me and then raised his hand in greeting. His bushy brows were creased and uneasy, an expression I did not see often on his face. The patron busied himself with drawing out his money pouch and signaling to the scribes to prepare the lists for him to record my sale.

The man from the ship stared at me.

"What goes here?" he asked again. His eyes devoured me. I have never seen such an expression on a man's face before. Desire, yes, but not this open and utter adoration.

"Just a girl to be sold," Aesop said. "Tell me, how fare your wife and daughters?" Aesop looked at me--his eyes nigh bulged out of his head.

What did he want me to do?

"Fat and rosy as any Grecian princess, I assure you. But what loveliness is this and at such a price?"

"A rare adornment," said Aesop, that traitor. "She is temple-trained. The most wondrous dancer you have ever seen."

"So you say." The man blinked. I glanced away from the pair of them. They made me sick, circling me like a pair of dogs over a bone. Men are all the same under the skin.

"Yes, but alas, this cretin has sworn to break her of her spirit." Aesop gestured to the patron who curled his lip in our direction and continued to shake coin out of his purse.

What was Aesop doing? My supposed mentor was nigh setting this man's appetite to have his way with me! It was an outrage and I swore he would be punished later for his deeds. If not by me, then by the gods. I thought of the golden haired woman of the water.

Lady, if it be your will, I prayed.

"Break her? Surely not such a fine creature as this. I have never seen such eyes before. And a figure to make Aphrodite herself weep."

"Ah, yes. Much the same was said by your sister not two days hence, Charaxus."

Sister? *Sister?*

"You took her to see Sappho, did you? What said the great poetess?" Charaxus eyed my hair with interest.

"She wished to purchase this girl. She vowed she could love such a creature, but I have sworn to sell her only to a man who will keep her well. A man without sons."

"Here now," called the patron. "Away from my property. I have paid my gold and will make my mark."

"A treasure my sister could not achieve by either her coin or her witty tongue? Ha! I can scarce believe it. Hold!" called Charaxus. "I wish to bid on this girl."

"You cannot," said the patron. "I have already paid."

The brother of the great Poetess wished to bid on me. Would he give me to his sister lady, then, as tribute? I thought of Sappho and her desire, so much like Aidne's dark regard for my mother. I shivered, even under the hot sun.

"I will hear all bids," called Xanthes with a wry smile for Aesop. He tightened his grip on the club and glared at the rude patron.

"I have no sons," said Charaxus. "And I will buy this girl for two hundred fifty drachma."

"What? No! Three hundred," retorted the patron. "Such was her initial price and I will not be outdone."

"Four," said Charaxus softly. His eyes turned to hard stone. "Four hundred for the girl." He crossed his arms over his chest.

I thought I would faint. It was an outrageous price for any slave. An educated Syrian had sold for three hundred that very day, and had been called out as overpriced in the process. Four hundred. I was a woman! Either this Charaxus was a very wealthy man or he was an extravagant fool.

"You...you cannot do this," said the patron. His eyes darted from Charaxus to rest on me. "Four hundred ten drachma."

"I will have her at any price," said Charaxus. His eyes never left me. "Five hundred."

"Done!" shouted Xanthes with glee. The patron bowed his head and clenched his fists as Xanthes returned his coin purse with a toss.

My new master removed the leather thong from my neck and crushed the pottery shard beneath the heel of his sandal. I wondered at his boldness. What was to become of me? I wrote my name, and the tally was paid.

With that, I was sold.

"Come," Charaxus said, gently leading me from the scribe. "I have no home to take you to, just yet. We are set to sail this very hour and you will accompany me. Will you join us, Aesop? I have heard you are a free man now."

"Word travels quickly. But, no." Aesop shook his head. He turned his gaze away from me. "No, I do not think so. I may visit you one day, if you will have me."

"You are welcome anytime, Fabulist. I thank you for this gift."

What an odd word to choose for a newly purchased slave. And at such a price! Though not quite the king's ransom my father saw, still a gift in Charaxus' eyes, at least.

Aesop raised a hand. "Farewell, Little Flower. Remember the Crab." He handed over my satchel containing a few personal items and the _hetaera's peplos_. My eyes pricked with tears, but I could find no words to voice farewell. He turned away.

Sea birds screeched as we bordered Charaxus' trireme. The gangplank wavered before my eyes. Once again, I was sold.

"What are you called? Surely you have a name, as lovely as yourself," said Charaxus, grinning broadly.

"Do you not wish to call me a name of your own choosing, Master?" I asked, dully.

His teeth flashed against his sun dark skin. Silver threaded his dark hair though he had a fit physique, making him far older than I had given him credit for.

"I wish to know your name," he said, most unexpectedly.

"I am called Doricha." I made the customary bow to him, my hair slithering over my shoulder to brush the gangplank.

"Doricha." He fit his tongue around my name. "Come now," he scolded. "No more obeisance. Let us retire to the foredeck."

Charaxus took my arm and led me to a wooden bench near the front of the ship. "I am Charaxus of Mytilene. My sister, you know, of course. But my wife and daughters also reside on Lesbos. Perhaps one day I shall present you to them. Mytilene is a fine city, but a bit small for my tastes. I prefer to roam abroad and thereby fill my coffers. You shall make it a far more pleasant journey. Have you traveled this far south before?"

"No," I replied.

"You will accompany me to Egypt. We are transporting Lesbian wine to the Pharaoh's table. It seems Aesop has been tutoring you some?"

I nodded.

"Well, we shall have plenty to discuss along the trip, eh?" Charaxus smiled again. "You will see. It will be a pleasant journey."

I could not help it. Pleasant for whom, I wondered. Still, I smiled back,

just a little, for Charaxus was kind and gentle.
   Perhaps Aesop was right after all.

CHAPTER 13

Charaxus had many faults, but he was a generous man. He drank overmuch, and was a bit of a braggart, but wooed me with a single-mindedness that made him an enemy of his sister and a target for crude jokes from slaves and freed men alike. Indeed, in true Grecian form, he had a love of that which is beautiful.

He ensured the journey to Egypt was pleasant for me, which was a surprise. The sailors were instructed to treat me with deference, and I was fed by his own hand--a luxury which, I'm sorry to say, was lost on me at the time. The other slaves were sent below and chained to the oars, but it did not stop them from making crude jests under their breath whenever they thought he was out of hearing. I inched closer to my new master's protective shadow and pretended not to hear.

The seas were rough near the northern coast and we spent the final night aboard the ship, lest we be dashed to pieces against the rocks littering the shore. Tomorrow, my feet would touch the soil of another land, a land more ancient than my own. Charaxus had told me Greece was but a babe as compared to mother Egypt, which had endured for thousands of years. A mother that drew people of all nations to her, to offer tribute to the mighty king of Egypt, the Pharaoh--a man reputed to be a living god.

But such thoughts were above me for a slave has no worries save for those of her master. Charaxus was a wine trader, and my survival depended on his acumen. Thus we made for Egypt. Waves tossed our ship about that night, as if we were indeed a god's plaything. By the next morning, I was sick with the motion of the deck. Sea salt crusted my hair and clothing and I rejoiced when we docked.

My first view of Egypt was black and green and gold.

It was wondrous.

For any who have not seen the glory that is Egypt, it is a rugged desert the further one travels from the great river, the one we call the Nile. Polished bronze sand stretches as far as the eye can see and there are few trees to shade us from the glare of the sun or blowing grit that pervades every city. It is a land hotter than the fire pits of the Underworld, in the great kiln of limestone buildings and heat waves.

The very earth was black as pitch near the Nile. On either side, unfamiliar green frond plants blew in the breeze, and reached up to tickle the pale sky.

I tried my best to stay out of the way of the sailors unloading casks of wine and other goods for trade. Charaxus kept me at his side for most of the morning. We'd stopped in the main trade port of Egypt, a city called Naukratis. I felt both sickened and grateful when I saw the rows of men he'd brought emerge blinking into the bright Egyptian sun. They were poked and prodded onto the platform. When the slavers began assigning prices, I turned my face away.

The city was a veritable festival of boats and people, odd smells and sights.

"Their eyes are so large and mysterious!" I pointed to a group of Egyptian men working on the dock.

"Their eyes are no larger than ours." Charaxus laughed at me. "They use kohl to line their eyes. It keeps out the grit and the sun's rays.

How weird and wonderful! Despite my disgust at the slave trade, I couldn't stop staring. I'd never seen so many shades of skin color, so many odd forms of dress. The clamor and noise of people and animals lasted all day, until my ears ached.

Whips cracked, men shouted in unfamiliar tongues, and insects buzzed around my face in annoying profusion. My head grew light and I wrapped my clammy hands around Charaxus' arm to steady myself. He aided me past the dark soiled backs near the docks, to a low, mud-brick building where he'd secured lodging for us. The sailors and oarsmen were to remain on board until all was unloaded and the slaves were sold.

Like most of the other dwellings, the inn was coated with white plaster and sported a series of very small, strategically placed windows that let in little light but allowed for air circulation. We entered on the main level that housed a small alcove where the proprietor slept. After ascending a narrow flight of dark stairs, we emerged, blinking, into the common room. Two patrons smoked and drank. The pipe smoke reminded me vaguely of the smoking flames of the Bacchanal, with the same sweet, spicy odor.

Then we climbed yet another set of stairs. The proprietor pointed out our room and a door that led to the rooftop where our meals would be served to us, away from the heat of the streets below. I was tired and too anxious to eat, so I left Charaxus guzzling a cup of amber liquid and retired to our rented chamber.

With great trepidation, I prepared myself, wondering if my respite had ended. For here, in this room, there were no coarse sailor's eyes to follow my every move and no chance of being seen by any man who was not my master. Charaxus had allowed me leeway from congress on the ship, where we could hear the belches and worse of the many men aboard. I would not be so fortunate now, I was certain. A man did not pay so much coin for a woman and expect her not to submit. And if I did not please him, I would be led to the slave docks myself. I had only my experience with The Swine to arm myself. My hands shook and my stomach clenched.

I had not long to wait. In good time, Charaxus reentered the room, whistling faintly through his teeth. He poured some fresh water from a jug into a low bowl and rinsed his hands and face. I was unable to look directly at him.

"Is something amiss?" he asked.

I shook my head to indicate the room was fine. And it was fine, by my standards. A small chest for our belongings crowded one side of the room, supporting a jug and basin. There was a wide reclining couch that served as a bed with a raised crescent shaped headrest. A straw mattress covered the surface. It was much finer than a bedroll on a swaying vessel amidst the stench of men and brine of the sea.

"You seem displeased." Charaxus frowned.

I took a step backward. I was a slave. I could not afford the luxury of emotion. "The room has been prepared, and you have had your meal. What more is required from me?" I bit my lip and fisted my hands to stop them from shaking.

Charaxus seemed less confident than he had appeared to me before. He stared at me for a long moment before speaking.

"You are mine to do with as I wish, Doricha."

"Yes," I agreed solemnly. Four years with Iadmon had taught me my place.

"I wish to avoid discomfort. You are a beauty unlike anything I have ever seen, and I would not quench your fire." I did not respond. Charaxus sighed. "You could lay here, next to me, for a start," he said. "We could talk if you like."

"As you wish," I replied. I stretched on the wide couch, closed my eyes, and awaited his next directive.

"Well." Charaxus cleared his throat. "You cannot mean to rest with your body as stiff as a wooden plank and your fists knotted in the linen sheet. Come now, open your eyes."

I felt him sink onto the couch beside me; the heat of his body warmed the air. His hand reached out to touch my arm, soft and soothing. Gorge rose in my throat. I did not want him. Tears formed behind my eyelids.

"Look at me," he commanded.

I did, as tears leaked down the sides of my cheeks and dripped into my ears. His brows rose. He looked horrified.

"You have been mistreated. I can see this. But you will see, I am not so very bad," he said. He kissed the trail of one tear, his breath hot against my skin. "You will see. I will be gentle."

His hand clasped my left shoulder and he continued to kiss my cheeks, my neck, my hair, my brow. He murmured soft words to me all the while, until at last I relaxed. He nestled his knee between my thighs. The crisp hairs on his legs prickled at my skin, but it was not too unpleasant. When he pawed at my chiton, I knew the time had come. Resignedly, I sat up and he helped to pull it over my head.

"You are lovely," he said, his eyes feasting on my naked, pink flesh. "Pink as a flower petal. Shall I call you that, Petal?" he said and unwrapped his own robes.

I sniffed and drooped on the couch, a gesture he must have taken for assent, for that is the name by which he called me. Petal.

"Now," he breathed and eased his body to cover mine.

His arms cradled my head. I could feel the length of him against my thigh, which terrified me. When I did not move, he scrunched himself downward until his head was level with my breasts where he began a tender assault.

My nipples puckered as the heat of his mouth moved away from them and up to my throat, my chin, and to my lips. At that, I turned my head. I couldn't stand the taste of him in my mouth. Charaxus gave a disappointed grunt but satisfied himself with the rest of my body. He shifted his hips and I felt his stiffening phallus poking at my nether lips.

I clenched my jaw and waited for the moment when the piercing pain would take me.

"You are so beautiful," Charaxus said. "So beautiful."

He thrust his hips, the tip of his phallus rubbing in the soft hollow joint where my inner thigh met the mound of my womanhood. His breathing became very heavy. "You are so unlike my wife, that acerbic cow. No, no, you are lovely. I am sure this time it will...*unh*!"

He stiffened, his head thrown back in pleasure or torment. Had I injured him? I was so unknowledgeable. I was sure I'd done something wrong, by not opening myself up to him.

Then I felt it, the warm sticky wetness spurting onto my belly as he wriggled against me. A tangy salt scent of man wafted up to my nostrils and I realized he'd spent himself on me, not in me. I had only a brief second to digest this information when his full weight crashed down on top of me.

"I'm sorry," he mumbled into my neck and hair. "It doesn't always happen like this."

I didn't know what to say. Awkwardly, I raised an arm and patted him on the back.

"We will try again. In the morning." Charaxus yawned and rolled off of me. "Sleep next to me, Petal. There are deadly insects crawling about in this land."

I waited until I heard his breathing become slow and deep. Then I rolled onto my side, putting my back to him, and wiped his disgusting seed from my abdomen with a corner of his discarded robes.

In the morning, I thought. *I must do this again in the morning.*

But in the morning, Charaxus forgot his earlier promise. He arose early and went out before I awoke. I'd spent much of the night lying awake in anxiety, unused to sharing a sleeping space, until at last, I'd drifted off. When I rose the next morning to his cheery whistle, my eyes were gritty and raw.

"Good morning, Petal," he said.

"Master," I replied, dutifully. I tried not to look alarmed when he drew nearer the couch and rested on the side closest to me. What were my duties in this strange land? I had no routine and no other servant to ask. "What shall I do?"

"Come and look." He tossed me my chiton and told me to hurry. I dressed and followed him to a common room, where an old Egyptian man awaited us.

"Khefti will take us to the market place," explained Charaxus. Khefti smiled back at me, his teeth ground down to blackened nubs. I looked away quickly. I'd bartered for household goods in Abdera many times. I would learn what Charaxus wanted of me.

He led me to a strange conveyance that was part cart, part litter. When we had settled ourselves inside the box, Khefti took up the long poles on either side of him and hefted the front end of the cart, strong and sure as any beast. I made to hop off, certain he could not carry us both, but Charaxus explained the lengths of the poles allowed the old man the leverage to both lift and haul us the distance to the market stalls.

I had walked much further to get to the marketplace in Abdera, but I did not mention this to Charaxus. In the already stifling, bug-infested heat, I was content to be carted by another.

"This looks like the _agora_," I waved my hand in front of my face. I loathe insects, especially these annoying tiny ones whose bites stung like an artisan's needle.

"It is. Naukratis was founded by the Ionians. It's one of the few truly Grecian settlements, although the city is governed by Egyptians. Of course, so many men of the world come through here, you'd have trouble finding a true Egyptian."

Charaxus paid Khefti to wait for us, and we spent some time wandering through the stalls of wares, both familiar and not. Various kinds of merchandise were on display: vegetables, fish, sycamore figs, drinking cups, beverages and cloth. Merchants, male and female, crouched by their wares, which were laid out in baskets. Customers carried a pouch slung around their shoulder.

"What coin do they pay with in this Greek city of Egypt?" I asked.

"They rarely pay with coin, except here in Naukratis. Most goods are bartered for, by trading one for another. Wheat for oil. Oil for beer. Beer for fish and so on."

"Who decides the value?" How would I know if I was being cheated?

Charaxus laughed. "They do, I suppose."

"Then I will do my best to learn their ways."

Charaxus nodded. He paused by a man who poured a glutinous amber liquid from a jug into an earthen cup. Small sediment, like chaff, floated on top.

"What is this?" I wrinkled my nose.

Charaxus tossed the man a coin and handed me the cup. "It is beer."

"Beer?" I repeated. I sniffed the cup suspiciously. It smelled sweet and yeasty, almost like bread.

"Try it," Charaxus urged, his eyes gleaming with delight.

I did. After one sip, I rolled the taste of it on my tongue. It was thin and fruity, but I was not fond of the grit.

"It is made from fermented bread loaves," said Charaxus, taking the cup from me and downing a huge swig. "They bake the wheat into loaves, and then crumble them into water with certain ferments. Then they drain away the bread and drink the beer."

"They need a better sieve." I frowned at the cup.

Charaxus laughed. "That they do. But in Egypt, most everything will have some grit or sand. You cannot stop it anymore than you can stop the sun from shining." He belched loudly and rubbed his stomach.

"Hmm. I think I prefer wine," I said.

He nudged me towards another stall. "In Egypt, very few can afford wine. The best of my cargo, we will take further down river to the city of Sais and Pharaoh's table. But I shall reserve one or two casks for you, my Petal. Stop here. I wish to buy you a gift."

Iadmon had not purchased half so much for me in four years' time. This Charaxus was an extravagant man, if a bit imprudent. He pointed to a few small brass boxes and ceramic jars with lids. The trader jumped up to hand them over to Charaxus who opened each and sniffed deeply.

I shielded my eyes. The rising sun baked the air. Annoying insects buzzed about my head and eyes. The more intense the heat, the more they swarmed. I wished I had one of those horsehair whips that I'd seen a man use to swat at them.

"What do you think of these?" Charaxus asked.

He handed me two containers, each the size of my palm. Inside was a white creamy substance that looked much like a salve. Both stunk with appalling pungency, one like burnt wood and the other a spoiled fruit.

"I am not eating that!" I exclaimed. Charaxus burst into laughter.

"You do not eat this," he guffawed. "You wear it. It will protect your lovely skin from drying in this accursed heat."

I sniffed again, cautiously. "I think I will take my chances with the sun," I said. "Unless there's another scent I may choose."

"It will also keep the insects away." Charaxus looked a little crestfallen, but he motioned the man to open and offer me another container.

One after one, we opened until my nose grew stuffy and my head began to ache from the overpowering scents. At last, I settled on one with a warm herbed scent that reminded me of my mother. I forced myself to smile at his eager face.

"You are most generous, Master," I said.

"Please, please," he pleaded. "I would hear only my name from your lips, lovely Petal."

"Very well," I said, uncomfortable with his unusual request. "Charaxus."

"I must return to the docks to oversee the trade of my wine. There have been more Persians this season than in any I have seen. I must make certain to get the best price for my goods, or they will glut the market with their swill." He mopped his forehead. "You may linger a while, if you like. Here is some coin for you to barter for whatever pleases you. I should like to see you in a new garment. That rag does nothing for your figure. Egyptian linen will do. No more coarse fabrics."

"Yes, master...er...Charaxus." I accepted the coins.

"Khefti will take you back when you have concluded." He touched my cheek without speaking, his eyes drinking in my face like a drowning sailor sighting land. "I shall return soon, my Petal." Then he was gone.

I must admit, I felt a little forlorn when he left. Perhaps it was the lack of women in the *agora*. Perhaps it was the fact that I'd scarce been alone in my lifetime. Or it could have been the way strangers ogled me, russet skinned Egyptians with their liquid eyes. I wondered what they thought of me, with my fair skin and red-gold hair, alone in a sea of darkness, but I never found out. Khefti shook a large stick at anyone who gave me more than discreet scrutiny.

The marketplace was so unfamiliar--the smells of unfamiliar spices in the food and drink, the people, the diaphanous clothing, the desolation of the everlasting sands beyond the river's banks. I actually felt a pang of homesickness for Abdera, for in Egypt, everything was strange. Even the insects were odd, especially the skeletal plated ones that scuttled into the shaded recesses of the stalls, waving their poison-tipped tails and crab-like claws. Charaxus had warned me their sting could kill a man, and yet these Egyptians danced around them and continued their business, as if they did not mind flirting with death.

My mind wandered a little, back to Aesop's words. I wondered if he'd reached his far off destination and what would he think of Charaxus' attention to me.

Remember the crab.

The coins Charaxus had given me jingled pleasantly in their sack.

I would try.

CHAPTER 14

"Very lovely," Charaxus said. He drew out the syllables so his lips, rosy and scented with Egyptian beer, curved in a predatory smile.

We had been in Naukratis for a month and his attentions to me had only increased. I was beginning to understand my role as his slave was less a concubine and more of a wife to run his household in Egypt. Well, I thought, not so much a wife, for a proper Greek woman would never clothe herself in such scanty finery. And I could never bear him legitimate heirs.

Charaxus was most pleased with my choice of dress. His eyes gleamed and he rubbed his hands together as he circled me twice, once very quickly and the second time, slowly, as if savoring every inch of my scarcely covered flesh.

I knew now why he wished me to purchase a new garment.

Still, Egyptians are a beautiful people. With skin like polished copper, they are thin and graceful as a valley willow, with a peculiar purring accent when they speak. Their eyes are liquid night--dark and slanted as an almond is shaped, and their hair, when they have not shaved it all away, falls in a swath of fine black silk. Egyptian hair is soft, unlike the rough kinked tresses of the Nubians, who hail from further south. Soldiers, laborers and slaves wear coarse linen skirts called _shentis_, when they bother to wear any clothing at all, which is almost never. The more expensive the weave of the cloth, the finer the material, until the finest of Egyptian cotton and linen fiber is woven so sheer, one could adorn one's self in the spider silk of Arachne's web and be afforded more covering. The gossamer fabric reveals more than it conceals, as Charaxus must surely have known.

No more rough fabric, he'd cautioned me.

The thin material of my gown was fashioned in pleats that draped from my neck over my breasts and hips to fall in a tight, fitted skirt. I had to adjust my stride to accommodate the skirt, which persisted in wrapping about my knees every time the wind blew. My shorter steps lent a roll to my hips I knew Charaxus found provocative. Well, it could not be helped. There were no other clothes to be had in Egypt—at least not for me.

Charaxus placed a warm hand on my bare shoulder. "Come, Petal."

He drew me toward the couch and began a tender barrage of kisses designed to lull me into desire--a thoughtful but futile gesture. I could not help but remain "stiff as a plank" as he'd likened me.

Then he poised between my thighs, spreading my legs apart to enter me. His hand groped impatiently at my sex. He leaned forward and balanced his torso against my abdomen. I braced myself for the entry of his member, but his fingers began the assault.

First one, then the other, prized my nether lips apart and probed within for the slick dew that would ease his invasion. He rubbed and fondled, making such gruntling noises that I was reminded of a rutting pig. The image did nothing to ease my anxiety.

I wrapped my fingers in the pleats of my new gown and waited for it all to end.

His fumbling hand remained between the two of us. Sweat dripped off his forehead as I felt him withdraw his meaty fingers. He took his phallus and tried to cram the head into me. I winced and sucked air sharply between my teeth. His finger slipped between my folds. He mumbled a curse and bucked his hips, trying to push into me.

"Petal, no...here, wait...let me," he gasped. He ground his pelvis into me, as if he could force his way into my body through sheer will. "It's...I can't!" he groaned.

He stopped and rolled off me, pulling his robes over him with a snap of his robes. I lay there scarce daring to draw breath. Charaxus didn't speak for some time, but knelt facing the wall.

"Gods, why have you cursed me like this, woman?" he muttered, finally.

What was I supposed to say? His attentions were certainly unwelcome and unpleasant. It wasn't near the drowsy pleasure I'd shared with my near sister, but it could have been so much worse.

"I'm sorry," I said. "I don't know what it is I should do."

As a slave, it was my duty to serve my master, however distasteful it may be. What if he were to sell me to some foreigner? I bit my knuckle to keep from crying aloud in protest. Perhaps my stiff refusal to aid him had rendered him useless. A slave who did not earn her master's keep would not survive long.

I reached out and patted his back. His skin quivered under my touch and he turned to face me. I kissed him. Not a passionate kiss, by any means, but I could taste his misery on my tongue as clearly as I could taste the salt of his tears.

Charaxus touched his finger, still scented with my sex, to his lips. "You have never kissed me before, Petal."

"No," I replied.

"You are so lovely. Surely, you love me just a little, do you not?" He looked at me with such fervor, that I did not turn my face away when he kissed me again. "I am good to you, yes?"

I did not burn in the soft delta between my legs as I had during my nights with Mara. No, this sensation was pleasant warmth stoked in my breast, like a task completed well. I recognized it. I felt valuable, and perhaps, even a little treasured.

Charaxus needed me. He desired me. To find oneself worthy of desire after so long is such a heady emotion.

So, I softened towards him. I molded my body against his. He sighed against my mouth and eased me back to the couch. After a few moments, he reared up and tossed off his robes to reveal his phallus, as straight and true as one of Eros' darts. With it, he pierced me and a sweet song of triumph shone in his eyes. I felt no pain.

And I would never feel as benevolent as I did that afternoon when Charaxus thought I loved him.

In the morning, he took me to the bathhouse. The Egyptians are even more fastidious than the Greeks, and they go to such lengths to be clean that the gods themselves must be jealous.

"These remind me of the bathhouses in Mytilene," I said.

"They are very like the ones in Syracuse, as well," he replied. "Pharaoh has allowed us to install our own customs here, in this city. It is reported he has a fascination with all things Greek." His eyes sparkled.

"What is that place?" I asked and pointed to a building near the bathhouse.

"Where they go to be shaved." He squinted at the Egyptian picture writing, called *hieroglyphs*, on the wall near the entrance. Men and women, slave and free alike, pluck and shave every hair from the bodies and scalp. Many of them wear wigs.

"Surely you don't mean to cut off my hair?" I fairly shouted at him. Not my lovely red-gold hair, my father's legacy?

"Ah, Petal, I shall pay for you to bathe as often as you like. There will be no need to shave your tresses, so you may keep your fire, my flower. I would not have your petals plucked for any price." He laughed at his own jest.

He was in a fine mood. I relaxed a little and smiled at what I knew to be the cause of his light heart. He flashed his white teeth at me, mistaking my mirth for amusement at his bawdy humor.

He spent what I thought was an obnoxious sum of money on a private bath for the two of us. When I emerged from the tepid pool, scented and pink all over, he pulled me onto his lap and kissed me heartily. I dripped water all over the floor. Charaxus laughed again and rubbed me with a cloth of Egyptian cotton. Then he motioned for a pair of nubile girls to come and rub me with scented salve until I reeked. Still, it did feel nice to have the sand scrubbed from my scalp and my hair freshly oiled and dressed as neatly as a queen.

He might have taken me right there in the bath house but his excitement at showing off his adopted homeland overrode his desire for me, at least for the moment. Or perhaps they did not allow congress in public, as they did in Greece. I certainly was not going to ask.

When we emerged into the harsh sunlight, he motioned and a litter was brought round. Nubian slaves carried us to the *agora*, where he made a final accounting of the sales of his wine.

How strange the Nubians were. I wanted to touch the litter bearers with their smooth, black skin, just the color of soot from my mother's hearth. I sighed, and Charaxus patted my hand.

"I have yet another surprise for you, Petal," he whispered in my ear. The rasp of his breath against my flesh reminded me of a stinging fly, and I forced my hand into my lap to keep from slapping him away.

"You are full of surprises." I said knowing Charaxus appreciated a bit of jest.

Charaxus chuckled even louder.

"You will like this, I think," he said, fairly glowing with excitement. "I decided this morning. We sail for Sais on the morrow. I shall present you at the Pharaoh's palace. I told you he has a love of all things Greek. I am willing to bet he would have paid three times the amount I doled out for you."

I was dumbfounded.

"I am not a Greek," I said. "Nor am I fit to be presented to any god-king."

"You are Greek enough for Amasis' eyes, I'll wager. Do not be alarmed, Petal," Charaxus patted my hand. "If the gods are willing, we shall find you suitable clothing and jewels to wear before you see Sais."

"You have already purchased me this gown," I murmured.

I was so tired of my life not being my own. Was this my fate, to be passed from man to man until I withered? Aesop was right. This world was no place for a woman.

"Yes, yes, this gown pleases me but it pleases me more to buy you another. A neck as elegant as yours deserves gold to circle it. And earrings that dangle, and something with which to bind up your hair, like they do in Athens…yes, I think Amasis will enjoy a lovely Greek goddess. You will do me much credit."

My eyes watered and I blinked to clear them.

What a fool I was! Charaxus did not love me! He merely thought to make good on his investment. No wonder he'd felt confidence in purchasing me for such an exorbitant amount of money. A man so well-versed in Egyptian culture would know the king of this land, this demigod, would covet me.

The next day Charaxus took me to the _agora_, but I could not enjoy such indulgences, so filled with worry I was at being sold against my will once more. He stopped at a heavily tented spot just off the main venue. This was no market stall that exposed fabric to wither and bleach in the bright eye of the sun. It was a cool, welcome interior. The perfume was too strong, but I kept my face neutral as he labored over his choice.

"I think this one," he said at last. He held up a garment for me to try-- one that bared my left breast and draped over my right with such pale, transparent pleats, it might as well be uncovered. If my figure was not so fine, I might have held some shame in wearing it.

The seller prattled on in a language unknown to me, but Charaxus seemed to understand him well enough. He laughed as I removed the gown, and scribed something on a sheet of very smelly fibers smashed to form a single mat that was far more pliable and lightweight than carved stone tablets. It was called papyrus. Well, miracle or not, it stunk! When he finished, the merchant rolled the dried papyrus with a nod. I was not sorry to leave.

We exited with the gown, which I could take no pleasure in, draped over Charaxus' arm. Next was the jeweler's stall. Again, he took unearthly care and time with his selection, until I was weary of standing and having all manner of bronze, copper, and polished stone beads draped over my neck and head.

"Charaxus," I interrupted his conversation with the jeweler. "Master," I said again, so he might know my displeasure. "I am weary from the sun and noise. I beg you, allow me to return, so I may better serve you in the hours of evening, when your need is most pressing."

His cheeks paled. I wondered if I'd angered him.

"My apologies," he directed to the merchant. "Your pardon, but I do not wish my delicate blossom to fade in this heat."

The merchant made a gesture that could have been taken for assent or irritation, but in either case, Charaxus had no eyes for it.

"You should have told me you found the merchandise inferior," he said when we'd quit the stall. "There are other places we might look."

"There was no fault with the adornments. I am truly unwell."

He compressed his lips, but took my arm with the utmost care, as if he might crush me in his gentle grasp. We moved towards the litter and he barked an order to return to the inn.

The Nubians leapt into position. They trotted with a languorous grace like the furry creatures that slunk around every corner and block of Egypt. Cats, the Egyptians called the creatures, and very much like them are the people from the south. I understood why the Egyptians have made a goddess out of the beast. I was a great admirer of beauty, myself.

I choked on the blowing dust, coughing and gulping air to clear my throat.

"Soon, now," Charaxus said. He patted my hand. "By week's end, you shall see the great city of Pharaoh."

When we reached the inn, I had a long rest. Charaxus was most solicitous of me. He requested a variety of dishes, many of which were prepared in Greek fashion, I suppose to entice me. Well, for all that it was a faked illness, I _was_ sick. Sick at heart. The food tasted like ash in my mouth.

"Forget the jewels, for now. We leave for Sais in the morning. The grandness of it will please you, I'm certain. Do not fear," he whispered. "I will watch over you until morning."

I thought of his plot to parade me in front of Pharaoh.

"I fear only the time when that will not be so." I turned my back to him. It was the closest thing to truth that I could safely speak.

CHAPTER 15

The palace of the Pharaoh in Sais was enormous. An expanse of limestone and porphyry, interlocking hallways led to the public rooms and, I supposed, to the Pharaoh's more private residence. Columned porches allowed the breeze to sift through the interior, but sunlight seemed forbidden, for all that they worship the sun god, Ra. As we were escorted further into the palace, the sizzle and pop of torchlight reminded me of a Bacchae temple, for it was so cool and dark in the halls of Pharaoh's inner sanctum that torches were lit, even in the daylight. Chill bumps raised on my flesh. No sun's glow could warm the depths of the inner palace.

Charaxus patted me on the shoulder as we were escorted through the cool halls to where Pharaoh awaited us.

I'd spent the previous evening performing a private dance and creative seduction of my master, using the _kelēs_ I'd learned at the temple many years ago. I'd hoped my efforts would endear me to him enough so he might keep me for his own and not sell me to the Egyptian king's household. It did me no good, for in the morning, we dined and dressed and were ushered in to the Pharaoh's hall.

Amasis, or Nesu Ahmose as Egyptians called him, kept many beautiful women, most of them inherited from his predecessor, the unlucky Apries. Charaxus smiled and assured me none could be as lovely as me--not even Ladice, who was herself a Grecian princess garnered from the Greek settlement of Cyrene in Libya.

It was rumored Ladice was so unattractive that Pharaoh could not perform his duties. Public sentiment named her a witch, but I could not believe a man as powerful as Pharaoh would tolerate a wife who was not comely. Surely, if my own master needed such assurances, the great god-king of Egypt would also. I hoped, for her sake, that she might have some features that bordered beauty. If Ladice wished to be the Great Wife of Pharaoh, she would do better to pray to her love goddess, the lusty Aphrodite, for the powers of seduction, then to emasculate him.

My station in life was due to the nature of my sex, more than anything else. But Charaxus was an easy man to please and most often was sated by my attention, rather than enthusiasm. After my years of drudgery, it was an easier life. I was satisfied to remain in his possession and not to be tossed to the whims of a cruel and barbarous foreigner. Besides, it would be an easier thing to earn my freedom from Charaxus, when he tired of me, than to live as concubine to an Egyptian king.

And that is what I most hoped to do.

Rumors of Persian invasions in the outermost edges of Egypt had reached us even here, in the tranquility of Sais. I thought back to Charaxus' comments on the dock in Naukratis and worried for our future. Despite his calm exterior, I knew Charaxus was concerned, for if Egypt fell to Persian rule, his trade here could be finished. The Persians had their own sources of wine through dealings with the nomadic Canaanites, the Hittites, and the Babylonians. Perhaps he hoped to make me gift to Amasis to cement his position with the king who rose through the strength of his spear and who loved Grecian wine.

The servant led us to a large area, where visitors lounged in various stages of wait. The cavernous room was supported on all four sides by large carved stone pillars, quite unlike those from Greece. Bands of colored patterns painted at the ceiling level gave the illusion of even more height and the painted figures on each column depicted Egyptians in various activities. I suppose it gave the Pharaoh a sense of watching over his subjects. Or perhaps he thought the public would be more at ease amidst such bucolic art.

Well, I could not be less composed. Sweat trickled down my back despite the cool air.

We were not the only merchants to be invited. There were many gathered that day. We retreated to a far corner to bide our time until our names were called. There was a trader of grain, and two Ethiopians bearing speckled and striped animal skins such as I had never seen. They recognized Charaxus and hailed a greeting, eyeing me with curiosity. A few scribes took copious notes, sitting cross legged and using their stretched linen skirts as a surface to write on papyrus scrolls. Others my master did not know lounged in the empty corners--all of us awaiting the pleasure of the most powerful man in Egypt.

The floor was a combination of soft beige, ivory, and rose variegated porphyry imported from the quarries to the south, Charaxus pointed out. Clusters of small gilded and onyx couches were scattered about the room. Servants passed by a burbling fountain. Along the walls in alcoves, were several bronze or granite sculptures of unfamiliar Egyptian gods--some in the form of men, some animals, and some a frightening combination of both. I imagined them looking down on me with displeasure.

"Stop fidgeting, you'll crease your gown." Charaxus hissed at me.

He must be as nervous as I. Perhaps he worried his investment would not pay off. I did not wish to be sold, but I could not continue to clench my dress in my sweating palms under his disapproving gaze. I forced myself to be still.

One hour passed. Then another. I sighed. The tiny red grains of the Egyptian time keeper--the hourglass--filtered with agonizing slowness. In all that time, only the Ethiopians were called away. Two men began a quiet dispute over who'd arrived first. I eyed the two guards posted at the front of the room and feared the worst. Neither of them moved an inch, but another servant poked his head in and uttered something to one of them. The guard shook his head and the servant went away. I sighed again.

I've never been a patient creature. I was even less, now, with the threat of new ownership looming over my head like a spear poised to strike.

I tried to content myself with observing the other occupants, but they all seemed as agitated as I, except for an obese trader who slurped his wine noisily and waggled his eyebrows at me.

I focused on the guards. They were very alike, both with the smooth copper skin and generous lips of their race, and shaved heads. Their eyes were lined in black kohl and they wore a sort of tunic made of white linen, slightly coarser than my own. Neither wore any jewelry or adornment, though even cheap trinkets were available in the streets.

At last, Charaxus and I were summoned to the front. There was much grumbling, as many had yet to be called. I tried not to consider that Pharaoh might be more eager to see Charaxus' offering than a cattle trader's wares.

We were shown into a smaller private chamber, lavishly decorated with vivid painted designs in gold, red, and black bands. An elderly Egyptian man, who I could only assume was Pharaoh, steepled his fingers together on a small table cluttered with faience glass jars of cobalt and green. An open work collar of gold and precious stones circled his neck and rings gleamed in the torchlight on his hands. He tugged at his finely made, ill-fitting wig as we entered, and I noticed the hair was a much darker shade than this man's eyebrows. He looked false. I smothered a wave of repulsion and fear.

I could tell, even from his seated position, I would tower over him. He was quite short in stature, with a slouched, craven posture like a stunted poplar trunk. I wondered how he'd gained much luck on the battle field. In Thrace, it had been a man's height that gave him the opportunity to strike first. This man looked hardly capable of hefting his paring knife, let alone a spear or axe.

Beside his wrinkled fingers lay several rolled papyrus scrolls, hollow reeds, and slung over his shoulder was a round leather container of ink as red as the man's carmined cheeks and lips. Comparatively, my current master was a demigod. Disgust filled me.

Charaxus bowed low. I knelt beside him and kept my eyes lowered.

"You may rise," said our host.

Charaxus looked around expectantly. "Where is the Nesu, Rising Son of Neit?" he asked.

I gaped at him. This was not the mighty Pharaoh Amasis?

"Nesu Ahmose is away. I will hear your petition, today." His gaze flickered towards me. "I am Neferenatu, the Nesu's most trusted advisor."

"Great Vizier," Charaxus bowed again. "I have journeyed from Greece to bring wine to the table of the great Pharaoh, may it please him."

Neferenatu inclined his head a fraction, his eyes still not leaving me. "You are not unknown to us, Charaxus of Mytilene. We have heard of the quality of wine you carry, and its taste is palatable to our...beloved ruler."

He lifted the reed and made to mark on the scroll in front of him. I speculated on the importance of his pause. His eyes slid from me to Charaxus and back to me.

"How much?" Neferenatu asked.

Charaxus blinked, clearly at a loss. The garish red color of the walls blossomed in his cheeks. I breathed deeply to calm my racing heart.

"I asked 'how much'. How much wine have you brought with you to sell?" The Vizier tapped the reed against his yellowed teeth.

Charaxus recovered and answered.

"It is not enough," said the Vizier, marking on the papyrus. "We must have at least twice that amount, and before the next season's festival. Leave us what you have now and bring the rest."

"That is quite a sum to bring all the way from Lesbos. I do not know if it can be done before the Inundation." Charaxus stroked his chin. "The ship will be much laden down with the weight of the wine. And great Nesu has never requested so much, not even in the days of his military doings."

"Such discussion is unseemly. Sell what we require or take your business elsewhere." The Vizier signaled to the servant at the door, who disappeared. Our audience was clearly coming to an end.

"Hold," Charaxus called out anxiously. "If it be the will of Nesu, I will bring the rest. But you must agree to settle on a price now and advance me for the portion I leave behind."

"You do not trust my word?" Neferenatu's face darkened like a thundercloud.

Charaxus threw his hands up in protest. He was clearly being forced into a position he did not like. "I have taken a house here in the city, and I have some debts." His eyes flickered towards me. "I trust your word and the words of any man so beloved by the Nesu. But I do not have the coin I need to transport such a large amount of wine from Lesbos. I will need a portion of it before sealing the agreement."

"Very well," said the Vizier, sitting back on his stool. They agreed upon a price, and Charaxus seemed pleased by the offer. A great chest was brought forth by two slaves. Neferenatu's eyes rested again on me as he weighed out the portion of gold ingots demanded by Charaxus. I could tell my master was satisfied, which made my heart lighter. I smiled at the wrinkled vizier, blessing my good fortune for I'd thought Charaxus meant to sell me.

Neferenatu closed the chest with an expression I could not read. His hand paused upon the lid. "Give me the girl and I shall double this amount," he said, as if in passing. "She is yours?"

My smile froze.

"She is," Charaxus answered. "I brought her anticipating audience with Nesu Ahmose. She is an exceptionally fine dancer." He signaled and I dutifully rose from my kneeling and assumed a ready stance for dancing.

Grand Vizier Neferenatu called for music, and within moments, drums and whistles were brought. I took a few shaky breaths before forming my body to the steps that I knew would impress him. Though Charaxus shone with pride, the leathery vizier's face remained as blank as sandstone. Well, perhaps he was just too old to be much moved, by the sight of me. Still, I was glad for his perceived sour displeasure, until the audience was ended.

"Oo-yay." The vizier tipped his chin. "A fine dancer, indeed. You could erase most of your debts with her. So? Sell her to me along with your fine wine. You can pick up another woman when you return to Lesbos."

I drew a sharp breath.

Charaxus rested his hand on my shoulder. "I thank you for your offer, but I must refuse."

"That seems unwise." Neferenatu's lips firmed, but Charaxus did not amend his rebuff. "So, then. As you wish." The vizier dismissed us with a curt lift of his chin.

We left in somewhat of a hurry. I rejoiced that I would not be sold today, especially to the leathery vizier. How easily Charaxus could have used me to gain the royal advisor's favor. And yet, surprisingly, he did not.

I stumbled through the rest of the afternoon in a state of amazement. That night I made love to Charaxus with such fervor he promised to bring me back a special gift from Naukratis. If he did not guess at my reasons for being so passionate, I would not tell him.

As the sun broke the next morning a flurry of preparations were made for Charaxus' journey back to Lesbos. Missives had to be sent to his wife and daughters to prepare them for his arrival, for it would take weeks just to send word. He had to secure transport to Naukratis, where he would then hire the vessel and crew that could haul a large quantity of wine back to Egypt. All would take time, and time was not a luxury Charaxus could afford.

"I must move quickly to capitalize on this sale, Petal. The whims of Egyptian nobility are as changeable as the sands. With the speed required to make it back before the festival, much of the wine may need transport over land, rather than by barge. It will be a rough journey." Charaxus finished rubbing his teeth with a small horsehair brush with an ivory handle.

"How long will it take?" I asked, signaling one of the slaves to bring me Charaxus' satchel. Much I desired to return home to Greece, I loathed sea travel.

Charaxus sighed. "A day or two to Naukratis. Then a few weeks to get passage back to Lesbos. After that, I don't know. Who can say if the quantity Pharaoh requires can be bought at this time of year? It will be months, at the very least."

Months, I thought. And what was to become of me?

"Am I to go with you?" I packed the last of his belongings.

Charaxus thought for a moment. "Such a journey will not be short, nor pleasurable. And I wish only to give you pleasures. Best that you stay here and mind my household, safely away from the clutches of those who would steal you away."

"Oh, please let me come," I begged. I did not want to be left alone in a strange land. What if he should never return? Travel was difficult even in the best of places, and Charaxus was certainly not a young man. "I could wait for you in Naukratis if there is no room for me aboard the ship to Lesbos."

"What has gotten into you, Petal?" He rubbed his chin. "No," he decided. "I dare not leave you in the port city unprotected. There has been talk of trouble, especially with the damned Persians sending emissaries every other week between Egypt and Greece. Besides, some wiser man than I could capture you and sell you off for a fortune, instead of spending one to keep you."

I paused. My fingers quivered on the knot of the satchel.

"But you were planning to sell me yourself." I straightened and faced him. "To Pharaoh."

His brows drew together in a frown. "Whatever gave you that idea?"

"But you…you said…" I tried to remember what he'd said. Had he stated forthright he planned to sell me? I couldn't remember. "You bought me clothing and adornments," I finished lamely.

"I'd have purchased them for you in any case." He kissed me on the cheek and bent to shoulder his belongings. "I merely wanted to display the best of my treasure to Pharaoh. I will never give you up."

I barely saw him off. My mind was fixed on his words.

He never meant to sell me. And he meant never to give me up.

The joy I felt and not being sold to the Pharaoh was tainted by the knowledge that Charaxus also never meant to free me. What could it mean when a Greek master should refuse his slave the chance to buy back her own freedom? My heart was crushed.

Oh, how I was tired of being another man's property to do with as he wished. Me, the child of a great warrior and a Bacchae. Me, who was trained to walk the paths of the gods. Someday, I vowed that I would find a way to live free as my father bade me.

Please Lady, I prayed. *One day, let it be so.*

Outside, I heard a bird cry. I hoped it would carry my words to my Golden Lady that she might deliver me as she had once before.

For the sake of my father's dying wish, I wished it to be so.

The next morning, when Charaxus boarded the ship to Naukratis, I raised my hand and dutifully waved my scented scarf until the ship disappeared from view. In truth, I could not wait to see him gone. Then I followed the other slaves back to our rented abode. He would be away some many long months, if he returned at all. In his absence, I would have the run of the household and would speak in his name—with his coffers to support me.

For the first time in almost five years since becoming a slave, I would live on my own. I scuffed the toes of my slippers on the sandy pavers, and felt almost free.

CHAPTER 16

The first month since Charaxus' departure, I spent exploring Naukratis. I brought offerings of wine and emmer wheat to the temple of Neit and admired the graceful paintings and hieroglyphs, many of which I recognized. Still, I despaired over the language barrier that separated me from the Egyptian people. For though I no longer feared Charaxus would sell me, I was still determined to somehow regain my freedom. A free woman would need to survive, and to find purchase back to Greece, so I must dedicate myself to learning everything I could in preparation for that day.

I asked Rada, a young, pretty servant who spoke some Greek, to teach me to speak Egyptian. She laughed at first, but when she saw I asked in earnest, she taught me a few common words. I learned the names for some of the fruits and some animals and plants. I learned "go" and "stop". Mostly, I listened to her wonderful purring voice and tried to emulate the sounds she made. I do not know if I was accurate. There are a few throaty inflections that sounded more like a hacking cough than a syllable. A Thracian tongue isn't made for such sounds, but I did try.

Another two months passed. My Egyptian was getting quite good. Sometimes Rada came with me to the _agora_, and I would practice my new words. I made a few mistakes, like the time I meant to ask for an onion and was rewarded with a sack of sesame instead, but I was much improved. And I began to feel like a true citizen of Sais, as I had nothing else with which to occupy my time, save to keep the household and wait for word from Charaxus.

At least, she reminded me a little of Mara.

Rada was a young woman from a nearby village. Charaxus had hired her out, hoping to keep me company. Rada was a good domestic, and like any concubine, attended to my grooming and such small tasks as I saw fit to give her. I wondered if she could ever be as close to me as my near-sister. Mara would be a Bacchae, by now. I felt a stab of jealousy prick my heart and I mumbled a hasty prayer for forgiveness. It was not Mara's fault I was now a slave.

At last, word of Charaxus was brought round—some many weeks old. He professed his misery at being without me, but I think he was happy to see his daughters, if not his wife. There was an obscure reference to his sister Sappho, something about a poem circulating in the upper echelons. He sounded quite angry and I wondered what it was about him to inspire his elder sister to such unkindness. Of course, if she carried on with her brother as she had with Aesop, then it was no great surprise to me that Charaxus was weary of her theatrics.

And what did it matter if the Poetess of Mytilene scorned us? A man was wont to harbor slaves, especially attractive young females. With the attention I received daily in the streets, I'd no disillusions about my desirability. Greek or no, the Egyptians had no qualms about indicating their interest in me. I suppose I was something of a rarity this far south, with my light eyes and fair skin, and Charaxus had certainly liked to flaunt me around the city. Although I'd seen slaves of decidedly non-Egyptian origin, few could boast Thracian heritage so far from our homeland's shores. My bright red-gold locks were a beacon in a sea of dark braids or shaved pates.

Later that season, I ran into Neferenatu, the Grand Vizier--this time outside the palace walls. A litter passed through the streets, and I, on my way to the fish sellers with Rada, was forced to pause and bow as he passed. The litter stopped and the thin linen draperies flicked open. Neferenatu motioned me closer.

"Where is your master, girl?" he asked. Rada tittered behind me.

"He has gone to fetch the wine you purchased, Great One," I responded, bestowing him the deep bow to which his station entitled him.

"The wine Nesu Ahmose has purchased," Neferenatu corrected. "May He Ever Walk in the Light of Ra."

"As you say." I bowed again. I have never favored long-winded epithets overmuch, but for Egyptian nobility, it seemed almost an art. Black flies bit my ankles and I wished I could move to the shaded area of the stalls.

"Send your girl home. You may attend me at the palace, whilst Charaxus is away at sea." Again, his words were belied by a face as inscrutable as a stone statue.

I glanced at Rada. Her eyes were huge with surprise.

"I...I cannot, Great One." I tried to be as placating as possible with my refusal. Gods above knew what would happen to me if I angered the powerful vizier whilst Charaxus was away. "Only my master may bid me to come or go. I must beg you to wait until I have received his command." There. It was not unheard of for a command to take several months to reach Lesbos and back.

Neferenatu compressed his lips, a sure sign of his displeasure, but he could not flout the social mores of our positions. "So be it. Move on," he ordered the litter bearers. The draperies snapped back into place and obscured his frowning countenance.

I waited until they'd completely left the market before I rose from my position.

"Can you believe?" Rada whispered reverently, nudging my shoulder. "You have gained the notice of the Grand Vizier!"

"Fie." I shooed away another fly. "Say nothing to Charaxus. It would displease him. Come, we have garments to buy." A man's interest in me was nothing new. And though the commoners such as Rada held the Vizier, the nobility, and Pharaoh's household in reverence as a messenger of the gods, I held to no such illusions myself. I also knew our visit to the marketplace would motivate Rada to swifter action, as I'd give her my things once I'd garnered new items.

Without Charaxus to guide me, I could not say which merchants were cheating me. I depended on my servants, mainly Rada, to help me purchase foods and drink, and the cloth for a new gown for I'd lived in Egypt for almost a season, and grown at least three finger's width. I am already a good deal taller than most Egyptians, male or female. My old clothing, while suitable, was no longer becoming. Before sailing, Charaxus had given me leave to purchase a new everyday gown and, since my feet had grown, we were to purchase my first Egyptian sandals as well.

I relied on Rada to guide me through the marketplace to the artisan district, for there is nothing so base in Grecian culture as a shoe seller, except perhaps a man who sells his time to other men. The experience was sure to be unpleasant without my master, so I'd brought Rada for security. At last we turned down the final alley and entered a cool, shady interior shop off the side alley.

"We must be on our guard, Rada." I cautioned, taking firm hold of her arm. "For a mere craftsman of sandals is sure to be dishonorable. Indeed, it is considered one of the lowest of professions."

"It is not the same, here, Flower." Rada wore a strange smile as she sauntered into the small workshop.

At the opposite end, a man labored with his back to us, seated at a small bench. In front of him, a long table held a variety of supplies, tools, and half-finished treasures. Rada giggled and he turned.

My breath caught in my throat.

He was young. Not much older than I, from what I could tell. He wore only a loin cloth of hemp and his body was cleanly shaved, his skin slicked with sweat or scented oils. But this man had a face to rival the gods. This was the sandal maker? He deserved to sit on a throne of gold and ivory from Kush.

The whole room seemed small and unaccountably hot. He stared at me and a slow smile spread across his lips. Rada shifted and cleared her throat.

"Hori," she said. "This is the Greek's woman. You are to make new sandals for her."

Hori jerked his head towards the bench. He gestured for me to sit. Then he crouched and took out a scrap of animal hide. He pointed to my foot. I lifted my skirts, revealing much of my bare legs, and placed my unshod foot upon the hide.

Hori's fingers stroked the delicate skin of my ankle as he held my heel in place and traced the outline of my instep. When he finished, his hand lingered on my calf. His warmth surprised me. He was as hot as Hephaestus' furnace.

Large eyes dominated his features; in the shadows, I could scarcely see his pupils, they were so dark. Like most Egyptians, he had a full mouth, and I could not stop from staring at his lips as they curved around syllables I could barely comprehend. He was the most finely sculpted man I'd ever seen. He reminded me of Dionysus, young and lithe and beautiful. I'd never been gently touched by a man that was not ravaged by time or ugliness.

Heat flared in my middle, as he stroked my ankle with his long, tapered fingers. I took a deep breath, and the spicy scent of his skin and cedar flooded me.

"Hori!" Rada snapped. And then she said something in her native tongue that I did not understand.

Hori gave a guttural response, and his eyes never left mine. He smiled. His teeth were white against his copper skin. I found myself smiling back. Really, he was too beautiful by half.

"Hori," Rada said again, her voice stiff with anger. "You forget yourself. Come, Flower. We go now."

She jerked me up by the elbow. I turned my head to watch Hori run a hand over his shaved head as we left. His eyes trailed over my bottom as I passed.

"Who was that?" I asked, breathlessly. Rada took a sharp turn down the nearest alley. Her lips were pinched in a tart expression.

"No one. He is just a craftsman. Sometimes he works in metals for the royal court, but mostly he makes sandals and such for the rest of us, when Nesu Ahmose is away. Pay him no mind." She sniffed. "He smiles at everyone like that."

Shoe seller or not, I thought about Hori's smile all the way back to the house.

In the evening, Rada would not brush out my hair, complaining she had too much work to do. And in the morning, she went to the market early without me. I was prepared to scold her, but when she returned, her eyes were glowing, and she was so sweet that I could not help but forgive her. I did not tell her how much I thought of Hori, though. I was not certain of their relationship, but he'd been so divinely formed, so handsome, that I felt certain there was no harm in just thinking of him the tiniest bit.

At least my thoughts could be my own.

The following season, Charaxus returned. He arrived, creased and worn from travel, in stained robes still crusted with salt from the sea. After long months apart, I'd forgotten how old and tired he was.

He was delighted to see me. He gathered me into his arms and I tried not to flinch as his roughened hands caressed me as he took me. I recalled the soft touch of Hori hands on my legs and tried not to compare them. Still, Charaxus did not seem to notice anything different about me. Well, what could harmless daydreaming about the sandal maker alter?

I was still Charaxus' property--the Greek's woman.

He'd brought me a special gift from Naukratis. A cat, sleek and lean, whose dun colored short fur deepened to black at the tip of his long tail and face. He had eyes as green as the Nile and six toes on his left paw and he gazed at me with the same tranquility and superior beauty of all his kind. I named him "Ankh" which means "life" in Egyptian. I think Charaxus was pleased with my choice; I was certainly pleased with his.

Ankh kept us in stitches with his antics as he clambered from ground to wall to rooftop and back again. For all that he was named 'Life', he was the harbinger of death to the rats in the granary and so quickly became a favorite of the servants. I adored him. There is something intensely satisfying about napping with a soft, purring body to keep you company in the long evenings. Though, I could not say the same for my newly returned master.

After a near sleepless night in which he snored and tossed about until I poked him in the ribs, I was in no fine mood the following morning when he called to me.

"Petal," he said as I passed the courtyard garden.

I sighed. Once my favorite place in the house, I was loathe to intrude. Too many months apart had inured me to prefer my own company and to come and go as I pleased.

"Yes?" I plastered a smile on my face.

"Rada tells me you saw the Vizier, Neferenatu. In the _agora_?" He raised his brow.

I nodded. So, Rada was not quite as discreet as I'd thought.

"And?" He popped a piece of bread in his mouth and swallowed it down with more warm beer. There would be no living with him this evening, I thought. That fermented drink would give us both another restless night.

"He asked me to visit him in the palace." I shifted my weight, impatiently.

"And what said you?" Charaxus studied me intently.

"I told him it would be for you to decide, and that he must await your return." I gave him a disapproving look as he gulped down the last of his beer and signaled for me to pour more.

"Did you wish to visit him? In the palace?" he asked.

I sighed. "In truth, I did not." I thought of Hori's quiet little workshop, with the sunlight streaming on motes of metal dust and wood shavings.

Ah, if only Charaxus knew the questions to ask.

"Good." He seemed mollified. "That is well. You seem downcast this morning, Petal. Shall we pick up your new sandals today?"

It was as if he could read my thoughts. I tried to caution him my sandals would not be ready, for I'd hoped to retrieve them on my own. The thought of the two men in the same space of my vision was almost enough to make me weep. One man I longed to see; the other I would be comfortable never seeing again. Oh, the unfairness of it all, that my life should not be my own!

But Charaxus insisted on visiting Hori's workshop, to see for himself that all Rada had assured him was true--Hori was a master craftsman and therefore worthy of his patronage. She begged to go with me, but I was hurt by her report to our master and bade her stay behind. I knew the way well enough, I traveled it in my memory many times.

We entered the shop after the morning meal. Hori was again at his bench, his shoulders gleaming from exertion as he toiled at what looked like an exquisite tiny box, no more than the size of my thumbnail and crafted of electrum--a pleasing mixture of silver and gold. I wondered at who would have a need for such a tiny treasure, but Hori put it aside as we entered. When he looked up, I swallowed and turned my face away. It wouldn't do for Charaxus to see how my cheeks burned. I'd one quick glimpse of Hori's smile before I fixed my eyes to the icon in the alcove nearest the door. Ptah, the long bearded god of craftsmen. I feigned intense interest in it.

"I wish to see what work you have created for my lovely Petal. Tell me, do you think yourself worthy of adorning one such as her?" Charaxus sounded very self-assured.

"Please. Sit." Hori bade us in clipped Egyptian. He motioned for me to put my foot up on the bench as he rummaged around at the back of his small shop. My skin tingled, anticipating his touch and I swallowed hard. I snuck a glance at Charaxus who was whistling faintly and looking around the room with a smug expression.

"Do you speak Greek?" Charaxus asked.

"Yes, a little." Hori returned, his hands behind his back. "Our Nesu has sent his scribes among us to make the language known." He cleared his throat and tossed me a confident smile. I averted my gaze before Charaxus caught me gawking.

"A wise man, your Nesu Ahmose," said Charaxus, nodding.

"Here," Hori said. "You called for sandals, Great Man," he said deferentially. "And sandals I can make. But not for one so lovely as she. She dances with every movement of her body. I have made these, instead. They will fit her and no other."

With the flourish of a performer, Hori revealed his handicraft--the most exquisite pair of dancing slippers I'd ever seen. Crafted of acacia wood, Hori had sculpted them in cunning fashion to curve against my arches just so. He'd lined them with animal hide, so despite the wood they were as comfortable as could be. The outer surface of the slippers was adorned with metal--and not just any metal. I'd thought it to be bronze, but my disbelief multiplied.

"Now see here…." Charaxus began.

"Rose-gold, fit for a queen." Hori interrupted. "I have smelt the yellow gold with copper to give it strength. The pink hue suits her skin, do you not think? And see the bells? They are made like this." He demonstrated how he inserted bronze pellets into a tiny rose gold cup and flattened a second cup on top. The effect was delicate. They were the most beautiful things I'd ever seen. Opportunist that Hori might be, they were too dear. Charaxus would never buy them.

I slipped on the treasures and twirled before him in one of my most pleasing dance positions. Charaxus' eyes softened. Hori stood discreetly to the side and let me mince about for Charaxus, but his eyes burned and never left me.

The jingly bells filled the small workshop with music as I pranced. The sunlight streaming through the high windows glimmered on my feet and turned them to solid honey. I felt molten and alive! Oh, how I desired the slippers!

They were more than incomparable in their beauty. They were a product of Hori's craftsmanship. How many hours had I spent daydreaming of the sandal-maker? Me, the daughter of the gods! Perhaps in this way, I could believe he'd thought of me--that he'd dreamed of me as he tooled and fashioned the wood, leather, and metal into treasure.

"They are lovely. Even more so on limbs like hers." Charaxus agreed, and clapped me on the bottom as I passed. I felt heat rise to my cheeks and Hori smothered another smile. "But they are also very dear, to be sure. I ordered sandals, not golden dancing slippers." He crossed his arms.

My heart sank.

Humiliation and rejection all in one. I was mortified, but I couldn't make myself remove the treasures from my feet. I sketched a few steps more, certain I'd never dance in them again.

"Gold is common as sand in Egypt, since the conquer of Nubia." Hori exaggerated. "I have not used so much to coat her slippers. It is only a thin sheet, see? Perhaps an arrangement could be made, for these will fit none but your woman." He emphasized the possessive ever so slightly.

Clever, clever Hori.

Charaxus' eyes lingered on me, still twirling like a whirlwind in the sunbeams. I stopped and gave him my most appealing smile. "And what of sandals?" he asked. "She cannot wear such slippers to the market."

"She should have music wherever she walks," Hori said. His eyes were hot. "These will last you well beyond any sandal. Think of the number of sandals you would have to buy to compare with sturdy wood and metal."

Charaxus did think. For some long moments he was silent. My gaze darted from him to Hori, who I dared not look at for long, and back to Charaxus. I wondered if my master calculated sums in his head. I wondered if he knew I wanted the slippers as much because Hori had created them, as I did because they were beautiful.

"What say you?" he asked me.

What else could I answer? "Oh, please," I said. "I-I desire them. Very much." I could not help but eye Hori as I said that last bit. "I hardly go out anyway. Let the servants go to the market. I shall dance!" And I twirled again.

Hori rubbed his lips together and looked at me with an expression I could not read.

Charaxus laughed at my childish desire. "She is a treasure to behold, is she not? Well, fetch us some beer, Petal. I would settle on a price."

"You are so good to me." I kissed his cheeks and minced towards the door to get his drink from the nearby stall. I did not even care he would break wind all night. I left with wings of happiness on my heels and felt Hori's eyes on me the whole way out.

CHAPTER 17

The rest of the week I spent dancing and satisfying the lusts of Charaxus. The man truly was an extravagant fool. I should have recognized the trait when he'd purchased me in Samos, but I'd never realized the extent of his profligacy until he agreed to Hori's fabulous rose-gold slippers. Charaxus was a weak man, and I am ashamed to say, I encouraged his weakness then for it led me to my own desires.

What can I say, but that I am Thracian and thus governed by my passions?

The city was abuzz with the news the Greek had ransomed a queen's treasure for his woman. We were invited to various homes of the lower echelon Egyptian nobility, a physician and his wife, and to attend the house of Isesi, a minor scribe, who had invited half of the young bureaucratic families to dine as well. Isesi's wife Wakheptry was kind, however, and knew some of the niceties of Greek culture. So, I passed a pleasant evening. I think they were satisfied to see me dance. It gave them fodder for gossip. The Greek and his beautiful flower--the girl with the rose-gold slippers.

As we departed, Charaxus made promises to Isesi to dine again next week. Still, I feared one day Pharaoh himself would ask us to attend him and then all Charaxus' reassurances I would not be sold would be set aside for the god king of Egypt. I was relieved to hear the Pharaoh was not even in Sais--he'd gone to Memphis some months ago.

I wondered if Charaxus knew of Pharaoh's absence. Surely he must, for it seemed he knew of everything that went on in the city. Well, almost everything.

He did not, for instance, know that I saw Hori again.

I was in the courtyard tending the jasmine and sweet winding roses when I heard a distant clatter. Puzzled, I went to the far wall to investigate.

It was a chunk of plaster the size of my palm. I scanned the high wall looking for any flaw in the smooth white surface. There was none. Who would throw a clod of broken limestone into my garden?.Some prankster, no doubt.

"Who goes there?" I called over the wall. "Be gone or I shall call for the guards to thrash you."

"Flower?" said a faint voice from the other side of the wall.

My heart leapt into my mouth. It was the warm, liquid purr of my dreams, the voice of the sandal craftsman.

"Hori," I called, as softly as I might without anyone inside the house to hear. "What are you doing here?" I'd not seen him since the day Charaxus had purchased my treasured slippers.

"Please, Lovely Flower, do not send me away. I pine for the sight of you. Is your man at home?" he asked.

"Yes," I whispered, as loudly as I dared. My heart leapt. He pined for me? "He is in the house tallying his stock."

"Tell him you wish to go to the market."

"I can't!" But, could I? After so many years of being prey for other men, I wanted Hori with a passion I'd never experienced before.

"Please," he begged. "I must see you."

I thought for a moment. "I could tell him I need to go to the market, but he will send a servant with me. I suppose I could bring Rada," I said doubtfully. I wasn't sure I trusted her.

"No," Hori called. His voice sounded strained. "Not Rada. Bring the old one, the one they call Menekhet. He's almost blind and lame besides. You can lose him in the throng. Meet me at my workshop." Then his voice was gone, before I had time to reconsider the wisdom of our plan.

"Charaxus," I called once I was inside. My heart pounded with the weight of my deceit. I'd never lied to him before…well, not truly lied outside of the niceties I used to stroke his manly pride. "I must go to the market. I wish to buy…I wish to purchase you more beer. Our casks are almost gone." That should do it.

He did not even look up from tallying his figures. "Take someone with you," he said. "The streets will not be safe for you alone."

Rada set down the linen she was mending and made to rise.

"Not you, Rada," I said, as calmly as I might with my heart leaping into my throat. "The casks will be too heavy for you, and besides," I moved towards the door, "I need you to finish the washing. I will take Menekhet."

And I disappeared before she could raise any objections, with my slippers jingling like an alarm.

Hori was right. I'd scarcely left the house when I left poor old Menekhet puffing behind me.

"Wait," I heard him call plaintively.

But I could not wait.

My heart and feet had wings. Hori of the divine face wanted me, he wanted to see me. He was but a seller of shoes, true, but he more than made up for his lack of station with his charm and handsome form. My skin tingled in anticipation and I felt almost free as I rounded the alley and turned towards his door.

"Hori," I called softly as I entered. What if he was not here?

He pounced on me the moment I entered. His full lips covered mine, and wicked creature that I am, I welcomed him without protest. I was on fire as his tongue surged into my mouth. How good it felt to be desired by such a handsome man as he.

"Oh...." He moaned into my mouth. "Oh, Sweet One, how I have longed for you."

I wrapped my arms around him. How strong he was!

His skin was warm cedar and musk. He lifted me up and set me atop his workbench, the very workbench he'd crafted my treasured slippers on. Leather scraps, wood and a half-finished electrum trinket slid to the floor.

"Hori." I sighed. I'd thought of little else but him for weeks now. I'd dreamed of this moment, never thinking it could actually be, but hoping for it just the same.

My pulse raced through my veins like unwatered wine. I should not let him please me like this, but oh! He tasted like honey and spice. His strong palms rubbed my breasts through the thin fabric of my shift until my nipples beaded. Then he moved his hot mouth from my swollen lips and suckled me right there--through the linen and all.

"Ah," I whimpered with pleasure. This was the lover of my dreams. What Mara and I had whispered about, so long ago in the temple. Surely I deserved this after everything I'd suffered. Some small measure of happiness not begot by my master's purse. My hands slid up his broad shoulders, and I reveled in the feel of his silken copper skin. A woman's cry broke into our interlude, a moment before I recognized the soft tread upon the doorstep.

"Hori!" It was Rada. What on earth was she doing here? Her face was as red as if she'd just been slapped.

"Rada," croaked Hori. I hopped off the bench and pulled my skirts into place. How had they become bunched up over my hips?

She glared at us both. "Your master is waiting for you at home, Flower. Go to him." She could not order me around like a servant! I was Charaxus' woman and not hers.

"I will go when I please," I said hotly. "You are the servant here."

"You will not hold such esteem when the Greek knows of your business here," she threatened. She turned on her heel to leave.

"Wait, Rada," Hori called. "It is me you are angry with. Please, do not go."

"You?" I turned to my would-be lover. "Why should she care?"

"He is my man, promised to me this past season." Rada smirked. "He will not have you, Little Flower. He plays with your petals, but he will take a true Egyptian woman to wife."

Wife. I had not thought that far ahead. Never in my fantasies was I a wife to some base sandal maker. In fact, I was no wife at all, for a true wife has but little worth other than to tend a household and bear heirs. In Greece, it was forbidden for a slave to marry. I'd thought only of gaining a little pleasure for myself, but marriage? I had not thought of it.

Still, here was an interesting prospect. If Hori wanted me, he would have to purchase my freedom. Perhaps, I could entice him to bargain for my freedom.

I could not breathe easily.

"Enough," Hori said. "Go, Flower. I will talk to Rada."

I didn't want to leave Hori to face a jealous Rada, but I could not risk Charaxus finding me here. I fled the workshop with a silent vow to return to Hori when I could.

All was well at the house. Menekhet had returned with a cask of beer, and Charaxus, still fiddling with his figures, said nothing. I supposed he thought the fresh cask was my doing. I gave Menekhet a string of glass beads and a kiss in exchange for his silence, something he would have given me at any rate.

Rada returned after some long hours with an exultant smirk and a spring to her step. She said nothing to me and, as far as I knew, nothing to Charaxus. I wondered at her strange expression, but what could I say aloud that wouldn't bring suspicion onto myself? And after all, Hori had sought out my company, not hers. Perhaps she'd lied. Why should she return with a smile? Oh, I could not bear to think of the two of them together.

"Petal," Charaxus called out the next morning as I passed. My heart leapt into my throat. "Come here. I've had word from your friend."

"My...my friend?" My voice squeaked. Rada had told.

Charaxus frowned at my hesitation. "Yes, your friend Aesop, the Fabulist. It seems he will be in Sais in a few weeks. He travels by way of Naukratis. Shall we invite him to visit?"

My limbs grew weak with relief. Aesop. How long had it been since I'd seen my old friend and mentor? I wondered what he would think of his Little Crab, finding happiness at last.

"Certainly." I kissed him on his stubbly cheek, and tried not to think of my smooth Egyptian lover as my master's hand slid up my buttocks. "I should love to see him." I disengaged his hand. "I shall make preparations."

Charaxus turned back to his tally books, and I exited, bumping into

Rada on my way out.

"Rada," I said, taking her arm and leading her away from Charaxus. "We need to prepare for a guest. He will be here in a few weeks."

Rada gave me a filthy look.

"Another man to satisfy your lusts?" She tossed her silky hair.

I sighed. I should try to make peace with her, for my own sake, if not hers.

"I'd no idea Hori was your man, Rada. And no action from him would have given me cause to believe it. He invited me to his shop yesterday, not the other way around."

Rada's brow furrowed. "I don't believe you."

"Believe it or not. Hori invited me there and kissed me of his own will."

Suddenly Rada looked much less certain of herself. "But, but...he said...." Her voice trailed away. She stopped and gave me a hard glare. "Stay away from Hori," she warned.

"Or what?" I could not help retorting as she sauntered down the hall.

She did not answer.

That night I begged off Charaxus attentions, citing my woman's time which was still a week away. I marveled that despite my regular cycles and his attentions to me, I'd not conceived a child. It was a blessing from the gods, I was sure, but strange nonetheless. I wondered if he ever questioned my fertility, as I had his.

I lay in my own bed and tried to recapture the heat from Hori's touch by stroking my fingers in a lazy circle around my nipples. I should not think of him, I knew this. But, I was naive then, and knew only that I desperately wanted for something more—something of my own design.

So, I tried to conjure up my passion with Hori. When that failed, I stuck my hand between my legs and rubbed myself as I had not done since my time with Mara. It did not relieve the ache clenching my womanhood. Without a lover, I could not gain release. I needed a smooth, hard body pressed against me, so I left off and tried to sleep.

It was far too hot this evening. My skin prickled all over as if I slept on a bed of needles. I tossed and turned until my pleated gown became a twisted rope between my legs. I felt guilty for lying to Charaxus; really, my master treated me better than any man had. I owed him my honor and loyalty. What did it matter that I was his property?

But, it did matter.

Ah, Lady, I prayed. *You promised that I should live free. Can you not share some measure of your grace?* My eyes ached for respite. At last, I fell asleep with my hand still tucked between my thighs. I dreamt as I had not done since leaving Abdera.

The fair haired lady stood before my cosmetics chest. She admired herself in a gilded mirror. When she caught me peeping at her from under my bed linen, she raised an immaculate brow.

"You have forgotten me," she said with a sigh. Her voice rang in my head like a thousand brass bells. Or perhaps it was the rush of a thousand sparrows' wings.

I tried to protest but found I could not speak. The Lady raised her hand to my pots and I watched in fascination as she lined her azure eyes with Egyptian kohl. Her finger dipped into the pot and came away red with carmine. She rouged her cheeks and lips, quite unnecessarily for they were as lush and red as berries.

"I could never forget," I began. My mouth went dry at her beauty. "You are truly the most beautiful, the most desirable of women." I ached and trembled anew.

"So, I am." She smiled. "And so you will be. You have gained my notice. My attentions are not an easy load to bear. Yet all I have placed upon your shoulders, you carry. All and more."

"Wh-o...?" I licked my dry lips. "Who are you?" For, I was afraid she might be offended I did not know her.

"I am called by many names, in many tongues. I am 'She of the Sea'. I am the Cyprian, the Goddess, the 'Man Killer', the 'Lover'. I am 'She who Gives'. I am 'Yours'."

Cunning, crafty, beautiful woman. She would twist even Aesop's reasoning with her pretty pink tongue.

"A name!" I cried, my arms aching to hold her. "Give me a name, so I may sing your praises."

"A name?" said she. "I have many. I am Freyja, Urania...I am Astarte, Aphrodite, and Isis. I am Ama-no-uzme, I am Ishtar. I am Anat. Which of these names would you choose?"

I swallowed hard. Was this a test?

"I will have none of these," I said. My voice was thick with longing. "I will call you 'Love' and follow you all of my days."

The Lady drew nearer to my bed. My legs turned to liquid fire and I sighed as she kissed my brow. I swear my forehead burned from her touch.

"You have named me well. I shall make you a gift." And she drew from her gown two things.

One was a girdle of silver and gold. I gasped at its finery. It was rich and encrusted with gems, many of which I had no names for. The jewels gleamed in the moon's light, like fiery stars fallen from the night sky. Gold and silver ropes twined together in sinuous harmony between the jewels. The girdle seemed a tad narrow for my figure. Indeed, I thought it might just barely fit over my hips. She held it up for me to try.

I was right. It settled over my linen shift as if it were a second skin. I wore a true queen's ransom around my hips. No, not a queen's ransom--a treasure fit for a goddess. I wept as the bands embraced me. I'd never seen anything so fine as the goddess' girdle. She held up her gilded mirror for me to see.

"Oh, Lady," I whispered and admired my reflection. Tears poured down my face. What could possibly compare to this precious gift? I was more than just a slave. I was Beauty. What a treasure! What a fine, fine gift.

"Ah," she cautioned and waved her fingers before my eyes. "You must make a choice." With trembling fingers and much regret I released the girdle's clasp. I exhaled as the weight of it slipped free from my body for I had not realized how heavy it was.

She seemed amused. Her other hand extended from the folds of her pleated gown. When I saw what she offered, I did not know what to say.

A rose.

A single, perfect, living rose of the purest white. It was whiter than the untainted dove, paler than the foam on the waves....even purer than the white of my lover's pearly grin. Her fingers nestled cautiously between the sharp, spiked thorns on the stem. The scent of the rose was rich and sweet.

When she offered it to me, I cradled the fragile blossom between my palms--afraid even my skin might stain it. The stem wound around my arms like a serpent. I felt the prickle of thorns and loosened my grip. I took one last whiff of the rose's sweet scent and placed it back into her hands.

"Which of them will you choose?" asked the Lady. "Which of them suits you?"

Well, there could be no indecision! My hands reached eagerly for the fine golden girdle, but just shy of grasping it, I paused.

Was this yet another test? Could the two gifts really be what they seemed?

All my life I've reached for what I could not attain without forethought to the consequences. I dared not incur a goddess' wrath now. The hairs on the back of my neck prickled. There was more to this, I was certain.

"A moment," I begged and walked a few steps to the edge of my cot.

CHAPTER 18

Aesop had ever cautioned me to think before I acted.

Well, I could not afford to scorn a Goddess. The girdle was a treasure to be sure, but it was also an object of binding. Was it meant to constrain me in more than one way? And here was the rose she offered, wild and sweet, but thorny. A living plant grew and blossomed, reseeded and died, and grew again.

Did I deserve a goddess' treasure? Surely not. The Lady wished to see if my eternal pride would cheat her out of my loyalty. I weighed my options with no small measure of indecision.

The girdle served a purpose. That counted for something. It could be used. What use did a rose have other than adornment and adoration?

The Lady watched me pacing back and forth before my window. I caught her sly smile and the way her fingers tightened on her girdle. Slightly, yes, but I saw her. Did she loathe to part with it? Or was it the gift she wished for me to choose? Oh, the indecision was driving me mad. Where was Aesop with his logic to guide me?

"Your choice," the Lady cooed. "What is it?" She smiled archly.

I thought a moment more.

Thanks to my master Charaxus, I had treasures aplenty. The girdle was a lifeless thing. And I had been raised to treasure life and freedoms. The rose was alive, and so therefore, more precious to me. So, I made my decision.

I grasped the Lady's hand, the one holding the white rose. The thorns scratched my hands, and a jagged, painful line of crimson bloomed on the side of my marriage finger--the one leading to the heart.

"This is my choice," I gasped. I winced as the stem curled around my palms and more thorns stung me like a serpent. This is what I deserved from a goddess.

"So be it," said the Lady. I could not tell if she were pleased.

She drew my bleeding fingers into the hot, moist cavern of her perfect red lips. Her tongue laved the blood from my finger tip. In an instant, I arched in ecstasy, and my body convulsed and flooded with release. When she withdrew my finger to smile at me with blood-stained teeth, I awoke with a jerk in my cold, narrow cot. I glanced at my hands, but there was no mark from the thorns on my palms. The throb of fulfilled desire strummed through me like a lyre and the sweet scent of roses clung to the air.

I slept soundly the rest of the night.

The next morning Charaxus sailed to Naukratis, to check on the arrival of his Lesbian wine. With my master away, I'd decided to try out more of my new language by haggling for some new plants for my courtyard garden.

I successfully negotiated for a scraggly, white climbing rose, which reminded me in a vague and pitiful way of the Lady's gift. The blooms were ivory, rather than white, true, and the perfume not as potent, but still it would do. Some careful tending and I was sure I could make it grow.

"Flower." Hori caught my arm as I turned down a narrow side street. He pulled me against the nearest wall and crushed my potted plant between us. "I pine for you," he said and kissed me hard and quick on the mouth. He tasted like cinnamon. "Why do you not come to see me?"

The air between us was thick with heat and roses as the squashed petals released their fragrance into the air.

"Hori, please." I pushed him back and busied my quaking hands by fussing over the crooked stems. My heart took flight from his nearness and the touch of his mouth on mine. "You are Rada's man. I have no business with you."

Hori looked thunderstruck, as if Boreas had speared him with a lightning bolt. "No business?" he cried. "No business! What of love, sweet Flower?"

Love. The word buffeted around my thumping heart until I was sure my soul would leap from my chest and into Hori's arms. Perhaps this was the gift of my Lady? Was not the very symbol of it, the rose, here in my arms?

"You are promised to Rada." I protested.

"I am yours." Hori stroked the hair from my face. "Meet me in your garden courtyard when the moon is high." And he turned the corner and was gone.

I don't know how I found my way back home. Thank the gods it was a familiar route. Rada quirked her brow at me, but I turned away and went to the courtyard to plant my rose where the fragrance could waft into my room. As I raked the soil and watered the roots, my fingers trembled. What was I doing? Regret and anticipation warred within me. I should not have offered to meet Hori. No, wait, I deserved this. This is my goddess' gift.

Hori of the smooth copper skin and the pearly white teeth.

I could not eat the evening meal, for indecision made me ill. The servants cleaned up without comment and retired for the evening, leaving only old Menekhet and Rada. How I wished Rada would go home to her own family. But she and the old man Menekhet lived at the house. Still....

"Rada?" I caught her in the hall. "I wish you to visit with your family tonight. Your mother must be longing to see you."

I caught a flash of yearning, quickly replaced by suspicion in Rada's kohl-rimmed gaze.

"Why?" she asked.

My heart sank. I am a horrid liar. "Charaxus is away." Why not state the obvious? "I am retiring to bed. I...I haven't felt well all day."

True enough. I'd been unable to sit still for longer than the briefest of moments and I'd eaten nothing all afternoon. My stomach churned to burning froth and butterflies.

"You should take this opportunity to visit with your family." Ha! She could not turn down my offer without appearing to be ungracious. I felt a stab of guilt. Hori might not want her, but I still wished her to be happy.

Rada considered me for a long moment. Then, she smiled. "Thank you. I will."

I watched her depart until the swaying outline of her silhouette faded into the sunset sky. Then I paced the hallway until Menekhet gave me a toothless grin. I shooed him towards the slave quarters with a stern glare. His shoulders drooped as he trudged out.

The moon crept across the indigo sky. I brushed out my hair and put on my best gown, wondering if Hori was as anxious as I. His lithe form danced through my thoughts as I rubbed cosmetics into my nipples in Egyptian fashion. I imagined his hand caressing me and they beaded with the pressure. Would he think me alluring? I hoped so.

He must want me, I thought. I needed Hori to buy my freedom from Charaxus.

Moments stretched to minutes and minutes seemed like hours. I tried to chart the moon's path through the sky as I had been taught in the temple, but there were far too many stars. I jumped at every sound, so I lit a small lamp hoping for comfort from night's cool blanket. Chill bumps puckered my exposed flesh.

When the moon was directly overhead, I began to worry. What could be keeping Hori? Had he been attacked by thieves? Or, far worse, was he already in the arms of another woman? Rada had been exceedingly eager to leave. Perhaps she...a soft thump at the far end of the courtyard interrupted my thoughts. I leapt up from the bench, wishing I had something with which to protect myself. I brandished my garden trowel, abandoned earlier that afternoon.

"Mrrrrow?" Ankh stalked from the shadows and rubbed his stiff whiskers and furry head on my ankles. Weak with relief, I tossed the trowel into the bushes and laughed at my own foolishness.

"Naughty beast," I whispered as I gathered him into my arms. His soft, furry body smelled like oleander and dust. He squirmed and leapt to the ground.

"Oho," I said. "My ankles will do, but not my embrace, you capricious thing!" Ankh padded into the darkness, his tail upright and twitching.

"Hello?" called a soft voice from just beyond my lantern's glow. "Flower?"

It was Hori!

I ran to him with my slippers jingling welcome. We embraced beneath the stars. Hori ran his hands through my hair and down my shoulders. He tweaked my nipples, cupping my bare left breast in his hot palm, and whispered unintelligible words into my mouth as he kissed me.

Oh, how sweet the taste of forbidden flesh! Hori should not be here, I knew this, and yet I could not resist the surge of my blood. At last I would lie with a man of my own choosing!

Hori felt warm and strong. His arms encircled me and I inhaled the scent of his skin rich with cedar and spice. What did I care if the weave of his *shenti* was not fine? The whites of his eyes shone like stars, beacons in the darker rims of kohl lining them.

"Your hair is soft as the feathery papyrus and your eyes as bright as the sun on the Nile," he said. His hand inched up my thigh. His hand squeezed my breasts urgently. "Kiss me, Flower."

I did, but perhaps Hori was not as practiced in the arts of love as I had dreamed, for my passion was not roused. Indeed, I did not feel anything. I tried to focus on him, many times I tried, without success.

Hori's hand crept again and again up my thigh. I don't know why I persisted in shifting away, but something was not quite right.

"Here, let us not stand as strangers," I said and pointed to the bench. We sat together. Hori kissed the back of my neck, but he did not please me.

"What is wrong?" Hori asked.

I did not know how to answer, save that this was not the greater glory I had imagined in my head. Still, I needed to entice him, for how else would a man wish to purchase me, if not for desire?

"Wait." I smiled to soften the blow. "Let me come to you tomorrow. I need to think."

"What is there to think of, but me?" Hori smiled winningly.

"I am in earnest, Hori. Go now, before we are discovered." I put my hands against his smooth chest and pushed him lightly to his feet.

He reached for me again, but when he saw I would not relent, he scowled like a child denied a favorite toy and clambered back over the wall without bidding me good night.

In the morning, Rada stomped about the dining hall. She plunked the platters of food in front of me. I kept my eyes and face neutral, but Menekhet stared at the pair of us as if we'd grown goat's horns.

As the morning meal drew to a close, I fled from Rada's temper and delivered some food to Hori. He had no woman to cook for him, and after last night, I wanted to play the part of an adoring lover. Perhaps it might entice my heart to be more moved by Hori's caresses. This might be my only chance to gain some measure of happiness that was not purchased or decided for me.

The thought of gaining freedom after so many years made my heartbeat quicken as I turned down the alley to Hori. As I entered the workshop, I saw Hori with his hands up the skirt of a pretty young Egyptian girl. She couldn't have been much older than I was when I'd left the temple. I watched his buttocks flex as he pushed into her. My stomach lurched. With each pleasured moan, every shred of interest I'd felt for Hori's affections dissipated like steam rising from the desert sands, along with my hopes for being free. I thought I might be sick.

The bread I'd brought slid onto the floor followed by the beer which sprayed over the effigy of Ptah, the artificer, in the alcove by the door.

Hori whirled, his eyes glazed with lust. "Flower?" He jerked away from the girl with an unmanly squeak, his upright phallus pointing like a spear at my heart.

It was then I realized that I was a mere vessel for his lust. He did not want me—he wanted anyone who was willing. Surely, this could not be the promise of my Lady!

Hori would never want to see me freed.

"Flower," he began. The girl turned her face to the wall.

"Don't." I backed away. "Never darken my house with your shadow again." I turned and ran up the side street before he could come after me.

If he even planned to come after me at all.

I'm not certain how I made my way home. My mind reeled, and I think my feet moved of their own accord to the paths of slavery where I was most accustomed. I wandered through the marketplace for some time, until Rada found me and dragged me home. She must have been spying on me again. She clutched my arm and pushed me into the house of Charaxus, scolding me all the while.

Well, if she knew my shame, then so would the entire city, and if the city knew, then Charaxus would find out soon enough. I did not care. My heart was swallowed up in misery. Why was I so lacking that I should not inspire love, even in a lowly craftsman? I'd hoped his love would win me my freedom.

I crawled onto my bed and would not eat for the rest of the day or night. How much I wanted to cry, and yet I found I could not. I was as dry and empty as the vast desert beyond my courtyard walls.

I stared up at the ceiling of my room and prayed to the Lady. Aside from a dream rose, my prayers had gone unanswered, and while the dream was as vivid as the roses growing in my garden, it was of little consequence to me. Perhaps she held no power here, but I prayed nonetheless.

Lady, I am your servant. I do not understand why you withhold your gifts from me.

I was so desperate to be free I would have given myself over to an unfaithful craftsman. I was worse than unworthy of my goddess. I'd called her Love, and yet I had not followed my heart. Truly, I was a desperate and stupid creature.

Charaxus arrived home the next day. I should have seen what was to come, but I was too full of my own grief to notice. My goddess had abandoned me.

"Doricha?" He found me by the pool. He looked tired. I swear he shriveled before my eyes.

I tried to muster some emotion that he had returned to me safely, but I could not. I was shackled, perhaps forever to be his woman. And no proper woman at that, for my heart was dead.

I looked away.

"Petal? What is it? What is wrong?" He knelt and embraced me. The scent of salty brine was still on his robes, and his hands left filthy smudges on my skin. At that, inexplicably, tears pricked behind my eyes. I began to cry. I could not help it.

"Shh, Petal! I am here now. There is no need for tears. I am safely home." He rocked me in his arms.

I am ashamed now of the way I clutched at him--at the way I let him cradle me. How I fooled him into thinking the tears I cried were for him. I sobbed. I wailed. I pulled at my hair.

He lifted me in his arms and kissed me. He led me to the pool's edge and we sank into the water together, while my clothing dragged at our twining limbs. He kissed my cheeks, my lips and my eyes. I let him. I did more than let him.

I suckled his bottom lip. My fingernails marked his back as I clung to him and I panted like a wild creature, like the Maenads of my forbearers. I wanted him inside me with a desperation I'd never felt. I welcomed the bite of the pool's stone edge against my backside as he pawed aside the fabric floating between us and thrust into me. His tongue plunged into my mouth and I cried out with pleasure. I moaned and thrust my hips against him.

I wanted to feel something, anything....

"Ah, Petal, my love...my love..." Charaxus sank his teeth into my soft shoulder before he released his seed.

I reveled in the pain. I _felt_.

"Yes, yes!" I shouted as he spent himself inside me. "You <u>do</u> love me. You love me, Charaxus." I held him tightly, until his senses returned.

He stiffened and pulled away, staring at me with an odd expression. His eyes became suspicious. "You are different, Petal. What goes here?"

I could not bear to look at him. I slogged out of the pool and peeled the sodden clothing from my skin. I hoped the sight of my nakedness would distract him, but it did not. The haze of lust had already faded from him.

"Petal? What has happened while I was away?" His brows drew together.

"Nothing," I lied. "Nothing happened." _I thought to love an Egyptian craftsman who did not love me_, I finished in my head.

Charaxus frowned and pushed me towards the house. "Get dressed."

I sloshed to my room, spattering droplets of water like tears the entire length of the hall. With shaking hands, I pulled on my second best dress. I heard Charaxus call to Rada and the other servants to make a report. What would they tell? What could they say? I had not done anything with Hori, really. Just kissed his supple lips and stroked his smooth, copper skin. I'd let him touch me, but not for long. Let Rada make her report. I told myself I did not care but I crept nearer to the doorway and strained my ears for any sound.

Silence fell over the house. After a few moments, I went back and dried my hair. I tried to arrange it; without Rada's hands to help me, I could not train my long locks into any semblance of order. I let it dry, long and flowing as a young girl's. Then I waited and waited longer still.

I was about to abandon my wait and seek out Charaxus for myself, when he appeared in the doorway. His eyes burned and the hair stood out on my arms.

"Tell me," he said softly. I could not face him. "Tell me the truth, now. I would hear it from your own tongue." He moved towards me and trailed a finger over my love-swollen mouth. "Your own...lying...tongue."

I began to cry again, this time out of fear. "Please," I whispered. "Please."

He drew his hand back and slapped me full across the face. I fell to the ground. Shock raced through me, but I did not feel the pain of his blow.

He'd never struck me before. _Never_.

"Charaxus, master...please," I sobbed. "I never meant to...to hurt you. He was a boy, just a boy. I did not lie with him. I'll never shame you again, I swear."

He yanked me to my feet by my hair. Pain singed my scalp, a thousand needles of flame. He released my hair with such force I stumbled backwards against the wall. He grabbed my shoulders and shook me brutally.

"How could you? I gave you everything! Everything!" And he shook me harder. I cracked my head on the mud bricks. My vision wavered. "You were mine to do with as I pleased. How could you dishonor me, dishonor my household, in such a way?"

"I'm so-or-ry. Charaxus, please. Forgive me." I put my hands up and tried to protect myself, but he struck me again.

His open palm slammed against the side of my face. Blood gushed from my left nostril and I fell to the floor. I curled into a ball and waited for the next barrage of blows.

"Aaagh!" He whirled away from me and upended an inlaid chest, spilling my cosmetic tray to the floor. "Why?"

I cowered as he yanked my polished bronze mirror from the stand and smashed it atop the corner of the chest. The bronze disc crumpled, distorting the image of my fearful face. He tossed it aside.

"Why, Petal, why?" Charaxus raked his hands through his hair. He staggered towards me.

I feared another blow, and shrank in fear, but he knelt instead and cupped my bruised chin in his hands.

"*Why*?" he asked again, softly. His eyes raged.

"I…I thought he loved me. He said he did."

Charaxus flinched as if I'd struck him.

"I loved you." He sat back and put his hand over his eyes. "Wasn't that enough?"

Words formed for the emotions I'd kept bottled inside me for years.

"You own me. I am accustomed to lying with you because it is my duty. No, it was not enough. It was never love."

Charaxus wiped his nose with the back of his forearm. I flinched as he reached out to help me stand, but his touch was gentle once more.

"And today?" he asked quietly. "In the pool? What of that?"

I thought for a moment. "As you said. I am your woman to do with as you please."

Charaxus' face turned red. "You sound like a whore."

"I am your slave. If I sound a whore, then you have made me into one."

He paused. His chest heaved from the force of his exertions. Then he took me by the elbow roughly. "So be it."

He led me none too gently into the hall and called for papyrus, reed and ink. Rada brought it to him with a satisfied smirk. She made a rude gesture to me behind his back as she left.

"If merely speaking words of love was the key to opening your heart, I could have saved myself much time and effort." He pushed me roughly onto a stool while he wrote. "You imprudent girl, have you not learned how words can lie? No, no…you have not yet. But I will show you truth. In this last thing, I shall yet be your master."

His hands shook as lines of crabbed hurried script materialized on the papyrus like scorpion's marks in the sand. When he had finished, he blew on the scroll and turned it for me to read. There was a passage in Greek and one in hieroglyphs.

"Be it known to all from this day hence," I read aloud, "the slave girl, Doricha, is a slave no longer. She is freed by Charaxus of Mytilene, who loved her."

I stared at him.

His eyes were terrible to behold. "You are free, Doricha. For love of you, I offer your freedom. But for the shame of what you have done, I disown you. I want you out of my sight. I will no longer be responsible for you or your debts."

Just like that, I was no longer a slave.

I was free.

"Get out." He stood and turned away from me. "Go find this man. Perhaps he will have you now. You will find out soon enough how much freedom costs."

I stood. My legs trembled so badly I did not think they would hold me. I feared what words I might say, so I kept my jaw clenched tight. I reached for the papyrus from his limp fingers. His eyes dared me to take it. He let the scroll fall before I could take it and it fell to the ground.

I dropped to my knees, scooping the precious scroll and clutching it to my chest.

I was free.

Charaxus did not look at me as I left.

I packed only a few things including the *hetaera's peplos*--it was so tattered it was scarcely suitable to carry my few unbroken cosmetic jars and some trinkets, but I kept it. It was a healthy reminder I should never trust on the attentions or generosity of a man.

I looked once more at the cedar chests of fine Egyptian linens, the scented unguents, and the adornments Charaxus purchased me. Then I closed the lids, and shouldered my small pack. I would take as little of his gifts as I dared.

I kissed Ankh and stroked his soft fur one last time. He scampered after a loose feather without so much as a final 'Mrrrow' to bid me goodbye. Beautiful, fickle creature. He was just like Hori. I would never trust such soft beauty again.

The belled, rose-gold slippers, I left sitting in the middle of my chamber, a terrible reminder of following blindly the shame of my passion. My heart still ached at Hori's betrayal, but I forced myself to swallow the pain. For I vowed, I would need no one.

I shouldered my small pack, filled with only the essentials by which I would start my new life—a few trinkets, some of my cosmetics, and a linen wrap. When I was halfway down the street, someone called my name. Rada huffed and puffed after me. With a sharp motion, she thrust the jingling slippers into my hands.

"Here," she said brusquely. "Do not forget these! Take them so all the world will know, 'Here comes the whore!'" Then she spat on my bruised, swollen cheek and sauntered away.

I wiped her spittle away and felt better than I had in years.

I was free.

CHAPTER 19

I was free! As dawn broke, I ran to the marketplace with wings on my feet. Perhaps Hori would allow me to sell back the slippers for coin to send me home to Greece. At last, I was my own woman again. I wanted to see his face when he discovered I was no longer a slave to any man.

When I turned the corner to his workshop, there was no activity. No sounds of scraping or hammering, no clatter as he worked. Curious, I peered inside. The room was dark and empty. Gone were the bench and tools. Gone were the unused supplies laid neatly in rows. Gone even, was the effigy of Ptah from his alcove. The faint scent of beer clung to the air, but the workshop was dead.

"Where is he?" I asked the man in the nearest stall.

He shrugged. "Gone." His eyes returned to his work. "Yesterday."

So, Hori had disappeared last evening while I'd cried out the ache in my soul to an unmoved goddess. I didn't know what to think. Hori had vanished as surely as his affection for me. I had neither the desire nor the means to follow. In fact, I had nowhere to go at all. I was alone in a strange land with little money and even less understanding.

I trudged between the market stalls for hours. As the sun crept across the sky, my mood lifted. I'd no coin, but at least I could go where I wished, do what I liked, and speak to whomever I pleased. After years of slavery, I'd achieved my father's dying wish. My life was again my own. The familiar sounds of traders hawking their wares, the babble of heated conversation, even the buzz of the insects seemed alive and gay. I breathed deeply, inhaling spices and sweat and dust with lusty joy. I was free.

But when the sun reached its zenith and the flies became unbearable, my mind turned away from my freedom to a much more pressing concern.

I should leave this city, I thought. I will go home to Thrace. But how to get there with little to barter for passage?

My stomach rumbled. I'd no food, no shelter, and only the clothes on my back. I had little to barter with other than some cosmetic pots, a few trinkets, and my rose-gold slippers, all carefully hidden in my knotted _peplos_. Why had I not thought to take more?

I should trade my cursed slippers for something more useful. But when I pulled out Hori's treasures to barter for some dried fish and figs, my heart seized in my chest. I could not give up my slippers, yet. Such a treasure would be worth far more than sustenance; it would be the means to deliver me home. I needed them to buy my passage back to Greece.

Where to go now?

A rising chant emanated from the temple, rising over the noise of the marketplace. It mingled with the rising joy in my heart. Despite my guilt over having shamed Charaxus, I owed the gods my thanks, so I went to the temple to pray. Charaxus had told me Egypt was the mother of all religions, I felt certain I would be welcome. Perhaps not in the innermost sanctuary where only the most influential and devout were allowed, but a courtyard would suffice. Surely my Lady would find me here and guide my footsteps. How long had it been since I'd made an offering to her? I do not think the goddess could live on dreams alone.

I traded away my pot of rouge for three long, thorny stems of white roses. Market stalls closed for the afternoon as I passed. I could only hope there would be few penitents at the temple, for I was uncertain of how I'd be received, especially without the influential Charaxus beside me.

Wearily, I drifted into the temple. Few Egyptians paced the inner courtyard. None of their attire was particularly fine, and I breathed a sigh of relief. I would be less noticeable, as the upper echelons I'd traversed at Charaxus' side would have worshipped in the morning, long before the day's tasks began.

The lesser priests and scribes' dark kohl rimmed gazes passed over me with lingering interest and more than a little curiosity, despite their vows of celibacy. I could not tell if it was my foreign features or my bruised cheeks that gave them pause. The chief priest, denoted by a spotted animal fur, directed the others to separate the offerings for purification in a line of wide ceremonial vessels. A scribe made a tally mark on papyrus and when the lot was finished, he rolled it up and dropped it into a huge alabaster jar. Such vessels are used by Pharaoh to make an accounting of offerings; I'd seen them in the temple many times.

I handed the priest my three twined roses and his brow furrowed. I suppose my offering seemed odd compared to the usual wine, emmer wheat, and lotus blossoms. The sun gleamed off the priest's shaved head, reminding me of Hori and I averted my gaze.

The priest purified the pile of offerings in a large grey calcite bowl of water. He waved the other supplicants inside, but when I rose to follow, he shook his head.

"I wish to pray," I said in halting Egyptian.

He scowled and stalked into the shaded overhang, leaving me with the remaining two priests and a scribe who tallied the offerings. I caught one of the priests staring at me. He saw me looking and ducked his head.

I had to get into the temple. I'd been allowed inside before, when we came with some of the wealthier patrons. And I was no less humbly dressed than others who came in after me. Well, if they would not let me pray here, I would not leave my offering. So much for Charaxus' theory that all nations are welcome in Egypt. If I did not fear his revoking my freedom, I should march back and tell him so.

I moved to take back my roses, when a warm hand covered mine. It was the same priest who'd sneaked looks at me. He shook his head at me, motioning for me to take the roses and follow him. My heart thumped in my chest, but I followed him as he meandered towards a small side garden, nearly hidden by the outer wall of the temple complex. He turned the corner much quicker than I, and when I followed hard on his heels, I nearly ran into the back of him.

He faced me and grasped my shoulders to keep me from stumbling backwards. Then he put a finger to his lips, motioning for silence. Would he lead me into the temple in secret? When the priest checked over my shoulder once more, he pointed to an alcove against the side of the temple. In the alcove was a small bronze statue of a goddess. I whispered my thanks.

The effigy was the warrior goddess who protected this city--Neit. I hoped my Lady would not be offended.

Lady, if it be your will, remember me, your lost flower. I am dying here in this unforgiving desert. I give myself to you...I give myself to your will.

I pressed my head against the rough plastered mud brick and extended my arms, prostrate before her. Moments passed, but I neither heard nor felt anything, save for the tickle of insects when they landed on me. I raised my head and glanced back into the courtyard. The priests and scribes and supplicants had disappeared. I wiped the sweat from my forehead and resumed my prayers. For long moments I waited for my Lady to speak, but no sparrow called, no dove cooed. Perhaps she could not find me here? I prepared to leave, but I did not know where to go.

Voices murmured in the courtyard. One in particular sounded familiar. I stood and brushed the grit from my skin. Peeping around the corner, I saw Isesi's wife emerge from the second hall of the temple. None of her daughters were present, but two slaves carried loaves of bread, an amphorae, and lotus flowers--offerings for the goddess.

"Wakheptry," I called as she passed me in the temple courtyard.

She started and turned at the sound of my voice. "Greetings, Doricha." She scanned the crowded courtyard and she tipped her chin at the tattered *peplos* knotted to hold all my possessions. "Where is Charaxus? Have you brought offerings to Neit?"

I licked my parched lips. "I am alone, today." I stepped out of the shadows of the courtyard wall.

"Light of Ra, what happened to your face?"

"I...I was attacked." It was hard to force the words out of my dry mouth. I did not want to lie to Wakheptry if I could avoid it--I did not think it right.

"Come with me." She took my arm and led me to her home, which was not far from the temple.

When we reached the home of Isesi, Wakheptry called for sesame bread, honey spiced with cumin and, bless her, beer. I was so parched, I did not even care that she did not offer me wine.

I placed my bundled *peplos* on the ground and drank the cup of beer while Wakheptry's servants cleaned my cuts and put a cool wet cloth on my cheek. All the while, she muttered about thieves and murderers roaming the streets.

"I pray they will be caught." Wakheptry's eyes flashed. "Isesi says that Nesu Ahmose will tolerate no man's attack on property, but as he himself was once a...." She stopped and gave me an odd look.

I waited for her to finish, but she didn't. "What does Isesi say?" I asked, wondering what a scribe would have to say about thieves and murderers.

"Nothing." She fanned her hands in front of her face. "It is nothing. Here, let me pour you some more beer."

"Neit's Blessings upon you. It was fortunate for me that you brought a late offering to the temple." For nobility usually preferred to be the first in their adulations.

We made small talk for a while, until my head began to swim from the heat and the beer in my empty stomach.

"Poor girl." Wakheptry clucked her tongue. "Why don't you rest? The Greek will not be pleased if I let you wither away before he returns."

She meant well, but her words curdled my stomach. I hated to accept her kindness under false pretense, but I forced myself to agree. Besides, I was overtired from the day's activities. If Wakheptry wished me to rest here, it would be rude to depart now. At least not until the scandal of my freedom had reached her stratum of society.

I rested for a few hours in the shade of a huge pomegranate tree in her courtyard. The slaves brought us a plate of figs and palm dates. I watched fish swim to and fro in the pool, while her slaves fanned me and she directed her two eldest daughters to dance for me.

"They are not so fine at dance as you, of course," Wakheptry said with a sigh.

"Nonsense. They are perfectly lovely." I popped a date into my mouth. Wakheptry smiled broadly and poured me another cup of beer.

The heat of the day began to ebb. As the sky leached of color, Wakheptry called for the evening meal preparations and my nervousness grew. What if Isesi should have heard of my disgrace and found me here with his wife? I knew very little of Egyptian customs, but I was certain that disgrace would be punished, no matter the local customs.

"Wakheptry," I called, moving aside my emptied plate. "I am well, now. I-I should return. The others will be worried."

Wakheptry patted my arm and escorted me to the door. And while she protested, I thought she might have been relieved. "Let us meet again soon. I shall ask Isesi to give another feast in your Greek's honor."

I managed a weak smile, shouldered my _peplos_ and fled from her house of comfort.

Dusk fell. All around me market traders wearily packed away their goods. Some called out as I passed, hoping for a last minute barter. Little did they know I had nothing to give, without the benefit of Charaxus' deep coffers.

I wandered until it grew difficult to see. The streets were eerily quiet now the din of the crowds had subsided. The Nile lapped at the banks and splashed against the stone jetty. I slipped from alley to alley, feeling like a shade from Hades. At last, with no one to say 'nay', I crept into Hori's abandoned workshop and crawled into a ball on the floor for the night.

The workshop was musty with old memories. I could still smell the scent of spice, cedar shavings, and beer lingering on the air. Tears formed behind my eyelids. When I opened them, I saw the moonlight streaming in through the high slatted windows. It turned the dust to stars.

What is the point of such sorrow, a small voice inside me whispered. _You were meant to please gods, not craftsmen._

The small voice reminded me of another voice long ago--the words of Merikos the priest. My mother had been trained to pleasure the gods. And yet she was as blind as I when it came to the struggle of love. Was I destined to her same fate? To betrayal?

I wished I had Mara to comfort me. She was older than I, and certainly a woman by now. How many nights did we whisper to one another about the dreams and desires of our hearts? She would have known what to do, even if my mother would not.

For the first time in many years, I was completely alone, without even a master to order me about. It had been four years since I was free. The elation I'd felt earlier at my freedom melted away to uncertainty and fear. I found myself longing for Thrace, for the rocky hillsides and rough hands of Thracian warriors. I ached for the language of my forefathers, spoken from the tongues of dour Perperek women. What would the forests look like at home? How did the villagers fare after the Greeks attacked?

Home. How long had it been since I'd seen my beloved homeland? If only I could reach Naukratis, surely I could find a way to gain passage home. I was so heartsick for familiar sights and sounds. I needed to leave Sais, with all its memories of Charaxus, Hori, and unfulfilled dreams.

Tomorrow, I vowed. *Tomorrow I will find a way to Naukratis.*

In the morning, I rose well before the sun, lest someone spy me hunkered down in the empty workshop. I was stiff from my night on the floor, and hungry besides, but I dared not barter my cosmetics and trinkets for food or drink. I had a more important purchase to make--passage home.

I slunk through the alleys toward the river where a few slaves already awaited cargo barges. Several young men trapped birds and fish with nets for the daily market. Much further down the bank, a band of ragged women dug up cattails and papyrus roots, keeping a close eye on the docks. No doubt they'd be shooed away.

I moved closer, thinking I would be more welcome amongst my own sex. Perhaps they could tell me how to buy passage to Naukratis.

The women glanced at me, but said nothing. I suppose my grimy skin and bruised face gave them enough of a reason to include me in their company. One by one, they dropped the starchy roots in a battered pot. When I saw one woman feasting on the flesh of the cooked tuber, my stomach rumbled again.

I rubbed a hand over my empty belly, and one of the women jerked her chin towards the rushes. When I dug up some roots of my own, she nodded to the pot. I scraped off the mud before plopping it into the hot water. In a few minutes that felt like forever, she handed me a cooled, white root on a flat lotus leaf. The meal was bland, but filled my growling appetite well enough, though my mouth watered at the smell of the fresh fish and the sight of fowl trussed not twenty paces away.

I wandered along the market's edge as they unloaded cattle, people and goods from the various docked vessels. Further out on the quay, a barge floated listlessly in the river's current, biding its time until space cleared on the dock. A thin Egyptian man made marks on papyrus as slaves massed a pile of goods, spices, and temple furnishings at the edge of the market. When one of the men pointed to the barge, the thin man nodded his head and said a word that stopped me in my tracks.

Naukratis.

The barge intended to sail for Naukratis, a one day journey by barge upriver. I could secure passage to Greece--perhaps even Abdera or Perperek! My heart pounded. How to get aboard?

"Excuse me," I said to the man with the papyrus. "How much to sail?"

He frowned at me and said something in rapid Egyptian. I shook my head indicating I did not understand.

His brow furrowed deeper. "No," he said, pointing to my hair. "Not for you."

Not for me? I didn't know if he meant because I was a woman or because I was not Egyptian, but his words stung. I had to get to Naukratis. I retraced my steps, this time calling out to the various skiffs and boats along the water's edge.

"Naukratis?" I called hopefully to each. My heart sank lower with each response. I trudged up and down the sandy dock, scuffing my heels as I went. No one, it seemed, was headed to Naukratis, save for the thin Egyptian man's barge--which I could not barter passage on.

I returned to the thin man, this time determined to win my way onto the barge.

"Please," I begged him. I drew my trinkets out of my knotted *peplos*. "To Naukratis?" I smiled winningly, in the same manner that had gained me favor in Charaxus' eyes.

The Egyptian man pushed my hands away. "No," he said. His eyes were hard as granite. He made an abrupt motion with his hand.

So, he would not be moved. I retreated to a shady overhang to think.

Several slaves gathered as the barge at last made its way to the dock. Under the orders of the thin Egyptian, black Nubians, pale Greeks, and golden skinned foreigners from a country I could not name hefted amphorae and sacks of grain to be loaded. As I watched them, I formulated a plan.

The thin man strode off towards the barge captain, shouting and gesturing in the air towards the sky and the diminishing pile of goods. The slaves mounted the gangplank to the barge, emerging from the darkened interior minutes later for another round. No one took the slightest interest in what they did, save for me. Who would notice if there was one more slave in the bunch? It would be dangerous…what if I couldn't find a way to escape? No, I had to try. This could be my only chance to leave the pain of Sais behind me, my one opportunity to find a way back to Greece.

I tore a piece of linen off the bottom edge of my long skirt. The ragged threads now hung to my knees, a perfectly acceptable length for a laborer, no matter their sex. The scrap I tied around my long hair to hide its color and length. There was little I could do about my pale flesh, but hope to be lost in the mass of Greek, Nubian, and Egyptian slaves huddled around the gangplank.

I hunched my shoulders to disguise my height, and shuffled along with the other slaves towards the huge pile of goods waiting to be loaded on the acacia barge. There were a few sacks of grain left, carved temple effigies of stone or metal, several goats and sheep huddled together, dozens of amphorae filled with flax oil or beer, hemp rope, papyrus rolls, coiled baskets and chests of spice and more. Once I was aboard, perhaps I could find a place to hide during the journey.

When it was my turn, I hefted a medium sized basket of cumin seed. My mouth watered at its musty scent. Balancing the basket on my hip, I shuffled up the wobbly gangplank into the lower hull, where men and women deposited their loads and returned for more. The ceiling was very low and I immediately felt cramped into the small, dark space. The bottom of the boat bucked and heaved. I stumbled into the woman in front of me. She did not even turn around, it was so crowded, but I heard her murmur something sounding like a curse. The air inside was hot and stuffy, and reeked of sweat and spices, but I did not care. I had to secure passage to Naukratis.

On the first trip, I scouted the belly of the ship for any cranny that might conceal me. Already, three double deep aisles of carefully stacked ceramic vessels of various sizes were positioned so they would not tip. They ranged from knee to chest high and were piled almost to the ceiling to create an aisle. In between the aisles of goods, narrow walkways were left uncluttered so someone could count the cargo and inspect it during the journey downstream.

As I positioned my basket, I glanced into the almost completed third aisle. In the farthest shadowed corner gleamed two huge alabaster jars, each easily as high as my waist, similar to the ones I'd seen in the temple of Neit. When the season ended, the jars would be shipped back to Sais for Pharaoh to peruse.

"Move," grunted the slave behind me.

I ducked my head and returned back to the quay to heft another load. I wondered if the jars were already filled--surely not for they were headed away from Sais, not towards. Alabaster is quite heavy. The jar would not tip or wobble during the voyage for the Nile is fairly smooth, unlike the cresting sea. I could hide inside without tipping it over.

I made another trek into the barge, this time with a small wooden chest carved with four winged goddesses. I glanced over my shoulder at the gleaming alabaster jars.

Each jar bore a pearly cap, as papyrus will spoil if it becomes damp. This could work to my advantage. I returned to the diminishing pile of goods on the dock, thinking all the while. I could leave the lid propped just so and still breathe during the day's journey. My legs might cramp, but I could manage it. Did anyone stay below deck during the voyage? With the heat and stench, I doubted it. And if they did, well, I could be silent as a mouse when I wished.

At the end of the journey, I could escape when the other slaves began to unload the cargo. It would be a great risk if I was discovered, but at least I had the opportunity. I could get to Naukratis and sail for home.

I was forced to make five trips before an opening came for me to hide myself. We'd neared the last loading of the amphorae, and all that remained were pieces of statuary. I'd almost given up hope as I scooped up a carved, painted statue. But, when no one followed on my heels, I swallowed hard and scooted towards that third aisle, now completely covered by a fourth, fifth, and sixth row. I could hear the slosh of water against the boat's hull. It sounded very near my feet. Hastily, I removed the lid and crawled over the edge of the translucent jar, replacing it so I was completely concealed.

My heart pounded in my chest. All was dark. My head brushed the top of the jar, even with my bowed posture. The walls were completely smooth, and I had to balance with my knees touching my nose in order to fit all the way in. I wondered if anyone could tell the jar was now filled. Did my red-gold hair show through the near translucent stone? What if someone noticed?

I heard guttural Egyptian and almost cried out in fear. What if they came looking for me? Oh, the punishment that would befall me if I were discovered. The muffled voices sounded close, very close.

There was a horrendous scraping, followed by a pronounced thump. The pat-shuffle-pat of retreating footsteps. Then silence. While the interior surface of the stone jar was smooth and cool, the air inside rapidly became unbearably hot. I forced myself to slow my breathing. Sweat beaded on my forehead and soaked my underarms and back. I crouched with my knees touching my chin and my back against the hard curved side of the jar. Minutes passed and felt like hours. Then I heard the far off shout and the barge lurched.

We'd set sail for Naukratis.

CHAPTER 20

I curled in my alabaster hideaway as the rocking of the barge and the stifling heat made me drowsy. I don't know how long I slept, but it wasn't long enough to dream. I awoke with a start of fear, confused and disoriented, only to realize I was still undiscovered in my cramped jar.

After a few more moments I had to ease the ache in my back. My legs were numb as I carefully braced the backs of my heels against the smooth surface. I paused, gathering my courage and straining my ears for any sound. Hearing none, I maneuvered the lid off the jar and stood. My knees were stiff. One minute passed, then two, before I dared to slip over the edge and onto the floor of the swaying craft.

With a sigh of relief, I stretched my limbs, just as I had long ago in Lukra's dance class. Could there be any water aboard? I wished I knew which amphorae held wine; my throat was so dry! I dared not risk peeping into any of the vessels, for surely the whole stack would tumble down if I were to unsettle them.

I poked my head around the corner, fully expecting to hear a shout of alarm. My nervous heartbeat hammered my chest like Boreas' forge. But there was no one about. I paced a few turns up and down my hidden aisle. My heart fairly leapt out of my chest when I heard the scuffle of steps above my head and I dashed back to my jar, climbed over the edge, and pulled the lid on top.

Three times during the voyage, men came to check on the goods. The last time, I'd barely made it inside my jar when I heard someone sneeze at the far end of the aisles.

I gritted my teeth and tried to slide the lid as over the opening. To my own ears, the grind of stone on stone sounded impossibly loud.

"What was that?" I heard a voice say. Footsteps drew nearer.

Lady, I prayed, *save me*. I held my breath. There was a long pause, where

I imagined them hovering over my jar, ready to capture me.

"Filthy rats," the voice said at last.

When their footsteps retreated into silence, I exhaled and swore not to leave my jar again.

It was a short-lived promise, although I did my best to stay hidden as long as possible. The trip to Naukratis took most of the day, and when the heat of my confinement grew unbearable, I propped the lid on the edge and gulped the cooler air like a hooked fish. At times, my back and legs cramped so much tears poured down my cheeks. I tried flexing my fingers and toes to keep blood flowing into my numb extremities. My throat was so dry I had not even enough moisture in my mouth to lick my dry lips. I thought I would die of thirst before we ever reached Naukratis.

As luck would have it, I did not die of thirst, but awoke from my second heat-induced nap to the bump of the barge striking the dock. Shouts sounded from outside, and I breathed a sigh of relief. We'd reached Naukratis at last!

I waited until I heard the rustle of slaves descending into the far aisles of cargo. There would be no way to tell if someone stood within view, so I whispered a prayer and eased the lid off the top of the alabaster jar. Nothing happened. I exhaled and gathered my courage. One, two, three...I stood up.

The hold was empty.

Whispering thanks to my Lady, I replaced the lid of my jar and moved towards the diminishing aisles of amphorae. Two slaves descended and loaded themselves with sacks of grain. One of them gave me a questioning look as I emerged from the dark recess of the ship's hull, but I ignored him, straightened my kerchief and hoisted the nearest vessel. The liquid inside sloshed against the sides of the amphora, much like the river crested against the barge.

I breathed deeply as I walked down the gangplank towards freedom. How thankful I was, when at last I could draw a breath that was not musty or rank with rat feces or body odor.

The cool breeze sifted over my sweaty skin as I waited my chance to tread on dry land. The air reeked of pitch, fish, and wet rope, but to me it smelled like freedom. I balanced the amphora on my hip, and tucked my knotted _peplos_ under my arm. Sweat began to dribble down my forehead. I shook my head like a dog, but the salt of my skin stung my eyes and blinded me. I yanked off my damp linen kerchief to wipe the stinging sweat out of my eyes.

"You!" shouted a voice behind me.

Dread raced through my veins like chilled wine.

The thin Egyptian man hovered over my shoulder, his hollow reed still poised above the papyrus where he marked the tally of each load. Our eyes met, and his gaze was as cool and slimy as the oil I carried.

"Guards," he said, not loud enough for any of them to hear. I think the angry shock of finding me aboard had closed his throat so only a furious hiss escaped his thin lips. His dark glare bored into my skull.

I dropped the amphora. It shattered and oil splashed my ankles and the stringy hem of my torn gown. Pale golden oil coated the gangplank and dripped into the Nile rippling below. The thin man's mouth opened wide to shout.

In a flash, I took to my heels, slipping a little on the oily, sun-baked gangplank. The Egyptian bellowed in rage. Clutching my sodden bundled _peplos_, I pushed a slave carrying a large wooden chest out of the way. The unfortunate wretch tipped off the end of the gangplank and into the swampy shallows near the docks. Curses broke out behind me, but I did not stop. I ran as fast as I could, with no clue to what direction I headed.

The streets were a blur of white plaster buildings, copper bodies, and hot sandy streets burned my bare feet. Scents assaulted me as I gulped for air--the fishy brine of the river, burning pitch, and animal dung, gave way to the clearer scent of spices and baking bread.

My chest burned like flame. I turned a quick corner and paused to catch my breath, my back pressed safely against a building. Over the din of the marketplace, I could not tell if I was being pursued. A sharp pain in my left side flared each time I gulped for air and my legs started to cramp. Here, in Naukratis, I was free and yet more afraid than ever of being caught. I laughed until I cried.

Once the tears started, they would not stop. I slid down the side of the building and collapsed on the sandy ground. I wept for those I'd left behind at the temple--friends, teachers, and family. I wept for the sorrow of slavery, for the years I'd been beaten and starved into submission. I wept for love, for the loss of Mara, my near sister, for my family. I wept for passion, for Charaxus, a man in search of love himself, and for Hori. How much I'd misjudged them both!

I sobbed until I had no more tears left in me. Thank the gods there was no one about then; they would have thought me mad, although I would not have cared.

At last, with my eyes almost swollen closed, and my nose running, I ceased weeping. Though I could hear the clamor and din of a nearby market, the noise and stench were muted. I rested against a private home. The houses here were further from the stink of the river. I could hear children laughing around the corner.

I did not know how long the thin Egyptian man would be on the docks. No doubt he planned to stay the night in Naukratis; it was already late in the day. Egyptians fear to travel the Nile at night for it is a perilous undertaking with hidden sand bars and floating islands. I could not go back to the docks, so I spent the few remaining hours of light searching the area to get my bearings. I discovered a cold, dark corner nestled between two ramshackle buildings where I could rest, hoping I would not be accosted by thieves.

The night passed without incident, although I shivered both from fear and the cold. Hunger gnawed at me and thirst choked my throat. Though at last I grew numb to the discomfort, I was still much too afraid to sleep. I jumped at every sound, from the scratching of rats to the murmur of voices from three streets over. Heat leaches from the air when the sun sets. My joints were stiff when I roused the next morning, and my eyes bleary from lack of sleep. I needed to find water, so I set out towards the market near the river.

Everything was familiar and then not, in this city. Naukratis was far different than Sais, and I felt a little lost among the conglomeration of races. There were so many people here. I prayed at least one vessel headed from Egypt.

I traded my cosmetics palette and mixing sticks for some beer, dried fish and bread, figuring I could smear kohl around my eyes with my fingertips. My mouth watered as I crouched by a trader of grapes, but I dared not snitch even the fallen ones. I did not want to be chased out of this city before I gained passage home, for then I truly would have nowhere to go.

I packed most of my food into my knotted _peplos_, contenting myself with only a few bites of bread. I needed a plan to get to Greece. First, I went to the docks, still leery of the thin Egyptian man, but the space where his barge had been moored was empty. A heavy weight lifted off my shoulders. I was safe.

I meandered between the traders and sailors, trying to find a vessel I could barter passage on. Tongues babbled in odd dialects, and everywhere was the noise of people. Cats streaked up and down the dock and slaves loading and unloading goods took care not to tread upon them, which is no easy feat with so many about. No wonder the rats kept a wide berth on the quays, preferring to infest the houses or cargo boats instead.

By afternoon, my head rang with the noise of the crowds. As the market began to shut down, I drew an irritated breath. I'd learned nothing about gaining passage to Greece. Worse, when the market cleared, the docks cleared as well. So, I trudged through the maze of streets and alleyways, pausing at familiar doorsteps here and there until I found my corner from the previous night. Hours crept by, as I crouched and swatted insects and ignored my groaning belly.

As evening fell, I shadowed a group of sailors as they ambled wearily to brothels and inns. Perhaps I could overhear who sailed towards my destination, as the men guzzled their beer and wine. The innkeeper eyed me as I padded up the narrow staircase. A few Egyptian girls trailed behind me, their eyes heavily lined with kohl and cheeks rouged so fiercely they almost appeared feverish in the dark interior. I envied them their well-fed forms and finery.

Foreigners supped and drank inside the tavern. The men at one table in particular stood out as quite unusual. They wore armor over their midsections, and all had long, dark locks that cascaded like a horse's tail past their shoulders to their waists. One man had a young boy with him whose sole job, it seemed, was to care for his master's hair. He brushed it out and arranged it, even at the table. The other men took no notice, but I thought the grooming to be quite out of place. They were obviously not from this country, nor any part of Greece that I could remember.

I tried to slip into the shadows, but the long haired man spotted me and motioned me over. "Here, girl," he called in a heavily accented Egyptian.

The other men hooted and babbled in a tongue I did not recognize. One of them pulled his slanted eyelids into huge circles. The effect made hideous work of his brown, pockmarked face.

The long haired man called again. I did not wish to make trouble. The innkeeper jerked his chin at me, so I went.

"How much?" he asked in broken Egyptian.

His question angered me. Had I changed so little since Charaxus had freed me? Did I still look the part of a slave? Well, I suppose I did. Still, who was he to barter for me? I was not a common street whore! I was not one of those women who chased men for money!

I shook my head, but he repeated his question with more insistence. One of the Egyptian girls went to him and sat on his lap, glaring at me all the while. A second trod on my foot as she passed, though she moved as gracefully as the rest of her race and had no reason to stomp on my poor bared foot. I backed away, aware that this girl wished to encourage the man's attention.

My retreat seemed to satisfy them for the time being, for they ceased to pay me any attention. I tried to listen to the conversation, but all too soon, the long haired man and the girl rose and went downstairs. He gave me a dark look as he passed and tightened his hold on the girl's waist. I tried to melt into the shadows of the nearest corner, where I hoped to discover the ship that would sail me back to Greece.

The remaining patrons grew increasingly rowdy, and sweat trickled down my back. I realized just how precarious my situation was. Who would care if one of them should try to have his way with me? I was not such a fool then that I had forgotten the lessons of Young Iadmon. A man would have his dominance. I slipped away from the tavern feeling weak and lonely.

On my way out, I heard a grunt and shuffle from around the corner. I froze. There was a small cry and then nothing, save for the rustle of palm leaves in the breeze. I crept between the buildings, just in time to see the long haired man thrust his hips against the plaster wall. No, not the wall.

She was bent forward, her buttocks high in the air, while he mounted her from behind like the animals do. I heard her sigh. It had been a long time since I'd heard the sounds of desire. A budding tension coiled between my thighs as I watched them. I think it was the heat of the day, or the lack of food, but I was dizzy by the time they finished.

The long haired man withdrew and fished out a bauble from his robes. I could not see what it was, but the Egyptian girl rubbed her nose to his and straightened her skirts with a laugh. She clutched it to her chest and murmured, low and guttural.

Well, I would not be so low! I tried to picture myself trading such trinkets and sailing away to Thrace. It would not be such a bad bargain, but my flesh crawled at the thought.

The next day I had even less luck finding passage home. The seas were rough, and there were fewer ships moored at the docks. I called and called to the sailors, but no one was headed out of Egypt. Two weeks, they told me. The harvest will be finished in two weeks and ships will sail from Egypt. It seemed an eternity to me, with hunger, thirst and fear shriveling my body. But I would wait. I had to.

The docks were well patrolled and I could not dig for cattail or papyrus bulbs to boil. I was so famished I could think of little else but how to fill my belly. I eyed my knotted *peplos* bundle, thinking of the rose-gold slippers. Surely they would be enough to trade for passage home. I parted with the last of my cosmetics, my precious, eye-protecting kohl, to buy some beer and bread. I'd not noticed, sheltered in Charaxus' home, how much the kohl protected my light eyes from the glare of the sun and blowing grit. Out on the streets, my eyes watered and burned and I stumbled about like a blind drunkard.

To make matters worse, I was forced to trade away my last trinkets, a small tattered fan and a green faience cat, for a place to sleep. My corner had been discovered. Peacekeepers prodded me with staffs until I got up and moved. I wandered blearily through the moonlit streets, fear driving my weary steps until daybreak when I sank into the sandy marketplace and dozed for a few precious hours. During my nap, a thief tried to pry my knotted peplos from my grasp, but I woke and he ran off. I was too exhausted to shout for help. Besides, the peacekeepers would only ask me to move on.

I knew I would not last long without rest, so I bartered for two weeks' space on a filthy hovel floor. I dared not leave my *peplos* there, for there were a number of unsavory characters, twenty of us in all, packed into a tiny, sweltering room. How different than the rented room I'd stayed in with Charaxus. I took to drowsing in the afternoon, instead of evening; there were fewer bodies crammed on the dirt floor.

The first week passed like grains of sand in the wind—timeless and dreary. My shoulders and forehead blistered from the sun's rays. My stomach ached constantly for food, and my mouth was too dry to even wet my chapped, bleeding lips. Once, I went to drink from the *shaduf*, a bucket contraption that drew water from the Nile. After a few swallows of scummy, foul-tasting water, I left. That afternoon, my stomach rumbled audibly and my bowels turned to water. My limbs trembled and I was sick. I vowed not to drink of the river water again.

I went without food for the next three days, and my bowels stopped their cursed cramping. And then luck found me the next morning. I overheard some sailors discussing a barge set for Cyprus on the next day. Cyprus was not so very far from Thrace. Infused with excitement, I dared to approach one of the sailors.

"Please," I begged. "I wish to go to Greece. How much for a place on the barge."

The men eyed me with interest. Their dark eyes traveled up and down the length of my body.

"You alone?" one asked. I did not like his tone, and although I counted them as dangerous, this was the best and perhaps only chance I might get to barter passage to Greece.

"I am a slave," I lied. "My master, Charaxus of Mytilene, bids me come to him in Greece. H-he is waiting for me." I forced my chin up a notch.

"Why does he not send a ship for you himself?" asked the other, stroking his whiskered chin. His eyes narrowed.

"He...he did. I was separated from our household. And...and now my master is ill. I must get to Greece. Please, I can pay." My lies grew more convoluted by the minute. These men would surely see right through me.

The first man raised his brow at the other. "She says she can pay."

"Show us then," replied the other.

Did I dare to hope? Swiftly so they might not walk away, I unknotted the *peplos* and drew out my slippers. I saw their faces change from skepticism to disbelief to awe. The slippers were magnificent. They would believe me now.

"Fine," said the first, wiping his hand over his cheeks. He threw a glance over his shoulder. "But we have no use for slippers. There is a trader who deals in goods at the end of the next street. You get the coin for these, and passage you shall have."

Oh, great fortune! I thanked the men profusely before racing to the recommended trader. The men waved before heading towards a knot of sailors mending ropes near the docks. They gestured to me and grinned, no doubt telling their companions a place should be reserved for me. I strode down the street, filled with purpose, and scanned the signs for the trader's mark.

The interior of the shop was cool and dark. It smelled of earth and metal. Piles of goods were stacked haphazardly--polished granite effigies, bronze baubles, bright blue and gold faience cosmetic pots, papyrus and hollow reeds, and some jewelry.

The trader was shrewd. He took one look at my ragged appearance and said, "Get out. I have no use for you."

I cleared my throat. The merchants in Sais, well aware of Charaxus' deep purse, had been quite accommodating. What a difference, now that I had only myself to rely on. Still, I remembered my lessons from haggling in Abdera. I must not appear overeager, or he would short my exchange. I straightened my shoulders and used my most graceful walk to draw near to him.

"I wish to trade." I pulled out my slippers.

He blinked. "Stolen, no doubt," he replied, crossing his arms over his chest.

"They are not, they are mine. See here!" I put the slippers on so he might see they fit me well. His eyes glimmered when I did a little dancing step. The bells on my slippers jangled and a wave of guilt and heartache took me. I stopped mid-position and let my hands fall to my sides. I'd been loved once, not by the man who made these, but by the one who purchased them. I took the slippers off and handed them to the trader.

He named a price that was obscenely low. I could be insulted and leave, but then I might never have another chance to barter for I knew no other traders.

"I'd heard you give an honest price." I took back the slippers. He released them with slight hesitation. "I paid over three times that amount for them, from a craftsman to the Pharaoh himself! You will find nothing like them anywhere in Naukratis."

"You are tall for a woman," he said with a shrug. "And your feet are large. A buyer will not be easy to find."

My feet were not large! I was taller than most Egyptians, true, but my feet were delicate compared to some I'd seen in the temple. His words were an attempt to cover his ridiculous offer under the guise of sensibility. Well, I knew how to barter.

"We shall see what the next trader has to offer, then. Perhaps his wife has large feet, too." I moved towards the doorway, straining my ears for the sound of his voice, but he did not speak. A bead of sweat trickled down my forehead. Would he let me leave? Perhaps he really did not want the slippers? What was I to do now?

I took one step outside of his shop before he stopped me.

"Wait," he called. I turned to see him shuffling after me. "Wait! I might've been mistaken. Ah, see! The sun shines here, and your feet are not half as large as I thought. My old eyes." His eyes bulged and he blinked. I could not help but smile. We returned to the shop to haggle on a price.

In the end, he gave me much less than what Charaxus had paid, but I did not care. The sailors had marked him as fair, and so I hoped the coin he gave me was enough to satisfy them. I fidgeted as he counted out his offer, coin by coin.

I started back to the docks with the coins clutched to my chest. I ran as fast as I could through the alleyways and narrow side streets, avoiding the throng of the market and thinking all the while that tomorrow I would be closer to Thrace than I'd been in years. Something snagged my foot, and I tripped.

The coins flew onto the alley as I toppled face down. Quickly, I scrabbled in the sand for them, just as a foot stomped on my hands. I jerked it away with a yelp and looked up.

Three men stared at me, their mean eyes full of greed. I recognized them. They were companions of the two sailors who negotiated passage with me. I'd seen them in the crowd mending ropes.

"Tell them I'm coming," I said, thinking they'd been sent to hurry me along. I nursed my sore fingers.

One of them grunted and hauled me up by the arm with a grimy, chapped hand. "Give 'em over." He jerked my arm.

A second man gathered up the rest of my fallen coins, while the third looked beyond us to the corner.

"Please," I said. "I will take them now. If you just let me go, I will br-"

His hand clamped over my face. He shoved me back against the plaster wall and placed his other hand around my neck. Then he started to squeeze.

I could not breathe. His palm covered my mouth and his fleshy fingers smashed my nostrils. I squirmed, trying to get free, but he held me fast. The second started to look nervous.

"Give us the coins!" growled my attacker.

I shook my head as much as I could with his meaty palm holding me in place, and tried to kick him in the groin. He sidestepped and his fingers slipped off my nose. I gulped a mouthful of air before he clamped over my mouth again. My heartbeat pounded in my head. It felt as if my skull would burst.

He called for the others to search me and clamped his hand around my throat. Black fog clouded the edges of my vision. My lungs ached for air. I wheezed, trying to suck air between his fingers. The second man whispered a curse and pried my balled fists apart. His nails dug into my palms, like burrowing insects. One by one, he pilfered away my precious hopes.

When the all the coins were stolen, my attacker laughed. I gathered my strength and kicked him, this time connecting with his kneecap. He yelped and released me. My lungs felt like lead. I fell to my knees, gasping for air. The ground spun beneath me, and pounding pressure mounted behind my eyes. If I'd had anything in my stomach, I would have been sick.

"Someone approaches. We go, now!" called the third, who'd watched me with pitiless eyes. I heard the pounding of footsteps and dust sifted into the air. I pushed up to my knees, trying to stand. The sand burned my hands and stuck to my bloody scratches.

"Stay away from the docks," my attacker threatened as he made his escape.

I could not let them rob me of my homeland!

As soon as I was able to follow, I went to the docks. My knees trembled, but I had to try. With no money, and nothing left to barter, my last chance rested on the ship bound for Greece in the morning.

The sailors were nowhere in sight. I walked up and down the docks and poked my head into the inns, but I did not find them. I checked the long stone jetties and weedy fields along the river bank. I even went to the Egyptian whore house, but they would not let me in. So, I waited outside and scanned the face of every man until I could not see their faces, even by the faint light of the crescent moon.

I stumbled to my rented, stinking hovel and crawled into a miserable ball. Then I cried. I'd lost my dearest treasure--my rose-gold slippers. I'd bartered them for passage home, and even that had been stolen from me. What would I do now? How would I survive?

In the blackness, a voice echoed in my memory. *Live free. Live free.*

I would. I swore I would.

Tomorrow, I would rise before the sun and go to the ship. I would demand passage from those treacherous brutes. They could steal my coin, but they could not take my spirit.

CHAPTER 21

I went to the docks the following morning, well before daylight broke over the sand dunes to the east. A group of sailors gathered there. My knees trembled, but I searched for the pair who had promised me passage. At last, I found them, lounging near the jetty.

"You promised me passage," I said to them. "But your companions stole my coin before I could pay it."

"Do you recognize this woman?" one asked the other. The second picked at his teeth and looked me up and down.

"No," he said. "I've never seen such a sorry creature before."

"You have!" I protested. My heart raged with injustice. Just then, I saw a familiar man swagger down the gangplank. His mean eyes widened when he saw me. It was the man who'd kept watch in the alley.

He whistled over his shoulder. A flock of sea birds shrieked in the distance and the faces of my two attackers popped over the edge of the ship. They'd cheated me. This pair had set me up and stolen my livelihood.

The sailors began to laugh and one of them cracked the knuckles of his hammy fists as he strode down the gangplank. I took to my heels with my heart pounding, certain they meant to kill me. When I hid around the corner, I heard the creak of wood and calls of farewell on the dock, I knew my last chance to leave Egypt sailed with the sunrise.

For the next hour, I battled black despair. With nothing left to trade, I had no way to live, let alone barter my way back to Greece. My cheeks were bruised where the thief had ground his meaty fingers into them, and my palms stung from scratches. I had no food, no drink, no shelter and no way to gain any of them. I'd never felt more forsaken in my life.

So, this was freedom. Aesop was right.

I begged for work along the side streets, where I'd be less likely to find respectable homes bursting with plenty of slaves. I rushed over to an old

187

woman setting out lengths of woven linen and hemp, but she shooed me away, muttering curses. I must find work. I raced to the market, where I located the nearest spice stall.

"See here," I called to the crowds, giving the spice merchant my most winning smile over my shoulder. "The finest spice in Egypt. Here! Here!" If I won him customers, perhaps he would give me a little spice to trade in exchange for my efforts.

"Get away," he growled. "I have no need for you." His hands reached out to push me away, but I persisted.

"Look," I called, desperate to show my worth. "Smell the cinnamon. Who needs some red cumin?" I danced just out of his reach. He hefted a stick and shook it at me, clearly at a loss between chasing me off and staying near his stall. The sweet smell of melons from a nearby stall clogged my nose. I wanted to faint from hunger. I must show this trader how useful I could be! A few slaves going about their business chuckled, but no one came to buy.

"Ah!" I cried. "Have you ever seen such cloves? Just the thing to scent a lover's kiss. Who will buy?".The spice trader was just behind me now. I could feel his anger radiating over my bare neck. I sidled away and the crowds laughed louder. A few shook their heads, but still no one made a purchase. My shoulders slumped in defeat as the last of them moved away.

"You've cost me a morning's trade with your antics." A hand manacled my upper arm.

"Please," I begged. "I need to work. I have nothing."

He shook me until my teeth rattled. "Get away," he snarled.

I fled from his anger and crouched in an alleyway as far away from the food market as I could get. I must stay close to the docks or the market, in order to find work. The smell of spices and roasting meat made my mouth water. I heard a soft jingle, and I glanced toward the nearest side street.

A young woman with tattooed breasts sauntered past me in the direction of the docks. Her perfume tickled my nostrils. I watched her sidle up to a man coiling rope. She muttered to him and he paused and shook his head. She shrugged and moved onward, passing like a shadow over the alley until at last, one man nodded. She jerked with her chin over to the side street where I'd seen her emerge. I remembered the girl I'd seen at the tavern and had no question what she was about. She was a _pornai_, a common street whore.

Naukratis was a busy sea port. Every ship wishing to send cargo for trade into Egypt had to dock and make an accounting of his goods. The streets of Naukratis teemed with traders who were willing to bargain, and after so many weeks at sea, hungry for a woman's company…I bit my lip. No! I could not. She was not a priestess, who gave honor to the gods through her body, and I was a temple devotee no longer. This was a base occupation. And yet, what would be the difference between what I did for Charaxus and selling myself, save for this time, the choice would be my own? Aesop and my old master were right—I'd truly discovered the price of a woman's freedom.

I'd achieved my father's dying wish, and yet I'd never been sorrier. Pitiful, but at least I still retained the power to choose my own path. I was my own master. I could choose to curl into a ball and die here on the streets, or I could live. Surely my Lady had other plans for me, even if I could not see them yet?

Yes, I decided. My fate was my own. A whore Charaxus named me. A whore I must become. Until I gained enough wealth to barter my way back to Thrace I would humble myself. I would not honor the gods with my service, but I would fill my aching empty stomach. I watched the Egyptian woman emerge time and time again until I was certain how she'd done it.

I strode towards the morning throngs about the docks. A large ship had recently unloaded and there were an unbelievable number of traders swarming the quay--all of them haggling, passing goods, and tallying debts on papyrus and pottery shards. Surely one or two of the departing sailors would be enticed by the sight of my scantily clad form. I tore a strip of my linen dress, this time until the hem reached well above my knees. I used the strip to tie up my hair, in some semblance of style.

Crowds of people clogged the docks, making it difficult to move further than two paces at one time. Perfumed women flirted with haggard men of the sea. I swallowed the hard rush of panic clogging my throat. I did not think I could do this…a man caught the back of my skirts as I tried to escape the throng. By his features and voice, he was a Greek.

"See here, a Thracian flower!" he called. He wrapped his arms around me and I struggled as he planted a sloppy kiss on my cheek. "How much?" He shouted over the din. "How much for you?"

Bile rose in my throat. I could not answer, but I let him lead me into an alleyway, where he pushed my head low against the mud brick wall. I turned my face away as he fondled my breasts. His hands grasped my waist and he splayed my legs apart and speared me with his phallus.

"Ah," he groaned as he pushed inside me. "Ah, your sweet rosy flesh."

He took me there, with unsurprising quickness. It is my opinion all men are quick when they take no pride in their attentions. The juncture between my legs was sore when he finished, for I was as dry as the desert. But he, drunk and delighted, handed me a coin and staggered out of the alleyway. Coin. Coin meant food and drink for the next few days at least, but I could not help but feel a twinge of anger my attentions were worth so little.

'*Rhodopis*', he'd called me. *Rosy cheeks.* I suppose after the tawny, sun darkened natives, my pale pink flesh was a welcome draw. I'd use it to my advantage. I bought some beer and dried fish, and tried not to think of the sums Charaxus had squandered on me.

How foolish I had been.

I had many men in those early weeks. Faceless, nameless men, sailors who escaped the solitude of the sea and the company of other men. Foreigners who dreamt of home and called me by any name they chose. Egyptians who cursed my unfamiliar features even as they plunged themselves into me. I was a mere receptacle to assuage male lust.

The other whores roaming the streets spit on me when they sauntered past. I did not care. I hoarded my coins to buy only the scarcest amount of food necessary to live. The rest I spent on dried crocodile excrement and a tincture of honey to prevent unwanted babes from forming in my womb. The pungent mixture stung when I inserted it, but since my Lady had not visited me since I'd left Charaxus, I was not certain if her promise to "close my womb until Love should open it for me," would hold true. I suspected Charaxus was infertile and I'd never tested my faith by lying with Hori; as much as fertility is revered in Egypt, I must be cautious now.

I serviced sailors and tradesmen who stank of fish and sweat. Sometimes one, sometimes many at one time. I pleasured them without adulation to the gods on my lips, true blasphemy. At the end of each day, I crawled into a filthy corner of the deserted market. How well I deserved this fate! To eschew a fine home and adoration of a kind man, to be the whore of multitudes.

A season passed, endless days of living in the slums and whoring in the back alleyways. I never seemed to have enough coin to feed my growling stomach. For being a common street *pornai*, meant the lowest of coins to be paid to use my body. I was a thing, an object—nothing more. How I lamented the memory of how Charaxus had tried to woo me with gifts!

Though the air and heat were stifling, a deep, barking cough kept me awake, even when I prayed for rest. I grew thin and snappish. Ill humors rattled in my chest when I breathed, and I was hot and cold by turns. I suffered on a ragged mat until the sun burned high in the sky. The few times I dozed, I dreamt of my poor dead family.

Doricha, my treasure. It was my father's voice. *Do you hate me for it?*

"No, Papita," I whispered. I awoke with a jolt, disoriented in the afternoon sun. "Papa?" White flashes speckled my vision. I blinked them away.

The trader in the nearest stall traced the Eyes of Ra in the air.

My reddened eyes and fevered brain kept most of the potential patrons at bay. The few times I did manage to snag a sailor too drunk to be concerned with my appearance were not enough to sustain me. My once lovely hair was lank against my skull.

As dusk threatened overhead and the breeze grew chill, I lounged against a shaded spot near the docks, but not so near as to be tempted by the smell of food and drink in the nearby _agora_. Flies buzzed around my eyes. I was too listless to shoo them away.

Plying my services became nigh impossible, as the Egyptian whores had banded together like a pack of jackals. They lived in a rented house like queens where they could lure the wealthiest clients into congress away from the stink, noise, and heat of the crowds. I was not Egyptian, so they would not accept me into their den. They laughed and hissed and sent the derelicts and the worst of the men out to prowl the streets for women like myself, too heartsick and weak to fend them off. I loathed the smell of laborers and sailors, their unwashed bodies, rough hands, and the fishy salt of their seed, but hate or no, I had to work, though I could no longer remember why.

The traders in the market grew tired of my loitering.

"Get away," they yelled. "You're frightening the customers!"

I shuffled away, desperate for something to fill my empty belly and to quench the burning thirst in my throat. The only free drink was the Nile water, where animal offal, human waste, and any number of other undesirable things were tossed from the ships in the docks. A person would become more ill from drinking unclean water as from not drinking at all. Besides, I had nothing to gather water in.

As I moved towards an alley, I stumbled into a corner stall. A pile of pomegranates tumbled to the street.

"Oh," I mumbled, my mouth watering at the sight of the red skinned fruits. "My apologies, I…"

I reached a hand out, fully intending to clean up my accident. When my fist closed around the firm fruit, I felt the spittle stick in my throat.

I risked one look at the angry trader, bent over and gathering his wares. Then I stared at the fruit, round and fragrant, clutched in my palm. I could almost taste the fruited seeds, bursting sweet and tangy in my mouth.

"Hie!" shouted the trader. He hovered over me with his cheeks mottled. "Thief!"

"Wait," I tried to say. "I'm not steal-" but the words would not come. I dropped the fruit into the dust and fled with fever pounding in my head like a club.

They caught me just around the next corner. One man raised his hand and struck me in the face.

"Thief!" he yelled.

My nose gushed blood, as crimson as pomegranate juice. Another brandished a stick and clubbed me in the side. I stumbled backwards into the dust and scrambled to my feet clutching my side. More shouts came from the nearest alleys and I darted away from the noise.

I turned left, then right. I couldn't breathe through my nostrils without sucking blood into my throat. I panted like a dog, with my mouth open, and darted down another side street and turned again. There were so many dead end streets. My lungs ached and I coughed so hard tongues of flame spread along my back and ribs. Pink sputum flew from my lips.

"Over here!" I heard a muffled cry. My heart leapt into my mouth. I forced my trembling legs to move. *Please, please*…. I prayed as I ran. *Let them never find me.*

Another cross-street lay just ahead, and by the noise I'd reached the marketplace again. I might lose them in the crowds.

I raced around the corner and ran headlong into the hard bulk of a man. My side hurt so much I thought I would faint. He grabbed me by the shoulders. I yelped and stumbled away, seeing little but the flutter of his robes. Had my pursuers cut me off? I could not tell.

In my haste, I fell backwards into the closest market stall and overturned a ceramic jar of preserved black olives. The trader cursed me with such vehemence that I lost my balance. I slipped in the spilled oily juice and collapsed to the ground.

Oh, I was tired, so tired. My body ached. The hard pits of the olives and broken pottery shards bruised my hip when I fell, like a hundred sharp stones. The trader kicked me, spewing curses all the while. I groaned and covered my face with my hands. My limbs trembled and the sand wavered before my eyes.

"Father," I groaned in my native tongue. "Protect me."

A pair of rough hands hauled me to my feet. I flinched, awaiting another blow, but none came. Instead, a voice struck me harder than any fist.

"Great Zeus! Doricha? Is it you?" After my shock wore off, the melodious voice settled over my ears like music.

It was the most beautiful sound I had ever heard.

"Aesop," I gasped, cracking an eye open to see. The noise of the market roared in my ears. My head felt thick and I was woozy from my attack and lack of food. I staggered a little and he, bless him, caught me in his arms.

He hugged me fiercely and I inhaled the dear scent of his stale sweat, dust and wine.

"Aesop," I wept into his robes. Relief made me weaker. I clutched at him, half afraid my pursuers would find me, and half because I did not think I could stand without his aid.

He patted my back and I felt the beloved scratch of his whiskers prickle the top of my scalp. "Your skin burns like fever," he whispered as he held me tight. "And your face? What has happened to my lost little Crab?"

I cackled like a crone, and pain flared along my ribs. "Living free."

The trader rounded on us. "Stupid fool! Who will pay for this mess?"

"I will pay, you buffoon!" Aesop shouted back. "Can't you see the girl is ill?" His voice echoed in my head like thunder.

I thought I would faint from the pressure in my skull and chest. Tiny lights flashed in my vision. A thousand insects buzzed in my ears.

"Here." Aesop tossed the man a coin. The trader eyed it greedily. "I am housed not far from here," Aesop said, leading me away. Black clouds encroached on the edges of my vision. "Can you walk?" His voice sounded very far away.

I tried to nod my head. "Yes," I whispered through dry, cracked lips. My legs were so heavy and then suddenly, they felt as if they'd no weight at all. "Yes. Of course."

"Doricha? Dori?" Aesop called.

Why was he so far away?

The sand turned to mush beneath my feet, and I had the oddest sensation of falling, though I could not see anything beyond the haze of black clouding my vision. I waited for the moment when my body would strike the ground, but it never came.

It was the last conscious thought I had.

CHAPTER 22

My body floated through an impenetrable black void. Voices whispered, just out of reach. I tried to call to them, but could not form any words.

How you will pay. The dulcet voice of my Lady reverberated in the aching cavern of my skull like a thousand golden bells.

My Lady? I thought. *I am here!*

She did not answer.

Pain…everything hurt. I sweated and itched. My ears were clogged with the rushing wind. Was I dead? Had I passed to the Underworld? Did my family await me?

"She's coming round," said a deep voice.

I struggled against black waves that bore me onward toward a prick of light in the distance.

"Doricha, can you hear me?" Something brushed my cheek. I knew that voice.

I floated towards the glow. "Aesop?"

"I am here." His deep voice soothed me. "You've been unconscious. How do you feel?" I heard him move nearer.

I cracked an eye. We were in a small, darkened room with little furniture. Moonlight beamed through the wooden grill of the high narrow window.

"Better, now you are here. Where are we?" I tried to sit up, and found I could not muster the strength. My ribs ached.

"My room. At least until the end of the week. After that…." He shrugged.

"Have you any coin?"

"I did. It was stolen." I coughed hard enough to make my back ache. Pain sliced across my ribs like knife. I thought they were broken. "Everything I have is gone. I do not think freedom agrees with me."

Aesop winced. "And I have used the last of my goods to barter for a healer from the temple. He will be here soon. You should rest."

"You used the last of your coin on me? I cannot let you..." I coughed again. "I should go, Aesop."

"Go? Where?" he asked. His gaze held me and I realized I had nowhere to go.

I tried to sit up again, only to fail a second time. Aesop dipped a scrap of linen into a basin and held it to my forehead. The cool wet cloth soothed me.

"We will think of something," he promised. "Do not worry."

The healer grumbled at being called in the evening but pronounced me in need of purging. He wanted to slather cow excrement on my forehead, but I couldn't tolerate the stench on an empty stomach. In the end, he prescribed a tonic of honey and calves' blood, which was horrid.

"I will bind her midsection." The healer pointed to a purpling bruise on my ribs. He used a wide piece of linen to wrap my aching torso. "It should heal in a few weeks."

"I must leave this place, Aesop." I said when the healer left. "I want to go home."

Aesop stared at me as if I'd grown horns. "Why? What fond memories can that place hold for you?"

"It's the last place I remember being happy," I said. The last place I felt loved and safe.

"And who will take you in, now your family is dead? Ah, Doricha, have you never listened to my wisdom? In avoiding one evil, care must be taken not to fall prey to another. Greece is no place for a woman. In Greece, you will be subject to even less freedom than you had as a slave. Is that the life you would choose?"

"It is better than being a whore!" I raged.

"You truly think so?" When I glared at him, he put both his hands in front of him and said no more.

Well, he was a man and could know nothing more than what he felt in his own skin. He did not suffer as a woman. He was not a target for every brute that trod upon the earth. I rested in sulking silence well into the evening.

Later, after my temper cooled, we sat together and sipped at the last of our beer.

"Do you remember the night you danced for me, in the garden?" He took a swig.

How could I forget? "Yes."

"I was struck then, by your loveliness." He took a swig of beer. "And later, by your mind. We could make a life, here--you and I."

I stared at him and could think of nothing to say.

"This Egypt is not the land of our forefathers. But it has its own beauty, does it not?" Aesop toyed with his cup.

"I suppose." I thought of my journey down to Sais with Charaxus, the glorious green and gold desert. "I have not noted its beauty, as of late."

Aesop took my hand. "Did you know, here, a woman can own property, just as a man? That is heresy by Grecian standards."

"What you are suggesting is heresy to my ears," I said. My stomach rumbled. "Please, no more. I am too hungry and tired." I pulled away from him and rolled onto my unbruised side.

Aesop sighed and left. I tried to stay awake until he returned but I'd been without a safe place to rest for so long, my eyes closed almost before our door did.

"Come with me," Aesop said the next morning.

We stopped to clean our hands and faces by the river. I was bruised and underfed, but healthy enough to walk. He took my hand and led me to, of all places, the Egyptian brothel. This time, they opened their home to me, and I could not help but wonder what Aesop had done to change them so.

I wandered through rooms of half-clothed, perfumed and painted beauties. They eyed me with little interest but tittered behind their hands at Aesop. I felt a pang of jealousy. Why should I be so beneath them? Once, I'd been beautiful and beloved.

Two of the women came over to me. One of them put her arms around my neck and kissed me on the lips, but Aesop called them away. I rubbed away the taste of her honeyed lips and slipped free of Aesop. I meandered into the next room, my mouth watering.

The tables were loaded with all measure of delicacies, nothing overly fine, but still extravagant to my hungry gaze. I knew the food was for patrons with coin, but I snitched a fig and a few grapes. I was desolate and famished. Here they had a low set of benches surrounded feasting tables, a sweet little courtyard garden with a round pool.

These women seemed more than content. When Aesop returned with carmine smears all over his cheeks and lips, I did not comment. He whistled as we walked back to our rented room. We had two days left of shelter, and no food. I thought back to the grilled fish, salat, and wine I'd seen at the Egyptian brothel. I'd done worse, much worse, alone on the streets.

"How did you pay? We have no money for food and yet you squander resources on women."

"We came to an…arrangement. I let them ply their trade during my assembly yesterday." Aesop gave me a sidelong glance, and wiped the carmine from his cheek. "You could be like them. Better, for you are a rare jewel in this desert. Egyptian women are as common as dust. Why even the Pharaoh himself de-"

"Oh, do not start in on me again. I do not wish to hear about the god-king's love of Greece." Why must Aesop nag me so?

"Give it thought, Doricha."

We walked on in silence, but my head was full up with the thought of a fine house and good food and wine to drink. As we turned onto our shabby street, to a shabby inn we could not even afford past tomorrow, I realized Aesop was right. I'd been so angry at being forced into being a whore, I had not taken advantage of opportunity. Perhaps, I could have been so much more…if only I'd used my head. This time, no man would force me into servitude; I would make my own choice. I'd given up on thoughts of Love, that which Sappho sang of, and focused my arts on my own survival.

"I will consider it," I said, as we passed under the wooden lintel of our threshold.

"I thought you might." Aesop patted the edge of the cot. "Now, listen well. This is what I propose…."

I sat next to him on the cot and tried not to close my mind to his words.

"It is a complicated illusion, this catering to man's desire. To be a true *hetaera*, you must accept only gifts from your patrons, and never coin, for Naukratis is a truly Grecian settlement here in Egypt," he said. "Coin is crass and low; you must be above such to be a respectable courtesan. So, we shall accept only wooing and gifts from your patrons. Each gift must come after an appropriate time, so as not to be unseemly. It must never be seen as repayment for services rendered. And we determine which assignations to take and which to refuse."

"I do not understand the difference," I grumbled. My head ached with understanding of the complicated system of selling myself. "They send the purported 'gifts' because of my services. What illusion is that?"

"Illusion, my dear Crab." He tweaked my nose. "Is everything. You will see."

So, we went round, turning our rented abode into a brothel, and making promises that I hoped we could keep.

"We will pay by the week's end," Aesop promised the beer maker, leveraging his notoriety against the necessary supplies for our plan. "Have you never heard of the great Greek Fabulist?"

So, the symposium was prepared. We waited until I'd healed enough to cover my fading bruises with meager cosmetics. The banquet was held in the inn where Charaxus and I had stayed my very first night in Egypt. Aesop sent word he would be in the tavern later, and so by the time we arrived the rooftop was bursting with a large number of Greek patrons who had heard of the Fabulist and wished to see for themselves if his tongue was truly magical.

Ah, how it was.

I think I am truly wooed by the words a man speaks, if not the face behind them. My limbs were as pliant as melting wax. When Aesop had heartily charmed and insulted them all good naturedly with his tongue, he called for me to dance and serve.

We set a decent table, if not so very fine. The wine was Egyptian, not Greek, but the patrons we invited seemed not to care. The prosperous tradesmen, minor politicians, and merchants laughed heartily at Aesop's fables, pounding on the long benches until musicians were called. When the music started, I slipped from my role of servant to seductress with the ease and long practice of my years as at the temple and as Charaxus' slave.

Make your spine a sarisa, I heard Lukra say in my memory. I held my chin high as a priestess and met the gazes of men without fear.

If I fretted over the amount we owed for food and drink, it lent my eyes a hunger the men found irresistible. Trouble, it seemed, agreed with me, for I carried an air of sadness, despite the smiles I used to encourage our patrons to beg for more.

"We yearn for Greece as much as she," they declared to Aesop.

He masked a smile, knowing full well I cared not for the glory of Greece, but my own skin.

I used every ounce of my temple training to seduce them--from the languid sway of my walk to the graceful sweep of my wrists as I danced. The men, so far from Greece, hooted and shouted for me. They offered goods to Aesop, for a kiss or more. He was discreet and shrewd in his dealings; I will credit Aesop with that. Just as my days on the stocks, he insinuated a gift-price that made my head spin.

"It is too high," I whispered furiously to him.

"They will pay it," he said. "Wait and see."

"They won't! They could've had me for less than a twentieth of that a week ago."

Aesop looked at me for a long moment. "You were a *pornai*, then. Common and cheap. Now, you are more. Act like it. Do not forget--we have pledged to repay the debts for all this food and drink. We'll need a little for ourselves as well."

How could I fail to remember how he'd pledged both our services to our extravagant bills? If the men did not pay, we'd be thrown into prison, or worse, sold back into slavery to pay our debts.

I returned to my subtle flattery and fawning, certain the patrons would be furious when they discovered how Aesop manipulated them, but the men paid all Aesop asked and more. I could not believe how they sweetened their offerings with gifts for me. By week's end we had enough resources to pay our bills and rent a small house not far from the docks.

The house was small, with no courtyard and no garden, which I missed most of all. There was only a single window. The air inside was dank and musty, but at least it was shelter for us. What did I care if it was not the fine accommodations I'd enjoyed in my past life as Charaxus' slave? I was buying my freedom daily, one assignation at a time. What did I care if we ate only enough bland food to sustain us? I dreamt at night of honey and figs, and roasted garlic and wine. Oh, I dreamed of wine, the good honest blood of Dionysus.

But there was only enough coin for beer and meager rations of bread. The rest we hoarded for our little gatherings. No gatherings meant no patrons. After another week of modest comfort, I was not so willing to return to my life on the streets. At least the men were somewhat worldly and they had more coin to spare on gifts, than the cheap, rough sailors and traders who littered the docks.

Another season passed. Our fame grew--Aesop's and mine. Not the name my mother and father had given me. I'd chosen a new one, one to signify the change in myself--Rhodopis. _Rosy Cheeks_. I must confess I blushed with pleasure to hear my name spoken as often if not more than his.

"You must continue to rise above the common _chamaitype_," Aesop instructed. "A man will pay far more for that which he cannot get elsewhere."

"And what can I offer? I have two legs, two breasts to suckle, and this," I cupped my pubic mound, "the same as any woman."

"You have a mind, Doricha, if only you would stop to use it. Put yourself to this riddle. What does each man want?"

I yawned and waited for him to tell me. "Yes, well…what is it?"

"I grow weary of playing your tutor. When will you learn to think for yourself?"

"When you are no longer here to do it for me," I jested. "I'm tired, Aesop and you <u>are</u> here. Tell me what a man wants." I trailed my fingers over his chest.

"Do not toy with me, for I am not so easily swayed by a pretty figure." Aesop swatted my hands away and glared at me. "You should know I will not buy your favors." His sharp words cut me to the quick.

"Aesop! I did not mean to-"

He brushed aside my apologies, with an irritated sweep of his fingers. "This is your question to answer, if you wish to grow your fortune beyond the men and women in the sex stalls."

I thought for a moment. "Like the _hetaerae_?" A vision of the cultured, entertaining pair of women at Iadmon's flashed behind my eyes. I'd meant to ask them if I could be worthy of them, once.

Aesop's eyes lit up like stars. "Exactly so. Use more than your body. Use your eyes, your ears, and your wit. Use your clever tongue for more than a whore's empty kisses. You will find the answer, I am willing to bet."

"Ha." I pressed a sulky kiss to his stubbly cheek. "You are only willing to bet because you have nothing overmuch to lose."

He gave me a sharp look. "You find the answers, and they will pay whatever you ask and more."

Aesop was right. On our next feast, I watched how the dock master's eyes followed my bottom and his eyes gleamed at every bawdy jest. I plied him with innuendos as he drank. A light flared in his eyes. When he paid his coin and lay with me, his passions for me were so pronounced I was a bit sore, but the following morning, a chest of precious frankincense was delivered in his name--with a request for another meeting.

"I cannot believe he sent this. For *me*." I did a little dance.

Aesop frowned. "We can use this. Give it over." He took it to the market and traded the frankincense for wine for the next party. The next gathering was even more successful. The room was crowded with admirers and intellects.

"Rhodopis," they cried. *Rhodopis*.

My lovers' gifts were carefully hoarded until in less than a year's time, we were able to pay for a sweet house with a tiny garden, near enough to the docks to be accessible, but not so no near as to be in the stench and din of the river. I hired servants as a customary show of status, but no slaves--for Rada had taught me trust is not easily offered as earned, and there was no one left in Egypt I trusted, save for Aesop. I vowed never to house a slave.

And true to my tutelage in temple hygiene, I summoned a female healer mentioned to me by an Egyptian whore I'd hired to serve lesser guests at our last feast. In shy secret whispers, the whore reported that the woman had much knowledge of more desirable concoctions for preventing babes-- a necessity to my industry. When the old healer crept into my home, as withered a crone as I had ever seen, I thought perhaps the whore had made me to look a fool. The woman was not Egyptian at all--but Greek.

"The gods will close your womb, I promise." The old crone gave me a toothless grin. "I was not always as wretched as I am now. Remember that, Beloved Woman. Mortal beauty and youth will fade, but what is inside remains." With a wink, she directed me to write on the papyrus I had prepared.

My reed poised above the papyrus, and a fat drop of ink spattered it. I was not sure if what I was inside would be worthy of admiration later, but for now, it must be enough.

I could not help but smile at the secret gleam that sparked her eyes. "Tell me what I must do."

"Grind together a measure of acacia dates with some honey. Moisten seed-wool with the mixture and insert it in your womb. Then, there are herbs you must dose yourself with after every assignation." She unrolled a leather bundle and held up a long stalk with clusters of white lacy flowers. "Mark this, the wild carrot. You can use the seeds. It is not the most effective, but the most plentiful to be sure."

I shook my head. "I want certainty, Wise One. Price is not an issue at the moment."

"Then...pennyroyal?" She moved to pick it up.

"No." I would never douse myself with the destruction of my mother. "It makes my nose itch."

"Ah, then perhaps this. It is very rare and costly, thriving only in a single area in Libya." She selected a stalk of a deeply divided leaves and clusters of yellow blossoms as golden as my goddess' hair. "Silphium. From the mountainsides, near Cyrene. Dry the blossoms and grind them into a fine powder. Mix it with a bit of honey to form a pellet no larger than the tip of your smallest finger. In exact proportion, blend this with myrrh and pomegranate seeds and take with a cup of water. Mix it precisely or the result will be a brew that makes your breath reek and stomach void, and not your womb." She laid out each herb and measured the correct amount. I stared at her tidy little heaps and committed it to memory.

The healer ground the dried silphium and myrrh until they formed a fine powder. Then she sprinkled it in a cup of water and bade me to drink it.

"How can I tell if my tonic is true?" I asked, sniffing the cup speculatively. After dousing my mother with a fatal dose of pennyroyal, I was loathe to ingest a hag's concoction. I caught a musty blend of flowers and...earth. "It would be easy to make a mistake."

"If you mix the tonic wrong, the odor of foul breath will give you away. Bitter as death, and as pungent as an unwrapped corpse. Drink it, and such a scent will linger on your lips for half a day or more." She cackled again. "And the sickness will last for much longer."

I drained the cup in one swallow, tasting only the sharp tang of the myrrh. "Why should anyone drink something that smells foul?" I placed my hand in front of my mouth and blew.

"I always mix correctly. You have no need to check." The healer packed her satchel and made to leave, looking slightly disgruntled with my lack of faith. "We are not all so fortunate or wealthy to set aside a poorly mixed potion. As I said, silphium is very dear. Foul or no, the properties are the same. It is only the taste and the accompanying illness that mark it undesirable."

"Then silphium it is."

Smarting slightly at her comment on my rise in financial status, I placed my newly purchased herbs in a cedar case and paid the healer generously for her time before resuming my plans for the next feast.

As the Inundation season loomed along with the waters of the life-giving Nile, I found myself once again near the shop of the trader who'd accepted my rose-gold slippers. I wondered if he still had them, for I mourned their loss. The novelty of them alone would be worth the repurchase, as I'd not seen their equal.

"You!" the trader said when I entered his shop. "Have you more useless baubles to trade?" His eyes flickered over my finery.

"No." With shock, I saw the slippers on a pile of carved wooden chests. "I have come to buy them back from you."

His eyes took on a greedy light. He named a price that was outrageous, considering what he'd offered me for them.

"Ridiculous," I scoffed. "I will not pay half again over the amount you offered me."

"I have housed them, and I gave you coin when you were in desperate need. You would begrudge me a little profit?" His face was a mask of woe.

I laughed. No wonder he was successful. He could wheedle venom from a serpent. Still, I was not so well off as to be able to spend so much on my pride and vanity.

"Very well. I suppose they will have to remain in your care." I put on my best stern expression. "And I shall have to tell my patrons how poorly I've been treated by you."

The trader looked puzzled. "Your...er...patrons?" He eyed the gold gleaming at my throat.

"Yes. The city will soon know how you have dealt with Rhodopis."

It was the first time I'd thought of myself as anyone other than Doricha, the slave. The name flowed out my mouth like honey, and the trader's tongue darted out to wet his lips as if he could taste the sweetness in it.

"Rhodopis, you say." He made a short bow. "I had no idea...of course, a bargain should be struck. Perhaps if I were to offer you a more amenable price, your opinion would improve?" He smiled ingratiatingly.

"Perhaps," I returned the grin, showing my teeth.

In the end, I paid less for my rose-gold slippers than he had originally offered. I ran home to show them off to Aesop.

"I thought I told you not to spend without consulting me? You are becoming quite unruly these days." Aesop grumbled.

"Oh, don't be angry with me Aesop. Look!"

There had been enough left over from our feast preparations to splurge on a flagon of wine for Aesop and myself. When the last drop was gone, I twirled about the room in a giddy fit. His eyes sparkled when he saw me dancing in the precious jingling slippers.

I took another mincing step. "I never thought I would own them again. Who would have thought we'd grow so wealthy?" I sang.

"You mean, you have grown so wealthy," he said, sounding irritable. He eyed my delicate ankles. "I do not think these men come to hear me half as much as they do to see your fine pale body."

"Don't be silly," I clasped his hands and tried to lead him into my stumbling dance. The room whirled in front of my eyes, and I ended up collapsing in a giggling heap on his lap.

He sucked air between his teeth and his hands went around my waist to steady me.

"Hush, you scoundrel. I am not heavy." I leaned back against his chest and closed my eyes to block out the whirling room.

Aesop's hands tightened. "Have I complained?" he asked. "Doricha, we must talk." His voice was odd, but I did not care. The night was a rollicking dance of moonlight, jasmine breeze, and wine.

"Fa, I don't want to talk. After listening to the Assyrian prattle on in his stilted Greek, I think I shall never want to talk again. I cannot believe you accepted an offer from him. Get up!" I stood and tried to yank him to his feet. "I want to dance!"

Aesop did stand but he grabbed me about the waist again, and pulled me close to him. "Little Flower." His voice was thick. I dimly registered his body pressing against mine. "Come here." He covered my mouth with his own.

Clarity pierced through my wine fogged brain. I pushed him away. "Aesop," I said. "Stop that. What are you about?"

He stepped back and ran a hand through his hair. "I know not. Only that you drive me wild with the need to be near you."

"Oh!" I cried and clapped my hands over my ears. "Stop this. I don't want to hear anymore of men and their desires. I am full up of desire!"

It pained me to push him away, Aesop, my only friend. I cared for him, but not as a lover. He'd kissed me once before, long ago in Iadmon's home. The outcome was no different. I was alarmed by his ardor, not enticed!

"Doricha." He struggled to pull my hands away from my ears. "Dori, please. Let us make a new plan. We can finish our business here. I will take you back to Greece if you wish."

"And what is my business, but to become a *hetaera*? The first in Egypt, I think!"

"You could be a wife," he suggested, almost too softly to hear.

His words hit me like a fist. Aesop, the only one I trusted in all of Egypt wished to shackle me to a respectable house in Greece? I had long since given up on marriage proposals to secure my freedom.

"How dare you make me such an offer? Was it not you who bade me stay and live free in Egypt? Did you not warn me it was the only place I could live as I wished?"

"I will protect you."

"Protect me from whom? I am your friend, Aesop. I do not wish to be your chattel in Greece. I have a mind of my own!"

He swiped a hand over his sweating forehead. "Please, I-I cannot watch these other men snarl over your sweet young body anymore. I want you for myself. No other woman has touched me here," he pointed to his forehead, "as you have. I'd not thought it possible. But…."

"And what of your dear Sappho?" He stared at me blankly. "Did she not tantalize you with her mind? She warned you to set me free. Whoever loved me would be cursed by the gods. What of that?"

A pounding ache massed behind my eyes and I thought I might be sick. The wine churned in my stomach. I could not believe Aesop, my only friend, should turn on me like this.

"I…I…" he turned away from me, but said no more. I'd struck the great Fabulist dumb, and I'd never felt worse in my heart. "I care for you, girl. Do you not feel the tiniest bit inclined to love me in return?"

I put my arms around him, resting my head against his broad back. "Sappho herself warned you. I am not meant for love. You are my dearest friend, my savior. Do you remember when you kissed me long ago in Abdera?" I felt him nod, or perhaps he merely trembled beneath my cheek. "It was wrong, even then."

After a long moment, when I felt certain my heart would break, he turned away from me. "Yes, yes, of course. You are right. It is nothing. Forget I mentioned it." He glanced at the door. "I'll be back soon." He quit our house as if nothing at all was amiss.

But, I did not sleep for a long time, and Aesop had not returned by the time I closed my eyes for rest.

The following year was filled with new patrons. The Inundation swelled the Nile's banks and ships sailed easily to and fro throughout all of Egypt. Trade was brisk, and my business was no exception. Aesop began to absent himself from the banquets, so I was forced to negotiate on my own behalf.

I hired a few of the prettier Egyptian girls full time to entertain my lesser patrons, while I jested and recited some of Aesop's fables. I took fewer and fewer assignations myself, until the day came, when I had enough wealth and influence, my name was spoken in the upper echelons. I was the foremost courtesan of Naukratis, and I lay with fewer than a handful of men in any given season. A mock rivalry surfaced amongst my patrons, and I delighted in their transparent attempts to curry my favor. I, who once had to beg in the streets…what a short memory the city has!

All in all, infamy was not so difficult to maintain. There was the tailor who declared my dancing to be legendary and sent me a gown so fine the Greek wife of Pharaoh, Ladice, would have been jealous. Then the butcher, who pinched my soft flesh with his hammy fingers, and sent round a brace of roasted geese dripping with honey. The jeweler who draped my pale, naked body with ropes of gems and precious metals.

When I knelt and took him in my mouth, as Young Iadmon had once bade me, the jeweler sucked air into his lungs so fast, I thought I'd bitten him. He clenched his fingers in my long hair. A moan of pleasure escaped his lips as I used my soft hands to finish him. When he departed, he left everything, even the wide bronze collar of jasper and carnelian that he'd spent himself on.

It was almost a breach of etiquette, payment for services rendered. Such would ruin my reputation as a courtesan and could reduce me back to the streets. So, I sent it back with a sharp reprimand for him to consider our dealings more carefully. After a week's time, the response was an ill-crafted poem in my honor, and an elaborate diadem of electrum and onyx to hold back the veils in which I draped myself from Egypt's burning red sun. This was a far better gift, to be sure.

Only one night out of the next ten banquets did Aesop attend, draped three times over with a bevy of Egyptian girls who fawned over him as if he'd strung stars across the desert sky. I wondered how many of his "gifts" to them were paid with from my own labors. I snapped at him when he returned the next morning, reeking of fine perfumes. He cursed me as a harpy and stormed out, with angry eyes.

The following week, Aesop received an invitation from the Babylonian King Nebuchadnezzar, who wished to meet him and become more worldly though Aesop's tutelage.

"Will you go?" I asked. I already knew his answer.

"I have always wished to see his miracle gardens," he said, "although I'm sure they are nothing compared to yours, Doricha."

Ah, Aesop, ever the flatterer. "Then you must tell me of them, when I see you next."

He opened his mouth to speak and closed it again. Finally, he said an abrupt farewell and kissed me once on the cheek. Tears stung my eyes as I watched him pack his things and leave.

Though my heart ached, I knew it was for the best. We could not continue, once he'd proclaimed his love. He had too much pride and I too much guilt to live together now.

Men of great importance all pass through Naukratis. Soon it was said every Greek knew my name. Tales were spread far and wide, only half of which were based in truth. I perpetuated the rumors, by making extravagant gestures and throwing the most intriguing banquets. Coin flowed like water from the Nile. I hired acrobats and revelers from the East, Nubian dancers and jugglers. I bade a seamstress to attire me Grecian finery, Persian silks, even a costume made of spotted cat fur that only just covered my breasts and crotch.

"Rhodopis," my patrons cried, "You must go to the home of Rhodopis!"

I would say I was a far more equitable host than given credit, for I did not dance for only the Greeks. I danced and pleased anyone who had enough coin or gifts to offer.

Now I had only myself to feed and clothe, I rented a new house, away from the memories of Aesop, with a larger garden already displaying the first green shoots of new growth. And every coin spent on luxurious plants and furnishings only enhanced my reputation and returned to me a hundred fold. My latest patrons, no longer common merchants and traders, now included the son of a minor nome leader, a prince from Punt who brought ivory and exotic spotted and striped animal skins of orange and black and gold, and Setis, a bureaucrat.

Setis offered me the use of two servants which I accepted. I trained the young girl to arrange my hair and serve, and the man I put to work in the kitchen. The garden I tended myself. As I could afford to be selective in my pursuits, I busied myself with creating my own paradise. My days as a slave and a common street whore seemed very far away, indeed.

One day all the world will know your name as a symbol of beauty and grace, my mother had promised.

I smiled as I patted the soil around my new olive tree. Though I did not think this was quite the infamy my mother had dreamt of and the name was not truly my own, still, her words rang true. I was far better off here, than in a vulnerable village in Perperek or cramped underneath a mountain in a temple nest of vipers. But, I missed Aesop's presence, for without him, I was truly alone despite unending invitations from the curious and the carnal.

I arranged for dancing girls to perform, and for those lucky individuals with enough coin or influence, I donned my rose-gold slippers and rendered them speechless. There are those who say my own influence grew in those days, but as one who makes her living by satisfying the many passions of others, I cannot say it is so.

I wanted for nothing, true, except for the one thing denied me. I'd stopped praying for love with the fateful end of my affair with Hori. What a silly girl I'd been to trifle with a charmer's affections and to think it love. Love was not for one such as me, no matter what my dream goddess had promised. But freedom, ah yes, sweet freedom was quite another thing. And wealth--a new advantage I distributed among my servants and the other girls with equal aplomb. It kept them more loyal to me than any law of Egypt.

Finally the day came when my world turned golden and bright. I'd gone to the *agora* early for there was aught I would buy. I cannot remember now what it was, perhaps a new plant for the garden.

I crossed the slave stocks as I went, and happened to notice a number of new arrivals standing there for sale. Many of them bore the familiar features of Greece and a few sported red or gold hair. I pitied them. I could not help myself, I drew nearer. As I did, one figure stood out from the rest-

-a figure that made my heart leap into my throat and my hands clench.

"Mara!" I cried.

She turned her head dully at my voice. Her eyes focused blearily on me, and then to my horror, she crumpled right there on the stand. A trader strode over to her and began to prod her.

My feet grew wings. I hitched up my skirts and ran, heedless of the men whistling at me. It seemed I would never reach her. I ran all the way up on the platform and threw myself over her rousing form.

"Stop!" I shouted as the trader moved to deliver another blow. "Stop, I will buy her. I wish to buy this girl." The words rushed out of my mouth. Me, who swore never to house a slave.

"She is a lazy slut, and ill besides," called another trader. "Have a look at my stock instead."

"No." I fumbled with my full coin purse. I tried to regain my composure and help the still silent Mara to her feet. She looked about her in a daze, and I saw her cheeks and eyes redden in a way that meant tears would follow. "No, I want only this one. Here," and I thrust some coins at the dumbfounded trader, before he could react. "Here, she is mine, now!"

In a fit, I yanked the leather cord off her neck guided her off the platform. I scarce recall making my mark, but somehow the deal was done.

"Safe," I murmured to Mara. "You are safe, now."

Mara stared at me. "You're alive," she said. Her unsteady hand reached out to stroke my hair. Gods, but she was pale and thin. "You're alive," she repeated, and crumpled again at my feet.

CHAPTER TWENTY THREE

"Merikos went mad after you were forced out of the temple," Mara croaked. "He raved up and down the hallways shouting your mother's name and tearing at his robes."

"I don't believe it." I set a cup of warmed wine with honey next to her. The healers I'd hired assured me Mara would heal with rest and care, and I meant to give her the best of both.

She took a sip and winced as it hit her raw throat. "It's true. He threw himself off a ledge outside the temple. I saw his body, broken and bleeding at the bottom of the cliffs." She shuddered. "Such a waste. The gods will not have him, now. Aidne ordered him buried without a blessing. She took complete control of the temple afterwards. She blackened the names of you and your mother, and I was afraid, so I ran away."

"You were very brave." I smoothed her hair away from her face. "Aidne was too powerful. She would have given you trouble, I am certain. You were wise and brave to cheat her of that pleasure."

Mara grabbed my hand and held it tight, as a drowning man reaches for a low branch.

"No, Dori. I was _foolish_. I was frightened of Aidne, when I should've been more frightened of what exists outside our temple...." Her voice trailed off and she looked away. "Ho-how did you...I mean, how could you...stand...what they did?" I waited for her to finish, but she did not speak for a long moment and she would not meet my eyes.

The hairs on the back of my neck prickled. "What _who_ did, Mara?"

I put my fingers under her chin and tipped her face so she could not look away. Her blue eyes were shadowed. My heart felt as if it would break. I wanted to know the whole story, I _had_ to know, and yet I knew deep down this was an experience I never dreamed I'd share with my near sister.

"Slavers caught me on the roadside. There were three of them. Horrid, stinking, filthy beasts. They did things to me...and for so long afterwards." She shook her head fiercely just as the first of her tears plopped onto her flushed cheeks. Her eyes closed and her breath grew rapid and shallow as a sparrow.

I gathered her to my bosom. "I know, my dearest, I know," I crooned.

And I did know.

We were alike, she and I, in so many ways. But I refused to succumb to despair. Aesop said this world was not for women. Well, I would make it so, if only here in Egypt, in my own little sphere of influence. And I would protect Mara in the process. I had more wealth than I could imagine, and patrons who were even more wealthy and influential. The city lauded me, and commoners bowed as I passed them in the streets. All I had at my disposal I could offer to Mara, my near sister.

My voice was steady as I described my plight with Cyrus, Iadmon, and Aesop. She gripped my hands in her icy fingers and nodded her head. Young Iadmon, the Lady, Sappho and Charaxus, Hori...I told it all from beginning to end. What happened back then, and what I did now, to live freely.

When I finished, she lay back on the bed and stared at me.

"So," she said at last. And nothing else.

"So," I responded.

"How can you bear it?"

Oh, what a complex question. "Because I must? I don't know, Mara. This is not the life I was trained for in the temple, but I find I can bear it better than my bonds of slavery."

She made a displeased snort. "You are still a slave. You just don't recognize what binds you."

I stared at her. "No, Mara. _No_. I am mistress, here. For all that I am built for pleasing, it is I who demand pleasure--in all its forms. Look around you. Should I give up my home, my garden, the fine food and drink? Tell me?"

"You are a slave to your passions." She shuddered again. "Your god-given talents should be used for more than mere base pleasures." Her eyes welled anew.

"What will I do then?" I asked. "If I find these so-called shackles tolerable, will you begrudge me some measure of contentment? After all I have endured?"

Mara's cheeks turned pink. "I will not."

"Good. Tomorrow, then, I will go to the docks and proclaim you are free."

"Oh, Dori." Mara gasped. "You cannot! What would I do then? Will you expect me to earn my keep as you have chosen?"

"Don't be ridiculous!" I began, but Mara cut me off.

"I won't do it. I will never dance for any man. And I am not suited for anything else, but to be a slave."

"Mara, no! You can live here. With me." The very idea of slavery was abhorrent to me. I would _not_ allow it, not for her.

"And make myself another burden for which you must ply your trade? Never!" Mara coughed violently and I waited until she took another sip of honeyed wine.

"You would never be a burden to me, near sister." I stroked her soft cheek. It was true. Mara was as dear to me as my own life.

"Then let me stay under your protection. Do not free me. If not your slave, I can be your concubine, then. And I can tend you better than any of these dark-eyed strangers."

"Mara!" I did not think of Egyptians as strangers. Not anymore.

"You must think of your reputation. There are places a woman of influence cannot traverse," Mara urged.

"Fah! This is not Greece, Mara. Women have more freedoms, here. You will see. I am safe enough in Naukratis."

"Just the same. I will stay as your handmaiden." Her blue eyes filled with tears again. "Say you will let me, Dori. I don't want to be parted from you ever again."

I thought for a moment. Perhaps it would be best to allow this. It would keep Mara near to me, and we would be much happier together than we could ever be apart.

"As you wish, dearest. But for now, you must let me care for you."

Mara's eyes lost a little of their sadness. "I never knew you were so strong, Dori. I am glad for it."

I found myself cursing the men who could injure her so, for this was not the Mara of my memory. It would take time to heal her, and in more than just her body.

"We will both be strong, dearest." I whispered.

When Mara finally closed her eyes and slept, my shoulders ached from tending her. I left her slumbering peacefully, with what I hoped was a lighter heart.

My near sister was home.

The following week, Pharaoh's barge docked in Naukratis. After all my careful avoidance, it seemed I could avoid his notice no longer.

I was well-established as Egypt's foremost courtesan by that time and made many offerings to the temples of Isis and Ra. I entertained in true _hetaerae_ fashion, throwing elaborate banquets and feasts. I even hired a few reported poets and philosophers, though they were nothing compared to my Aesop. I bested them easily and my patrons loved me for it. I hired the best musicians, offered the finest food and drink, and toyed with potential assignations, which only made my would-be admirers work harder to earn my notice. Life was good for me. My coffers were full to overflowing. And yet I found myself strangely dissatisfied, for Mara's words still echoed in my soul. There was something missing, some greater glory absent from my designs.

It would be many long weeks before I would discover it.

I did not go to the docks when the god-king landed in Naukratis, but I heard a firsthand account from one of my hired servants who possessed a flair for dramatic storytelling. As he spoke, I saw images in my mind's eye-- Amasis' gilded barge, the attendants, servants, and priestesses posed in perfect formation around his throne. When they unloaded the vessel and Pharaoh retired to his prepared residence, the servant claimed every furnishing transported from the barge bore gilding of gold and electrum, and those that did not were encrusted with precious gems and costly paint. It sounded like Pharaoh was indeed a man who appreciated beauty and luxury. Well, I could not fault him for that which I, myself, held dear.

An invitation to Pharaoh's welcoming feast came from one of my patrons, a Greek by the name of Praxitlytes, who traded in wool. And I, no longer fearing to be sold, found myself somewhat curious about this lover of Greek cultures, this god-king. Praxitlytes, my patron, was brash and over-concerned with gossip, as a young man can be when he has made a fortune early in life. And since the city could talk of nothing else but the festivities surrounding the Pharaoh's arrival, even he could not keep his mind on our business.

"Praxitlytes, if you will not recline here next to me, at least stop pacing. You remind me of a lion trapped in the sand caves." I eyed the servant who brought a fresh amphora of Grecian wine and motioned for it to be set on the low bench next to me. "How about a game of _senet_?" I stood and moved to the chest that housed my wooden board.

The object of _senet_ is to be the first to clear the board of all your colored stone pieces. Even children can play, but there are trap positions and a deeper strategy at play on the board, for those who are clever enough to comprehend it. Praxitlytes did not, but I let him win often enough so his pride would not be pricked.

He whirled away from the balcony edge with his arms extended. "Rumor has it the Pharaoh's welcoming festival will rival the Feast of Horus. It will be quite a sight! Say you will let me escort you, Rhodopis."

"I will not. I have no desire to see this Pharaoh. The less notice he takes of me and my affairs the better. Besides, you yourself declare nothing rivals my own celebrations. The Pharaoh must not spend as readily as I, for he has an entire nation to govern, while I have only myself. Now, will you take wine or shall I call for beer?" I fiddled with the compartments of the board and released the game pieces, polished blue and black obelisks, into my hand.

"Ah, but you will have to make an accounting of all your affairs at the year's end, now Pharaoh has passed his law." He gestured for me to pour the wine.

"You are as ridiculous as you ever were, Praxitlytes." The polished stone pieces were cool against my palms. "I don't know why I allow your attentions."

In truth, I knew very well why. I'd begun a fine stable of horses, on his gifts alone. And he amused me, in his own way. I liked his vigor and he did have a good head for politics. Though Egypt governed the city, it was the Greeks who controlled most of the trade that passed through Naukratis. And Praxitlytes was swiftly gaining influence, which could only benefit me and my treasuries.

"There is no hiding what you are, Rhodopis. I think half the city will not function, unless it is by your sway…well, at least the Greek half." He reached out and stroked my shoulder. "You should make yourself known to Amasis. Come. Don't make me beg you."

I felt my cheeks heat. His invitation reminded me of Charaxus' determination to display me before Amasis. "How you jest, sweet Praxitlytes, when I am in no mood for jesting." I did not have to feign my displeasure. "You need not parade me before the god-king. Pharaoh has any number of desirable women in his court."

"He has many wives, it's true. And yet he spends so little time with them, his reputation as a lover of women is in serious jeopardy. Last week he prayed to his gods to give him a wife worthy of being queen." Praxitlytes guffawed before he downed a huge gulp of wine. "Perhaps you can influence him, when others cannot. I've heard of his fondness for Greece."

I snatched up my small feathered fan and waved it impatiently in front of my face. "He has Ladice, a Grecian princess to keep him company."

"Ha, she has the face and figure of a pig! He will not make her Mistress of the Palace."

"Then he is a fool," I said. "The Greeks do not take insults well."

"A fool? No…certainly not. He's passed his law, where each man must report to his nomarch and make an accounting of his chosen trade. It's a clever idea, for it keeps an accounting of where the nation earns its coin. We should do just the same in Greece, for I swear half the government would be forced to decry themselves as thieves and liars!" When I smiled, as I knew he wished me to, he slapped his knee and chuckled. "No, Amasis is less a fool than you or I might think." He moved to my chaise and drew up a stool on the opposite side of the gaming board.

I'd heard rumors of displeasure circling the upper echelons of Egyptian royalty. I wondered if that is what Wakheptry had alluded to in her garden, on the day of my release long ago. "And what say the noble families to this new law?" I tossed the sticks and moved my first piece.

"Some approve. Others…well, they would not approve, even if Amasis paved their courtyards with gold from the new taxes that will come of such a system. I've heard the nobility is in open dissent. There is talk of giving over to the Persian king Kourosh." Praxitlytes moved his own piece and frowned at the board. "I don't know why I play you, Rhodopis. You are sure to best me."

"You play because like most men, you enjoy the challenge. Would not the nobility support the increase of their wealth, whatever the cause?"

Praxitlytes drained his wine cup in a gulp that would have left me, a Thracian, reeling. "There are some who feel Amasis is beneath them. He was a soldier. His family was not well connected. Even a lowly man can attain wealth and power in the army, if he is strong, but Amasis had no claim to nobility, when he conquered Apries. I think they resent him." He frowned and moved his next piece into position. "He is certain to be unusual, my sweetling. Are you not the least bit curious?"

I sighed. "You paint a very compelling picture."

"Then, you'll come with me? Pharaoh will weep to see such beauty."

So, the mighty god-king of Egypt was but a commoner. What did I care? My next toss was lucky. I made a noncommittal noise and moved a majority of my pieces around the board.

"Great Zeus, I'm losing before I've half begun!" Praxitlytes sighed and rubbed his eyes. "Come here, Rhodopis, I tire of this game."

I stood and set the board aside. "How can the nobles recant his decrees, when they have declared Pharaoh is a god?" I moved to pour him more wine, but he waved me onto his lap instead.

"I do not know. You must take your dispute to an Egyptian." His breath was heady with the rich scent of wine. Praxitlytes trailed a hand over my cheek. "For I owe my allegiance and good fortune to Poseidon's grace."

Perhaps Pharaoh was not as fearsome as I believed. My heart warmed a little for this soldier who was given a king's power. He had much to overcome, if he wished to rule over the bureaucrats in Egypt. They who controlled the purse strings of the nation and could smite this former soldier without ever lifting a spear.

Praxitlytes' hands cupped my buttocks. He shifted the position of his knees, spilling senet pieces off the board and onto the floor.

"Amasis must be a consummate game player to have withstood the displeasure of Egyptian nobility for so long," I said, allowing him a healthy squeeze. "They can be as close knit as a pack of jackals guarding a scrap of meat."

"Ha! Spoken like a true _senet_ lover. Tell me, would you care to match your wit against the Pharaoh's, lovely Rhodopis?"

It was an enticing thought. I am quite good at games, especially _senet_, which is deceptively simple. But such a meeting could not have a positive outcome, I was sure.

"I can only imagine Pharaoh would best me, as he does the rest of Egypt." I feigned an innocent shift in his lap, and felt his body stiffen beneath his robes.

Praxitlytes' eyes twinkled. "Come with me to the banquet and see for yourself." His hands stroked the small of my back.

Well, I could not help it. My vanity and my curiosity were piqued by this bit of gossip, for all that it came from the boisterous Praxitlytes. What would the Pharaoh be like? He was once a soldier and thus likely to be fierce. An image of my father's broad shoulders flashed before my eyes. It had been a long time since I'd met a true warrior, a man to rival my father's memory.

"As you wish." I slipped off his lap and stood. "But you must furnish me with jewelry and suitable finery to be presented to Pharaoh. I will not be seen in this." I gestured to my outrageously expensive pleated gown.

Praxitlytes unwound my shawls and veils, loosened the ties of my girdle and let the cloth puddle on the marble floor with a whisper. "So be it."

Praxitlytes brought me a present in addition to the fine clothing and jewels he sent before the feast. Perhaps he felt guilty over nagging me into attending. Whatever his reasons, he presented me with a cunning little grey monkey on a golden leash. The monkey had a white face and quick brown eyes. I named him Kyky.

Mara helped me prepare for the feast in Pharaoh's honor, for in Egypt, much status is perceived by one's appearance and finery. Security could vanish in an instant if a courtesan was not careful, and I intended to keep mine for as long as possible. As Mara dressed my hair in an elaborate pile on top of my head--a thoroughly Grecian style--I sensed her unease.

"What is it?" I asked, admiring the long locks spilling from the top of my coif to halfway down my back.

"It-it's just this Pharaoh. He is the king of this land." Mara licked her lips. "What if he does not approve of you?"

"Why should he take notice of me?" I finished painting my eyes with kohl and white lead.

"How could he not?" Mara selected my finest golden necklace, the new one with lapis lazuli beads and tiny scarabs made of polished green agate. She let her hands linger on my bare shoulders as she clasped it on me.

I rested my hands over hers. "I am a courtesan, and nothing more. Pharaoh will have no reason to take notice of me." I studied my reflection one last time in the large polished bronze disk. Egyptians love to adorn themselves, and I must admit I quite enjoy it myself.

Mara rolled her blue eyes at me. "There are few who can withstand your beauty, near sister. I am the least of them." She kissed me on the lips. Her breath was sweet with thyme and mint. "You are as lovely as a goddess. Remember me, when the Egyptian king and his court are begging for your favors this evening."

"Of course, my dearest," I said, distractedly. For though I clothed myself in finery as light as gossamer, my heart was heavily weighted with more serious matters. "Mara, have you sent round the extra resources to the temple of Neit? I hear they have even more refugees swelling for charity. We should add them to my lists."

It disturbed me to see men, women and children sold into the hopelessness of slavery, as I passed through the streets in my litter and trappings. I understood that economic circumstances required it, but I still abhorred the very practice. I'd vowed never to house a slave, and after Mara (who was less a slave than my shadow), I never had. So, it was that often I'd secretly made donations to temples that housed the low and indigent. And I used my burgeoning coffers to support physicians that I knew attended those who could scarce afford to pay.

"As you asked, I have," she replied. "With a courier not from our household. I had Zahouri hire someone in the market that he knew to be reputable."

"Hmm, "I said. "I would rather remain anonymous. Advise Zahouri not to use anyone who can be traced back to us." Unlike my more public temple offerings, I did not know what this private support would do my standing as a _hetaera_. Still, if word got out, then so be it. I knew only that I must do something to aid those who could not help themselves, for I had been one of them--alone and unloved-- myself.

Kyky clambered up my shoulder quick as a wink and snatched a slice of melon from my fingers. Mara screeched at him. When he burrowed under my red-gold tendrils, I could not help but laugh, which made Mara a tad sulky.

"He will ruin your gown and void his bowels on your fine necklace." Mara put her hands on her hips. "What will Pharaoh think of you then?"

The thought sobered me. I unlatched my adorable monkey with some difficulty, and although he did not void on my shoulder, he did entangle himself in my long hair. Mara was forced to redo the whole elaborate coif while Praxitlytes waited for us with some measure of impatience.

At last, we departed. When Praxitlytes turned towards the door, Mara kissed me swiftly on the cheek. I saw the crease forming between her fine brows.

"All will be well," I promised her with a squeeze of my hand.

She looked doubtful, but gave me an unsteady smile which did nothing to allay my nervousness.

On the way to the festival, I fidgeted with my attire as the litter bearers rushed us to the god-king's door. The feast was in full swing by the time we were delivered to the temple. With trepidation, I allowed Praxitlytes to escort me to the dining tables. Men lined one table, and women, the other in traditional Egyptian fashion. Egyptians and foreigners mingled freely, eyeing one another's finery with thinly veiled calculation. I held my breath and glanced for anyone who might look the part of a god-king, but found neither clusters of sycophants gathered, nor any knot of royal guards in formation.

Praxitlytes noticed my preoccupation as we passed between the tables. He leaned over to make certain I heard him over the din. "Pharaoh has not made his appearance yet."

I could not tell whether it was disappointment or relief fluttering in my breast.

We circulated through the thronging crowds. Furthest from the dais were the more common folk of Naukratis, higher levels of craftsmen and minor politicians, all hoping to gain recognition, and thereby increase their status. The next echelon was the lesser nobility, of which I navigated easily through a wave of their awed sighs, for I was well above their status, now.

Wives whispered behind their hands and eyed my attire. By the week's end over half of them would have gowns and jewels made just the same. Several of the women even sported elaborate wigs. They imported henna from Assyria and rinsed it through their black hair. I supposed I should be flattered, but in truth, it was a poor comparison to my red-gold locks, and leant their copper skin no favors.

"May I come to see you tomorrow?" A man whispered into my ear. I tore my gaze away from the women. It was the governor of Naukratis. He was not particularly clever or comely, but he had much influence in the city.

"We shall see," I responded with a smile, wondering what the governor of Naukratis might offer. Perhaps I could entice him to establish more support from the temple priests to help the sick and the destitute. Through the governor, support could be given, without attaching it to my name.

The governor rubbed his hands together and gave me a short bow, before moving away.

Praxitlytes chuckled beside me. "And so the sphere of Rhodopis grows," he said without rancor.

"We are all whores in our right, Praxitlytes. Even bureaucrats."

"Most especially bureaucrats!" He laughed and led me away.

The festival continued for another hour, as the guests feasted and drank, forgetting the rumors of invasion from the mighty Kourosh of Persia. More than once, I heard voices lifted in heated debate, and not song. They argued over what should be done, what could be done and I blessed our god-king his military training. It was tiring, and I began to lose hope that for tonight at least, I could forget playing politics.

At last the musicians stopped their playing. A great expectant pause arose from those seated nearest the raised dais. Feast goers elbowed their way into a better position of the dais and courtyard.

"What?" I whispered to Praxitlytes. "What is it? Is it him?"

My heart thudded in my chest.

"It appears the game has begun, Rhodopis," he murmured and grasped my elbow. "Shall we play?"

CHAPTER TWENTY FOUR

I did not see Pharaoh enter the festival, but the rushing whisper of homage marked his arrival. As the last sistrum jingled and fell silent, I found my nerves tingling with anticipation. At last, I would see this god-king of Egypt. I felt certain he would not live up to my expectations. After all, he was only a man, and I had those in droves.

What did Amasis look like?

I had one quick glimpse of him as he passed through the colonnade, clad in a fine linen _shenti_ that hung to his knees. Armed guards lined him on all sides. He wore a huge pectoral of gold and a headdress that brushed his shoulders, which were unusually broad for an Egyptian. He seemed rather tall, although from my prostrate position, even the craven vizier would've seemed a giant. It was a very imposing sight.

The courtyard fell silent. I focused my gaze on the rosy compacted gravel and swallowed the lump lodged in my throat. Would he speak? Would he have an affectation I found annoying or the high, whiny voice of so many of the royal families?

"Rise and be welcomed," said a deep, gruff voice. "Oh Nile, whose Waters Embrace Us. Be Fruitful. The Exclusive One Shine his Rays upon you Forever!"

I cannot tell you how his voice went through me like a thunderbolt. When the people stood and cheered, nervous sweat broke out on my palms and my stomach fluttered as if I'd swallowed a moth. We sang the prepared song and Amasis spoke another blessing in Egyptian. I had trouble hearing, over the cheers of the people. Then the throngs surged forward, some towards Pharaoh to make obeisance, and some towards the tables laden with food and drink. Slaves flooded into the area, laden with sweetmeats and pastries, wine and beer.

I lost Praxitlytes in the crowds. No matter, I thought, he would find me soon enough. I slipped away to the beverage casks and a slave offered a brass cup filled with sweet red wine.

The musicians struck up a lively tune and crowds parted to make room for the scantily clad Nubian acrobats and dancing girls. I envied them their gay eyes and long limbs, so dark against the white of their linen tunics. They had no pressing concerns to make their steps heavy. I moved to a spot under the open colonnade where I could enjoy the performance without scrutiny from half the noble houses. But even better, across the open courtyard of entertainers, I had a much clearer view of the god-king Amasis.

He was a dynamic man, powerful and dark, and bore his years well. He wore a blue and gold _Menes_ headdress. His white teeth flashed in the torchlight when he smiled, which was not often. I wondered whether he was naturally somber, or just cautious. Heavy kohl, drawn out to his temples, lined his eyes and gave him a very feline appearance. His eyelids were painted with jade. An aquiline nose, hooked like a falcon's beak, dominated his face, but I did not find it to be unattractive. Quite the contrary.

He looked every inch a warrior; and unlike most of my patrons.

My mouth went dry.

Here was the epitome of a worthy adversary, I thought. I would not be able to wend him round the crook of an elegant finger. For this man was, as my father had been, a fighter at heart.

His was not the softened beauty of a politician or even a lowly craftsman!

Amasis was all long-limbs and hard, angular planes. He was muscular, sitting straight and tall as a soldier would, without shifting on the cushioned seat of his gilded throne. Still, he seemed pleased by the festival, which boded well for Naukratis. A high priest came and Amasis gave over the symbolic crook and flail. The priest deposited them into a finely carved and painted wooden box. The music ended with a flourish and the dancers pattered away to disappear into the night beyond the torches' glare.

I decided now was the time to make my obeisance, to offer him homage as was his due. I stepped out of the shadows of the column, and wiped my hands on my skirt. My stomach fluttered nervously. How much easier this meeting would be, if he were ugly.

Amasis clapped his hands. "Oo-ay, Oo-ay." Silence fell. "Well done."

He signaled the musicians to play again, but the performers had exited. We waited, but they did not return. The crowd began to murmur in puzzlement, for the festival was far from ending. Even the lowliest among us could sense something was amiss. Amasis turned to his advisors.

"Bring on the entertainment," called a wizened priest. A sheen of sweat marked his face. He clapped his hands, but the dancers did not return.

Amasis' brow furrowed. Unlike the other nobility he did not puff his chest or hoot his displeasure, the mark of a subdued man. His reserve pleased me. For certain, the upper strata in attendance did not hold to such decorum.

"Where are the girls?" called the princes of Egypt. The minor nobles took up the cry.

"Who is to entertain Him who Shines with the Morning Sun? Who will dance for Nesu Ahmose?" I thought I heard a note of sarcasm in their pleas.

The crowds grew restless, and the musicians picked up the threads of another hymn. Again, no dancers came. The music died away. I saw one of the priests frown and gesture to a set of guards behind the throne. They marched off. The murmurs grew louder. People began to mill about in some confusion, and there was more than one angry face on those closest to Pharaoh.

I scanned the crowd, just in time to see several of the noble princes and princesses smother knowing looks. My heart skipped a beat. Those simpering serpents had designed this plot to embarrass the Pharaoh. And just like _senet_, I feared an underlying purpose.

For, this was no game. Word would spread that the city of Naukratis had insulted the god-king...oh! I leaned against the limestone column and struggled to see beyond the haze of anger clouding my vision. Pharaoh's power must be absolute, to hold the public together against the impending threats from invasion. He could declare our city to be razed to the sand dunes. How was this to play out? Who would use this to their advantage?

I risked a glance at Amasis. His eyes seemed to penetrate the crowd, and though I knew he could not see me, hidden half behind the column as I was, a wave of nervous perspiration slicked my hands.

"Is this the best Naukratis can offer?" said a wizened priest. "To offer insult to the gods?"

Amasis stood, his body a stiff arrow of displeasure, on the point of exodus.

Naukratis was doomed.

"Great majesty," a voice from the crowd called out. My heart stopped. It was Praxitlytes! "Beloved son of Ra, demand that which is worthy of you. The Treasure of Naukratis. She is with us tonight. If only you will bid her dance, she will please you as no other in our city can."

I had a sudden sinking sensation in my stomach, as if I'd been pushed off a cliff.

"Who has spoken?" asked the priest angrily.

"Yes," called another voice. The governor! "To honor Him Who Holds the Light, we call for Rhodopis, the Treasure of Naukratis, to dance!"

Whispers behind me crested like a wave, engulfing my ears with their rasping accusations. I saw the commoners on the fringes begin to nod. Some pointed towards me. A few shouted approval. I felt a little dizzy and set my cup of wine on a stool before it sloshed on my fine attire. I motioned to a slave with a large ostrich feather fan to come and fan my hot face, but he did not see me.

I put a hand to my head. It could not be! Just as Charaxus had intended so many years before, it seemed now that I should be called to serve upon the Pharaoh's pleasure.

I would strike that idiot Praxitlytes down for bringing me into this!

Rho-do-pis, some took up the chant. *Rho-do-pis*. They clapped and chanted until I was sick of my own name.

I turned and put my forehead against the cool pillar and thought I would be sick. Those nearest me grabbed my arms and thrust me forward calling:

"Here she is! Here comes the 'Treasure of Naukratis'. Make way!"

My cheeks burned. I heard my father's voice echoing in my memory, like birdsong. *You are my treasure, Doricha. Do you hate me for it?*

"Papita," I whispered.

People moved aside. Praxitlytes emerged, whispered loudly, "Go!" and pushed me forward.

I had only a second to gather my courage before I stumbled into the courtyard facing the dais of Amasis.

I stopped and tilted my chin high as I'd been trained. Silence fell like a thunderclap. The chanting and clapping ceased. The governor nodded at me, his face pale and sweating.

Amasis stared. No one spoke a word. Even the cicadas were still. I forced my trembling legs to still beneath my skirts. In truth, all I wanted to do was to flee back to my safe garden and weep to Mara. No, that is not quite true. First, I wished to smite Praxitlytes for his cruel joke. Then, I would run home and weep. Instead, I knelt and bowed so low, the long hanging tail of my hair slithered over my shoulder to tickle the dust and gravel.

"Rise," Amasis bade me. I could tell nothing from his vocal inflection. Every eye fixed upon us. He looked very stern. "You are she? This...Rhodopis of Naukratis?"

Well, he was a soldier once. I looked him squarely in the eye as my father had taught me, and fixed a smile on my lips. "I am."

A priest whispered furiously in his ear. A flicker of amusement passed over the Pharaoh's face and he waved the priest away.

"We have...heard...of the legendary charm that Rhodopis possesses. Will you dance for Pharaoh's pleasure?"

"No!" said a voice from beyond the throne. With some difficulty, I wrenched away from Amasis' gaze and saw a royal scribe step forward out of the shadows of the dais. No, not a scribe.

"I say this <u>Greek</u>," Neferenatu, the Grand Vizier, spat the word as if it were a curse, "is not a suitable tribute to the mighty Nesu, may He live Forever." He glared at me, and his cheeks were flushed, but in my mind I saw him as he'd appeared in the Sais marketplace--greedy and utterly arrogant atop his curtained litter. He'd wanted me then. "Call for your ladies, Nesu Ahmose, call for our Egyptian Princesses!"

"She is the Jewel of the City," yelled a man behind me. I think it was a patron from two weeks prior who spoke. "Let her dance."

"She disgraces Egypt," called a reedy Egyptian nomarch bedecked in gold. "Where are the royal women? Let them perform!"

Discord reigned over the courtyard, a cacophony of jackals' howls. I surreptitiously scanned the crowds looking for Praxitlytes so I could give a few angry glares myself, but he had wisely hidden himself from view. At last, Amasis held a hand up for silence. The noise ceased.

"You have been questioned. Will you answer?" Amasis asked me.

I glanced at Neferenatu, who shook his head. His posture was so taut that his earlobes touched his shoulders. I could not think of a way to refuse gracefully and without offending half the court. And the city of Naukratis needed me.

"I dance for the gods' pleasure, Oh Honored King of Egypt. If it pleases Nesu that I should dance, I shall." And I bowed again.

Amasis nodded once. "She speaks like a devout subject." He settled back onto his cushion and crossed his arms over his chest. "I will allow this."

Angry crimson blotches bloomed in the Vizier's cheeks and he turned his back to me as the musicians lifted their pipes and drums to play.

I danced as I had never had before. I called on every ounce of my temple training to perform a complicated, and thoroughly Grecian, dance. Somehow I knew in my heart my adulatory tribute would endear me to Amasis, though it might infuriate his vizier.

I spared one brief second to mourn the fact that I had not worn my rose-gold slippers to the festival. Then I was lost in the rhythm, twisting my figure to its best position in time to the music. I twirled and leapt. I let my limbs sway like a graceful willow. Naukratis wished me to honor them with dance--I would do more than that. I used my eyes, my hips, and my smile to entice the Pharaoh. My fingers curled gracefully, my feet skipped through the steps like sunlight upon the Nile. My hair was the fronds of the grasses on the riverbank. My arms were the arch of the waves. I was a woman in her element, and I danced solely for the pleasure of one man—the god-king Amasis.

When the song ended, I froze motionless in position. The silence was deafening. I paused, my arms trembling as I held my stance, and waited for

Pharaoh to condemn or applaud me. Every inch of my body tingled in anticipation as Amasis opened his mouth to speak.

"So," he said, while I drew a shuddering breath. "If she is the treasure of Naukratis, then the city is wealthy beyond belief. Such beauty demonstrates the blessings of the gods. You have done well, Rhodopis of Naukratis. By the Light of Ra, I say it is so."

The Greeks in the crowd burst into cheering, and I felt my cheeks burn anew at his fine praise. Naukratis was redeemed. Pharaoh could have ruined me forever with the slightest insult, and yet I knew my substantial business would be trebled by the morning.

I reveled in the joy of the crowds, the frown on Neferenatu's face, and yes, even the smirk of Praxitlytes. He wished to gain notice for himself through me. Well, I would allow him this moment, but he would have much to atone for in my eyes. I beamed at Amasis the god-king, unable to contain my pleasure, and swept a graceful genuflection. He smiled back without showing his teeth and leaned over to speak to his nearest advisor. I peeped through my lashes and read his lips.

"Have her brought to me."

Pharaoh's apartments in Naukratis were indeed luxurious. I was surprised by how little notice he took of the fine artwork and gilded chests, for I would think a former soldier would appreciate such treasures, having taken spoils of war from afar. He prowled into the room, motioning for the vizier and priests to attend us. I knelt before him and waited for the guards to meld discretely into the background, like shadows. Amasis bade me rise and led me to a low cushioned bench carved in the likeness of a lioness. I sat and then regretted it, for he remained standing over me like a hungry jackal guarding his kill.

The man radiated power. I tried to quell the fluttering in my stomach. We made some simple talk for a time. The weather, perhaps, or the status of the Nile. In truth, I do not recall. Everything seemed to pale around Amasis, as if he was, indeed, the focus of all Egypt. I watched the tilt of his head as we spoke lightly. His look was appraising and direct. It thrilled me. I felt my body go hot and cold by turns, and cursed myself for being so weak.

At length, a servant presented him with a goblet. He sniffed the cup and swallowed before indicating I should be served.

"It seems you have some enemies, as well as admirers." My heart skipped a beat.

"The same could be said of you, Great One." I grasped the cup with both my hands to keep them from shaking.

He paused. An awkward silence filled the room.

"You speak plainly," he said, at last.

I swallowed hard. "My apologies, Oh Great Nesu. I fear it is a fault I have always possessed." I felt naked and foolish beneath his gaze, though only my shoulder was bared.

Amasis moved towards the bench. "I do not find it a fault." His body filled the space next to me. He sat, but I could see he was not at all relaxed. The fingers of his hands were curled into a loose fist on the bench between us.

"You are beautiful." He reached up to finger a lock of my hair. I could feel the heat of his hand on my back. "Very beautiful," he repeated.

I shivered and tucked my skirts around my knees. "The Son of the Sun has many beautiful things." He frowned again and dropped the lock of my hair. I sighed, inwardly. Curse his soldier's face, he was so hard to read! Well, if he wanted me to be honest, I would not disappoint him. "Yes, I am."

He nodded. I could smell the oils and unguents rubbed into his skin. He smelled of sweet almond. "There are many things of beauty in Egypt." He paused. "Some of them are very deadly." I wondered if his eyes would be so compelling without the layers of fine cosmetic paint to enhance them.

I did not know how to reply. My pulse raced. One misspoken word could mean disaster. "I am a simple courtesan, Nesu. I do my utmost to take care under the protection of the gods."

He did not look convinced. "We shall see."

The heat of his body dared the night air to chill us. My throat grew tight. What would he do with me?

I took a sip of wine. "This is not Grecian, Potent Sword of Ra," I said, to fill the silence with safe and easy conversation.

"No." Amasis set his cup aside, untouched. "It is not." He seemed uncomfortable. "And I do not care for flowering epithets. Speak only plainly to me."

So, he wished to dispense with formality.

"As you command, Nesu. Do you wish me to lie back now?" I asked. Well, I could not be more plain than that! Perhaps the sooner this night ended, the sooner I could go home.

"I have many lovely women to please me. And not one of them do I trust. No, I have no need to lie with you, at present." He smoothed with the pleats of his white *shenti*.

"Then how might I please you?" I asked.

He did not respond.

I could hear the sounds of the festival outside, the joyous songs and laughter. I wondered if anyone guessed at how the 'Treasure of Naukratis' failed miserably to seduce the god-king. Oh, the shame! I focused on the lovely apartment, the rich furnishings scattered about the chamber, anything than to face his probing eyes.

"Do you play?" he asked, suddenly.

I jumped a little in my seat and realized I'd been staring at a gilded gaming box. "I do."

He surprised me with a smile, and by pulling a stand over. My heart hammered in my chest. Amasis carefully set the _senet_ board and allowed me to select the color of my choice. I tossed the sticks and moved my first piece around the board.

The game had begun.

He played well, avoiding the trap positions through a series of lucky rolls. I scarcely noticed when he called for more wine and food. I must admit, he was a good match for my skill, for his stint in the military made him a strategist. A fighter to the heart of him, I thought.

We were at evens by the time our final pieces reached the end of the board. I eyed the tidy pile of my lapis lazuli pieces, stacked beside the board. He had a haphazard mound of black onyx obelisks on his end.

"Your move." A brief smile touched his lips and he handed me the sticks.

I held my breath and tossed.

In an instant, I could see my throw was good. I moved my hand from my wine towards the board. I glanced at him. His eyes were still fixed on the game board and his lips compressed. Decorum bade me to lose the game. I _should_ lose.

My fingers lingered over my game piece, the one that must make a foolish mistake and cost me victory. Amasis shifted in his seat, leaning slightly away from the board. I could not read his expression, but the spark in his eyes seemed to dwindle and die. I drew my hand away from the board, masking my indecision with a small sip of wine.

"A difficult choice," he remarked. "One hardly knows what path to choose." He tipped his chin and looked down his nose at me.

"True." I wet my lips. "Sometimes the best choice is no choice at all-- to remain safe. For therein lies no risk."

He slapped his hands on his knees, startling me. "That is never the best decision! A player must act and reap the benefit or consequences of his choice. You must act. Now!"

I dislike being goaded, especially when I thought only to save his masculine pride.

"As you command, Great Nesu." I grabbed my final pieces and moved them off the board, winning the game. "I cannot make myself other than what I am. Here is my position. And now, I believe, I have won."

Amasis' eyes narrowed. His hand closed over mine and he twisted my arm. "You are a canny player. Who are you? Who has sent you? Was this some ploy to curry my favor?" The board and pieces clattered to the spotless marble floor.

"I am Rhodopis." I was surprised by how calm my voice sounded, for my pulse beat a steady tattoo. "No one sent me. I attended the feast by way of Praxitlytes the Greek who sought only to impress you."

Amasis stared at me.

Then, he released his painful grip and threw his head back, and barked a laugh so loud, he brought the guards. He wiped his forehead, smearing the kohl across his cheeks.

"As you say. You have done well twice this evening, Rhodopis of Naukratis." He leaned towards me. "Tell me, are you this honest with all your patrons?"

"Not all of them require such honesty, Great Nesu." I took the edge of my fine linen shawl and dabbed at his scented skin until the kohl was removed from his skin.

He caught my hand in his, and my breath jumped in my chest. The way he looked at me, I thought for certain he would kiss me.

"I require only the truth from you, Rhodopis. Will you swear to hold no artifice where I am concerned?" He squeezed my fingers.

Gently, yes, but enough that I realized how he held the whole of my being in his grip. He could order me to do whatever he wished, even imprison me for the slightest err. I would have to tread carefully.

"Honesty can be brutal." I swallowed hard.

"Egypt is brutal. But if you are strong and loyal, then you need have no fear." He released my hand, and reclined on his elbow, appearing unconcerned.

"I am loyal to you and to Egypt, Nesu. Only time will tell if I am strong."

Amasis leaned back and smiled. He unclasped a wide electrum band from his wrist and slipped it over my hand, up my wrist, and secured it around my upper arm. The precious metal was warm from his skin. "I have no mind for games this evening, it seems. Take this. The city will expect you to have some token of mine."

So, the soldier understood the social mores of my station. And, to my mind, he was a fine player of games. "Thank you. You are very astute, Nesu."

"Not half as much as I might wish, Rhodopis. Good night."

CHAPTER 25

I allowed Praxitlytes to apologize for his dangerous game playing.

After three weeks of returning Praxitlytes' missives, he sent round such a trove of gifts, including an orchard of potted persimmon trees, various jewels, a gorgeous cosmetic palette, polished bronze mirror, and a new brood mare for my stable, that I was forced to relent. Mara shook her head but refrained from commenting.

Praxitlytes' ploy had worked. Both he and I were commanded to attend the temple blessing. This time, the goddess Neit, a particularly favored shrine of the Pharaoh. There always seemed to be one feast or festival or another in Egypt. Indeed they are a most reverent and joyful people.

I let Praxitlytes escort me to the ritual, for I hoped to set up an exclusive brothel of trained *hetaerae* in Naukratis. Now that my own schedule was overtaxed, the additional girls would serve the lower echelons; a portion of the gifts they received would be donated to the governor to support improvements and repair of the docks and byways along the Nile.

All in the name of the people, of course.

On the way to the temple blessing, I tried to convince myself I had no qualms about meeting Amasis again. I was sure that after our initial encounter his interest in me would dwindle. After all, I'd done nothing more than play a ridiculous game of <u>senet</u>. What man would find that memorable? So, I was quite at ease when we arrived.

At least that is what I pretended.

I had dressed in an elaborate styled gown of costly net of polished blue lapis beads, extravagant and sensual, as I was completely nude beneath it. I felt decadent, scandalously so, but as the Egyptians were not overly concerned with nudity, neither would I be. I'd painted my eyes with kohl and rouged my lips and nipples, careful not to apply too much. The effect was stunning. The blue beads set off my light eyes and the cobalt patterns of my tattooed hands.

The noise of the feast was riotous. A bevy of Grecian girls danced to complex music. I singled out one or two who might make a suitable addition to my brothel. Perhaps the one with eyes like a doe, and that slim one there....Even I was impressed by their tireless dedication. Ever present rumors claimed the previous Master of Ceremony had disappeared, for he'd not been heard nor seen since the first festival. Someone made certain Pharaoh would not withstand another insult by hiring these devoted performers.

Wine flowed from amphorae in abundance. I secured foster of the girls, but after hours of fending off more persistent admirers and accepting a few assignations, my head began to ache. As I moved through the inner sanctum where only the wealthy and powerful were allowed to pray, I overheard more conversation that the mighty Kourosh of Persia had overtaken Drangiana, Arachosia, Margiana and Bactria just within the past month. So many within one campaign. Gods help us if he turned his evil eyes toward Egypt.

I moved through the crowds, unsettled by the smoke and noise. Plastering a false smile on my lips, I left Praxitlytes waxing poetic about the need for road repairs to increase trade routes, and I slipped away to the garden courtyard to clear my head.

How I love a garden at night! The breeze was scented with jasmine and smelled faintly of the smoke from the torches in the hall. It had been a successful evening and I was pleased by the results, but now I desired only solitude. The moon shone, round and full, overhead in the indigo black of the sky. Tension melted out of my body like the cone of perfumed wax that cooled my skin. I rubbed my hands over my arms to smooth the chill bumps away.

"Are you cold, Lovely Rhodopis?" asked a deep voice behind me. The scent of sweet almond oil enveloped me.

Amasis stepped out of the shadows.

My heart began to beat faster, and I told myself it was only because none may approach the Pharaoh without consent, and not because the sight of him speared me.

"Nesu." I dropped to a prostrate position. I had not meant to encroach upon his solitude. His private guards hovered like shades of the Underworld, just beyond his shoulder.

"Rise," Amasis said flatly. He stepped past me to the balcony and stared at the evening sky, the city of Naukratis only just visible below. Flickers of torchlight in each building spread like thousands of stars. "The moon is very full tonight."

"Are you enjoying the feast?" I stood and brushed the sand from my skirt.

His lips pursed a little. "As much as you," he said wryly.

"I-I think the dancers very fine," I said. What an inane comment! Could I think of nothing better to say to him? He would think me a babbling fool.

He glanced at me. "I have seen better."

My cheeks burned as I remembered the way his eyes had lingered on me at the festival.

He did not speak for a long moment.

"A thousand pardons for my intrusion, O Great Nesu. I-I should return to my escort." I bowed and awaited his approval to leave the courtyard, but he caught me by the wrist and I was forced to look up to meet his gaze.

"Do not leave." His eyes were dark and shadowed. His thumb stroke lightly on the inside of my wrist.

"As you command," I replied. In truth, I didn't want to stay on that cursed balcony, with his gaze devouring me. I shifted my weight and glanced at his hand still lingering around my wrist.

He removed it at once. "I do not wish to be alone, at present."

Well, I supposed his personal guards did not count for good company. We stood in estranged silence for some time while I tried not to fidget. At last he spoke again.

"I was not being courteous at the festival. I have heard of you, Rhodopis. Of your…influence in Naukratis."

My heart froze. I'd been found out.

"I am well known here, yes." I forced myself to sound unaffected by his words. I turned away so the moonlight might not betray my emotions.

"You give support. To the people. That is well, for it is the people who will bring Egypt her glory," he said.

I blushed at his praise. "As you say, Nesu."

"You are reputed to be clever." He paused. "I wish to gain Greek support so Egypt may hold against the Persians. What do you say to this?"

"I am but a woman, Nesu. What do I know of such things?"

He gave me a dark look which I well deserved. "I wish to hear your opinion, as a subject of Egypt. For as long as you remain here in Naukratis, you are under my," a strategic pause, "protection."

I wet my lips with a nervous tongue. "The Greek armies are known for their strength. You would do well to ally yourself with them."

He gave a half nod. "Such I have reasoned out for myself. I have asked for an alliance."

"And?" I asked.

"And they ask what I offer in return." He turned to look at me, resting his hand on the persimmon tree. "What should I offer them?"

Lightning raced along my skin. I swear I could feel the heat of him, though his hand no longer touched my flesh. "Something of value in trade for their aid. The Greeks are covetous of that which is beautiful. There is much of beauty in Egypt."

A more obvious answer could not be had! My mind was a jumble.

He sounded both defensive and interested, an odd combination. "I have questioned my viziers and yet none can come up with an agreeable offering. You are a Greek. What do you suggest?"

I did not think now was an appropriate time to point out I was not a Greek, but a Thracian. His fingers were stiff, though he curled them in a carefully controlled position on the tree trunk.

I swallowed the lump in my throat. "Surely you have some treasure with which to mollify them? Something of value to ransom their aid. Copper? Turquoise from the mines? Emmer wheat and barley?"

"We cannot. If Persia attacks, and I remain certain they will, I need to provide for the Egyptian people first. You see the value in this, I'm sure. I will not alienate my people for the sake of mercenaries, as did my predecessor Apries. Already the people clamor that foreigners overtake their cities along the mouth of the Nile. Not every place is as accommodating as Naukratis to those not Egyptian born."

I found it ironic that he consulted with me, a foreigner, on the subject.

"A gesture, then. Something of importance to Greece, but less concern to Egypt." Surely if all his viziers could not come up with a plausible offer, I could not either. I tried only to buy myself an end to this conversation.

"Such as?" Amasis would not let it be. Really, he was a most tenacious man. I suppose he must be, to have lasted so long despite the disdain and waning support of half the nobility.

"I cannot guess, Great Nesu. The Greeks are always fighting with one another; I cannot imagine what would bring them into battle in a foreign land, unless...."

I heard a drunken Praxitlytes laughing just inside. Something clicked in my head. The Greeks were ever in dispute, over lands, over women, over territory. What did it all come to? Hegemony. Power. Dominance.

How many times had I heard Praxitlytes complain of the Egyptians taxing their imported goods, and for what purpose? Because he resented the Egyptian control of what he considered his affair. Trade.

Nearly all trade cycled through our city; those who did not were forced into the lesser tributaries or to haul cargo over the treacherous desert wastelands. What if Amasis were to allow the Greeks governing control in Naukratis? The amount of goods taxed would be the same, and the coffers of Egypt would still swell. The issue at hand was who appeared to be in control of the ports in Naukratis.

"Great Nesu," I said. "Naukratis is nearly a Grecian city-state, save for the officials you have placed here. Have you not seen how many of us come to Egypt and settle here? What does it matter who is collecting the taxes as long as they are paid to your treasuries?"

"You wish me to give Naukratis over to the Greeks?" His entire body went very still. "This seems to countermand the very perception of the people."

I drew in a fortifying breath and forced my voice to remain steady. "I merely suggest you offer the Greeks a gift they half-own already. If a farmer toils the fields for his own sustenance, does that make his crops invulnerable to taxes? Is the ground any less yours to do with as you will?"

He stared at me for a long moment. Then, his fingers peeled away from the bark of the tree. "Rhodopis," he murmured, taking my hand up again. "The rumors are correct. You are quite… uncommon."

I wondered what it was that he had heard, but before I could ask, the blessing festivities spilled over into our quiet interlude.

"Have you seen the lovely Treasure?" called Praxitlytes from inside the colonnade. "Rhodopis? Where are you my sweetling?"

Amasis looked at me. His eyes were unreadable.

"I beg you to excuse me, oh Great One." I said, bowing low, slipping from his grasp once again. Decorum bade me to wait until he dismissed me.

Gone was the reserved grace from before, the assured possessive touch of his hands on my wrist. He flicked his hand toward the door. "I will think on what you have said."

I took it as an assent to leave and fled as quickly as I could. The guards turned away when I passed.

Days crawled by with no further word from Amasis or his court. As I was not called to attend Pharaoh or his court, I spent the following hours fretting over nothing. Mara suggested we sail down to Karnak and Giza to see the pyramids, but I opted to remain in Naukratis and accepted an assignation with a trader named Srensen instead. I still did not understand why Amasis had not tried to conquer my body. It was almost insulting, if one did not consider the sums this Srensen offered for my time. Srensen and many others, but not Amasis.

So, I focused on the business of increasing my business.

"There is no reason to accept this offer," Mara accused.

"Don't be ridiculous. Srensen trades all over Egypt. His word alone will more than pay for our trip to Giza later this season." I put my arms around her and kissed her until the frown left her face. I tried to tell myself that I wasn't staying simply to make myself available for a court summons.

Srensen was a thin man, with beady black eyes. Still, he had a ready laugh. Our conversation was light and easy over the evening meal—a marked difference than my fretful attempts to communicate with Amasis.

"I have heard you trade all over Egypt, Srensen. Tell me, in what do you trade," I asked, pouring over my platter of fruits.

"Poison," he said, with a wide smile.

I put down the piece of melon I'd selected.

Srensen grinned. "<u>Rat</u> poison. I hear Egypt is full of them." He slapped his knee.

What he found so amusing I could not say, but his smile was infectious. He was a pleasant patron, not overly generous or intelligent, but still, it was an evening well spent. He sent me on my way when our business concluded with a small cache of poison certain to rid my pantry of pests, which I did not think would damage my *hetaera* status.

"Be sure your servants use care when handling this, for it will kill a man as easily as a rat," he cautioned. I took the tiny red faience vial with some trepidation.

"Snake venom," he said proudly. "Sprinkle the powder and your troubles are over." He laughed again.

The cities must be full of rats from the amount he claimed to be importing into Egypt. Perhaps he was just inflating his own importance, a common enough habit among men without talent or skill in other areas. I returned home, tired and ready for the welcoming embrace of my courtyard pool.

"Here." I handed Mara the faience vial carefully. She quirked her brow and made to open it. I put my hands over hers. "It's poison to kill the rats. Give it to Zahouri, and tell him to keep it out of Kyky's hands. It's meant to rid my house of pests and you know how he feels about the monkey stealing the fruit."

Mara stifled a little smile. "I will."

"And be sure you tell Zahouri to wash after he distributes the poison."

I leaned over to give Kyky a kiss on his furry little head. Kyky screeched at Mara's retreating back, and I offered him a palm date. He leapt to my shoulder and his little paws snatched the fruit from my fingers. It was good to be home.

I rested that night with a clear conscience and awoke in the morning feeling at peace. Today I would go and visit the temples, and see for myself if my resources were being put to good use. And rumors stated Amasis would sail back to Sais within the week. I'd passed the test of his curiosity and now I would be free to continue my life in Naukratis.

Still, I couldn't help but feel the tiniest bit unloved, that I'd failed to seduce his interest, for he had certainly drawn mine. For Amasis was an extraordinary man. He gave credence to my words, as much as my fine figure—perhaps, even in spite of it. This made him most exceptional. I felt aglow with how much I wanted to draw his particular interest, an emotion I had not experienced in many long years, since before I returned to Naukratis. I drew an ivory comb through my hair, watching the red-gold strands shimmer in the morning light, wondering if Amasis wanted to touch me as much I desired him.

Sudden footsteps interrupted my grooming.

"There is a messenger at the door for you, Dori." Mara's eyes were wide. "One of Pharaoh's men."

I tried to quell the descent of my heart into my stomach, but failed. "What does he want?"

"He would not say. Shall I tell him you are out? You could sneak into the courtyard."

"No, if it is important, he will most likely search for me. How many were there, did you say?"

"Just the one." She worried her lip with her teeth. "What say you? Is it trouble for us?"

"One is not trouble. I will see him." I rose and dressed hastily. Mara trailed behind me, like a shade.

A royal messenger waited with stoic patience at the front gate. "You are Rhodopis of Naukratis?" he asked, through the bars of my outer gate.

"I am." I nodded.

"This is for you." And he passed me a missive through the scrolled bars.

I unrolled the papyrus scroll and read it. The paper trembled beneath my fingers.

"What is it?" Mara moved to peer over my shoulder. I did not mind; she could not read Egyptian.

"An invitation from the Pharaoh. He wishes me to accompany the court on the trip from Naukratis to Sais." I sighed heavily. I had not been back to Sais since Charaxus freed me.

"For how long" Mara asked.

"It does not specify. I think we must be prepared to be gone for some weeks."

"The Great Nesu also sends you this gift," stated the courier. He dug inside a leather satchel and removed a fine silken *peplos* of pure white linen, embroidered with gold thread. It was so thin and sheer it fit easily between the bars. The *peplos* settled as light as a bird's wing over my arm.

"Oh!" I caught my breath. "It's lovely!" I turned to show it to Mara.

She frowned at my new shawl. "Will you go?" she asked.

"I suppose I must," I replied. Mara's shoulders slumped. "When does the barge sail?"

"At dawn, two days hence." The messenger bowed and marched away.

I pretended to watch him depart, though in truth I wished to avoid facing Mara's displeasure. I could tell she did not approve. No doubt she would attempt to talk me out of going. When I could stall no longer, I turned and opened my mouth to speak.

"Mara, I…"

"I'm going with you," she blurted. Her lips compressed into an unyielding line.

I sighed. "It will not be a pleasant journey for you. Who knows how long he means for me to stay in Sais?"

"Precisely why I should come with you. You do not think to leave me behind?"

"Mara!" I felt my cheeks color. "I did not ask for this invitation! He is Pharaoh. I cannot deny him." I also could not deny that my heart trilled within my breast. What a glorious trip it might be, to finally have the chance to see him again. I was less excited to return to Sais, but who would refuse the god-king?

"Why not? You have not held to decorum so far!" Her cheeks flushed. "Who ever heard of a courtesan that defeated Pharaoh at *senet*? Why could you not just lie with him and be done with it?"

I saw Zahouri give us a curious glance from the courtyard. A wave of cold anger washed over me. I could ill afford to have such rumors as that bandied about the city.

"Do not make me sorry that I have confided in you, near-sister." I murmured. "I have been betrayed before."

Mara burst out crying and threw her arms around me, crumpling my new *peplos* against my body. "Ah, Dori! I am sorry. It is only my jealousy that makes me speak so, for I would have you all to myself. I love you. Please do not be angry. Don't send me away."

"I have no intention of sending you anywhere." I tossed my hair over my shoulder. "You are welcome to come with me, but only if you promise to voice no more objections. He is in a difficult position. Some of the nobility does not support his rule. My actions as a *hetaera* must be neutral and above reproach. One word spoken in jealousy could mean trouble for me. I will not have my name discussed in such a manner."

"Dori! I would never seek to harm you!" Mara's watery eyes grew wide.

It was true enough. Mara was not overly blessed with a clever mind, but I did not believe she would intentionally set out to hurt me.

"I know you mean me no harm, dear heart." I patted her shoulder and let my arm linger on her soft, warm skin. "Come, let us prepare. We have much to do and not a great deal of time to accomplish it."

The journey to Sais was not at all what I expected. After I set up Zahouri to watch over my house and stables and hired extra men to guard my gates in my absence, Mara and I climbed into the hired litter that would bear us to the docks. I was grateful for her support and company. We held hands behind the canopy of fine linen as the litter traversed the winding narrow streets to the docks.

"Look!" Mara gasped and pointed through the curtains towards the quay.

Pharaoh's immense barge was indeed gilded. It shone like the bright morning sun, gleaming on the desert sand. I looked around for Amasis but did not see him amongst the royalty, servants and dock hands milling about.

"Stop here," I called to the bearers when we'd drawn as near as we could. The litter was lowered, and the bearers helped Mara and I to stand.

A number of royal princes and princesses, nomarchs, and priests crowded the docks awaiting the signal to board, along with some of the finest aristocrats of Naukratis. I was the only courtesan and the only one without the stamp of Egypt on my features. Murmurs broke out as I passed, jeweled hands raised to cover whispers and speculative smiles, but I ignored them. I kept my chin high as a priestess would and my eyes sharp for Amasis, grateful for his fine gift draped over my shoulders. It made an impression on some of the court, at least.

We were herded onto the barge like cattle. I could feel Mara pressed up against my backside like a frightened calf.

"Mara," I whispered, as I almost tripped over her foot. "Step back." But she did not get off my heels until I bade her to straighten my attire.

Once we boarded the vessel, I saw that Amasis was already seated underneath a canopy of linen that fluttered in the river breeze. He nodded as the noble families made their obeisance, but scarcely looked at me. The procession of nobility and guests broke into small knots of conversation on the barge foredeck. Once or twice, I tried to edge in, but backs were turned or the conversation died as soon as I drew near. A few guilty glances shot in my direction and the groups reformed to new groups. Of Amasis, I scarcely saw him, closeted as he was under his own pavilion with the highest of Egyptian nobility, and, in which I was not invited.

The trip was an utter failure, save to rouse my ire.

So, I stood alone, save for Mara at my back. Well, I could withstand a little humiliation. I had survived much worse than the scorn of nobility, so I plastered a smile on my face and nodded pleasantly to anyone who passed. Once again, Amasis sat unmoving upon his gilded throne. I felt his eyes on me, though, even when I deliberately turned away from his stare.

I knew few of the other passengers, most by reputation. Most were from Sais and not my patrons, but I recognized Princess Therawejt, some ten paces away. Therawejt was a famous beauty, and Amasis' sister-cousin several times removed. She was the daughter of the wealthiest nomarch in Egypt, and indeed quite pretty with her lustrous skin and beaded braids. She stood next to her intended husband Snesuankh, Master of the Harvest, kin to Neferenatu the Grand Vizier. Snesuankh looked me up and down slowly before turning to glare at the Nubian dwarf attending Amasis, with his lips pursed in distaste.

"So," said Neferenatu, appearing suddenly at my elbow. "You _have_ joined us. I'd heard rumors."

I gave him my most polite smile. "As you can see, Grand Wise One."

Mara trembled beside me like a broken leaf. "Mara, fetch me some wine." Mara skittered away and I wished I could follow her.

Princess Therawejt glided next to the Grand Vizier and narrowed her black eyes at me. "Perhaps you can settle a dispute for us, Rhodopis. You are reported to be clever, for a Greek." She laughed a little too loudly.

I ignored her intended slight. "As always, I will do what I can for the royal families of Egypt, O Shining Star of the Morning." I inclined my head.

Princess Therawejt looked mollified by my flowering epitaph. She preened, tossing her braids over an elegant shoulder. Snesuankh smirked, and I sensed nearby guests turning their attention to our little group.

"They say that this Kourosh of Persia is unstoppable. That his hand is mighty and merciful." Princess Therawejt eyed my long locks blowing in the breeze as the barge sailed down the Nile.

"I heard he conquered Croesus with little trouble," Snesuankh replied. "Now he controls Lycia and Caria both."

"Did not Nesu secure forces from Caria to defend us?" someone asked from behind me.

Princess Therawejt waived her hand airily. "So he has said." Therawejt smirked. "But they say this Kourosh enjoys the company of Greeks in his household. They are treated like royalty. Tell me is that a common habit among rulers? To lift up the company of Greeks over one's own kin?"

My shoulders stiffened. It was well known that Amasis' predecessor Apries had promised too much to the Greek troops secured for protection in Egypt. But Amasis? I did not believe Therawejt felt any discomfort in attributing the sins of the former Pharaoh to Amasis to suit her own purposes.

"A ruler should be loyal to his subjects, of course." I placed a definite emphasis on that word--subjects. "Be they of like blood or not."

"And what if he should be betrayed with false promises to the detriment of his people? What say you then? Should he have remained loyal to the nation that birthed him?" Therawejt's eyes gleamed like polished ebony. "I have heard the Greeks are useful for little other than filling their own coffers."

Ah! She meant to embarrass me and rout Amasis as well. Well, I would not give her the satisfaction. But how to answer without offending the royalty present, nor inciting the Princess to further discourse?

"It is my experience that loyalty must be earned rather than bought." I glanced at Neferenatu, whose arms were crossed over his chest. "Or such loyalty is misplaced."

Snesuankh snorted. "How can loyalty be misplaced? It is either given or not. If a man buys you, you are bound to him."

"Are you saying that no amount of money could sway your loyalty, Great Master?" I asked.

Snesuankh glared at me. "Not I! I am a true man of Egypt."

"Take comfort in your own words, then. For if you check any city, even here in Naukratis, there are half or more who can boast the same. Does that make them any less a subject of Ra?" I gave him a small bow. "Perhaps they would not care to pay your taxes and work your land, then?"

Neferenatu frowned, crossing his arms over his chest. "Do you presume to gainsay the Master of Harvests? You are merely a talented harlot, not a court advisor."

"As you say. I am only a simple courtesan. What could I know of such things?" I moved away from them, feeling very much like a funeral barge gliding through crocodile infested waters.

It was a tortuous day.

After that, I was neither welcomed nor shunned outright. I spent most of my time standing silently on the fringes of conversation, scarcely tolerated for now. It was quite a blow after the many long months of adoration from citizens of Naukratis. Well, the royal houses would come to know me, to know that I stood for more than just empty beauty and grace. Still, I took care to avoid Neferenatu, Snesuankh, and Princess Therawejt as best I could.

And short of my brief welcoming nod, Amasis did not so much as glance my way, which only exasperated me further. I struggled to maintain an even demeanor. For all that I'd plastered a tight smile on my lips, my mood grew so sour that even Mara fled from me under pretense of airing out my *peplos* and I had to carry my own wine cup.

After the sun slid across the wide expanse of the skies, it was announced that we would reach Sais within the hour, though it could not be soon enough for me. I could not be more glad to get off this cursed barge. Mara was right; I should never have come.

I glanced at Amasis, who appeared hot and restless on his throne. He stared at me for a long moment. I could not read his expression. Then he inclined his head toward the side of the ship and stood up.

He wanted to speak with me!

I cursed my heart for soaring whenever he was near and strolled across the deck, past the laden feast tables and knots of curious or hostile glances. We moved in symmetry from opposite ends of the barge, Amasis and I, winding around the far side of the canopy where our conversation would be stolen away from eavesdroppers by the wind.

"Great Nesu." I made my obeisance.

Amasis drew nearer. We stared out at the river, the boats passing by, the young boys running along the banks, and the bundled papyrus skiffs that darted from island to shore like insects. The high chanting voices of priests echoed across the green water. We were very near Sais, by now. The bow of the barge dipped and water sloshed from the oars.

"You are a very skilled player of games." Amasis glanced at me.

Despite the throngs of people who surrounded the daily trappings of Pharaoh's court, Amasis projected an aura of solitude against the masses.

My head ached. "A game amuses only if one is aware of the rules."

He shifted his weight and the fine linen of his headdress brushed against my bare shoulder. "I am glad you are here, I think." The corners of his mouth deepened.

I meant to make a smart retort about how he could have shown me a little more welcome, but he turned and smiled at me--a genuine smile that turned his eyes to snapping brown sparks--and I forgot everything I was to say.

"Mistress!" Mara interrupted, pointing off the bow. A puff of white fluttered in the wind and was gone. My _peplos_!

I ran towards her, knowing it was already too late. Nothing could be done. I heard Princess Therawejt titter behind me.

"I'm so sorry." Mara stared at the deck. "The wind caught hold and it slipped away before I knew it was gone." Her face was reddened.

She was always a terrible liar.

"It is nothing," I feigned indifference. I could not help but mourn the loss of Amasis' gift. "Sometimes the wind will have its way, no matter what." I moved to the feasting tables without looking at her again.

CHAPTER 26

I did not speak to Mara until we landed in Sais, and then it was only to order her to stay close to me as we exited into a throng of citizens cheering the return of Pharaoh. My near sister was skittish in the crowds, and the order unnecessary save to express my anger.

Amasis had declared that I should stay until the Festival of Homecoming, which would take place in a little over a month's time. Mara meekly offered to stay behind on the docks and oversee the unloading of my things from the barge, while I hired a litter and inspected the few homes for rent near the palace, for I refused to lodge with that nest of vipers. The homes were outrageously expensive, but I contented myself with the thought of the wealth I would acquire as Pharaoh's favorite.

Mara sulked all the way to our new abode. I'd had enough rude behavior from the nobles on the ship, so I was not prepared to accept more from one of my own household.

"It was your choice to come to Sais, Mara. I warned you that the trip would not be enjoyable for you. Cease this childish behavior! It does not endear you to me."

"Why must you go to him tonight?" She slammed the lid of my carved wooden chest.

"Because he wishes it."

"We've sailed all day!" she complained. "You could use your charm to forestall him. You've done it before. Tell him you're tired and don't wish to go."

"Then it is because _I_ wish it! I have scarcely spoken to him since we left Naukratis. You swore to stand by me, once. Will you help me dress or not?"

Mara gave me a mutinous glare and stomped from the room.

I sighed. I suppose she had every right to be jealous of my time with

Amasis, but I had every right to enjoy such luxuries as were offered me. I told myself that I went because I was a dutiful citizen of Egypt and not because my heart fluttered like bird's wings when he was near. It was my job as a courtesan. Besides, I did not wish to insult Pharaoh by refusing his offer, for that offer could just as easily become an order.

I downed a cup of wine and soaked for a long time in the courtyard pool. A pair of languorous Egyptian girls rubbed my body with scented unguents until my skin was supple and fragrant. Mara entered my chamber with my best gown freshly pressed. She offered it to me with a silent, guilty face.

"Thank you." I removed the linen from my damp hair and let her arrange the pleats and select the jewels I would wear.

"Shall I wait up for you?" Mara asked when my last adornments were clasped in place. Her voice was raw, and I could tell she had been crying.

"Do as you wish. I am likely to be late." I gave her hand a final squeeze and headed to the waiting litter.

The night passed without incident. It was a small gathering. Neferenatu did not attend. I'd heard from one of the nobles that he and his wife were hosting a party of their own, to celebrate the joining of Princess Therawejt to Snesuankh. Well, that was a mercy, at least.

The women's table was crowded with a pair of languid, doe-eyed Kushites, a few ladies with pale skin not unlike my own, and many Egyptian princesses. These must be the wives of Amasis, and the daughters of royal houses, looking to gain Pharaoh's favor. I sat next to an overfed woman swathed from head to toe in pristine woolens. Imagine my surprise to discover that this nervous, sweating creature was none other than Ladice, Amasis' Greek wife. Ladice slouched miserably while the rest chattered in rapid Egyptian or picked at their platters of roast fowl, dates, and cool melon.

"Greetings, Star of Cyrene," I said in Egyptian.

"Oh." She peeped at me with huge brown eyes. "I do not suppose you speak Greek?" she asked.

"Of course, Princess." I responded, affording her the rightful title of her position--one of many wives of Pharaoh who had not attained the position of Great Wife and Queen.

Like his predecessors, Amasis followed tradition and gathered many wives. It was common for politics, not the heart, to govern his decision to marry. He currently had five wives--the daughter of his predecessor Apries by whom he'd already fathered two sons, two Kushite princesses named Semihib and Ootma, the Cyrene princess Ladice, whom was given in trade after Apries' unsuccessful rampage on that city, and a royal princess of Egyptian descent, whose belly was round with child and whose voice was so mild that I did not catch her name over the din. The wives lived in separate apartments, some at the palace, while other less favorite wives, like Apries' daughter, were allowed to live elsewhere, as she had no interest in court games, now that her sons' position, and thereby her own, was secure.

One of the Kushite princesses, Semihib, overturned a wine cup on the lap of a meek Egyptian girl scarce out of child's years, and then had her beaten. Sweat beaded my upper lip. I must not seem weak or easy prey to these cultured vipers, bred for the beds of kings. How I despise cruelty! Only sweet Ladice fussed over the distraught young girl, while the Kushites smirked behind their hands. I recanted my original assessment of the awkward Cyrene princess and vowed to champion her, if I could.

Ladice was rumored to be unconcerned with politics. It was said she was most unhappy in Egypt and she appeared as lost and lonely as I'd been.

"We can speak in Greek any time you like, Princess," I said, when the uproar was over, and the girl bundled safely off. I gave her a genuine smile. Her gaze wavered for a moment. What a discomfited, strange creature she was!

"Oh...oh! I am so glad," she babbled. "I have been half out of my senses trying to learn Egyptian, but...." Her voice trailed away at an odd point.

I had no idea what she was addressing, so I smiled and nodded as if I understood and took a sip of wine to cover the uncomfortable pause in conversation. I was not about to point out that most of the court and half the citizens of Sais spoke Greek in varying degrees. Amasis himself had ordered the scribes to educate the people.

"How do you find Sais, Princess Ladice?" I heard someone ask in Egyptian. "Do you miss Libya?"

Ootma masked a malicious smile, when Ladice's brow furrowed. Her lips moved as if she sought to translate words in her head, so I relayed the question quietly to her in Greek. Ladice's cheeks pinked, but she gave my hand a squeeze under the table.

Her brown eyes filled with tears and her trembling lip reminded me of Mara. I felt a twinge of pity for her. She was only slightly better off than the poor wine-stained Egyptian princess.

"Oh...oh. I suppose Sais is nice." Her voice was as flat as the sandy banks of the Nile. She gave away much with her tone if not her words. Ladice was not happy in Egypt. Perhaps it was only that which kept her safe from the plots of the Pharaoh's wives, for I did not trust the Kushites to keep their pranks restrained.

"There are some lovely gardens near the temple, Princess." I put my hand over hers. "I should be happy to show them to you."

"You have been in Sais before then?" Ladice asked. "I...I thought you arrived on the barge with...." Her voice trailed off again.

I felt my cheeks burn a little. "I lived here some time ago."

"I should like to accompany you to the gardens sometime." Ladice's quivering lips curved into a smile.

She appeared to harbor me no ill will. I don't think I could make the same claim, if I should be in her position.

The entire court was in a frenzy over the conquests of the Kourosh of Persia and over who would eventually position themselves as Amasis' Great Wife. For much of the people's opinion of Pharaoh's potency resided in his ability to master a powerful household. It had been speculated that perhaps the beautiful Therawejt would soon wed Amasis, but thus far, she remained promised to Snesuankh. I thought of her calculated snide remarks, and silently thanked the gods that Amasis had not thought to bed that coiled viper.

After the meal ended, I was asked to dance for the royal families. As there were many there who had not accompanied Amasis to Naukratis, I forced a smile to my lips and put my tired body through its paces. Three times I was called, and three times I danced with Amasis' dark gaze weighing heavily on me, but he did not speak openly to me. After the third dance, the Kushites hissed at me behind their hands. Their eyes shot daggers at me, when Amasis wasn't looking.

As the evening wound down, I moved restlessly through the clustered groups to the fresh air and solitude of the balcony. The moon bathed the garden courtyard below me with pale silvery light and the scent of jasmine and sweet mint scented the air. I felt a pang of longing to see my home, the familiar village paths of Perperek.

"I thought I might find you here." Amasis joined me on the balcony.

"Nesu." I bowed low before him. "It seems you always know where I am."

"Well…." Amasis said and then just, "Well." He chuckled.

I wondered what else he might have said. "Are you glad to be home?" I asked to fill the silence of the night air.

"Yes, I am now." Amasis seemed preoccupied. "Rhodopis, I have heard of you."

"So you said, Nesu, the other night."

"No, not the rumors of Naukratis. *Here*. In Sais. You were the woman of Charaxus, the wine trader, yes? But you had another name then." So, Amasis had spies everywhere. My heart pounded in shame, but Amasis fanned his bejeweled fingers. "It does not matter to me."

I could not believe he would so readily dismiss my past. I felt frozen inside, as cold as the peaks of mountaintops in Thrace.

When I did not speak, Amasis nodded again. "It is of no consequence. I had another name, myself, once. It seems very long ago." This news did not surprise me, as it was the custom of Egyptians to take a court name when ascended to noble status. It signified the attainment of a new life.

I'd taken a new name, myself. And though not royalty, it had been many years since I'd thought of myself as Doricha.

"Do you miss that old name, now that you have found another," I asked, fighting for calm.

"At times." His fingers clenched. "I was more certain then, of what was expected of me. Now...." he paused. "You saw them in there. The royal families treat me as if I were no more than that." He gestured to the brass chamber pot tucked behind a huge potted palm in the corner of the balcony. "A vessel to be used."

I blushed at his candor.

True, the royal families obeyed Pharaoh's every command. They served him, but I'd seen the subtle slights, a too long moment before acceding to his request, the slight shortcomings of some of their deference. I'd heard the whispers of dissension and felt the tension coiled in the room like a mesmerizing serpent. It angered me, when by all accounts, Egypt was more prosperous now than in any time in recent recollection. Why should he have to fight to keep that which the gods had given him to rule?

"The chamber pot?" I laughed with a lightness I did not feel. "No matter the use, is it not the same metal we use to craft our effigies? Is it not as finely carved and deserving of its place in the palace as, say, the goblet that graces your lips? Why should it be considered any less?"

And why should he be? He was Nesu, the mighty Pharaoh of Egypt, regardless of his origin. A man who stood alone against the legions of Persia's advances.

Amasis stared at me. I could not read the emotions playing across his liquid eyes. At last, a hint of a smile played across his lips, and he grasped my shoulders and pulled me hard against his body. I thought he would kiss me. Surely he wanted to kiss me, now. I leaned closer to him, savoring his warmth, his sweet almond scent. I parted my lips and waited for the feel of his mouth on mine.

It did not come.

For just then, his advisors came with their pinched faces to intrude upon our quiet conversation. I sighed with more regret than relief and felt my cheeks burn.

"Neferenatu has returned. Snesuankh and the Princess Therawejt have wed," they said.

Amasis plastered a wan smile on his lips. "May they be blessed with joy and long life under the Light of Ra."

My heart echoed his blessings. I felt his eyes on me as I made my farewells to the royal families and called for my litter bearers.

"Do not forget. The gardens? Tomorrow?" Ladice squeezed my hand. Her eyes were so filled with hope that I could not refuse her. I saw Semihib glancing at us and felt wearier than ever.

"As you wish, Princess." I crossed my left arm to my shoulder and inclined my head in the customary obeisance for her station.

Mara was waiting for me when I arrived home. I stumbled into my house, weary and sleepy from too much wine and too little food. I'd been so nervous I hadn't eaten much, and I was much surprised I had not tripped over my own feet through the dances.

Mara fussed over me, helping me to undress and releasing my hair from its elaborate coif. She brushed it with soothing, even strokes. I sighed in pleasure and did not complain when she drew off her own gown and bade me lay beside her on her bed. Not when she kissed me hungrily on the mouth, over and over, until I begged for her touch.

Afterwards, her long fingers drew soft patterns up and down my sore limbs as I recanted the evening's events--lonely Ladice, the scheming Kushites, the marriage of Therawejt and Snesuankh, my dancing, Amasis and the chamber pot. She giggled at my description of the fat, rosy princess sweating in her Greek woolens.

"She would do better to go home than to stay in Egypt," she said.

"Yes, but I do not think Amasis would allow her to leave Egypt." I answered. "Did you know that Apries sent him to attack Cyrene?" Mara shook her head. "Poor thing, her marriage was meant to curry favor between Cyrene and us, once Amasis gained the throne."

Mara's hands stilled. "Us?"

"Egypt is our home, now." I propped my head up on my hand. "Do they not remind you a little of Thrace? With their fire, their passion...their beauty?"

Mara stared at the straw mattress. "I cannot say they do."

"Oh." I felt a twinge of disappointment, for I'd thought our hearts were more similar.

"Besides," Mara continued. "You are far more lovely and graceful than anyone I have seen here in Egypt. Even with too much wine and not enough food in you." She gave my nose a playful tweak.

"Oh, Mara." I snuggled up beside her, grateful for her soft, warm body. My shoulders ached from dancing and my cheeks were stiff from the smile I'd plastered onto my face.

She smoothed the hair off my forehead. I listened to her breathe for some time before she spoke.

"Dori, have you ever considered leaving this place." Her voice had lost its teasing lilt.

"Hmm," I said with a half-laugh. "And where would we go, sweet sister? Back to Greece? Do you wish to return to the temple so quickly then?"

Her hand stilled. "No." She bit her lip. "No, not there. But I do not know how much longer I can continue, Dori." She shuddered.

I sat up and leveled my gaze at her. "What is the difference between these men and the temple *ktístai*? We were nothing in the eyes of Greece, simple chattel to be mastered and broken. We would not be proper women. And if we did marry, would you be content to live out your days imprisoned in your home?"

"You could be *hetaera*." Mara said. "Why settle for Egypt when we could go elsewhere?"

"I'm not settling." Somehow, the savage beauty of Egypt had wormed its way into my soul. "I'm happy here. You could be, too." I sighed. "My beauty will not last forever, sweet sister. At least here, we have some freedoms. I will not return to Greece to become any man's wife or concubine."

"We could go to Lesbos, to the Poetess Sappho. You told me she has a school for girls there. We could be together, Dori."

"No, Mara." I stood. "She is as dangerous as Aidne ever was, I am sure of it. And I am no longer the girl I once was. Her way is not mine, but if you wish to go, I will not stand in your way."

Indecision flitted across her face like shadows.

"Do you not love me?" she asked. Her voice sounded small.

"Of course, dearest," I hugged her fiercely, inhaling the scent of her sweet skin. "But I will not give up my hard-earned freedom. Not even for you." And I could not deny the strange attraction I felt whenever Amasis was near.

I watched her affection for me battle her loathing and wondered which would be the victor. Some long moments passed and she did not answer.

"This is not a decision you can make after an evening such as this. Think on it. I will abide by whatever your heart dictates you must do. But," I said as I put my hand over hers to soften my words. "Do not think that I will go with you, if that is your choice. I have my place here, in Egypt. Though it may break my heart, I will not go."

Mara's bottom lip trembled. I wanted to kiss her, to soothe away the unrest in her soft cheeks, and to put my arms around her slender waist. Instead, I walked away and left her with an uneasy decision.

The next morning, I had her decision. She left a white rose on the chest beside my bed. I awoke to the powerful perfume of devotion and two simple words scrawled in spidery Egyptian on a shard of pottery.

I stay.

The following day I'd gone to the gardens with Ladice, but she was so tongue-tied and uninteresting that it was nigh torture for me to think of how to fill the silence. After the umpteenth time of sending her servants for this sweet or a feathered fan, I promised to send an Egyptian tutor round for both her and Mara. Perhaps it would help my near-sister to receive the benefits to which I myself had applied. And for certain, it could only help the poor Cyrene, as one of Amasis wives. Ladice thanked me with the apathetic air of one used to needing extra tutelage.

The day was stifling, in her inner garden courtyard. No breezes blew, and the sand gritted beneath our sandals like shards of glass.

"You seem uncomfortable, my Princess. Perhaps you should try to adopt a more comfortable form of dress." I eyed her sweat-soaked chiton.

"I could never clothe myself in such indecent...." Her voice trailed off, but this time I sensed it was because she did not wish to insult me. "Well, I have not the figure for it." She gave a nervous laugh and swooshed the fabric of her dress back and forth. I could smell her body odor lurking beneath the multitude of perfumes she wore. "You are all swan-like grace in your...oh look!"

And she prattled on about a completely unremarkable olive tree. I could not wait to escape and take respite in my own courtyard.

I focused my attention on the blooming jasmine and nightshade, so vivid against the garden's plastered white walls.

"Oh, Rhodopis. I'm afraid I do not know people to ask favors and keep my secrets in Egypt. It was not so in Cyrene. Before they came, my sisters and I would chase the new ponies into the surrounding fields...oh, such times we had together, there."

"Cyrene is known for its fine steeds, Princess," I said, thinking of my own stables back in Naukratis.

"Yes, it is. Indeed, it is so." Ladice wiped her eyes and called for refreshment.

And that was the most interesting of our conversations that day.

Over the next week, Ladice requested me to escort her around Sais three more times. Those next visits were filled with her blatant frustration at being in the royal court of Egypt, a marked sign of her uncouth trust in me, a fellow Grecian. I could not help but feel sorry for her, being raised on a mountainside with her horses and sisters, and then sold as a peace bargain to the very throne that destroyed her home.

"Oh...oh!" Ladice said when I arrived. "I am so glad you are here. I have wanted to call for a healer woman and none of them," she gestured at her bevy of Egyptian ladies, "can understand me."

"A healer? Are you ill?"

"Oh! It is only my woman's time that pains me so. No," she waved her pudgy hand back and forth. "No, I am not ill."

"Well then." I smiled. "It is an easy remedy." I snapped my fingers at the Egyptian ladies who stood and bowed respectfully. Still, they were a trifle slow to respond and I caught their sly glances and covert smiles. "You there!" I said in Egyptian. "Shall I bring your name before our Great and

Holy Son of Ra as lacking in your duties to your honored Princess?"

At that, their faces blanched. I ordered them to bring Ladice refreshments and a large fan to keep her cool. They crossed their arms over their chests and scurried away like rats, while Ladice stared at me with open-mouthed delight.

"They poke fun and insult me, I know. I recognize their tone, if not the words. You do not know how grateful I am that you have come to Sais."

"Why do you not pick new ladies to attend you?" I asked.

"What would it matter?" She sighed and I pretended not to recognize her unhappiness. She was so filled with longing for Libya, that I thought it wise not to unleash the tempest of her tears. She was much like Mara in that respect.

"You should try to apply yourself to your tutors, my Princess. Your time would be easier spent here, if you became more accustomed to our culture." I urged, gently.

Ladice sniffed. "That is what you have done, yourself?"

I supposed I had. I was more than immersed in Egyptian culture. I'd troubled myself to learn everything I could, and in the learning, came by an understanding that I had lacked before. Perhaps that is why I couldn't bear the hungry faces of the orphans on the street, or hear the crack of a whip against a slave's back.

The next week Amasis sent an invitation for me to attend him, while he exercised his chariot horses. I was excited at the prospect of seeing him again. And having owned a fine stable in Naukratis, I was more than interested in seeing him race, and flattered that he should ask me to attend. Part of me wondered if he realized his Cyrene wife was learned in horseflesh, but I could not bring myself to ask.

He led me to a wide sandy track near the edge of the city. There were a few others gathered to watch, including Neferenatu, the vizier. I tried not to notice his angry, narrowed eyes as Amasis led me to the pair of fine white horses.

He encouraged me to stroke their gleaming bodies, while stable hands held their reins tight. The horses quivered under my touch, and my gaze darted back to the gathered royalty, clustered in loose knots of conversation. I identified with the horse's emotions. Fear. Distrust.

"Sha," I murmured low. "I won't hurt you." I blew gently into his nostrils that he might become familiar with my scent. The horse nickered in response and allowed me to catch hold of his rein.

Amasis put his hand on my shoulder and led me back to inspect the chariot. It was a wonder--great and golden as Apollo's sun chariot. The entire carriage was bedecked in layers of gold, electrum, and silver. The concave interior sported painted scenes of Amasis conquering a horde of kneeling Nubians, his foot placed atop their heads.

"Ride with me," he commanded.

This time, I did not hesitate.

I handed my cup of wine to the nearest servant. Amasis stepped up first, and I stood just behind. In the chariot there was enough room for us to stand side by side, but I was content to let more practiced hands hold the reins. He widened his stance, his muscular thighs straining at the tight pleats of his *shenti*. I braced myself, holding onto the sides of the chariot.

With a shout from the stable hands, we were off. At the first rushing jolt, I abandoned my hold on the wooden chariot and flung my arms around Amasis' midsection.

"Are you sure this is safe?" I called, over the rushing wind.

He laughed and called for the horses to go faster. I leaned against the strength of his broad shoulders, and let go my inhibitions. If he thought it safe, I would not gainsay him. The wind whipped through my hair, and my heart pounded in my chest in time to the beat of the horses' hooves. Once I'd let go of my fear, the sensation was indescribable.

We were flying!

We pounded down the sandy track, away from the city. I risked a glance over my shoulder and saw the white plaster buildings of Sais grow smaller. The wind whistled in my ears and I could not help but laugh. I felt as free as the falcons circling overhead. The sun blazed and turned the dunes to gold.

He tossed me a grin, and for a moment I saw the boy he must have been, eyes twinkling with delight and his tanned face creased with joy. No more the heavy cares of the throne of Egypt.

We turned a corner and he pulled back on the reins slowing the chariot. Gravel spewed from the horses hooves and we rolled to a stop.

"Well," he said. "What say you? Did you enjoy the ride?"

What could I say? That it was frightening and thrilling all at once? That the sensation mimicked the feeling in my stomach when he drew near?

"It...it was the most precious of your gifts to me," I smiled. I pushed the unkempt locks of my hair out of my eyes, not even caring that I looked a mess.

His expression grew serious and he pulled me close to him. His eyes fixed on my mouth. "Not many women of the court would share your enthusiasm for such coarse pastimes, Rhodopis."

I was dizzy from the speed of our ride and the nearness of his body. A wave of desire engulfed me; every inch of my flesh was attuned to him. Oh, why did I seem to go into heat every time he was near? Me, who'd never needed a man's touch!

"I was raised a soldier's daughter," I said. "I am not afraid."

His lips quirked. "And yet I feel your body trembling like a palm frond." He shifted his weight so that the length of him touched me from foot to chest. The hard muscles of his body pressed through my fine linen as if we were alone and naked before the sight of the gods.

"Only from the nearness of you, Nesu." I confessed.

His brow rose. "Rhodopis…" he murmured.

Now, I thought. Surely now he will kiss me. I felt my lids droop in anticipation. His lips were inches away. I felt his fingers grasp at my hands.

"Here." His voice was more a sigh against my lips, than speech.

"What?" I looked down and found he'd slipped the leather reins into my sweating palm.

He smirked. "Let us see how a soldier's daughter handles herself."

My nerves were a jangled mess by the time we reached the palace. My back and legs ached from bracing myself against the bouncing chariot and the surging horses. All the while, he balanced easily behind me with his hands resting lightly around my waist. He directed me through his words and his touch, showing me the easiest way to grip the leather reins, so that I afforded the horses enough room for the proud arch of their necks, while not allowing them too much freedom.

By the time we arrived, half the royals had departed for more interesting company. I was grateful, for my hair was a tangled mess, and my gown sodden with sweat. When Amasis gave me leave to depart, I limped to a litter. Then I spent the rest of the afternoon soaking my sore muscles in my courtyard pool, but the feel of his body against mine did not leave me.

When Ladice summoned me yet again that week, I am ashamed to say I sent Mara instead. Though I pitied Ladice, I could not stand the thought of listening to her mindless babble after I'd spent long lovely hours reveling in her husband's company. Besides, my coffers were in need of replenishing, and Mara did not seem to mind the Princess' company, so I was content to let her go in my stead.

Still, I found myself unwilling to accept any assignations. Which ones to answer first? Who would be insulted and who would gain notoriety by my selections? Stacks of gifts piled up in my chambers, but I felt too restless to answer any of them. My head ached with determining what decorum dictated I must do, and from wondering if Amasis thought of me at all.

I'd heard news that the Persian king Kourosh had captured Babylonia, taking the city by surprise. He was now master of an area that stretched far to the east of Egypt. If public rumors were to be believed, the Persian king crouched at our borders as if his gods promised him the world. It truly seemed so, for the Persian threat was now without equal. The whole of Egypt dithered with worry, and me doubly so, for last I'd heard my dearest Aesop had been sent to attend King Nebuchadnezzar of Babylonia. Without Amasis' strength and experience to protect us, I feared what would become of us all.

Still, by season's end, there was a new uproar in the palace. The marketplace was abuzz with minor gossip. It seems Amasis had installed a lovely new sculpture of Ra in an alcove of the palace rose garden. Many of the minor noble families, craving approval or simply wishing to be thought as such, had stopped to admire it, to kneel before it with offerings of food, drink, and adulation. That is, until Amasis let it be known that the brass used to smelt the god's image had come from an unusual source.

His chamber pot.

"From humble origins, great things can come," he proclaimed.

I was so amused I could not help but laugh as I went about my daily business. Especially when Mara rushed into my chambers with a gift of precious lotus-infused wine from Amasis.

"What can it mean?" she asked. It was not the typical offering of a lover. I shook my head, not wanting to explain for fear that my pleasure at his tribute would cause Mara pain.

I understood the gift of the lotus wine. It stood for clarity of thought. The Egyptians believed that to drink lotus wine gave them the power to commune with the gods. The message within the gift was clear. He valued my council. My heart soared.

Perhaps he did think of me, a little.

"I do not understand these people," Mara said.

"I am sure it is nothing." I patted her hand, but she drew away from me with a scowl.

A frown marred her pretty face. "I think you like him."

How could I not? "He is far different than I thought he would be," I admitted, feeling unaccountably cautious.

"You used to fear him. How can you change your feelings so quickly?"

"Oh, Mara." I sighed. "You will find fault with any man that interests me. Even the god-king of Egypt." I wrapped my arms around her to take the sting from my words. "You must admit there is much to admire about him." I tried to dispel the memory of his strong hands around my waist.

"I hear he is a drunkard. He fritters away half the day on drinking and games."

"Mara! Where do you hear such things?"

"It's true! He only holds session for part of the morning and then spends his afternoon guzzling wine and exchanging jests with commoners and royalty alike."

"Perhaps he wishes to discover the thoughts of the common people for himself. But, even if those stories were to be true, I should like some time to indulge in drinking and pleasantries myself if I bore the weight of a country on my shoulders. You cannot blame him for that."

"I don't. But the same could not be said for others." Mara pursed her lips.

"Mara!" I laughed, without meaning it. "What is it? What do you know?"

She shook her head and slipped out of my arms. I was half-tempted to call her back, to order her not to pay such heed to rumors and gossip, but it occurred to me that perhaps I could use her ears and eyes to Amasis' advantage. If she communed with those who plotted against Amasis, her insight could help strengthen his hold on the throne.

That I wanted to help him succeed surprised me more than I can say.

Two weeks passed in a blur of invitations to the palace, temple rites, feasts and court celebrations. Mara was not at home that morning. Her absence made me irritable as I was summoned to play _senet_ with Amasis that afternoon and without Mara I could not dress my own hair.

I'd escorted poor Ladice around the city once more, and accompanied her to the marketplace where she planned to try her newly acquired Egyptian words. But Ladice was not impressed with the market. She continued to compare everything to those of Cyrene, from the foodstuffs to the finery. I wondered if the Libyan markets were truly that much superior, or if it was only her lonely heart that made her so ungenerous. We left without making any purchases, though it would've done the common people much good to have her patronage.

I'd seen Amasis few times in those weeks, though we were never alone. We passed a few moments of polite conversation, or a shared smile. I watched for him everywhere, and kept my ears trained for any word of him, telling myself that I was only being a loyal citizen of Egypt.

Still, I found myself staring at his lips on more than one occasion, wondering what they would feel like on my skin. But he did not try to kiss me. He seemed content to merely watch me from across the room. He did not request I attend him in his private chambers again.

If my patrons' gifts were any indication, I was by far the most desirable woman in the realm. I'd received a stack of precious animal furs from Nubia, frankincense from Babylonia, and a reed cage of doves. Kyky, my monkey, screeched and taunted the poor birds, so I gave them to Mara to send to Ladice. My servants, commoners, and tradesmen on the streets stopped and made obeisance when I passed them in my litter. So why did Amasis not wish me to please him? Was he a lover of men, then, for all that Egypt rumored him to be a great womanizer? Perhaps that is why he did not wish to lie with me.

I worried that his lack of ardor would hurt my business, but it did not. Offers poured in, invitations to large feasts and quiet dinners. Still, I put off responding to any of them, for what if Pharaoh should request my company? My coffers were quite full. I could well afford to wait.

I busied myself by penning an Egyptian harpist's lay I'd heard at the palace.

> ...Revel in pleasure while your life endures
> And deck your head with myrrh. Be richly clad
> In white and perfumed linen; like the gods
> Anointed be; and never weary grow
> In eager quest of what your heart desires
> Do as it prompts you...

It reminded me of my promise to the goddess--to follow love all of my days. A noble endeavor, but difficult to hold to.

"Dori!" Mara rushed into the room.

I fumbled with my hollow reed, splattering red ink across the page.

"Where have you been, Mara?" I forced my tone to be even. "I came back from the temple and you were gone."

"I was at the market shopping for hair combs. Princess Ladice admired yours, so...never mind that. Dori, you must listen to me. I delivered the combs to the palace." She paused and bit her lip.

"Mara, what is it? What about the palace? Has something happened?" My heart leapt into my throat. "I can see from your face something is wrong!"

"It's not _him_." Mara answered my unspoken question without rancor. "It's Aesop."

"Aesop?" I breathed a sigh of relief. "Is he here? Quickly, get my _peplos_. Oh, I cannot wait to see him. I have so much to tell him...and you must meet him, of course...."

Mara did not move. "He is not here, Dori. He's gone."

The plea in her voice stopped me when her words would not. "What do you mean, gone?" I asked.

She would not look me in the eye. "He's dead, Dori. Murdered at Delphi."

CHAPTER 27

Mara went with me to see Ladice. If my near-sister had heard of Aesop's death at the palace, then no doubt Ladice, who was much prone to gossip, would have ferreted out the entire story by now. I followed hard on the heels of our escort through the maze of garden courtyards, past the pools of blue lotus and tamarisk trees to Ladice's chambers.

"Oh...oh! It is such a loss for Greece." She wailed and threw herself into my arms. Her eyes were puffy and red, and her cheeks streaked with tears. For once I did not mind her heavy theatrics. I felt like crying, myself.

"How did it happen?" I stifled my own tears. "Was there some dread accident with King Nebuchadnezzar?" Anger clutched at my chest like a falcon's claw.

"Had you not heard, Rhodopis? Aesop left Babylonia long ago. He was sent with an embassy to Delphi by Croesus, King of Lydia."

"Lydia? I thought he was in Babylonia." He'd made himself indispensable to two kings in short time. "Why did Croesus send him to Delphi?"

"To give out one hundred gold ducats to whoever proved himself worthy. But Aesop was so disgusted with the Delphinians that he lashed them with cruel sarcasms until Delphi was in a fury."

"I do not doubt it was so." I nodded. Aesop had a terrible temper.

Ladice agreed. "It was no more than they deserved. Everyone knows that Delphi is a den of liars and cheats. Only a barbarian would send them gifts, but I am certain Aesop did as he was bid by Croesus. He brought the ducats but could find no man worthy, so he vowed to pass out none and threw them into the sea, instead."

No man, I thought. But perhaps he should have searched instead for a woman. In Greece, that was sure to never happen.

"At this, the Delphinians became enraged. They chased him to

Hyampeia, the tallest cliff, near the Oracle's Temple. Then they threw him to his death onto the rocks below the Castalian Spring."

"Oh!" Tears sprang to my eyes. I pictured the bulk of his body broken on the jagged rocks and covered my mouth with a shaking hand. "What a horrid end to such a great man."

"True…true," Ladice said. "And I feel his loss, keenly. He was a kinsman of mine, of course."

I wanted to smack her. She did not know Aesop; she'd never even met him! My fingers clenched and Mara must have guessed what I was feeling because she pressed a cup of wine into my palms an instant later. I calmed myself whilst Mara poured one for Ladice, as well.

"So," the Princess continued. "Reports from Delphi say the city is cursed. They'd left his corpse to rot beneath the sun, those impious fools. Aesop was in the right, after all, for the gods have rained fire, famine, and death upon its denizens. There is hardly a soul who survived. Why, I have heard that the ground rumbles and shakes and great flames spew out of the streets until half the city has fallen to rubble! Can you imagine?"

I should never have let Aesop go to Nebuchadnezzar. I should have agreed to marry him…perhaps if I had, he would not have died in such a wicked manner. I could not stand to be in Ladice's chambers another moment. I desperately needed time to be alone in my grief, but Amasis expected me some time ago.

"Excuse me, Princess." I forced my voice to be calm. "I am late for an assignation that I fear I cannot refuse." Though I did not feel at all well, it would not do to insult either of them with an unexplained absence from a summons.

"Oh…oh!" Ladice's cheeks flushed. "I cannot bear to be alone in my sorrow. Can you not stay with me?"

"I am sorry, Princess." I tried to be gentle, to spare her feelings. "Pharaoh has summoned."

Ladice ducked her head and shot a wistful glance at my near sister.

I sighed and rubbed my eyes. "Stay, Mara, if you wish. You can escort me home later."

Mara gave Ladice a shy smile, and I slipped gratefully away from the Princess' cloying presence, feeling only a little guilty at offering my near sister as a substitute. It was my fault that Aesop perished. My skin prickled all over, as if I were about to weep. I willed my eyes to stay dry until after I'd met Amasis.

After following my escort through the palace, I found him in his outer chambers. He was dressed casually, without his headdress or wig. His cropped hair gleamed as if it had just been oiled and the scent of sweet almond and exotic sandalwood hung in the air. I hesitated, for thus far I had only seen the formal side of Pharaoh. Here was little more than a common man before me, and yet I found myself breathing deeply as if I could ingest the very sight of him.

"You are late," he observed, taking the draughts from the tiny drawer of the game box. "I expected you much earlier." His smile glinted at me from the dark copper of his skin, taking the sting from his rebuke. "Now, you will have to work twice as hard to please me."

"I…I am sorry." My nerves were a jangled mess. I did not make a proper obeisance.

For though my heart lurched at the sight of him, I could not withstand the guilt of Aesop's death. I needed to make an offering to the gods on behalf of Aesop's shade so that he could travel to the Underworld in peace. It was my fault he'd died, my burden to bear across the cold seas to Delphi.

Amasis set down the draughts and strode towards me. "You are troubled. I can see it in your face and the set of your shoulders. What is it?"

"Aesop the Fabulist is dead." I withered inside, just speaking the words aloud. I'd always thought my dear friend would return to me someday.

"Ah, I have heard of him." Amasis said. He stared at the ground for a long moment. "You knew him? Loved him?"

If only I had! "As a brother. He was a true friend to me when I needed him and now Delphi has killed him." If only I hadn't chased Aesop out of Egypt.

Amasis put a warm hand on my shoulder. "I am sorry for you, Rhodopis." He called a servant. "Let me send an offering to Delphi on your behalf. He was a great man."

Aesop *was* a great man, the best of them. Custom bade someone to make an offering to the gods--to appease the shade of Aesop's murdered soul. And he had no family to speak of, save for me, his Little Crab.

"No, please, Great One." I walked a few steps away from him. "I wish to do this myself." I expected him to insist on his own way, but he let me slip from his touch without comment. "I…I beg you to dismiss me from Sais, if only for a short time. I must appease Aesop's spirit."

He paused, and then nodded once. "You must go, of course. Will you return in time for the Planting Festival? There is something I would discuss with you…well, I cannot say it now when your heart is heavy with the loss of your friend. Will you come back to Sais for the Festival?"

The Planting Festival was only a few weeks away. I intended to sail to Delphi myself, to make peace with Aesop's memory, even if the Delphinians would not.

"I will try." I managed a weak smile.

"Then *I* will try to be patient until I see you next." He scooped the draughts and dumped them back into their drawer. "Not so easy a task, I assure you." And he leaned in and pressed a soft kiss to my mouth.

I was so startled I did not think to play the flirt with him as I ought.

How strange to think that even in my grief, I could be unsettled by him. Feeling somewhat dazed, I followed my escort to Mara and told her of my plan to sail for Delphi.

I did not tell her Amasis kissed me.

Instead, I listened to Mara prattle on about Ladice's menagerie of animals, her gazelles, her exotic birds and her fine spotted cats.

"You are very quiet," Mara commented as we left the palace. "Amasis took your news well? He was not angry with you for asking to leave Sais?"

"As well as he could. No, he was not angry." I thought of the feel of his lips on my skin and my legs trembled all the way home.

I would sail to Naukratis without my near sister by the week's end. Amasis would never consent to me leaving my Saisian home completely, so I asked her to watch over my affairs until my return. Mara protested at being left behind, but when Ladice sent a messenger inviting her to visit at the palace, she ceased her dogged arguments and acquiesced.

As our flat reed skiff caught the current upstream, I tried to think of a worthy tribute to Aesop's memory. There were the usual offerings of animals or grain. Perhaps I could send some spices? No…though costly and rare, none of that seemed appropriate for my friend and mentor. I needed a tribute that would placate his shade and appease the wrath of the gods or he would not be free to walk the Elysian Fields. I wanted him to find a place in the highest level of the Underworld. But what to give? There was a temple to Athena in Delphi, the goddess of wisdom…well, something for the temple, perhaps….

Once we landed in Naukratis, I had my answer. A pair of sacred cows was unloaded onto the quay while I waited and watched from my barge. They were magnificent creatures, each as high as the shoulder of the herder leading them to the temple for sacrifice. I would not send cows, but the very implement to offer their flesh to the gods. The sun's rays gleamed on their immense bodies as if Ra approved of my decision. I would give Athena the means to accept the finest sacred beasts Delphi could secure.

When my boat docked, I procured a litter to bear me home, surprised at the number of people who stopped their work and bowed as I passed. I'd been gone almost half a year, how could they still know me? I suppose my finery led them to believe that I was royalty. I was curious to know what had happened in Naukratis while I was away. More faces bore Grecian features than I remembered. The sight of them made me homesick.

Zahouri greeted me with marked enthusiasm, eager to show off how well he'd kept my home and chattel. He'd done more than a decent job. Everything was as tidy and well-kept as if I'd still lived there. Even Kyky, my monkey, was content to perch on my shoulder and chatter and scold me until I kissed his head and fed him honeyed dates.

Before I unpacked my satchel, I ordered Zahouri to send a tenth of my wealth to the forges. I wished to finance a group of rare beef spits--huge iron rods capable of spearing the carcass of an entire cow--to send to the Temple of Athena. They were both expensive and unusual. I did not know how many of them there were, nor did I care. It was enough that they would be a remarkable offering to honor a remarkable man.

Zahouri bowed and swore that all would be done to my specifications. I asked him to send in a servant with some wine before he left, while I reviewed my accounts. Sometime after the wine arrived, I looked up to find Zahouri had returned and skulked outside in the late afternoon shadows of the hall. I'd worked much later than I'd intended.

"Yes, Zahouri? What is it?" I blotted the ink on my papyrus scroll. My eyes strayed out the window to the curling leaves on my white climbing rose. He'd done a fair job running my household while I was away, but my garden was sorely in need of my attention.

"Naukratis has mourned your absence, great Mistress. There has been speculation that you would not return to us."

"Ridiculous. Who would make such a false statement?" I reached for the cap to my ink pot. "This will always be my home."

Zahouri licked his lips. "There have been many ships coming in, now that the Nile swells its banks and Nesu Ahmose has given Naukratis over to the Greeks for settlement. Ships that report Persia prepares for invasion."

So, he'd followed my advice, and allowed the Greeks dominion over that which they already held. I wondered what Neferenatu, the Grand Vizier, had thought of that.

"What does this have to do with me? Nesu is a skilled soldier. His troops are loyal." War was a bad business, even for courtesans to the king.

"It is said in the streets that Nesu must make a strong show to the barbarians. He must choose a Great Wife and forge an alliance that will unify our defenses against this Kourosh of Persia. The royal houses must be united to withstand." Zahouri stroked his chin.

"True. But such is outside of my concerns just now. I do not have the heart to set your mind at ease over which of the royal princesses will be suitable."

Zahouri huffed through his lips, clearly agitated that I did not agree. He waited for me to finish, with a patience that only a former slave could have. Still, Zahouri was a loyal servant. He seemed so earnest; I could not bring myself to insult his reasoning.

"Here." I gave him my mark to secure passage to Delphi. "Find me a ship. I promised Nesu I would try to return by the Planting Festival."

Zahouri shook his head, but took the papyrus from me. "It is good that you follow the will of Nesu Ahmose. But it will take you almost that long just to sail to Delphi, to say nothing of the wait for the iron spits. You will not make it there and back in time, unless the gods themselves fly you there."

"Then you'd best make haste, Zahouri. I do not know if Ra's arms can stretch all the way to Delphi, but we'd best try."

As soon as the iron spits were forged and ready, I sailed from Naukratis to Delphi--to the temple of Athena that stood there. The journey took us almost twelve days. The seas were rough and wicked. I must admit that I did not live up to my reputation as a famed temptress on that journey. When I was not sicking up my bread and beer over the side, I was huddled morosely at the mast, feeling cold and miserable. I wondered, quite uncharitably, if Mara enjoyed herself at Ladice's palace in my absence.

Love is a complicated and demanding mistress. Each time I thought I'd earned her notice, she saw fit to toss me to the wolves. Charaxus and Aesop had loved me, but Hori had not. I'd thought Mara loved me well, but she seemed distant as of late and determined to mother me as she had in the temple. Well, I was not a naive girl anymore. I had no illusions that Amasis might love me. He'd done no more than ask advice on matters which I'm sure he could have reasoned out for himself and offer me a chaste kiss. I rested my face in my arms and wondered when my life had become such a tangled skein of emotions.

For I could not fathom what might be wrong with me that Amasis did not wish to love me. I realized now that I more than desired him.

"Mistress?" The captain touched my shoulder.

I blinked back the tears that stung my eyes and lifted my head from my arms. "Yes, what is it?" Could he not see I wished to be alone?

"We reach Delphi by morning."

At last, Aesop would have his restitution, and I would be the one to pay it.

"Thank you," I said grateful for the knowledge. "I will go below and try to rest."

I tossed and turned fitfully on my rocking cot. One of my attendants brought me a measure of watered wine and a lotus petal to chew. My stomach settled and I drifted into a lethargic daze. At last, I closed my eyes to the swaying cabin. My ears felt stuffed with wool and my tongue seemed too swollen for my mouth.

I dreamed of my white climbing rose.

You have not tended me, it said. Its thorny branches quivered, and a few blackened leaves fluttered to the sandy earth.

I don't know why I was not more surprised that a rosebush should speak to me. Its voice was sweet and reedy, like the trill of pipes or birdsong.

"I am here, now." I touched a fingertip to one of the twisted brown branches. It felt warm and alive beneath my fingers.

"But is it enough?" It was the voice of my Lady. She sat beneath an olive tree, and sweet olive blossoms drifted down like snow around her face. "It seems a shame not to work such fertile soil." She gestured to my dying rose.

I was filled with a sudden anger. Why should such a lovely thing die, neglected and uncared for? Who had left it in such a sorry state?

I took a trowel and worked furiously at the earth beneath the splayed branches, content to feel the sun upon my shoulders and the earth in my hands. I yanked away the choking weeds that crowded the stems. When I finished, I set my trowel aside and discovered an amphora of water beside me. I sprinkled the glistening drops over the soil. I swore I could feel the roots take hold beneath the earth, and saw fresh, green shoots sprout from the gnarled and twisted stem above.

"See," cooed my Lady. "All that was needed was a little care." I heard the flap of wings behind me and turned but she was gone.

The flap of wings turned to sharp rapping of hands on wood.

"My Lady," called the ship's captain. "My Lady? We have arrived."

With great trepidation, I stepped off the ship with my entourage of servants, my two personal guards, and Kyky the monkey perched on my shoulders. The entire city had been rocked by an immense earthquake just a week prior. I was shocked by how rocky and pale Greece seemed, after years spent in the warm, vibrant company of the desert. Even the air smelled different.

It was no longer home.

The people were worn and tired. Despite the exotic luxury of my entourage, they stared dully at my finery, my servants, and the huge stack of iron spits piled on the docks. We made the journey from the docks up the winding hillside to where the city hovered near the foothills of the Phædriades.

"Have you come to save us?" asked a decrepit old man crouched in rags near what should have been the _agora_. The courtyard was nothing more than a pile of scorched rubble and broken timber. I wondered if he had joined the crowds that tossed Aesop to his doom.

"I come to make an offering." I forced away my righteous anger, for surely there were innocents within the devastated city. "You must save yourselves."

The citizens feared the gods' retribution after the first of the plagues, so they'd gathered up Aesop's corpse and sent his spirit to the sea with an honor procession that wound down every path of the mountain. They'd placed him on a funeral bier and set it aflame as it sank into the sea. The very sea now littered with Croesus' coins.

Nevertheless, I hired a guide to take me to the spot where Aesop died.

It took a good deal more gold than I thought, for they considered the spot cursed. Still, wealth will always have its way, and in the end, I stood at the cliff where Aesop had been tossed to his death. We wound up the jagged cliffs near the Castalian Spring where supplicants once bathed. I knew my friend had met his death on these sharp stones nearest the pool, so I did not offer such tribute to the gods.

I closed my eyes. Aesop rested with Poseidon, now. My wise and dear friend. Did he entertain the gods? Could he see me?

"Higher," I told our guide. "I want to go higher."

We hiked between the two highest peaks, until I reached almost the summit of the highest, Hyampeia. My days of climbing mountains had ended many years ago and I found myself laboring for breath. I was no longer a young woman, but a woman past her prime. I should have had a fine husband and babes, by now. Had it been my goddess' promise or the silphium that tainted my womb? I could not say.

The fact that I'd never conceived had never been a concern—certainly not in my profession. But I found the riches and luxury of my freedom hollow compared to the warmth of a husband's embrace and the laughter of a child. In my youth and arrogance, I traded away the greatest gift of the gods—the immortality of seeing one's children and grandchildren grow and prosper. What man would want a barren woman? Not even my famed beauty could diminish the power of a fertile woman.

For all that Aesop sang my praises and all that I was reported to be clever, in the end, I was nothing more than a fool. A slave to my passions, as Mara had cautioned me.

At last we reached the summit. I ventured near the edge of the precipice and peered down at the pool, only a glittering flash of silver from this distance.

Egyptians fear to travel, for they believe to die on foreign soil precludes them from the Great Afterlife. They say that Ra floats along the Nile bottom to collect those who have drowned and promises them a place at his table. We were not in Egypt, and Delphi was not the spot of Aesop's birth, but still I murmured a prayer in Egyptian, in case the Sun God was listening.

A bit of gravel skittered off my sandal as I rose. It scattered into the spring below.

"Please, Lady. Come away. Do not stand so near the edge." My guide shifted nervously from foot to foot.

"I do not fear this place." I raised my arms and did a little dance, just to show him. How Aesop loved to see me dance! I felt the warmth of the sun shining on my cheeks as I twirled.

I swear I heard Aesop's laughter rustling in the wind.

Little Flower, cried the wind. *Little Crab*.

The guide backed away from the edge and me, his eyes round with fear in his pale face. No doubt he thought me mad.

I sighed and dropped my arms. "Let us go. It is almost time for the ceremony."

After we climbed back down the mount, I heard that another had come to Delphi on Aesop's behalf. The city reported that Iadmon of Samos had arrived to claim restitution from the people of Delphi. My heart nigh stopped when his procession arrived and I was trapped in the streets by the rush of his party, but the young man I saw was scarcely sixteen years of age. He could not be the Iadmon my former master, nor even The Swine of my nightmares. I think it must have been his son, no doubt forced on some poor slave girl. One thing was certain, he had red hair.

I smiled ruefully at that bit, even as I pitied the mother.

The beef spits were piled before the altar of Athena, though half the central chamber stood in rubble. All of Delphi came to view them before the large stone effigy where the goddess dwelled, the citizens spilled out of the temple and down the stepped hillsides, each awaiting his turn to pray for mercy and forgiveness. The seas were unusually calm as the priests chanted the blessing.

I spoke only a few words to the assembly. When the Delphinian priests asked who gave such a generous gift, I surprised even myself.

"I am Rhodopis," I said. "Rhodopis of Egypt." It felt right. Surely thoughtless Doricha would've never made such a grand gesture.

A pair of young girls dressed in rags stared at me. Their eyes were wide and one sucked nervously on her finger. Gods, had I ever been so young? Grief and misfortune had pushed me beyond that reckless, self-centered child who thought only of her own comfort. Aesop would have been proud, I think.

Goodbye, my friend.

I hoped that his shade would go quietly into the afterworld, his death having been avenged. Perhaps he would join my Lady and watch over his Thracian flower. For the court of Egypt was a tangle of political turmoil-- who knew who would be the victor? I needed some watching.

I returned to Naukratis within the month, much sadder, but determined to learn from my mistakes. I vowed to use the gifts of reason and logic that Aesop had bestowed upon me.

I did not keep my promise to Amasis, however, which was not an auspicious start to my new life. I'd been away over a month. Though the seas were calm, our ship docked in Naukratis almost a week after the Festival. I'd missed it and, I realized with a shock, I missed Amasis.

Praxitlytes met me on the docks, with an entourage of servants.

"I'd heard you returned." He smiled broadly. "See? I have been made

Master of the Docks in your absence. Not a barge settles here that does not go through my accounting."

I was tired and crusted with salt from my journey, but I forced myself to smile. "I am glad for you, Praxitlytes. Your gamble at the festival has paid off."

"Yes," he chuckled. "I am sorry you were my gaming piece, though. Will you forgive me for that?"

"It is my own pride and folly that I cannot forgive, Praxitlytes. I have already forgiven yours." I signaled to a litter bearer.

Praxitlytes laughed again. "Still the consummate game player, lovely Rhodopis?"

I thought of what Zahouri had said about the ships bringing news. Sailors from many ports came through Naukratis. Perhaps there was news of the Persians.

"I keep my hand in. Tell me, Praxitlytes, how fares our Naukratis?"

"It is as well as can be expected. The people sorely miss you. Their numbers swell the temples. We are glad for the continued support, in your ah….absence." He shrugged his shoulders and helped me into the litter.

"Any news from the palace? What of the Kourosh?"

Praxitlytes stroked his short beard. "You heard he conquered Babylonia, did you?" When I nodded, he continued. "He sent an envoy to Pharaoh's palace, proclaiming himself King of the Four Rims. They came through here and that nasty fellow, the one who called you unworthy, came to greet the entourage."

"Neferenatu? The Grand Vizier?"

"The very same."

My stomach fluttered. "Neferenatu came to greet them?" I wondered if it was by Pharaoh's command, or by Neferenatu's own design.

"So it would appear." Praxitlytes turned and shouted at a pair of workers lounging in the shade. I sensed that he wished to make a show if his importance, but my endurance was running short.

"Blessings on your new appointment, Praxitlytes. I must go. Zahouri will have much for me to do before I sail back to Sais." I signaled to the litter bearers to lift.

"Zahouri is a loyal credit to your name. I'll call on you tomorrow." Praxitlytes bowed.

I waved what could be taken for assent and closed my linen curtains.

Zahouri greeted me at the gate. "Will you go to Sais, now?" he asked.

It felt good to be back in Egypt. "Yes, I suppose." I sighed. "Though Nesu will not be pleased by my late arrival."

"The people will rejoice to hear you've returned. And as for Nesu Ahmose," Zahouri's lips curved in a lascivious smile. "You can ease his displeasure, I've no doubt."

I raised my brows at him. Despite rumors that I was Pharaoh's courtesan, Amasis had never indicated any desire for me other than his chaste kiss. If only the people knew half of what went on behind the palace walls, what a laugh they would have.

I gave him a mock frown. "Such talk is unseemly, Zahouri. Even for you."

His face grew serious. "Truly, Great Mistress, I mean no disrespect. It is well that you should go to Nesu Ahmose at once."

"You are very eager to be rid of me, Trusted Servant," I said.

Zahouri's cheeks went pale. "No, Mistress. It is just that...well...the rumors say Nesu shall announce his Great Wife before the next full moon."

"Then Amasis has chosen his Queen?" My heart skipped a beat.

"So the rumors from Sais report. But nothing is set until the decree has been posted."

"There no secrets in Egypt. Who is it?" I asked.

I did not want to hear her name, but I found I could not help but ask.

"No one knows, but Nesu has been closeted with his viziers for days. Rumors say none of his advisors appear pleased, but the threat of invasion forces Nesu's decision. Our Great House must be strong." Zahouri's lips compressed. "The people believe Nesu Ahmose will do what is best for Egypt."

I wondered who the woman was, which one of the royal Egyptian ladies had deigned to marry a former commoner. I hoped for his sake that she was both clever and pretty. _Well_, I rubbed my eyes with the heel of my hands, _perhaps not too pretty_.

I forced my tone to be calm. "Then, I hope he shall get her with child and make our alliances secure in the eyes of Ra." My voice sounded sharper than I'd intended.

"You jest at what you cannot understand, Mistress." Zahouri's expression was strained. A man in his position could not express outrage at what he perceived was an insult. I felt horrible to have treated him so.

"I am sorry, Zahouri. I did not mean to belittle you. We are all children of Egypt, whatever our origins--you, by birth, and I, by choice. Let's not quarrel. Make the necessary preparations. I promise to head for Sais by the week's end."

"Or tomorrow, perhaps?" he wheedled. "Tomorrow would be a good day to sail. I've heard the weather will be fine." He sounded so hopeful.

I did not like to be hounded into action, nor did I wish to rush to Sais only to return when Amasis married his Great Wife. No Queen of Egypt would tolerate a courtesan as her husband's personal confidant. Lesser wives, such as all the Princesses, surely must bow to Pharaoh's decree, but a Queen? Her position would be as like to Pharaoh's own, and her power multiplied tenfold. Not only would I lose him, but I would be forced to leave Egypt altogether.

"No, not tomorrow. Would you have me appear before Amasis, thin and ill from the sea? Give me a few days of solid earth beneath my feet and decent food before I must go."

Zahouri bowed deeply. "As you wish, Mistress. It shall be done."

Oh, if only it were that simple.

Chapter 28

The day I sailed back to Sais, I decided to put an end to my foolish naiveté. I'd thought long about the lessons I'd learned from Aesop, from the misery of my life as a slave to my experience as the only Egyptian *hetaera*. Well, I was a woman now. I need seek my value from no one. If the goddess saw fit to send me love, it would not be the fickle attentions of some man too weak to make his own destiny. Surely not after all I'd learned.

Live free, my father bade me.

It was time to put away childish dreams and consider what lay ahead. To plan for my future, whatever future my Lady had in store for me. And here I had the very symbol of my misspent youth, stowed in my baggage. I handed Kyky to my escort and fetched out my lovely rose-gold slippers from the *peplos* stored in my satchel.

The afternoon sunlight glittered on the ripples of the Nile. The small barge moved through the green waters like an eel. I breathed deeply and glanced at the slipper in each hand.

I'd vowed to follow my Lady all of my days and she'd indeed led me to Love.

Perhaps mine was not the love of a god-king, or even a simple man. But Egypt, ah Egypt! Motherland of nations, she sang to me a song called *home*. After so many years, I'd grown to adore it. The endless copper sands, the swelling jade river that twisted through the black fertile land, the gleaming white cities, even the deliciously impudent people who kneaded clay with their hands and bread with their feet! They chose their own path and so must I.

What need did I have for empty tokens, when the goddess gave me riches in excess in every leaf, rock, and wave? For me, Rhodopis of Egypt, it would have to be enough.

I called upon all the gods of my memory, those of Thrace, Greece and Egypt. I called upon my Lady with the Golden Hair. Take back the treasures you have given, that I may honor you anew, as a woman.

I breathed deeply, drew my right hand back and flung one of my treasured slippers far over the water. It glimmered like a blazing star and arced toward the welcoming depths of the Nile with a soft tinkle of the brass bells. But just as the toe of my slipper touched the water, there was a piercing seven-scale cry and a flutter of cream and brown bird's wings. A predator swooped low over the water, hunting for his evening meal.

I cried out and lunged far over the side of the barge, but it was too late. I lost sight of my slipper beneath the feathered body of a crested falcon. His talons dipped into the river's surface and he lifted up, up and sailed away carrying a dripping treasure in his fierce grasp.

"My slipper!" I shouted. "Come back!"

What portent did this have for my return? Did the gods not accept my offering? I glanced at the remaining slipper. I thought I'd learned so much. I'd lost nearly everything I treasured in my life, if only to gain some measure of clarity. Did that count for nothing?

"How much more?" I shook my empty fist at the sky.

The far off, triumphant cry of the falcon rebounded across the water.

By late afternoon we docked in Sais. The docks were almost empty, surprising for midday.

"Where is everyone?" I asked the nearest dock worker.

The slave dropped his hemp rope and crossed his arm over his chest as if I were royalty. "The gods have answered our prayers, Great Lady. Nesu makes a proclamation at the palace."

So, Amasis would announce his wife today. My heart was so heavy, I wished I could pluck it out of my chest and drop it into the Nile. I was sure it would sink like a stone.

All I lay upon your shoulders you bear, my Lady had said. *All and more.*

Well, I did not think I could bear anymore. I was shaken by the portent of my lost slipper. And though I should be happy for the Pharaoh's marriage meant Egypt would hold against the Persians, I found I could not muster any joy.

I should go to the palace and wish him well. I should be relieved that the troubles of court would no longer plague me--that I could slip into the obscurity of my profession and fill my coffers for the days when Mara and I were old, when I would be fit for nothing but spinning yarn and tales from my youth. I should return to Naukratis, back to my garden, my stables, and my life.

I *should.*

But it is not in my nature to do that which I should.

All I could think of was the rumble of his laughter, the unfettered joy as we rode in his chariot, and the way his lips warmed my hand. I buried my face in Kyky's furry back. He cocked his head and squeaked at me.

"Take me home," I said to the litter bearers. No doubt Mara would be thrilled to pack up and return to Naukratis.

But Mara was not there. The servants reported that she attended the ceremony at the Temple of Neit. Feeling anxious and a little abandoned, I read over my household accounts for a few hours and reviewed a few patron offers while I waited. I tried not to think of what might be happening at the palace, to not speculate on which woman Amasis chose. Hours passed and I realized that this was a test of my earlier resolve. I must put this whole mess out of my mind. He had his Queen. It was time for me to leave Sais, to return to Naukratis and make my mark as Egypt's foremost *hetaera*.

Mara returned late in the day, with her hair arranged artfully. Ladice must have loaned her the use of a servant.

"Dori!" Mara kissed my cheeks. She smelled of myrrh. "I'm so glad you are back. I have so much to tell you."

"Do you?" I directed a servant to unpack my satchel and another to draw me a bath. I dreaded hearing who Amasis had selected. "Mara, I'm tired. Perhaps we can discuss this later?"

"But, you'll never guess what has happened. Someone tried to kill the Pharaoh!"

I froze. "What did you say?"

"Amasis went lion hunting with some of the other nobles this morning. I saw them leave; their chariots made such a racket as they left the palace!"

"You were at the palace, then?" My heart pounded. "Is Amasis well?"

"Well, yes, Ladice asked me to attend her." Mara waved her hand back and forth in the air. "But that is not here nor there. Settle your heart. He is well, Dori. The attempt did not succeed, nor did they catch the one responsible."

"How did it happen? Perhaps it was only an accident?" Oh, I could not bear to think of him injured.

"They'd cornered a lion out in the dunes," Mara said. "Someone miscast a spear and it almost hit Amasis, and not the lion in front of him."

My throat grew tight. "Who threw the spear?"

"The spear was unmarked. No one claims to have seen who threw the spear, not even the chariot drivers, though Neferenatu ordered them beaten to make them talk."

"I cannot believe the guards saw nothing." So many soldiers, all of them trained to notice small details. Pharaoh himself had described their training to me. And not one of them saw the culprit? Chill bumps raised on my flesh.

"So they claim. But Amasis has dismissed them and selected a new personal guard. I think the proclamation today was arranged to quell the fears of the people."

A hard knot formed in my throat. "Ah," I forced myself to sound nonchalant. "Who did Amasis name as his Great Wife?"

"He didn't." Mara's gaze darted to a plate of dried fish. She snatched one up and took a bite. "How was Delphi?"

"It was fine. What do you mean, he didn't?" Delphi was not fine, but I was too concerned with her news to elaborate.

Mara shrugged. "He said something about the sun god Ra and Horus...you know I don't understand Egyptian all that well."

"Ladice has interpreters. What did he say, Mara?" I stared at her.

Mara's hand dropped from her mouth. She set the fish aside. "If you must know, he never announced his choice."

"Why not?" I sat down, stunned.

"He sat on his throne on the central dais. All the nobility was present. Everyone waited for the moment he would speak the Queen's name. As for me, I thought he would choose Ladice. Amasis has visited her often since you left."

Did she think to wound me with her words? Was she still angry, then, that I'd left her behind in Sais? "Why should he not? It is a wise choice. She is already his wife and a Greek."

A declaration for the Cyrene Princess would cement relations between the Greeks and Egypt. I knew Amasis needed Greek support to fight back the Persian threat of invasion. I knew this.

I *did*.

So, I forced my tone to be even, though my near sister cut me to the bone with her hasty support of Ladice. It felt almost like betrayal, though I myself had no claim to him. Still, better he marry a kind and gentle Egyptian royal, than to raise up an awkward foreign Princess with little or no interest in Egypt or her people. I tried to picture Ladice standing behind Amasis on his sun chariot as the wind whipped around them or passing out resources for the temples to support the indigent and sick. Tried and failed.

"Why did he not make his intentions clear?" I asked. "His proclamation would be cause for great joy." *For some*, I amended in my head.

"There was a sign from the gods which precluded it." Mara fussed with her pleated gown. "Just as he spoke, a great bird sailed over the dais. It was a falcon, the very symbol of Horus. All present bowed their heads for its wings were twice the span of a man's arms, I'm certain! At any rate, the canopy bearers backed away in fear. The priests called out to their gods. Then, the falcon swooped down low and dropped something right into Amasis' lap."

"The falcon dropped something?" An image of brown wings stretched over the glittering Nile flashed before my eyes. My heart stopped.

"Yes," Mara stared at me. "It did. Your slipper. Right into the hands of the Pharaoh." Her voice was cold with accusation. "It was a neat trick, Dori. How did you manage it?"

I could not breathe.

"How did I...? I *never*!" The venom in her voice startled me. Did she think I meant to steal her precious Ladice's favor? I'd never set out to do any such thing!

"You did!" Mara retorted. "How else could such a thing have come to be?"

"I tossed my slipper into the water and the cursed bird fetched it back again. It flew away. I had no idea that it would drop it into Amasis' hands! How could I?"

Mara stared at me for a long moment and I watched the flame of accusation dwindle and die in her eyes.

"No," she mumbled. Her shoulders deflated. "I suppose not even the great Rhodopis could manage such a feat. I'm sorry, Dori. It might be the will of the gods, but still I worry for you."

I was so grateful that she believed me that I put aside her condemnation. "What can it mean?" I whispered, feeling sick. "What can the gods mean by this?"

Mara shook her head and moved towards the door. "I don't know. But Amasis claims the gods have spoken to him. He will marry none but the woman who fits the slipper." She paused and looked back at me. "And we both know that you can never be named Queen of Egypt."

Mara was right.

I can hardly deny that my blood pounded at the thought of being his wife, queen or not. I could not help but remember the way we'd laughed the last time we played at *senet*. The way his eyes sparkled and his face became animated when he discussed his plans to build a huge monument at Memphis. Any woman would be honored to bed him. But I was no temple priestess, beloved of the gods. I was not even an Egyptian princess. In fact, I had no royal ties at all, unless one counted my patrons.

And if my near sister thought I aspired to such greatness, then surely those who knew me less well would think the same. That could make my position quite tenuous when the Great Wife was named. So I kept my remaining rose-gold slipper. I hid it carefully away in my room, where it burned like a guilty secret. When no one was about, I unwrapped it from the shabby *peplos* and stroked the finely wrought workmanship.

Here it is. The answer to all my prayers. With this, I could be queen of this land, his Great Wife. And I would, if only Amasis wanted me.

I took special care to absent myself from his presence unless I was summoned, and I did not dance. If any in Sais remembered the origin of the rose-gold slippers, they did not speak it publicly. So there was no one to know that Amasis' proclamation named me as his Great Wife, save for those of us too heartbroken or frightened to mouth it.

The next week a second misfortune struck. I'd just finished praying at the temple of Neit, and honored the priests with offerings of oil and amber. As I went to put up my jeweled bracelets, I noted the lock was open on my cedar chest and the _peplos_ with the rose-gold slipper hidden inside was gone.

I called for Mara. Together, we turned my household upside down, but the fact remained that my treasure, my only connection to the greater glory of being Amasis' wife was stolen away from me. I doubled the guards in my household, and allowed Mara to hire new concubines to attend me. She was a comfort to me, my near-sister, and went about her business of tending me with a patient and kind efficiency. I was nearly inconsolable, for I felt I'd lost my last ties to Amasis. I sobbed my heart out in her lap, while she stroked my hair like a child.

The next day I nursed a sore head and a worried heart. I pushed aside my feelings for Amasis and vowed to accept one or two of the more interesting invitations. But my heart was not in it and before I knew it, two weeks went by without my answering any. Two weeks spent in restless activity--my garden had never looked so fine.

My seclusion only gave fodder to more speculation that all was not well between Pharaoh and myself, and Mara reported that whispers of my celibacy had reached the palace. Ladice had asked once again if I should attend her, but I demurred, giving a paltry excuse. Mara gave me a shrewd look and asked if I was still unwilling to leave Sais and Amasis behind.

But I could not.

I don't know what I waited for. I suppose for some foolish Egyptian girl to grow a foot large enough to fit my slipper. But only a Thracian woman was tall enough to fill the treasure. And I would not dare to approach him and claim to be his queen. Neferenatu and his lot would murder me before my words met Pharaoh's ears, even if I dared to speak them.

I spent long hours pacing in the courtyard of my own rented home. I feared that someone might remember days of the past when Charaxus and his lovely Flower danced for entertainment, but none came forth to denounce me. Days passed and Amasis did not visit me, nor did I go to him. What would be the point?

Still I ached for news of him.

I heard from Mara that the royal court bid him to begin his search in Sais. The falcon caught his treasure there, they reasoned. A great procession of women lined up, royalty and lesser nobles to try on the slipper. I watched them from my covered roof. Mara brought me some wine and slipped her hand around my waist as I spied on the proceedings.

"It is for the best, Dori." She sighed and leaned her head against my shoulder. "You know he must choose another."

I watched another litter depart from the palace, with some poor dejected creature no doubt weeping behind the linen curtains, her royal family's hopes no doubt scattered with a jingle of a slipper's brass bells.

"You always have my best interests in mind, near sister." I said, moving away from the view. She moved to kiss me, but I dodged her advance. "Not now, Mara. I'm tired, dearest." I patted her cheek and ignored her frown.

I felt old, well beyond my years. My heart ached.

"Dori," Mara said, taking up my peplos. "I can see your heart is heavy. I only ever wanted you to be happy. I think you..." She shook her head and began again. "I am truly sorry it is not to be with this man. For your sake, if not for his. If I could, I would make it so, for you." Her face looked strangely scrunched as if she were about to cry and she fled like a wraith from my sight.

That night, I mixed a measure of lotus wine and honey and drank deeply. I wanted to sleep like the dead. Instead, I slept fitfully, in small dozes where I would jolt awake for no reason I could name.

For once, I did not dream. Even the precious steeped lotus could not bring me serenity.

I thrashed about my fine bedclothes, drifting in and out of consciousness, until the dark early morning hours just before dawn. Unable to gain respite, I had just pulled back the linen sheet to fetch myself a drink of cool water when a soft thump sounded from the other side of my chamber, nearest the window.

"Kyky?" I whispered into the dark. No chattering response. No answer at all. "Who is there?" My heart pounded. Sweat trickled down the small of my back. I opened my mouth and prepared to scream for help.

"One who needs you," said a voice I never thought to hear in my bed chamber.

Amasis. My heart seized in my chest.

"Nesu?" I slipped from my bed and kept my back to the wall. My tongue felt heavy from the lotus wine. "Is it you? Where are your royal guards?" I heard someone moving towards me.

He bumped into the wooden cedar chest by my bed and whispered a curse. "I left them at the palace. They think I am sleeping."

"I can scarce believe you could sneak out of the palace undetected."

"You forget, I was a soldier. I am used to stealth." Though he jested, I sensed that his heart was heavy, for no mirth tinged his words.

"What are you doing here?" My eyes strained against the darkness.

"I hardly know myself." I heard him laugh without mirth. "Ah,

Rhodopis. What am I to do?"

He sounded so weary. I sat down on the edge of my bed.

"Come here," I patted my silk wrapped mattress, grateful again for the extravagance my profession afforded me. I felt the weight of him sink beside me. A warm cloud of sweet almond enveloped me.

"Did you know that I was once a thief?" he asked. "Long before I entered Apries' service...it seems ages ago. I was very young and poor. I snuck into the homes of the rich and stole fruit from their gardens. Have you never wondered why I sanction some temples and not others? Once Apries was defeated, I visited every temple to ask what sins I'd committed. Those that spoke truth--the ones who decried my thievery--they are the ones I have sanctioned."

I could not guess why Pharaoh stole into my house at night to tell me he was a thief.

I could not guess why he was here at all.

"I know how much you value truth and honesty." I said to make polite conversation. I heard him sigh.

"What can I do, Rhodopis? You have given me counsel before. Tell me what I can do?" His voice broke. Had the royal families overcome him at last?

"What is it?" My heart ached for him. "I will help you, if I can."

"I know," he said. "I know."

We sat for some time, while I waited for him to speak. The light became ghostly and birds began to rouse and twitter outside my window ledge.

"I have prayed, Rhodopis. All of Egypt has heard that I have prayed to almighty Ra to bring me a worthy wife to raise up as my queen."

I did not want to hear this. I could not...why could he not speak to me of other things?

"I have found her, Rhodopis. I know it. And yet I fear she may be lost to me."

I forced my mouth to work. "Surely that which is lost may be found?"

"Ha," Amasis said and paused. "I would lift this woman up as Great Wife, yet I cannot endanger the future of Egypt for my own selfish desires. We are on the brink of war. Kourosh of Persia masses his troops on the border. Without support from the royal families, Egypt will fall."

"And the royal families will allow Egypt to fall to this Kourosh, just to force you to favor whom they wish?"

Amasis gave an odd snort. "I believe some of them would sell off the palace stone by stone just to keep me from it."

"That cannot be."

"No," Amasis agreed. "They would not act openly of course, but they grow bolder each day that I delay my decision. In their arrogance, they believe themselves certain to overthrow the Persians, once I am safely ousted. That is not a new strategy. You were not here some seven years past when the Kushites gained the throne. Apries took it back for Egypt and now I have taken it from Apries. You might say we are all thieves, in that regard."

"What about the Greeks? Do they not send you aid?" Oh, I did not want to help him win this woman, but I could not stand to see him suffer so!

"The Carians and Greek mercenaries will arrive any day but I will not repeat Apries' mistake. I will not alienate my people to save their lives. Not when I have the power to avoid it." His warm hand covered mine.

"Will it be enough?" I asked.

Amasis inhaled deeply. "I have contracted with Polycrates of Samos to build a naval force of one hundred warships for Egypt. If Egypt and her allies can hold the seas, the Kourosh and his armies will never penetrate the deserts of the north without exposing his armies, no matter how much gold he sends to the Bedouins. Still, it will not be enough, for I have heard recent reports that Polycrates has sent an envoy to Cambyses, son of the Kourosh. If he has betrayed us, the Greek mercenaries alone could not withstand the Persian armies. We must have his warships."

"I see." Princess Therawejt's insults on the trip to Sais suddenly made much more sense. And it further made sense that Amasis would visit Ladice often, as cementing relationships with his Greek wife could only strengthen the support of this Polycrates. "I see," I repeated, nodding.

"Of course you do."

Something about the way he spoke that simple phrase warmed me through and through. I rubbed my thumb over the back of his hand. His fingers clenched mine and he drew my hand to his warm lips.

"Rhodopis," his voice was thick with emotion.

I felt him draw closer and scarcely dared to breathe, afraid that the spell would be broken and he would remember that he was a god-king and I, a courtesan.

"Rhodopis, I was never so much myself as when I was with you. I exist, pretending all is well and that I do not feel this hollowness in my middle. Curse you for finding me! Would it have been better to go through life without knowing you existed? I don't know. I just know that I've found the other half of my soul, and I cannot stay away."

Oh, sweet, silvered words!

My breath caught in my throat. I felt as if I'd been slapped.

"Nesu…." I began. But I did not know what to say.

A sudden gust of warm breath against my cheek signaled his position a scant moment before his lips covered mine. He kissed me. A true and honest kiss that a man gives to a woman. My senses reeled and I turned to molten gold against him.

This could not be! And yet, how long had I wanted him?

"No, please," I broke away. "Please do not torment me! I know you have your duty. You have given your word to the people, after all. You must stay the course of your decision, I know this. But, I do not want to hear the name of your queen. Not now, when you are here with me like this." I forced myself to push away from him.

"Rhodopis." He drew back as if he could see me in the dark. "I watch for you, did you know? I visit the Cyrene, Ladice, for I know of her fondness for you. Seeing your handmaiden, the Little Blue Eyed One gladdens my heart, for I feel as if you are there."

"Nesu…" I protested weakly. I could not breathe.

"It is so. I send my men to gather news of you in the city, to seek for signs of you at the palace. I smile at the very mention of you, even when we cannot steal away and talk. My heart lifts. I watch for you, and see you wherever I go. I hear your name on the lips of the people." I sensed him smiling now, beside me in the darkness.

"This thing between us cannot be." I was miserable. "You yourself have said it." At last Love had opened to me, and yet it was as far away from me as the stars in the skies above.

"Rhodopis," he mumbled against my lips and laid me back against the silk mattress. "Light of Ra, help me. Help me find a way to make you mine."

Oh, the swift prick of pain that speared my heart!

I had little trust in a man's words, but Amasis was a soldier—a man of action. And this man wanted me.

"Hush," I whispered back. "I want no more of words, only this…this time with you."

His lips took me with the force of a sandstorm. Every fiber of my body burned with desire. Amasis fumbled with our clothing, drawing my robes away with rough, desperate hands. His uncharacteristic awkwardness roused me even more. This was no hollow daydream, no whore's pretense. I wrapped my arms around his neck and pulled him to me.

The air was thick with the scent of sweet almond and desire. His mouth was a hot torrent of pleasure raining on my face, my neck, my breasts. I arched against him, straining to fill the ache within me.

He gave a little cry of wonder as he sank into me. I had never felt so complete, so whole, so _worthy_ before. What did I care of the goddess' glory? I had the love of this one man. And for me, it was enough.

"Ah," he sighed. I felt a warm drop against my lips and tasted the salt of his tears on my tongue. He lay there for a long moment without moving, allowing my body to adjust to the weight of him within me. His warmth infused me like sunlight. I was alive and on fire with him. Then he moved and pleasure speared my core.

When he thrust inside me, again and again, it was as if the waves of the Nile lapped at my body, warm and fluid and full. My hips lifted to meet him and I twined my legs around his long dark limbs. He felt so good within me, gods he felt so good! I am ashamed to say that I did not ply my trade with him. I did not think of the *hetaerae* schooling, of what the temple training declared I should do to please him.

I laid with him, a simple woman who desired him. I let the heat and rigid, silky motion of his body bring me to climax. When I cried out and shuddered against him, his body stiffened and I felt his phallus flexing within me as he spent himself.

"Ah!" Amasis leaned his face against my cheek and kissed my eyelids. "This is truth," he whispered. "This is real."

There was such raw emotion in his voice, such wonder. I wanted to lie with him forever. I wanted to shield him from worry and pain, and to bring him joys beyond measure. If only I could hear that awe in his voice...that truth.

Realization pricked me like a rose's thorn, sweet and despicably painful. *I loved him*.

I knew then, that I had never loved before. Amasis, the proud and clever god-king. Amasis, who cared less for my beauty than he did my counsel--who knew my past transgressions, and trusted me with his own. I wanted to be at his side, to help him bear the burdens of his throne, and to give him children to fill his life with joy. This was not the hollow dream of my youth. Egypt was my spirit, yes, and Amasis, my heart.

We satisfied ourselves with each other's bodies, and did not need to speak. Our minds and souls already joined. I did not know this man, and yet I felt I did. For to be with him was like staring into a clear pool. The other half of myself.

I gave myself to him completely.

It was many long hours before either of us could trust ourselves to speak again.

"Rhodopis. Do you love me?" he asked, at long last when we were finished.

"Oh," I breathed. "How could I not?"

"You know I must have my Great Wife. The people demand it." He sighed.

I did know, though my heart railed against it.

"Raise up whomever you must," I said. The languorous ease of our lovemaking now spent, I spoke the words that would give him away, and thus keep Egypt safe. "You must choose another, for Egypt to prevail."

"You are a beautiful woman, Rhodopis. And too proud, by half." He gave a dry laugh, a sound I never thought to hear. "I have decided. Do you not see? You are the goddess the people have dreamed of. They see your worth, as I do. They will support this—and they will support Egypt against her aggressors."

"Me? You cannot!" I sat up. "The others? The royal families will never agree..." I could not believe my ears.

We were quiet a long moment, there in the dark.

"Rhodopis, the royal houses cannot agree on anything. But the gods have already spoken to me of their choice. Horus has made all clear. I am but their humble vessel."

I sucked air between my teeth. How could I tell him I was the cause of the gods sign? Could it be true? My heart pounded. I could scarce draw breath for fear of shattering the perfection of this moment.

"The slipper." I said.

"It is a true herald from Horus," Amasis continued. "It cannot have been clearer than at the temple. Still, I am a man, Rhodopis. I am wise enough to know whose slipper I hold in my grasp. It is yours."

My cheeks burned and I hid my face in my hands.

"How did you know?" I asked.

"Did I not tell you I'd news of you? I knew that you were the woman of Charaxus the Greek. And there was another...a scribe of some kind. He and his wife have both come forth to declare you as the proper owner of the slipper, for they saw you dance long ago in their household. I should like to have seen that, I think." And he chuckled low.

My mind worked furiously. It must have been Isesi and his wife Wakheptry, she who had sheltered me so long ago. And now Amasis wished to pose me as the choice of the gods?

"Nesu, for all my careful hiding of the other slipper, I fear it has been stolen away. I cannot prove they were ever mine."

Amasis breathed against my cheek. "No matter. The slipper at the palace will fit you, Rhodopis. The people will see this for themselves."

"But is it wise? You must think of Egypt. I swear for my love of you, the people will not hear of this from my lips." I promised. "You are still free to choose another queen!"

"You are more than the 'Treasure of Naukratis', Rhodopis. You are the 'Treasure of Egypt'. No, the gods themselves have led you to me. I am certain." His fingers stroked my cheek. "Come to the Festival of the Harvest, and don the sign from the gods. I shall put you forth as my Great Wife."

Could it work? Egyptians were a reverent people. My heart swelled. I dared not hope it could be.

"Are you certain it is the will of the gods, then?" I asked. "And that is why you come to me now?"

Amasis made a noise, low in his throat. "You question my ardor? I come to you like a thief in the night, to steal kisses from your lips and it is my heart you question? I know you, Rhodopis and now I would know your heart's desire. What of you? Would you marry me now that Persia descends upon our nation like locusts? Our life will not be one of leisure. Would you give up your freedom for a marriage bed?"

Freedom? It seemed a paltry thing, compared to exquisite feel of his hands on my body. His voice in my ears. All logic flew from out of my head. A vision of Amasis and I playing _senet_ in our fine palace apartments flashed before my eyes. Our children leaned against my knees. Children with copper skin and grey-green eyes.

What could I say, but that my heart cared little for the scourge of the mighty Kourosh? His armies may not touch me, but I could not withstand the barrage of my own heart's longing. Amasis, a former soldier, would not appreciate such woman's sentiments.

"I am yours to command, always." I twined my fingers in his and pulled him toward me as the sun broke over the sand dunes.

I could see him now, a shadowy figure suddenly serious in the dawn. He moved atop me once again, his face scant inches above mine. "And if I ask you, not as your Nesu, but as a simple man? I want only truth from your lips, Rhodopis." And he kissed me again.

The whole of his body covered me, created a warm cocoon in which I felt certain and safe from harm. What did I care what the future held? I shifted in pleasure, and felt him stiffening against my womanhood. My thighs parted willingly and I wrapped them tightly around him, as if to shut out the world with my embrace.

And I would, too. I would have him, for any reason.

"You cannot be that other than what you are, Nesu. My answer does not change. I am yours."

Amasis laughed at that. "From your mouth to the gods' ears. So be it."

In the morning, none of the servants acted any different, but Mara avoided me during our meal. I waited until the platters were cleared and my near sister and I were safely ensconced in my chambers before approaching her.

"You seem out of sorts, Mara." I kept my voice neutral.

"I should say the same of you. Your lips are as red and swollen as grapes." She dropped the lid of my cosmetics case and latched it shut. "What did you think you were doing last night?"

"Mara, I'm sorry. I don't know how much you overheard."

"Enough. How could you do it?"

"I...I couldn't help myself. I love him, Mara."

"You said you loved me!" The look on her face seared me.

"I do, dearest. Ours is an affection long borne of a shared remembrance. You will always be my near sister. But...this is different." I could see by the set of Mara's jaw that she would not understand. As much as I loved Mara, her affection did not fill my soul. She was not enough. "There are things that I would share with him, Mara. Things that near sisters cannot."

"Like children?"

I could not deny it. I had dreamed of such last night in Amasis' arms. I stared at her without speaking.

"Forget it." Mara waved her hand. "Your face has blossomed like a rose in the morning dew. Here." She thrust my combs at me. "I will be gone most of the day. I must attend Ladice's preparations at the palace until evening."

"Mara, wait," I called to her retreating back. She pretended not to hear me.

She did not return to my household until the Festival of the Harvest began. Amasis planned to address the noble houses after the temple blessing; I was to attend and to try on the slipper before all assembled. In this way, we reasoned, the other royal families could not deny us their support.

That afternoon, as I called for a litter to be brought, Mara startled me at the door, fully dressed in her best gown with a thin necklace of beads around her neck. Her eyes were red rimmed.

"What are you about?" I asked. "You detest these celebrations."

Mara settled my _peplos_ around my shoulders. "I won't send you to the jackals alone, Dori."

"There is no need," I said. "You cannot protect my heart, and that is all I am in danger of wounding. Amasis believes the people will follow."

"I'm coming with you." She shouldered a small satchel and compressed her lips in a manner that meant she'd resolved herself.

I sighed. "As you wish."

We arrived just as the Festival at the Temple of Horus had begun. Hundreds thronged up the temple steps to the center courtyard. The city was in high fervor as the yoke of invasion descended our shoulders. For the will of the gods was upon us all. Moods were made falsely light and easy between the sects and a unifying urge for safety precluded old disputes.

As a favored guest, I was ushered to the front, nearest the entrance to the inner sanctum, where a dais had been raised. Mara trailed behind me like a shadow. Amasis sat upon his gilded throne, tapping his fingers on one knee, with the rose-gold slipper resting on a cushion in the hands of his royal bearer just behind. Torchlight gleamed along its fine surface, as if to beckon me forth. But decorum bade me wait until all of Amasis wives and half the courts should try it for themselves.

So, I waited.

I moved wordlessly through knots of courtyard conversations and the shadows of the immense columns of the temple. I tried to ignore the curious glances thrown my way. Mara materialized and slipped her hand in mind to pull me to one side.

"Ladice wishes to welcome you." She kissed my cheek and disappeared. I spied Ladice to the side of the courtyard with her back to me.

"Flower of Cyrene." I greeted her, kissing her cheeks.

"Oh…oh, you are here at last!" She turned and gave me a fierce embrace. "How little I care for these things. Still, it's all very exciting. Which woman do you think will fit the slipper? Anyone we know?" Ladice was an eternal court gossiper, despite her bucolic upbringing. Her dark eyes darted around the gathering.

"I cannot say, my Star." I replied, masking a smile. And I couldn't-- unless the ceremony proclaimed me thus-- if it worked to secure the support of the people at all. Nervous flutters twisted my stomach to knots.

"Whoever she is, she cannot be sweeter to me than you have been." Ladice replied, squeezing my hand. "I wish it were you," she said fervently. "You and your Mara, both. I do not care that Nesu Ahmose should bring another to the palace, as long as you say that you will continue to visit me, even after the Pharaoh has made his choice?"

It was kind that she should offer me welcome, if Pharaoh cast me aside for his new queen. From the awkward Cyrene princess, it was a mark of her regard—a royal gesture, indeed.

I bowed. "If it be the will of Nesu, I shall."

Ladice released me and took her place among the other wives of Amasis, to the rear of the dais. I wandered through the painted and bejeweled throng for an hour, searching for Mara who would be lost and uncomfortable in the sea of people. Neferenatu glared at me from his position on the dais. I turned my back to him and smiled politely at the revelers behind me. When the foremost Grecian mercenaries appeared, I knew that Amasis' announcement would not be far behind.

The sistrums jingled and my stomach clenched. At last the moment was at hand. Amasis signaled and the Chief Steward brought forth a huge amphora filled with lotus wine for the assembly. Amasis stood and spoke a blessing to the gods. He smiled at me over the rim. Then the ceremony was over and he sat upon his gilded throne, the symbolic crook and flail in hand.

"My people," he began. "Many long days have I prayed to find a worthy wife, one who shall rule over the hearts of the people. Let the gods speak to us now!" And he signaled for his bearers to bring forth petitioners to try the slipper. A royal bearer held the slipper on a fine cushion.

As the royal women were brought forth, each to have her turn, my mind turned to that day long ago in Hori's workshop, when his hands had traced the lines of my foot. *These will fit her and no other,* he'd promised Charaxus.

Well, I thought. It was truly so. For among the wives and princesses, the many royal women who were called and tried and failed, none could fit the slipper. Amasis scanned the assembly, and motioned again and again, until even the most minor nomarch's daughter had tried and been found lacking.

"Horus, Truth Giver, has sent me this sign." Amasis cried. "Is there none who will come forth to fit the slipper?" And bless him, his eyes cut a sideways glance at me.

Now. Now, was the time. I could embrace the opportunity the gods had given me, or I could hide in the shadows, afraid to make my own destiny.

But just before I moved forward to try the slipper, Neferenatu, the Grand Vizier, stepped forward.

"No! Not her! I denounce this as a trick and a lie!" And he stuck out his staff and tripped the royal bearer before I even drew near enough to be recognized.

The slipper dropped to the pavestones with a jangle of bells and clatter of wood.

"You seek to bring embarrassment to the royal women of Egypt!" Neferenatu hefted his foot and before anyone could stop him, smashed it down hard on the slipper, crumpling it like papyrus reeds beneath his feet. Someone in the crowd screamed.

"Stop him!" Amasis shouted. Guards rushed in and took hold of the grand Vizier.

I felt doused in sea water, cold and merciless.

Amasis knelt, and retrieved the golden slipper, but it was clear that the treasure would never adorn any foot again. He spared me one tortured look. The polished acacia wood was cracked and splintered, the finely wrought gold dented and crushed beneath the vizier's rage.

It was destroyed beyond repair, as much as any hope I might have had of becoming Amasis' queen.

I knew now the wicked vizier plotted to usurp Amasis. My ears felt stuffed with wool, as Amasis shouted for justice. The royal guards took hold of Neferenatu's arms and dragged him from the courtyard. The priests took up a hymn, chanting for the mercy of Horus against such blasphemy. I sank against the column, feeling my eyes well with tears.

There would be no proof now. No way to show my worthiness to convince the royal houses to support Amasis' choice. He must give me up, for the sake of all Egypt. To prevail against the Persian threat, it must be so.

I had to leave, and now, before he made an enemy of the royal houses. For his sake and the sake of all Egypt, I would for once do what I should.

"Mara," I grabbed her hand. "I am finished. We must go." I tried to lead her from the throng surrounding the dais. But my near-sister balked.

Her face was white.

"Dori," Mara whispered, as I tried to push my way forward through the crowd, away from the dais and away from Amasis. "Wait!"

She stopped and pressed something hard, half wrapped in a fine silk *peplos* into my hands. Something glimmered beneath her fingers, and my breath caught in my throat. I heard a member of the court next to me cry out in disbelief.

The other slipper.

"I'm sorry," she cried. "I thought perhaps if I took it, we could be together. But you would not leave him, even when you thought he would choose another." She took a deep gulp of air. "There are some things worth risking your life for. Love is the greatest of them," she said. "I know now that you love this man, as much as I love you. I am sorry I took it, Dori. I am sorry for everything."

Oh, Mara! She wished only to leave Egypt, but for her love of me she had almost cost me my greatest desires. Time seemed to stop. We stood there in silence, holding hands around the golden slipper and watching the torches flicker and pop. For a moment, we were those same young girls, as alike as to be called near-sisters. I closed my eyes and replayed visions of us together in the temple, dancing, sweating and dreaming of the paths our lives would take. That is how I choose to think of Mara, my beloved, my near-sister. I could never believe she set out to hurt me.

"Go," she whispered. And the moment passed. "For remembered affection and my duty to you, Dori. Go." And she pushed me toward the god-king's throne.

So, I left her there. The crowds quieted as I climbed the dais in a daze and made my obeisance to Amasis. From my prostrate position, I unwrapped my remaining slipper and placed the treasure of gold at his feet.

"O Great Nesu. If I may restore what wickedness has stolen from you. Behold, the gift of Horus." I said. "I present you with its twin."

Amasis froze. He might have been carved in marble. His face was a mask of disbelief. Then he bent his knee and with a single, deft motion, picked up the slipper. His strong fingers caressed the rose-gold surface, playing upon it as they had once played across my skin. Then he turned, and the corner of his mouth crooked upward in a slight smile.

He held up the pair for all assembled to see they were akin.

Two halves of the same whole. One damaged, and the other shining in its unblemished perfection. My throat ached with unshed tears as Amasis descended from his throne. He, himself, brushed the royal bearer aside and knelt before me to settle the slipper on my foot. The touch of his hand was splendid on my skin.

"A perfect fit!" he announced.

I raised my skirt and made a deep curtsy to the royal families, that all might see for themselves.

The council of advisors began to whisper furiously.

"It cannot be," I heard someone exclaim. It sounded like Princess Therawejt. Someone shushed her.

Amasis raised his head and scanned the assembly. "O People of Egypt, raise your voices. I call upon the royal families to heed my command. For the gods have spoken, and I would have this woman, this Rhodopis of Egypt." Amasis looked at me and then scanned the council of viziers. "What say you?"

There was a moment of utter silence.

Then, from somewhere in the back, someone shouted a name. My name.

Someone else took it up. And then many.

A cacophony of calls swelled from the people like the tide. They chanted my name, calling for blessings, calling for me to honor them, in voices as pure and as piercing as the falcon's cry!

As the crowds swelled louder, I saw Chief Scribe Isesi nudge his wife. They knelt down before me. The royal nomarchs took note. And slowly, incredibly, impossibly, one by one, the court and council sank to its knees, with Ladice at the first, and Therawejt and Snesuankh at the last. They kneeled, some with honor, some with mutiny, etched in their features. But each head was bowed, lower then Pharaoh's, lower than my own. Each forearm crossed over in obeisance.

"What the gods have proclaimed, I will not set aside." Amasis called. "Rhodopis of Egypt, I declare you to be my Great Wife. Accept the laws of Ra, of Isis, and of Horus and become Mother to all Egypt."

It was done. Egypt would hold.

Before all assembled Amasis took my hand. We led the court out of the inner sanctum and the cymbals sounded our exit. We returned to the temple, to the commoners, the soldiers and the citizens who championed their god-king.

Now that the matter was settled, Amasis and his troops joined the Grecian mercenaries and Polycrates' warships to protect our northeastern cities. For a proclamation of Great Wife had inspired the people to fight for our Egypt, and the Greek city-state of Naukratis was would heed the call to arms. A fearful month passed before we heard the joyous news. Kourosh had fled. Soldier reports stated that there was some trouble on the far borders of the Persian's domain and so the Kourosh turned tail and returned to his homeland, at least for now, to settle his own affairs.

We planned to wed by the following season. I moved into the palace with the other wives and princesses. Ladice was pleased to have me, although I daresay she was happier to have the company of Mara, who moved into the palace with me. Our troubles were now forgotten and my near-sister seemed at peace with our new situation.

Amasis returned home to me, a weary warrior, but rejoicing at the passion between us. I spent many days and nights bringing him welcome, not for my duty but for the sake of my own heart. I moved through the halls of the palace in a haze of joy. Me, who feared once to belong to any man, to give up my freedom for the slavery of a marriage bed.

I realized then that to live free is not so much about the bands around one's wrists, but to live by the dictates of one's heart. I would no longer dwell on what could be, for what soul can say where her path may lead? Today we were safe from the threat of invasion, but tomorrow everything I loved could turn to dust. I need not be bound by the choices that others made for me, but by the opportunities that were offered to me. Such was true freedom for a woman. And freedom, for me, was Amasis and Egypt.

Amasis and I were married with much pageantry by the Inundation season. It was a good choice, a time when the land is fertile.

During the ceremony, I bowed my head, so that I would not be shamed by the tears that wet my cheeks. The red gold curtain of my hair hid my burning cheeks, until Amasis tipped my chin and forced me to meet his gaze. With pride, I thrust my chin as high as a priestess and spoke the words that bound me to him and to Egypt forever.

Thus did a Thracian slave become Queen of Egypt.

Throngs of people, common and not, cheered for us. They stamped and shouted my name. An immense feast was given, and I was overjoyed to see most of the noble families attended. And not two weeks later the news came that the mighty Kourosh of Persia was dead. He'd dared to cross an eastern queen who did not take well to the death of her son on his battlefields. She took the life of Kourosh as recompense to her gods.

Egypt settled once again in to a routine of exports and trade. Life resumed its normalcy.

And, in true Egyptian fashion, I gained a new throne name, 'Nitocris', chosen by my husband. It meant "Beloved Treasure of Neit" his patron goddess. So, three names.

And I'd not thought such a number to be lucky.

"Honorable Wife of the Sun," Isesi, now made a vizier, inclined his head at my approach.

"Elevated One." I offered him a white rose from my hands. I heard Amasis laugh at something, just out of my sight. The sound gladdened my heart.

"It seems the gods favor you," Isesi said. "I hope you are worthy of their notice."

"I am a Daughter of the Gods and Mother to Egypt, Isesi." I would not think about what the royal houses might do if they thought me lacking. For today, it was enough that the sun rose and set, and Amasis loved me.

Just then, the sistrum rang and cymbals clanged and the air was filled with the flapping of wings as a score of birds took wing. Not sparrows, but doves, crated especially for the temple blessing. The afternoon sun blazed on their feathers and turned them to rose-gold. I felt the shackles of doubt, pain and misery fall away from me. For once, my future seemed bright and secure.

Amasis motioned for me to join him on the dais. His dark eyes sparkled. My heart leapt just looking at him.

"Excuse me, Vizier. My husband waits." I gave Isesi a smile, and he bowed and moved towards his wife Wakheptry who nodded to me, her eyes politely lowered. The sun glittered on the wide electrum band set on my heart finger, the one adornment I would never be without.

I joined Amasis near our thrones, a pair made of ivory from Kush. It took most of my will to hold myself to a sedate pace in front of the eyes of the noble houses. In truth, I wanted to fly into his arms.

"Are you happy?" Amasis asked. "I would have my clever Great Wife content."

The air was cool upon my skin. Gone were the worries of my past and the fear that I no longer had a place in this world. I had made one, here, in Egypt.

"I am more than that." I leaned my head against his shoulder, inhaled the sweet almond scent of his skin and watched the sun sink into the brilliant green waters of the Nile. "I am free."

ABOUT THE AUTHOR

J.A. Coffey has been fascinated with mythos and legend for as long as she can remember. She grew up in the Dustbowl of the Midwest-hence her flights of fancy. Since then she's lived in all parts of the country and traveled abroad. She currently resides in North Carolina with her husband and four large dogs.

J.A. holds a Bachelors Degree of Fine Art and a Masters Degree of Education in Educational Leadership. A popular presenter and conference speaker, she tries to write through the lens of an artist. When she isn't writing or reading, she can be found toiling in her raised bed gardens, painting, or "feathering her nest". She dreams of restoring a historic home. A former RWA Golden Heart finalist in the "Best Manuscript with Romantic Elements" category, J.A. is currently working on her latest historical novel.

For more information, please visit www.JA Coffey.com.